# THE WOMAN IN THE WINDOW

THE WOMAN IN THE WINDOW

**J. H. Wallis** (1885-1958) was born in Iowa and educated at Yale. He was a newspaperman in Iowa, later writing full-time in New York whose 1942 best-selling book *Once Off Guard* (later published as *The Woman in the Window*) was made into a film, *The Woman in the Window* (1944), directed by Fritz Lang.

## The yellowbacks... classics of popular fiction

The yellowjackets or yellowbacks were a great series of bestselling adventure and crime thrillers that had its origins in the mid to late 19th century following on from the 'penny dreadfuls'. They virtually began the mass market revolution of the early 20th century with a clear standard format and imprint/series livery (what would today be called branding). Hodder & Stoughton published the yellowjackets in two main series with series run dates of: 1923-1939 and later 1949-1957.

As the tagline ('where thrillers really began') on the back cover implies, the imprint and series focused on thrillers that were the bestsellers of their time. This current reissue or retro revival if you will, brings back many of these masterpieces, now classics in their own way and extends it further by including key titles from that period that were either great crime or thriller or even general commercial fiction (including sub-genres of noir, horror, gothic, romance, westerns, etc.) influences of their time. There are some perennial favourites and many rarities either lost or not easily available being revived in the current series. Writers and characters ranged from adventure heroes like Bulldog Drummond, Allan Quatermain, Richard Hannay or the Saint through thriller grandmasters Edgar Wallace and E. Phillips Oppenheim, crime and mystery maestros like Patricia Wentworth, G.K. Chesterton, Agatha Christie and the Detection club, to western and swashbucklers like Zane Grey, Max Brand, Captain Blood and even romance or general fiction classics like Hermina Black, Denise Robins, Marie Corelli or Stella Morton. These were books that had storytelling at their heart and always entertained.

The yellowbacks had both hardback (with varying design elements) and paperback (which built the series look) versions with the latter still carrying the imprint 'yellowjacket'. The current reissues pay tribute to both and use an amalgam of elements from both editions while retaining the complete yellow (or 'mustard-plaster') livery with the author's name in blue beveled type with a 'simulated emboss' effect and a white outer 'outline', and the book title in black. These reissues retain the distinctive size of the original mass market paperback and follow the three main category variations—the thrillers (crime, westerns, mystery, adventure) had blue lettering for the author's name, while Romance and softer general fiction had red; and other categories like humour had green.

For more details and a full list of titles visit https://www.hachetteindia.com/home/yellowbacks

# THE WOMAN IN THE WINDOW

J. H. Wallis

HODDER AND STOUGHTON
YELLOW JACKET

hachette

*The Woman in the Window*
First publishedby E.P. Dutton in 1942 as *Once Off Guard* and then republished as *The Woman in the Window* as a movie tie-in.

This Hodder Yellowback edition © Hachette India 2023
(Registered Name: Hachette Book Publishing India Pvt. Ltd.)
An Hachette UK Company www.hachetteindia.com

1



The texts in these editions in most cases have been reprinted as is, with minimal editorial changes and by and large no bowdlerizing for political correctness; though in some editions, a few words and phrases considered archaic, or those considered offensive now, along with archaic punctuation may have been modified in places to make the text more accessible to today's readers. The narratives, language, beliefs, social mores and/or cultural depictions, in these volumes are a reflection of their times and must be viewed as such. They may also contain certain cultural, racial and gender prejudices and stereotypes that may be outdated or clearly wrong then and wrong today; but their removal would be tantamount to claiming these prejudices never existed. The Publisher does not endorse or support those depictions or stereotypes; and these books have been made available for a discerning audience that will read it for entertainment value and a chronicle/record of popular fiction of past times.

Cover design by Priya Singh adapted from the original classic yellowjacket by Hodder & Stoughton.

Cover illustration by Ishan Trivedi.

Series note: Some of the books in the series (unless otherwise credited) may have cover or inside illustrations from the original yellowbacks or early editions, and while full restoration has been attempted, some images may be grainy or faded due to the condition of the original material. The end notes or bonus material or blurb details may have been sourced from the public domain or free use publications such as Wikipedia and attribution is hereby made also allowing similar free use reproduction from here. Sources requiring further specific attribution may write in and further detailing and/or corrections shall be made in subsequent printings/editions.

Reprint specifications may be subject to change including but not limited to finishes, paper, colour sections.

ISBN: 978-93-5731-177-9

Hachette Book Publishing India Pvt. Ltd.
4th & 5th Floors, Corporate Centre,
Plot No. 94, Sector 44, Gurugram - 122 003, India

Typeset in Electra LT STD 10/12.5 pt by Manipal Technologies Limited, Manipal

Printed and bound in India by Manipal Technologies Limited, Manipal

FSC www.fsc.org MIX Paper from responsible sources FSC™ C043100

# CONTENTS

# SUNDAY, OCTOBER 24

## 1

Her husband's almost home. He'll catch her this time.

There isn't a scrap of curtain, not a blade of blind, in number 212—the rust-red townhome that once housed the newlywed Motts, until recently, until they un-wed. I never met either Mott, but occasionally I check in online: his Linked In profile, her Facebook page. Their wedding registry lives on at Macy's. I could still buy them flatware.

As I was saying: not even a window dressing. So number 212 gazes blankly across the street, ruddy and raw, and I gaze right back, watching the mistress of the manor lead her contractor into the guest bedroom. What *is* it about that house? It's where love goes to die.

She's lovely, a genuine redhead, with grass-green eyes and an archipelago of tiny moles trailing across her back. Much prettier than her husband, a Dr John Miller, psychotherapist—yes, he offers couples counseling—and one of 436,000 John Millers online. This particular specimen works near Gramercy Park and does not accept insurance. According to the deed of sale, he paid $3.6 million for his house. Business must be good.

I know both more and less about the wife. Not much of a homemaker, clearly; the Millers moved in eight weeks ago, yet still those windows are bare, *tsk-tsk*. She practices yoga three times a week, tripping down the steps with her magic-carpet mat rolled beneath one arm, legs shrink-wrapped in Lululemon. And she must volunteer someplace—she leaves the house a little past eleven on Mondays and Fridays, around the time I get up, and returns between five and five thirty, just as I'm settling in for my nightly film. (This evening's selection: *The Man Who Knew Too Much*, for the umpteenth time. I am the woman who viewed too much.)

I've noticed she likes a drink in the afternoon, as do I. Does she also like a drink in the morning? As do I?

But her age is a mystery, although she's certainly younger than Dr Miller, and younger than me (nimbler, too); her name I can only guess at. I think of her as Rita, because she looks like Hayworth in *Gilda*. "I'm not in the least interested"—love that line.

I myself am very much interested. Not in her body—the pale ridge of her spine, her shoulder blades like stunted wings, the baby-blue bra clasping her breasts: whenever these loom within my lens, any of them, I look away—but in the life she leads. The lives. Two more than I've got.

Her husband rounded the corner a moment ago, just past noon, not long after his wife pressed the front door shut, contractor in tow. This is an aberration: On Sundays, Dr Miller returns to the house at quarter past three, without fail.

Yet now the good doctor strides down the sidewalk, breath chugging from his mouth, briefcase swinging from one hand, wedding band winking. I zoom in on his feet: oxblood oxfords, slick with polish, collecting the autumn sunlight, kicking it off with each step.

I lift the camera to his head. My Nikon D5500 doesn't miss much, not with that Opteka lens: unruly marled hair, glasses spindly and cheap, islets of stubble in the shallow ponds of his cheeks. He takes better care of his shoes than his face.

Back to number 212, where Rita and the contractor are speedily disrobing. I could dial directory assistance, call the house, warn her. I won't. Watching is like nature photography: You don't interfere with the wildlife.

Dr Miller is maybe half a minute away from the front door. His wife's mouth glosses the contractor's neck. Off with her blouse.

Four more steps. Five, six, seven. Twenty seconds now, at most.

She seizes his tie between her teeth, grins at him. Her hands fumble with his shirt. He grazes on her ear.

Her husband hops over a buckled slab of sidewalk. Fifteen seconds.

I can almost hear the tie slithering out of his collar. She whips it across the room.

Ten seconds. I zoom in again, the snout of the camera practically twitching. His hand dives into his pocket, surfaces with a haul of keys. Seven seconds.

She unlooses her ponytail, hair swinging onto her shoulders.

Three seconds. He mounts the steps.

She folds her arms around his back, kisses him deep.

He stabs the key into the lock. Twists.

I zoom in on her face, the eyes sprung wide. She's heard.

I snap a photo.

And then his briefcase flops open.

A flock of papers bursts from it, scatters in the wind. I jolt the camera back to Dr Miller, to the crisp "Shoot" his mouth shapes; he sets the briefcase on the stoop, stamps a few sheets beneath those glinting shoes, scoops others into his arms. One tearaway scrap has snagged in the fingers of a tree. He doesn't notice.

Rita again, plunging her arms into her sleeves, pushing her hair back. She speeds from the room. The contractor, marooned, hops off the bed and retrieves his tie, stuffs it into his pocket.

I exhale, air hissing out of a balloon. I hadn't realized I was holding my breath.

The front door opens: Rita surges down the steps, calling to her husband. He turns; I expect he smiles—I can't see. She stoops, peels some papers from the sidewalk.

The contractor appears at the door, one hand sunk in his pocket, the other raised in greeting. Dr Miller waves back. He ascends to the landing, lifts his briefcase, and the two men shake. They walk inside, trailed by Rita.

Well. Maybe next time.

# MONDAY, OCTOBER 25

## 2

The car droned past a moment ago, slow and somber, like a hearse, taillights sparking in the dark. "New neighbors," I tell my daughter.

"Which house?"

"Across the park. Two-oh-seven." They're out there now, dim as ghosts in the dusk, exhuming boxes from the trunk.

She slurps.

"What are you eating?" I ask. It's Chinese night, of course; she's eating lo mein.

"Lo mein."

"Not while you're talking to Mommy, you're not."

She slurps again, chews. "*Mo-om.*" This is a tug-of-war between us; she's whittled *Mommy* down, against my wishes, to something blunt and stumpy. "Let it go," Ed advises—but then he's still Daddy.

"You should go say hi," Olivia suggests.

"I'd like to, pumpkin." I drift upstairs, to the second floor, where the view's better. "Oh: There are pumpkins *everywhere*. All the neighbors have one. The Grays have four." I've reached the landing, glass in hand, wine lapping at my lip. "I wish I could pick out a pumpkin for you. Tell Daddy to get you one."

I sip, swallow. "Tell him to get you two, one for you and one for me."

"Okay."

I glimpse myself in the dark mirror of the half bath. "Are you happy, sweetheart?"

"Yes."

"Not lonely?" She never had real friends in New York; she was too shy, too small.

"Nope."

I peer into the dark at the top of the stairs, into the gloom above. During the day, sun drops through the domed skylight overhead; at night, it's a wide-open eye gazing into the depths of the stairwell. "Do you miss Punch?"

"Nope." She didn't get along with the cat, either. He scratched her one Christmas morning, flashed his claws across her wrist, two quick rakes north-south east-west; a bright grid of blood sprang to the skin, tic-tac-toe, and Ed nearly pitched him out the window. I look for him now, find him swirled on the library sofa, watching me.

"Let me talk to Daddy, pumpkin." I mount the next flight, the runner coarse against my soles. Rattan. What were we thinking? It stains so easily.

"Hey there, slugger," he greets me. "New neighbors?"

"Yes."

"Didn't you just get new neighbors?"

"That was two months ago. Two-twelve. The Millers." I pivot, descending the stairs.

"Where are these other people?"

"Two-oh-seven. Across the park."

"Neighborhood's changing."

I reach the landing, round it. "They didn't bring much with them. Just a car."

"Guess the movers will come later."

"Guess so."

Silence. I sip.

Now I'm in the living room again, by the fire, shadows steeped in the corners. "Listen..." Ed begins.

"They have a son."

"What?"

"There's a son," I repeat, pressing my forehead against the cold glass of the window. Sodium lamps have yet to sprout in this province of Harlem, and the street is lit only by a lemon-wedge of moon, but still I can make them out in silhouette: a man, a woman, and a tall boy, ferrying boxes to the front door. "A teenager," I add.

"Easy, cougar."

Before I can stop myself: "I wish you were here."

It catches me off guard. Ed too, by the sound of it. There's a pause.

Then: "You need more time," he says.

I stay quiet.

"The doctors say that too much contact isn't healthy."

"I'm the doctor who said that."

"You're one of them."

A knuckle-crack behind me—a spark in the fireplace. The flames settle, muttering in the grate.

"Why don't you invite those new people over?" he asks.

I drain my glass. "I think that's enough for tonight."

"Anna."

"Ed."

I can almost hear him breathe. "I'm sorry we're not there with you."

I can almost hear my heart. "I am, too."

Punch has tracked me downstairs. I scoop him up in one arm, retreat to the kitchen. Set the phone on the counter. One more glass before bed.

Grasping the bottle by its throat, I turn to the window, toward the three ghosts haunting the sidewalk, and hoist it in a toast.

# TUESDAY, OCTOBER 26

## 3

This time last year, we'd planned to sell the house, had even engaged a broker; Olivia would enroll in a Midtown school the following September, and Ed had found us a Lenox Hill gut job. "It'll be *fun*," he promised. "I'll install a bidet, just for you." I batted him on the shoulder.

"What's a bidet?" asked Olivia.

But then he left, and she with him. So it flayed my heart all over again when, last night, I recalled the first words of our stillborn listing: LOVINGLY RESTORED LANDMARK 19TH-CENTURY HARLEM GEM! WONDERFUL FAMILY HOME! *Landmark* and *gem* up for debate, I think. *Harlem* inarguable, likewise *19th-century* (1884). *Lovingly restored,* I can attest to that, and expensively, too. *Wonderful family home,* true.

My domain and its outposts:

*Basement:* Or maisonette, according to our broker. Sub-street, floor-through, with its own door; kitchen, bath, bedroom, tiny office. Ed's workspace for eight years—he'd drape the table in blueprints, tack contractor briefs to the wall. Currently tenanted.

*Garden:* Patio, really, accessible via the first floor. A sprawl of limestone tile; a pair of disused Adirondack chairs; a young ash tree slouched in the far corner, gangling and lonely, like a friendless teenager. Every so often I long to hug it.

*First floor:* Ground floor, if you're British, or *premier étage*, if you're French. (I am neither, but I spent time in Oxford during my residency—in a maisonette, as it happens—and this past July began studying *français* online.) Kitchen—open-plan and "gracious" (broker again), with a rear door leading to the garden and a side door to the park. White-birch floors, now blotched with puddles of merlot. In the hall a powder room—the red room, I call it. "Tomato Red," per the Benjamin Moore catalogue. Living room, equipped with sofa and coffee table and paved in Persian rug, still plush underfoot.

*Second floor:* The library (Ed's; shelves full, cracked spines and foxed dust jackets, all packed tight as teeth) and the study (mine; spare, airy, a desktop Mac poised on an IKEA table—my online-chess battlefield). Second half bath, this one blued in "Heavenly Rapture," which is ambitious language for a room with a toilet. And a deep utility closet I might one day convert into a darkroom, if I ever migrate from digital to film. I think I'm losing interest.

*Third floor:* The master (mistress?) bedroom and bath. I've spent much of my time in bed this year; it's one of those sleep-system mattresses, dually adjustable. Ed programmed his side for an almost downy softness; mine is set to firm. "You're sleeping on a brick," he said once, strumming his fingers on the top sheet.

"You're sleeping on a cumulus," I told him. Then he kissed me, long and slow.

After they left, during those black, blank months when I could scarcely prize myself from the sheets, I would roll slowly, like a curling wave, from one end to the other, spooling and unspooling the bedclothes around me.

Also the guest bedroom and en-suite.

*Fourth floor:* Servants' quarters once upon a time, now Olivia's bedroom and a second spare. Some nights I haunt her room like a ghost. Some days I stand in the doorway, watch the slow traffic of dust motes in the sun. Some weeks I don't visit the fourth floor at all, and it starts to melt into memory, like the feel of rain on my skin.

Anyway. I'll speak to them again tomorrow. Meanwhile, no sign of the people across the park.

# WEDNESDAY, OCTOBER 27

## 4

A rangy teenager bursts from the front door of number 207, like a horse from the starting gate, and gallops east down the street, past my front windows. I don't get a good look—I've awoken early, after a late night with *Out of the Past*, and am trying to decide if a swallow of merlot might be wise; but I catch a bolt of blond, a backpack slung from one shoulder. Then he's gone.

I slug a glass, float upstairs, settle myself at my desk. Reach for my Nikon.

In the kitchen of 207 I can see the father, big and broad, backlit by a television screen. I press the camera to my eye and zoom in: the *Today* show. I might head down and switch on my own TV, I muse, watch alongside my neighbor. Or I might view it right here, on his set, through the lens.

I decide to do that.

It's been a while since I took in the facade, but Google furnishes a street view: whitewashed stone, faintly Beaux-Arts, capped with a widow's walk. From here, of course, I can set my sights only on the side of the house; through its east windows, I've a clear shot into the kitchen, a second-floor parlour, and a bedroom above.

Yesterday a platoon of movers arrived, hauling sofas and television sets and an ancient armoire. The husband has been directing traffic. I haven't seen the wife since the night they moved in. I wonder what she looks like.

I'm about to checkmate Rook & Roll this afternoon when I hear the bell. I shuffle downstairs, slap the buzzer, unlock the hall door, and find my tenant looming there, looking, as they say, rough and ready. He *is* handsome, with his long jaw, his eyes like trapdoors, dark and deep. Gregory Peck after a late evening. (I'm not the only one who thinks so. David likes to entertain the occasional lady friend, I've noticed. Heard, really.)

"I'm heading to Brooklyn tonight," he reports.

I drag a hand through my hair. "Okay."

"You need me to take care of anything before I go?" It sounds like a proposition, like a line from a noir. *You just put your lips together and blow.*

"Thanks. I'm fine."

He gazes past me, squints. "Bulbs need changing? It's dark in here."

"I like it dim," I say. *Like my men,* I want to add. Is that the joke from *Airplane*? "Have..." Fun? A good time? Sex? "... a good time."

He turns to go.

"You know you can just come on in through the basement door," I tell him, trying for playful. "Chances are I'll be home." I hope he'll smile. He's been here two months, and I haven't once seen him grin.

He nods. He leaves.

I close the door.

I study myself in the mirror. Wrinkles like spokes around my eyes. A slur of dark hair, tigered here and there with gray, loose about my shoulders; stubble in the scoop of my armpit. My belly has gone slack. Dimples stipple my thighs. Skin almost luridly pale, veins flowing violet within my arms and legs.

Dimples, stipples, stubble, wrinkles: I need work. I had a down-home appeal once, according to some, according to Ed. "I thought of you as the girl next door," he said sadly, toward the end.

I look down at my toes rippling against the tile—long and fine, one (or ten) of my better features, but a bit small-predator right now. I rummage through my medicine cabinet, pill bottles stacked atop one another like totem poles, and excavate a nail clipper. At last, a problem I can fix.

## THURSDAY, OCTOBER 28

# 5

The deed of sale posted yesterday. My new neighbors are Alistair and Jane Russell; they paid $3.45 million for their humble abode. Google tells me that he's a partner at a midsize consultancy, previously based in Boston. She's untraceable—you try plugging *Jane Russell* into a search engine.

It's a lively neighborhood they've chosen.

The Miller home across the street—abandon all hope, ye who enter here—is one of five townhouses that I can survey from the south-facing windows of my own. To the east stand the identical-twin Gray Sisters: same box cornices crowning the windows, same bottle-green front doors. In the right—the slightly Grayer Sister, I think—live Henry and Lisa Wasserman, longtime residents; "Four decades and counting," bragged Mrs Wasserman when we moved in. She'd dropped by to tell us ("to your faces") how much she ("and my Henry") resented the arrival of "another yuppie clan" in what "used to be a real neighborhood."

Ed fumed. Olivia named her stuffed rabbit Yuppie.

The Wassermen, as we dubbed them, haven't spoken to me since, even though I'm on my own now, a clan unto myself. They don't seem much friendlier toward the residents of the other Gray Sister, a family called, fittingly, Gray. Twin teenage girls, father a partner at a boutique M&A firm, mother an eager book-club hostess. This month's selection, advertised on their Meetup page and under review right now, in the Grays' front room, by eight middle-aged women: *Jude the Obscure*.

I read it too, imagined I was one of the group, munching coffee cake (none handy) and sipping wine (this I managed). "What did you think of *Jude*, Anna?" Christine Gray would ask me, and I'd say I found it rather obscure. We'd laugh. They're laughing now, in fact. I try laughing with them. I take a sip.

West of the Millers are the Takedas. The husband is Japanese, the mother white, their son unearthly beautiful. He's a cellist; in the warm months, he rehearses with the parlour windows thrown open, so Ed used to hoist ours in turn. We danced one night in some long-gone June, Ed and I, to the strains of a Bach suite: swaying in the kitchen, my head on his shoulder, his fingers knotted behind me, as the boy across the street played on.

This past summer, his music wandered toward the house, approached my living room, knocked politely on the glass: *Let me in*. I didn't, couldn't—I never open the windows, never—but still I could hear it murmuring, pleading: *Let me in. Let me in!*

Number 206-208, a vacant double-wide brownstone, flanks the Takedas' house. An LLC bought it two Novembers ago, but no one moved in. A puzzle. For nearly a year, scaffolding clung to its facade like hanging gardens; it disappeared overnight—this was a few months before Ed and Olivia left—and since then, nothing.

Behold my southern empire and its subjects. None of these people were my friends; most of them I'd not met more than once or twice. Urban life, I suppose. Maybe the Wassermen were onto something. I wonder if they know what's become of me.

A derelict Catholic school abuts my house to the east, practically leans against it: St. Dymphna's, shuttered since we moved in. We'd threaten to send Olivia there when she misbehaved. Pitted brown stone, windows dark with grime. Or at least that's what I remember; it's been a while since I laid eyes on it.

And directly west is the park—tiny, two lots across and two deep, with a narrow brick path connecting our street to the one directly north. A sycamore stands sentry at either end, leaves flaming; an iron fence, low to the ground, hems in both sides. It is, as that quotable broker said, very quaint.

Then there's the house beyond the park: number 207. The Lords sold it two months ago and promptly cleared out, flying south to their retirement villa in Vero Beach. Enter Alistair and Jane Russell.

Jane Russell! My physical therapist had never heard of her. "*Gentlemen Prefer Blondes,*" I said.

"Not in my experience," she replied. Bina's younger; perhaps that's it.

All this was earlier today; before I could argue with her, she laced one of my legs over the other, capsized me onto my right side. The pain left me breathless. "Your hamstrings need this," she assured me.

"You bitch," I gasped.

She pressed my knee to the floor. "You're not paying me to go easy on you."

I winced. "Can I pay you to leave?"

Bina visits once a week to help me hate life, as I like to say, and to provide updates on her sexual adventures, which are about as exciting as my own. Only in Bina's case it's because she's picky. "Half the guys on these apps are using five-year-old photos," she'll complain, her waterfall of hair poured over one shoulder, "and the other half are married. And the *other* half are single for a reason."

That's three halves, but you don't debate math with someone who's rotating your spine.

I joined Happn a month ago "just to see," I told myself. Happn, Bina had explained to me, matchmakes you with people whose paths you've crossed. But what if you haven't crossed paths with anyone? What if you forever navigate the same four thousand vertically arranged square feet, and nothing beyond them?

I don't know. The first profile I spotted was David's. I instantly deleted my account.

It's been four days since I glimpsed Jane Russell. She certainly wasn't proportioned like the original, with her torpedo breasts, her wasp waist, but then neither am I. The son I've seen only that once, yesterday morning. The husband, however—wide shoulders, streaky brows, a blade of a nose—is on permanent display in his house: whisking eggs in the kitchen, reading in the parlour, occasionally glancing into the bedroom, as though in search of someone.

# FRIDAY, OCTOBER 29

## 6

My French *leçon* today, and *Les Diaboliques* tonight. A rat-bastard husband, his "little ruin" of a wife, a mistress, a murder, a vanished corpse. Can you beat a vanished corpse?

But first, duty calls. I swallow my pills, park at my desktop, knock the mouse to one side, enter the password. And log on to the Agora.

At any hour, at *all* hours, there are at least a few dozen users checked in, a constellation sprawled across the world. Some of them I know by name: Talia from the Bay Area; Phil in Boston; a lawyer from Manchester with the unlawyerly name of Mitzi; Pedro, a Bolivian whose halting English is probably no worse than my pidgin French. Others go by handles, me included—in a cute moment, I opted for Annagoraphobe, but then I outed myself to another user as a psychologist, and word swiftly spread. So now I'm thedoctorisin. She'll see you now.

*Agoraphobia:* in translation the fear of the marketplace, in practice the term for a range of anxiety disorders. First documented in the late 1800s, then "codified as an independent diagnostic entity" a century later, though largely comorbid with panic disorder. You can read all about it, if you like, in the *Diagnostic and Statistical Manual of Mental Disorders, Fifth Edition. DSM-5* for short. It's always amused me, that title;

it sounds like a movie franchise. *Liked* Mental Disorders 4? *You'll love the sequel!*

The medical literature is uncommonly imaginative when it comes to diagnostics. "Agoraphobic fears... include being outside the home alone; being in a crowd, or standing in a line; being on a bridge." What I wouldn't give to stand on a bridge. Hell, what I wouldn't give to stand in a line. I like this one, too: "Being in the center of a theater row." Center seats, no less.

Pages 113 through 133, if you're interested.

Many of us—the most severely afflicted, the ones grappling with post-traumatic stress disorder—are housebound, hidden from the messy, massy world outside. Some dread the heaving crowds; others, the storm of traffic. For me, it's the vast skies, the endless horizon, the sheer exposure, the crushing pressure of the outdoors. "Open spaces," the *DSM-5* calls it vaguely, anxious to get to its 186 footnotes.

As a doctor, I say that the sufferer seeks an environment she can control. Such is the clinical take. As a sufferer (and that *is* the word), I say that agoraphobia hasn't ravaged my life so much as become it.

The Agora welcome screen greets me. I scan the message boards, comb the threads. 3 MONTHS STUCK IN MY HOUSE. I hear you, Kala88; almost ten months and counting here. AGORA DEPENDENT ON MOOD? Sounds more like social phobia, EarlyRiser. Or a troubled thyroid. STILL CAN'T GET A JOB. Oh, Megan—I know, and I'm sorry. Thanks to Ed, I don't need one, but I miss my patients. I worry about my patients.

A newcomer has emailed me. I direct her to the survival manual I whipped up back in the spring: "So You Have a Panic Disorder"—I think it sounds agreeably jaunty.

Q : How do I eat?
A : Blue Apron, Plated, HelloFresh... there are lots of delivery options available in the US! Those abroad can likely find similar services.
Q : How do I get my medication?
A : All the major pharmacies in the US now come straight to your door. Have your doctor speak to your local pharmacy if there's a problem.
Q : How do I keep the house clean?
A : Clean it! Hire a cleaning agency or do it yourself. (I do neither. My place could use a wipe-down.)
Q : What about trash disposal?
A : Your cleaner can take care of this, or you can arrange for a friend to help.
Q : How do I keep from getting bored?
A : Now, *that's* the tough question...

Et cetera. I'm pleased with the document, on the whole. Would have loved to have had it myself.

Now a chat box appears on my screen.

SALLY4TH: hello doc!

I can feel a smile twitching on my lips. Sally: twenty-six, based in Perth, was attacked earlier this year, on Easter Sunday. She suffered a broken arm and severe contusions to her eyes and face; her rapist was never identified or apprehended. Sally spent four months indoors, isolated in the most isolated city in the world, but has been getting out of the house for more than ten weeks now—good on her, as she'd say. A psychologist, aversion therapy, and propranolol. Nothing like a beta-blocker.

THEDOCTORISIN: Hello yourself! All okay?

SALLY4TH: all ok! picnic this morning!!

She's always been fond of exclamation marks, even in the depths of depression.

THEDOCTORISIN: How was it?

SALLY4TH: i survived! :)

She likes emoticons, too.

THEDOCTORISIN: You are a survivor! How is the Inderal?

SALLY4TH: good, i'm down to 80mg

THEDOCTORISIN: 2x a day?

SALLY4TH: 1x!!

THEDOCTORISIN: Minimum dosage! Fantastic! Side effects?

SALLY4TH: dry eyes, that's it

That's lucky. I'm on a similar drug (among others), and from time to time the headaches nearly rupture my brain. PROPRANOLOL CAN LEAD TO MIGRAINE, HEART ARRHYTHMIA, SHORTNESS OF BREATH, DEPRESSION, HALLUCINATIONS, SEVERE SKIN REACTION, NAUSEA, DIARRHEA, DECREASED LIBIDO, INSOMNIA, AND DROWSINESS. "What that medicine needs is more side effects," Ed said to me.

"Spontaneous combustion," I suggested.

"The screaming shits."

"Slow, lingering death."

THEDOCTORISIN: Any relapses?

SALLY4TH: I had a wobble last week

SALLY4TH: but got thru it

SALLY4TH: breathing exercises

THEDOCTORISIN: The old paper bag.

SALLY4TH: I feel like an idiot but it works

THEDOCTORISIN: It does indeed. Well done.

SALLY4TH: thanx :)

I sip my wine. Another chat box pops up: Andrew, a man I met on a site for classic-film enthusiasts.

Graham Greene series @ Angelika this w/e?

I pause. *The Fallen Idol* is a favorite—the doomed butler; the fateful paper plane—and it's been fifteen years since I watched *Ministry of Fear*. And old movies, of course, brought me and Ed together.

But I haven't explained my situation to Andrew.

*Unavailable* sums it up.

I return to Sally.

THEDOCTORISIN: Are you keeping up with your psychologist?

SALLY4TH: yes :) thanx. down to just 1x week. she says progress is excellent

SALLY4TH: meds and beds is the key

THEDOCTORISIN: Are you sleeping well?

SALLY4TH: i still get bad dreams

SALLY4TH: u?

THEDOCTORISIN: I'm sleeping a lot.

Too much, probably. I should mention that to Dr Fielding. Not sure I will.

SALLY4TH: ur progress? u fit for fight?

THEDOCTORISIN: I'm not as quick as you! PTSD is a beast. But I'm tough.

SALLY4TH: yes u r!

SALLY4TH: just wanted to check on my friends here—thinking about u all!!!

I bid Sally adieu just as my tutor dials in on Skype. "Bonjour, Yves," I mutter to myself. I pause for a moment before answering; I look forward to seeing him, I realize—that inky hair, that dark bloom to his skin. Those eyebrows that bolt into each other and buckle like *l'accent circonflexe* when my accent puzzles him, which is often.

If Andrew checks in again, I'll ignore him for now. Maybe for good. Classic cinema: That's what I share with Ed. No one else.

I upend the hourglass on my desk, watch how the little pyramid of sand seems to pulse as the grains dimple it. So much time. Nearly a year. I haven't left the house in nearly a year.

Well, almost. Five times in eight weeks I've managed to venture outside, out back, into the garden. My "secret weapon," as Dr Fielding calls it, is my umbrella—Ed's umbrella, really, a rickety London Fog contraption. Dr Fielding, a rickety contraption himself, will stand like a scarecrow in the garden as I push the door open, the umbrella brandished before me. A flick of the spring and it blooms; I stare intently at the bowl of its body, at its ribs and skin. Dark tartan, four squares of black arranged across each fold of canopy, four lines of white in every warp and weft. Four squares, four lines. Four blacks, four whites. Breathe in, count to four. Breathe out, count to four. Four. The magic number.

The umbrella projects straight ahead of me, like a saber, like a shield.

And then I step outside.

Out, two, three, four.

In, two, three, four.

The nylon glows against the sun. I descend the first step (there are, naturally, four) and tilt the umbrella toward the sky, just a bit, peek at his shoes, his shins. The world teems in my peripheral vision, like water about to flood a diving bell.

"Remember, you've got your secret weapon," Dr Fielding calls.

It's not a secret, I want to cry; it's a fucking umbrella, wielded in broad daylight.

Out, two, three, four; in, two, three, four—and unexpectedly it works; I'm conducted down the steps (out, two, three, four) and across a few yards of lawn (in, two, three, four). Until the panic wells within, a rising tide that swamps my sight, drowns out Dr Fielding's voice. And then... best not to think of it.

# SATURDAY, OCTOBER 30

## 7

A storm. The ash tree cowers, the limestone glowers, dark and damp. I remember dropping a glass onto the patio once; it burst like a bubble, merlot flaring across the ground and flooding the veins of the stonework, black and bloody, crawling toward my feet.

Sometimes, when the skies are low, I imagine myself overhead, in a plane or on a cloud, surveying the island below: the bridges spoked from its east coast; the cars sucked toward it like flies swarming a lightbulb.

It's been so long since I felt the rain. Or wind—the caress of wind, I nearly said, except that sounds like something you'd read in a supermarket romance.

It's true, though. And snow too, but snow I never want to feel again.

A peach was mixed in with my Granny Smiths in this morning's FreshDirect delivery. I wonder how that happened.

The night we met, at an art-house screening of *The 39 Steps*, Ed and I compared histories. My mother, I told him, had weaned me on old thrillers and classic noir; as a teenager I preferred the company of Gene Tierney and Jimmy Stewart to that of my classmates. "Can't decide if that's sweet or sad," said Ed, who until that evening had never seen a black-and-white movie. Within two hours, his mouth was on mine.

*You mean your mouth was on mine,* I imagine him saying.

In the years before Olivia, we'd watch a movie at least once a week—all the vintage suspense flicks from my childhood: *Double Indemnity, Gaslight, Saboteur, The Big Clock...* We lived in monochrome those nights. For me, it was a chance to revisit old friends; for Ed, it was an opportunity to make new ones.

And we'd make lists. The *Thin Man* franchise, ranked from best (the original) to worst (*Song of the Thin Man*). Top movies from the bumper crop of 1944. Joseph Cotten's finest moments.

I can do lists on my own, of course. For instance: best Hitchcock films not made by Hitchcock. Here we go:

*Le Boucher,* the early Claude Chabrol that Hitch, according to lore, wished he'd directed. *Dark Passage,* with Humphrey Bogart and Lauren Bacall—a San Francisco valentine, all velveteen with fog, and antecedent to any movie in which a character goes under the knife to disguise himself. *Niagara,* starring Marilyn Monroe; *Charade,* starring Audrey Hepburn; *Sudden Fear!,* starring Joan Crawford's eyebrows. *Wait Until Dark:* Hepburn again, a blind woman stranded in her basement apartment. I'd go berserk in a basement apartment.

Now, movies that postdate Hitch: *The Vanishing,* with its sucker-punch finale. *Frantic,* Polanski's ode to the master. *Side Effects,* which begins as a Big Pharma screed before slithering like an eel into another genre altogether.

Okay.

Popular film misquotes. "Play it again, Sam": *Casablanca,* allegedly, except neither Bogie nor Bergman ever said it. "He's alive": Frankenstein doesn't gender his monster; cruelly, it's just "It's alive."

"Elementary, my dear Watson" does crop up in the first Holmes film of the talkie era, but appears nowhere in the Conan Doyle canon.

Okay.

What next?

I flip open my laptop, visit the Agora. A message from Mitzi in Manchester; a progress report courtesy of Dimples 2016 in Arizona. Nothing of note.

In the front parlour of number 210, the Takeda boy draws his bow across the cello. Farther east, the four Grays flee the rain, charging up their front steps, laughing. Across the park, Alistair Russell fills a glass at the kitchen tap.

# 8

Late afternoon, and I'm pouring a California pinot noir into a tumbler when the doorbell chimes. I drop my glass.

It explodes, a long tongue of wine licking the white birch. "Fuck," I shout. (Something I've noticed: In the absence of others, I swear more often and more loudly. Ed would be appalled. *I'm* appalled.)

I've just seized a fistful of paper towels when the bell rings again. *Who the hell?* I think—or have I said it? David left an hour ago for a job in East Harlem—I watched him from the study—and I'm not expecting any deliveries. I stoop, cram the towels against the mess, then march to the door.

Framed within the intercom screen is a tall kid in a slim jacket, hands clasping a small white box. It's the Russell boy.

I press the Talk button. "Yes?" I call. Less inviting than *Hello*, more gracious than *Who the hell?*

"I live across the park," he says, almost shouting, his voice improbably sweet. "My mom asked me to give you this." I watch him thrust the box toward the speaker; then, unsure where the camera might be, he slowly pivots, arms orbiting overhead.

"You can just..." I begin. Should I ask him to deposit it in the hall? Not very neighborly, I suppose, but I haven't bathed in two days, and the cat might nip at him.

He's still on the stoop, box held aloft.

"... come in," I finish, and I tap the buzzer.

I hear the lock unbuckle and move to the door, cautiously, the way Punch approaches unfamiliar people—or used to, back when unfamiliar people visited the house.

A shadow piles up against the frosted glass, dim and slim, like a sapling. I turn the knob.

He's tall indeed, baby-faced and blue-eyed, with a flap of sandy hair and a faint scar notching one eyebrow, trailing up his forehead. Maybe fifteen years old. He looks like a boy I once knew, once kissed—summer camp in Maine, a quarter century ago. I like him.

"I'm Ethan," he says.

"Come in," I repeat.

He enters. "It's dark in here."

I flick the switch on the wall.

As I examine him, he examines the room: the paintings, the cat spread along the chaise, the mound of sodden towels melting on the kitchen floor. "What happened?"

"I had an accident," I say. "I'm Anna. Fox," I add, in case he goes in for formalities; I'm old enough to be his (young) mother.

We shake hands, then he offers me the box, bright and tight and lashed with ribbon. "For you," he says shyly.

"Just set that down over there. Can I get you something to drink?"

He moves to the sofa. "Could I have some water?"

"Sure." I return to the kitchen, clear up the wreckage. "Ice?"

"No, thanks." I fill a glass, then another, ignoring the bottle of pinot noir on the counter.

The box squats on the coffee table, next to my laptop. I'm still logged in to the Agora, having talked DiscoMickey through an incipient panic attack a little while ago; his thank-you note is writ large across the screen. "Right," I say, sitting beside Ethan, setting his glass in front of him. I snap the computer shut and reach for the gift. "Let's see what we've got here."

I tug the ribbon, lift the flap, and from a nest of tissue remove a candle—the kind with blooms and stalks trapped inside like insects in amber. I bring it to my face, making a show of it.

"Lavender," Ethan volunteers.

"I thought so." I inhale. "I lav lovender." Try again. "I love lavender."

He smiles a bit, one corner of his mouth tipping upward, as though tugged by a string. He's going to be a handsome man, I realize, in just a few years. That scar—women will love it. Girls might love it already. Or boys.

"My mom asked me to give this to you. Like, days ago."

"That's very thoughtful. New neighbors are supposed to give *you* gifts."

"One lady came by already," he says. "She told us that we didn't need such a big house if we're such a small family."

"I bet that was Mrs Wasserman."

"Yes."

"Ignore her."

"We did."

Punch has dropped from the chaise onto the floor and approaches us gingerly. Ethan leans forward, lays his hand on the rug, palm upward. The cat pauses, then slithers toward us, sniffing at Ethan's fingers, licking them. Ethan giggles.

"I love cats' tongues," he says, as though confessing.

"So do I." I sip my water. "They're covered in little barbs—little needles," I say, in case he doesn't know the word *barb*.

I realize I'm not certain how to speak to a teenager; my oldest patients were twelve. "Shall I light the candle?"

Ethan shrugs, smiles. "Sure."

I find a matchbox in the desk, cherry red, the words THE RED CAT marching across it; I remember dining there with Ed, more than two years ago now. Or three. Chicken tagine, I think, and as I recall, he praised the wine. I wasn't drinking as much then.

I strike a match, light the wick. "Look at that," I say as a little claw of flame scratches at the air; the glow blossoms, the blossoms glow. "How lovely."

There's a soft silence. Punch figure-eights around Ethan's legs, then vaults to his lap. Ethan laughs, a bright bark.

"I think he likes you."

"I guess so," he says, crooking a finger behind the cat's ear and gently niggling it.

"He doesn't like most people. Bad temper."

A low growl, like a quiet motor. Punch is actually purring.

Ethan grins. "Is he an indoor-only cat?"

"He has a cat flap in the kitchen door." I point to it. "But mostly he stays inside."

"Good boy," Ethan murmurs as Punch burrows into his armpit.

"How are you liking your new house?" I ask.

He pauses, kneading the cat's skull with his knuckles. "I miss the old one," he says after a moment.

"I bet. Where did you live before?" I already know the answer, of course.

"Boston."

"What brought you to New York?" I know this one, too.

"My dad got a new job." A transfer, technically, but I'm hardly going to argue. "My room's bigger here," he says, as though the thought has just occurred to him.

"The people who lived there before you did a big renovation."

"My mom says it was a gut job."

"Exactly. A gut job. And they combined some of the rooms upstairs."

"Have you been to my house?" he asks.

"I've been a few times. I didn't know them very well—the Lords. But they had a holiday party every year, so that's when I'd come over." It was nearly a year ago, in fact, that I last visited. Ed was there with me. He left two weeks later.

I've started to relax. For a moment I think it's Ethan's company—he's soft-spoken and easy; even the cat approves—but then I realize that I'm reverting to analyst mode, to the seesaw give-and-take of Q&A. Curiosity and compassion: the tools of my trade.

And in an instant, for a moment, I'm back there, in my office on East Eighty-Eighth, the small hushed room sunk in dim light, two deep chairs opposite each other, a pond of blue rug between them. The radiator hisses.

The door drifts open, and there in the waiting area is the sofa, the wooden table; the slithering stacks of *Highlights* and *Ranger Rick*; the bin brimming with chunks of Lego; the white-noise machine purring in the corner.

And Wesley's door. Wesley, my business partner, my grad-school mentor, the man who recruited me into private practice. Wesley Brill—Wesley Brilliant, we called him, he of the sloppy hair and mismatched socks, the lightning brain and thunder voice. I see him in his office, slouched in his Eames lounger, long legs arrowed toward the center of the room, a book propped in his lap. The window is open, gasping in the winter air. He's been smoking. He looks up.

"Hello, Fox," he says.

"My room is bigger than my old room," Ethan repeats.

I settle back, fold one leg over the other. It feels almost absurdly posed. I wonder when I last crossed my legs. "Where are you going to school?"

"Home school," he says. "My mom teaches me." Before I can respond, he nods at a picture on a side table. "Is that your family?"

"Yes. That's my husband and my daughter. He's Ed and she's Olivia."

"Are they home?"

"No, they don't live here. We're separated."

"Oh." He strokes Punch's back. "How old is she?"

"She's eight. How old are you?"

"Sixteen. Seventeen in February."

It's the sort of thing Olivia would say. He's older than he looks.

"My daughter was born in February. Valentine's Day."

"I'm the twenty-eighth."

"So close to leap year," I say.

He nods. "What do you do?"

"I'm a psychologist. I work with children."

He wrinkles his nose. "Why would children need a psychologist?"

"All sorts of reasons. Some of them have trouble in school, some of them have difficulty at home. Some of them have a tough time moving to a new place."

He says nothing.

"So I suppose that if you're homeschooled, you have to meet friends outside of class."

He sighs. "My dad found a swim league for me to join."

"How long have you swum?"

"Since I was five."

"You must be good."

"I'm okay. My dad says I'm capable."

I nod.

"I'm pretty good," he admits modestly. "I teach it."

"You teach swimming?"

"To people with disabilities. Not, like, physical disabilities," he adds.

"Developmental disabilities."

"Yeah. I did that a lot in Boston. I want to do it here, too."

"How did you start doing that?"

"My friend's sister has Down syndrome, and she saw the Olympics a couple years ago and wanted to learn to swim. So I taught her and then some other kids from her school. And then I got into that whole..."—he fumbles for the word—"scene, I guess."

"That's great."

"I'm not into parties or anything like that."

"Not your scene."

"No." Then he smiles. "Not at all."

He twists his head, looks at the kitchen. "I can see your house from my room," he says. "It's up there."

I turn. If he can see the house, that means he's got an easterly view, facing my bedroom. The thought is briefly bothersome—he's a teenage boy, after all. For the second time I wonder if he might be gay.

And then I see that his eyes have gone glassy.

"Oh..." I look to my right, where the tissues should be, where they used to be in my office. Instead there's a picture frame, Olivia beaming at me, gap-toothed.

"Sorry," Ethan says.

"No, don't be sorry," I tell him. "What's wrong?"

"Nothing." He scrubs his eyes.

I wait a moment. He's a child, I remind myself—tall and broken-voiced, but a child.

"I miss my friends," he says.

"I bet. Of course."

"I don't *know* anyone here." A tear tumbles down one cheek. He swipes at it with the heel of his hand.

"Moving is tough. It took me a little while to meet people when I moved here."

He sniffles loudly. "When did you move?"

"Eight years ago. Or actually nine, now. From Connecticut."

He sniffles again, brushes his nose with a finger. "That's not as far away as Boston."

"No. But moving from anywhere is tough." I'd like to hug him. I won't. LOCAL RECLUSE FONDLES NEIGHBOR CHILD.

We sit for a moment in silence.

"Can I have some more water?" he asks. "I'll get it for you."

"No, it's fine." He begins to stand; Punch pours himself down his leg, pooling beneath the coffee table.

Ethan walks to the kitchen sink. As the faucet runs, I get up and approach the television, haul open the drawer beneath the set.

"Do you like movies?" I call. No answer; I turn to see him standing at the kitchen door, gazing at the park. Beside him, the bottles in the recycling bin glow fluorescent.

After a moment, he faces me. "What?"

"Do you like movies?" I repeat. He nods. "Come take a look. I've got a big DVD library. Very big. Too big, my husband says."

"I thought you were separated," Ethan mumbles, crossing toward me.

"Well, he's still my husband." I inspect the ring on my left hand, twist it. "But you're right." I gesture at the open drawer. "If you'd like to borrow anything, you're welcome to it. Do you have a DVD player?"

"My dad's got an attachment for his laptop."

"That'll work."

"He might let me borrow it."

"Let's hope so." I'm starting to get a sense of Alistair Russell.

"What sort of movies?" he asks. "Mostly old ones."

"Like, black-and-white?"

"Mostly black-and-white."

"I've never seen a black-and-white movie."

I make full moons of my eyes. "You're in for a treat. All the best movies are black-and-white."

He looks doubtful but peers into the drawer. Nearly two hundred slipcases, Criterion and Kino, Universal's Hitchcock boxed set, assorted film noir collections, *Star Wars* (I'm only human). I inspect the spines: *Night and the City. Whirlpool. Murder, My Sweet.* "Here," I announce, prying loose a case and handing it to Ethan.

"*Night Must Fall*," he reads.

"It's a good one to start with. Suspenseful but not scary."

"Thanks." He clears his throat, coughs. "Sorry," he says, sipping his water. "I'm allergic to cats."

I stare at him. "Why didn't you say so?" I glare at the cat. "He's so friendly. I didn't want to offend him."

"That's ridiculous," I tell him. "In a nice way."

He smiles. "I'd better go," he says. He returns to the coffee table, sets his glass on it, bends to address Punch through the glass. "Not because of you, buddy. Good boy." He straightens up, shakes his hands over his thighs.

"Do you want a lint roller? For the dander?" I'm not even sure I've still got one.

"I'm okay." He looks around. "Can I use your bathroom?" I point to the red room. "All yours."

While he's in there, I check the sideboard mirror. A shower tonight, for sure. Tomorrow at latest.

I return to the sofa and open my laptop. Thanks for your help, DiscoMickey has written. You're my hero.

I rattle off a quick reply as the toilet flushes. Ethan emerges from the bathroom a moment later, rubbing his palms on his jeans. "All set," he informs me. He treads to the door, hands stuffed in pockets, a schoolboy shuffle.

I follow him. "Thanks so much for coming by."

"See you around," he says, pulling the door open.

*No, you won't*, I think. "I'm sure you will," I say.

# 9

After Ethan leaves, I watch *Laura* again. It shouldn't work: Clifton Webb gorging on the scenery, Vincent Price test-driving a southern accent, the oil-and-vinegar leads. But work it does, and oh, that music. "They sent me the script, not the score," Hedy Lamarr once griped.

I leave the candle lit, the tiny blob of flame pulsing.

And then, humming the *Laura* theme, I swipe my phone on and take to the Internet in search of my patients. My former patients. Ten months ago I lost them all: I lost Mary, nine years old, struggling with her parents' divorce; I lost Justin, eight, whose twin brother had died of melanoma; I lost Anne Marie, at age twelve still afraid of the dark. I lost Rasheed (eleven, transgender) and Emily (nine, bullying); I lost a preternaturally depressed little ten-year-old named, of all things, Joy. I lost their tears and their troubles and their rage and their relief. I lost nineteen children all told. Twenty, if you count my daughter.

I know where Olivia is now, of course. The others I've been tracking. Not too often—a psychologist isn't supposed to investigate her patients, past patients included—but every month or so, swollen with longing, I'll take to the web. I've got a few Internet research tools at my disposal: a phantom Facebook account; a stale LinkedIn profile. With young people, though, only Google will do, really.

After reading of Ava's spelling-bee championship and Theo's election to the middle school student council, after scanning the Instagram albums of Grace's mother and scrolling through Ben's Twitter feed (he really ought to activate some privacy settings), after wiping the tears from my cheeks and sinking three glasses of red, I find myself back in my bedroom, browsing photos on my phone. And then, once more, I talk to Ed.

"Guess who," I say, the way I always do.

"You're pretty tipsy, slugger," he points out.

"It's been a long day." I glance at my empty glass, feel a prickle of guilt. "What's Livvy up to?"

"Getting ready for tomorrow."

"Oh. What's her costume?"

"A ghost," Ed says.

"You got lucky."

"What do you mean?"

I laugh. "Last year she was a fire truck."

"Man, that took days."

"It took *me* days."

I can hear him grin.

Across the park, three stories up, through the window and in the depths of a dark room, there's the glow of a computer screen. Light dawns, an instant sunrise; I see a desk, a table lamp, and then Ethan, shucking his sweater. Affirmative: Our bedrooms do indeed face each other.

He turns around, eyes cast down, and peels off his shirt. I look away.

## SUNDAY, OCTOBER 31

# 10

Weak morning light strains through my bedroom window. I roll over; my hip cracks against my laptop. A late night playing bad chess. My knights stumbled, my rooks crashed.

I drag myself to and from the shower, mop my hair with a towel, skid deodorant under my arms. Fit for fight, as Sally says. Happy Halloween.

I won't be answering any doors this evening, of course. David will head out at seven—downtown, I think he said. I bet that's fun.

He suggested earlier that we leave a bowl of candy on the stoop. "Any kid would take it within a minute, bowl and all," I told him.

He seemed miffed. "I wasn't a child psychologist," he said.

"You don't need to have been a child psychologist. You just need to have been a child."

So I'm going to switch off the lights and pretend no one's home.

I visit my film site. Andrew is online; he posted a link to a Pauline Kael essay on *Vertigo*—"stupid" and "shallow"—and beneath that, he's making a list: Best noir to hold hands through? (*The Third Man*. The last shot alone.)

I read the Kael piece, ping him a message. After five minutes, he logs out.

I can't remember the last time someone held my hand.

# 11

*Whap*.

The front door again. This time I'm coiled on the sofa, watching *Rififi*—the extended heist sequence, half an hour without a syllable of dialogue or a note of music, just diegetic sound and the hum of blood in your ears. Yves had suggested I spend more time with French cinema. Presumably a semi-silent film was not what he had in mind. *Quel dommage*.

Then that dull *whap* at the door, a second time.

I peel the blanket from my legs, swing myself to my feet, find the remote, pause the movie.

Twilight sifting down outside. I walk to the door and open it.

*Whap*.

I step into the hall—the one area of the house I dislike and distrust, the cool gray zone between my realm and the outside world. Right now it's dim in the dusk, the dark walls like hands about to clap me between them.

Streaks of leaded glass line the front door. I approach one, gaze through it.

A crack, and the window shudders. A tiny missile has struck: an egg, blasted, its guts spangled across the glass. I hear myself gasp. Through the smear of yolk I can see three kids in the street, their faces bright, their grins bold, one of them poised with an egg in his fist.

I sway where I stand, place a hand against the wall. This is my home. That's my window.

My throat shrinks. Tears well in my eyes. I feel surprised, then ashamed.

*Whap.*

Then angry.

I can't fling wide the door and send them scurrying. I can't barrel outside and confront them. I rap on the window, sharply—

*Whap.*

I slap the heel of my hand against the door.

I bash it with my fist.

I growl, then I roar, my voice bounding between the walls, the dark little hall a chamber of echoes.

I'm helpless.

*No, you're not,* I can hear Dr Fielding say. In, two, three, four.

No, I'm not.

I'm not. I toiled nearly a decade as a graduate student. I spent fifteen months training in inner-city schools. I practiced for seven years. *I'm tough,* I promised Sally.

Scraping my hair back, I retreat to the living room, yank a breath from the air, stab the intercom with one finger.

"Get away from my house," I hiss. Surely they'll hear the squawk outside.

*Whap.*

My finger is wobbling on the intercom button. "*Get away from my house!*"

*Whap.*

I stumble across the room, trip up the stairs, race into my study, to the window. There they are, clustered in the street like marauders, laying siege to my home, their shadows endless in the dying light. I bat at the glass.

One of them points at me, laughs. Winds his arm like a pitcher. Looses another egg.

I knock harder on the glass, hard enough to dislodge a pane. That's my door. This is my home.

My vision blurs.

And suddenly I'm rushing down the stairs; suddenly I'm back in the dark of the hall, my bare feet on the tiles, my hand on the knob. Anger grips me by the throat; my sight is swimming. I seize a breath, seize another.

In-two-three—

I jolt the door open. Light and air blast me.

For an instant it's silent, as silent as the film, as slow as the sunset. The houses opposite. The three kids between. The street around them. Quiet and still, a stopped clock.

I could swear I hear a crack, as of a felled tree.

And then—

—and then it bulges toward me, swelling, now rushing, a boulder flung from a catapult; slams me with such force, walloping my gut, that I fold. My mouth opens like a window. Wind whips into it. I'm an empty house, rotten rafters and howling air. My roof collapses with a groan—

—and I'm groaning, sliding, avalanching, one hand scraped along the brick, the other lunging into space. Eyes reel and roll: the lurid red of leaves, then darkness; lights up on a woman in black, vision blanching, bleaching, until molten white swarms my eyes and pools there, thick and deep. I try to cry out, my lips brush grit. I taste concrete. I taste blood. I feel my limbs pinwheeled on the ground. The ground ripples against my body. My body ripples against the air.

Somewhere in the attic of my brain I recall that this happened once before, on these same steps. I remember the low tide of voices, the odd word breaching bright and clear: *fallen, neighbor, anyone, crazy*. This time, nothing.

Arm slung around someone's neck. Hair, coarser than my own, rubs my face. Feet scuffle feebly on the ground, on the floor; and now I'm inside, in the chill of the hall, in the warmth of the living room.

# 12

"You took a tumble!"

My vision fills like a Polaroid print. I'm looking at the ceiling, at a single recessed light socket staring back at me, a beady eye.

"I'm getting something for you—one second..."

I let my head loll to one side. Velvet fizzes in my ear. The living room chaise—the fainting couch. Ha.

"One second, one second..."

At the kitchen sink stands a woman, turned away from me, a rope of dark hair trailing down her back.

I bring my hands to my face, cup them over my nose and mouth, breathe in, breathe out. Calm. Calm. My lip aches.

"I was just headed next door when I saw those little shits chucking eggs," she explains. "I said to them, 'What are you up to, little shits?,' and then you sort of... *lurched* through the door and went down like a sack of..." She doesn't finish the sentence. I wonder if she was going to say *shit*.

Instead she turns, a glass in each hand, one filled with water, one with something thick and gold. Brandy, I hope, from the liquor cabinet.

"No idea if brandy actually *works*," she says. "I feel like I'm in *Downton Abbey*. I'm your Florence Nightingale!"

"You're the woman from across the park," I mumble. The words stagger off my tongue like drunks from a bar. *I'm tough*. Pathetic.

"What's that?"

And then, in spite of myself: "You're Jane Russell."

She stops, looking at me in wonder, then laughs, her teeth glinting in the half-light. "How do you know that?"

"You said you were going next door?" Trying to enunciate. *Irish wristwatch,* I think. *Unique New York*. "Your son came by."

Through the mesh of my eyelashes I study her. She's what Ed might call, approvingly, a ripe woman: hips and lips full, bust ample, skin mellow, face merry, eyes a gas-jet blue. She wears indigo jeans and a black sweater, scoop-necked, with a silver pendant resting on her chest. Late thirties, I'd guess. She must have been a baby when she had her baby.

As with her son, I like her on sight.

She moves to the chaise, knocks my knee with her own.

"Sit up. In case you've got a concussion." I oblige, dragging myself into position, as she sets the glasses on the table, then parks herself across from me, where her son sat yesterday. She turns to the television, furrows her brow.

"What are you watching? A black-and-white movie?" Baffled.

I reach for the remote and tap the power button. The screen goes blank.

"Dark in here," Jane observes.

"Could you get the lights?" I ask. "I'm feeling a little..." Can't finish.

"Sure." She reaches over the back of the sofa, switches on the floor lamp. The room glows.

I tip my head back, stare at the beveled molding on the ceiling. *In, two, three, four.* It could use a touch-up. I'll ask David. *Out, two, three, four.*

"So," Jane says, elbows on her knees, scrutinizing me. "What happened out there?"

I shut my eyes. "Panic attack."

"Oh, honey—what's your name?"

"Anna. Fox."

"Anna. They were just some stupid kids."

"No, that wasn't it. I can't go outside." I look down, grasp for the brandy.

"But you *did* go outside. Easy does it with that stuff," she adds as I knock back my drink.

"I shouldn't have. Gone outside."

"Why not? You a vampire?"

Practically, I think, appraising my arm—fish-belly white. "I'm agoraphobic?" I say.

She purses her lips. "Is that a question?"

"No, I just wasn't sure you'd know what it meant."

"Of course I know. You don't do open spaces."

I close my eyes again, nod.

"But I thought agoraphobia means you just can't, you know, go camping. Outdoorsy stuff."

"I can't go anywhere."

Jane sucks her teeth. "How long has this been going on?"

I drain the last drops of brandy. "Ten months."

She doesn't pursue it. I breathe deeply, cough.

"Do you need an inhaler or something?"

I shake my head. "That would only make it worse. Raise my heart rate."

She considers this. "What about a paper bag?"

I set the glass down, reach for the water. "No. I mean, sometimes, but not now. Thank you for bringing me inside. I'm very embarrassed."

"Oh, don't—"

"No, I am. Very. It won't become a habit, I promise."

She purses her lips again. Very active mouth, I notice. Possible smoker, although she smells of shea butter. "So it's happened before? You going outside, and... ?"

I grimace. "Back in the spring. Delivery guy left my groceries on the front steps, and I thought I could just... grab them."

"And you couldn't."

"I couldn't. But there were lots of people passing by that time. It took them a minute to decide I wasn't crazy or homeless."

Jane looks around the room. "You definitely aren't homeless. This place is... wow." She takes it in, then pulls her phone from her pocket, checks the screen. "I need to get back to the house," she says, standing.

I try to rise with her, but my legs won't cooperate. "Your son is a very nice boy," I tell her. "He dropped that off. Thank you," I add.

She eyes the candle on the table, touches the chain at her throat. "He's a good kid. Always has been."

"Very nice-looking, too."

"Always has been!" She slides a thumbnail into the locket; it cracks open, and she leans toward me, the locket swaying in the air. I see she expects me to take it. It's oddly intimate, this stranger looming over me, my hand on her chain. Or perhaps I'm just so unaccustomed to human contact.

Inside the locket is a tiny photograph, glossy and vivid: a small boy, age four or so, yellow hair in riot, teeth like a picket fence after a hurricane. One eyebrow cleft by a scar. Ethan, unmistakably.

"How old is he here?"

"Five. But he looks younger, don't you think?"

"I would have guessed four."

"Exactly."

"When did he get so tall?" I ask, releasing the locket.

She gently shuts it. "Sometime between then and now!" She laughs. Then, abruptly: "You're okay for me to leave? You're not going to hyperventilate?"

"I'm not going to hyperventilate."

"Do you want some more brandy?" she asks, bending to the coffee table—there's a photo album there, unfamiliar; she must have brought it with her. She tucks it beneath her arm and points to the empty glass.

"I'll stick with water," I lie.

"Okay." She pauses, her gaze fixed on the window. "Okay," she repeats. "So a *very* handsome man just came up the walk." She looks at me. "Is that your husband?"

"Oh, no. That's David. He's my tenant. Downstairs."

"He's your tenant?" Jane brays. "I wish he were *mine*!"

The bell hasn't chimed this evening, not once. Maybe the dark windows put off any trick-or-treaters. Maybe it was the dried yolk.

I subside into bed early.

Midway through graduate school, I met a seven-year-old boy afflicted with the so-called Cotard delusion, a psychological phenomenon whereby the individual believes that he is dead. A rare disorder, with pediatric instances rarer still; the recommended treatment is an antipsychotic regimen or, in stubborn cases, electroconvulsive therapy. But I managed to talk him out of it. It was my first great success, and it brought me to Wesley's attention.

That little boy would be well into his teens now, almost Ethan's age, not quite half mine. I think of him tonight as I stare at the ceiling, feeling dead myself. Dead but not gone, watching life surge forward around me, powerless to intervene.

## MONDAY, NOVEMBER 1

# 13

When I come downstairs this morning, sloping into the kitchen, I find a note slipped beneath the basement door. *Eggs*.

I study it, confused. Does David want breakfast? Then I turn it over, see the word *Cleaned* above the fold. Thank you, David.

Eggs do sound good, come to think of it, so I empty three into a skillet and serve myself sunny-side up. A few minutes later I'm at my desk, sucking the last of the yolk and punching in at the Agora.

Morning is rush hour here—agoraphobes often register acute anxiety after waking up. Sure enough, we're gridlocked today. I spend two hours offering solace and support; I refer users to assorted medications (imipramine is my drug of choice these days, although Xanax never goes out of style); I mediate a dispute over the (indisputable) benefits of aversion therapy; I watch, at the request of Dimples2016, a video clip in which a cat plays the drums.

I'm about to sign off, zip over to the chess forum, avenge Saturday's defeats, when a message box blooms on my screen.

DISCOMICKEY: Thanks again for your help the other day doc.

The panic attack. I'd manned the keyboard for nearly an hour as DiscoMickey, in his words, "freaked out."

THEDOCTORISIN: Anytime. You better?

DISCOMICKEY: Much.

DISCOMICKEY: Writing b/c I'm talking to a lady who's new and she's asking if there are any professionals on here. Sent her your FAQs.

A referral. I check the clock.

THEDOCTORISIN: I might not have much time today, but send her my way.

DISCOMICKEY: Cool.

DISCOMICKEY HAS LEFT THE CHAT.

A moment later, up pops a second chat box. GrannyLizzie. I click on the name, skim the user profile. Age: seventy. Residence: Montana. Joined: two days ago.

I flick another glance at the clock. Chess can wait for a seventy-year-old in Montana.

A strip of text at the bottom of the screen reports that GrannyLizzie is typing. I wait a moment, then another; either she's whipping up a long message or it's a case of senioritis. Both my parents used to stab at the keyboard with their index fingers, like flamingos picking their way through the shallows; it took them half a minute just to bash out a hello.

GRANNYLIZZIE: Well hello there!

Friendly. Before I can respond:

GRANNYLIZZIE: Disco Mickey gave your name to me. Desperate for some advice!

GRANNYLIZZIE: Also for some chocolate, but that's another matter...

I manage to get a word in edgewise.

THEDOCTORISIN: Hello to you! You're new to this forum?

GRANNYLIZZIE: Yes I am!

THEDOCTORISIN: I hope that DiscoMickey made you feel welcome.

GRANNYLIZZIE: Yes he did!

THEDOCTORISIN: How can I help you?

GRANNYLIZZIE: Well I don't think you can help with the chocolate I'm afraid!

Is she effervescent or nervous? I wait it out.

GRANNYLIZZIE: The thing is...

GRANNYLIZZIE: And I hate to say it...

Drum roll...

GRANNYLIZZIE: I haven't been able to leave my home for the past month.

GRANNYLIZZIE: So THAT is the problem!

THEDOCTORISIN: I'm sorry to hear that. May I call you Lizzie?

GRANNYLIZZIE: You bet.

GRANNYLIZZIE: I live in Montana. Grandmother first, art teacher second!

We'll get to all that, but for now:

THEDOCTORISIN: Lizzie, did anything special happen a month ago?

A pause.

GRANNYLIZZIE: My husband died.

THEDOCTORISIN: I see. What was your husband's name?

GRANNYLIZZIE: Richard.

THEDOCTORISIN: I'm so sorry for your loss, Lizzie. Richard was my father's name.

GRANNYLIZZIE: Has your f ather died?

THEDOCTORISIN: He and my mother both died 4 years ago. She had cancer and then he had a stroke 5 months later. But I've always believed that some of the best people are called Richard.

GRANNYLIZZIE: So was Nixon!!!

Good; we're developing a rapport.

THEDOCTORISIN: How long were you married?

GRANNYLIZZIE: Forty seven years.

GRANNYLIZZIE: We met on the job. LOVE AT FIRST SIGHT BY THE WAY!

GRANNYLIZZIE: He taught chemistry. I taught art. Opposites attract!

THEDOCTORISIN: That's amazing! And you have children?

GRANNYLIZZIE: I have two sons and three grandsons.

GRANNYLIZZIE: My sons are pretty cute, but my grandsons are beautiful!

THEDOCTORISIN: That's a lot of boys.

GRANNYLIZZIE: You're telling me!

GRANNYLIZZIE: The things I've seen!

GRANNYLIZZIE: The things I've smelled!

I note the tone, brisk and insistently upbeat; I clock the language, informal but confident, and the precise punctuation, the infrequent errors. She's intelligent, outgoing. Thorough, too—she spells out numbers, and writes by the way instead of btw, although maybe that's a function of age. Whatever the case, she's an adult I can work with.

GRANNYLIZZIE: Are YOU a boy, by the way?

GRANNYLIZZIE: Sorry if you are, it's just that girls are sometimes doctors too! Even out here in Montana!

I smile. I like her.

THEDOCTORISIN: I am indeed a girl doctor.

GRANNYLIZZIE: Good! We need more of you!

THEDOCTORISIN: Tell me, Lizzie, what's happened since Richard passed?

And tell me she does. She tells me how, on returning from the funeral, she felt too frightened to walk the mourners beyond the front door; she tells me that in the days following, it felt like the outside was trying to get into my house, and so she drew the blinds; she tells me about her sons far away in the Southeast, their confusion, their concern.

GRANNYLIZZIE: I've got to tell you, all joking aside, that this is really upsetting.

Time to roll up my sleeves.

THEDOCTORISIN: Naturally it is. What's happening, I think, is that Richard's passing has fundamentally altered your world, but the world outside has moved on without him. And that's very difficult to face and to accept.

I await a response. Nothing.

THEDOCTORISIN: You mentioned that you haven't removed any of Richard's belongings, which I understand. But I'd like you to think about that.

Radio silence.

And then:

GRANNYLIZZIE: I'm so grateful to have found you. Really really.

GRANNYLIZZIE: That's something my grandsons say. They heard it in Shrek. Really really.

GRANNYLIZZIE: May I speak to you again soon, I hope?

THEDOCTORISIN: Really really!

Couldn't help myself.

GRANNYLIZZIE: I am really really (!!) grateful to Disco Mickey for pointing me to you.

You're a doll.

THEDOCTORISIN: My pleasure.

I wait for her to sign off, but she's still typing.

GRANNYLIZZIE: I just realized I don't even know your name!

I hesitate. I've never shared my name on the Agora, not even with Sally. I don't want anyone to find me, to pair my name with my profession and figure me out, unlock me; yet something in Lizzie's story snags my heart: this elderly widow, alone and bereaved, putting on a brave face beneath those huge skies. She can crack jokes all she wants, but she's housebound, and that's terrifying.

THEDOCTORISIN: I'm Anna.

As I prepare to log out, a last message pings on my screen.

GRANNYLIZZIE: Thank you, Anna.

GrannyLizzie has left the chat.

I feel my veins rushing. I've helped someone. I've connected. *Only connect.* Where have I heard that?

I deserve a drink.

# 14

Tripping down to the kitchen, I roll my head against my shoulders, hear the crackle of my bones. Something catches my eye overhead: In the dim recesses of the ceiling, at the very top of the stairwell three stories up, there's a dark stain glaring at me—from the trapdoor of the roof, I think, right beside the skylight.

I knock on David's door. It opens a moment later; he's barefoot, in a wilted T-shirt and slouched jeans. I just woke him up, I see. "Sorry," I say. "Were you in bed?"

"No."

He was. "Could you look at something for me? I think I saw water damage on the ceiling."

We head up to the top floor, past the study, past my bedroom, to the landing between Olivia's room and the second spare.

"Big skylight," David says.

I can't tell if that's a compliment. "It's original," I say, just to say something.

"Oval."

"Yes."

"Haven't seen too many like that."

"Oval?"

But the exchange is over. He eyes the stain.

"That's mildew," he says, hushed, like a doctor gently breaking news to a patient.

"Can we just brush it off?"

"Not going to fix it."

"What will?"

He sighs. "First I need to check out the roof." He reaches for the trapdoor chain and tugs. The door judders open; a ladder slides toward us, screeching; sunshine bolts in. I step to one side, away from the light. Perhaps I am a vampire after all.

David drags the ladder down until it bumps against the floor. I watch him as he mounts the steps, his jeans taut against his rear; then he disappears.

"See anything?" I call.

No response.

"David?"

I hear a clang. A plume of water, mirror-bright in the sunlight, pours onto the landing. I draw back. "Sorry," David says. "Watering can."

"It's fine. Do you see anything?"

A pause, then David's voice again, almost reverent. "It's a jungle up here."

It was Ed's idea, four years ago, after my mother died. "You need a project," he decided; so we set about converting the rooftop into a garden—flower beds, a vegetable patch, a row of miniature boxwoods. And the central feature, what that broker called the pièce de résistance: an arched trellis, six feet wide and twelve long, thick with leaves in spring and summer, a shady tunnel. When my father had his stroke later on, Ed placed a memorial bench within it. *Ad astra per aspera*, read the inscription. *Through adversity to the stars.* I'd sit there on spring and summer evenings, in the gold-green light, reading a book, sipping a glass.

I've scarcely thought of the roof garden lately. It must be wild.

"It's totally overgrown," David confirms. "It's like a forest."

I wish he'd come down.

"Some kind of trellis over there?" he asks. "Tarp covering it?"

We'd sheathe it in its tarp every autumn. I say nothing; I just remember.

"You should be careful up here. Don't want to step on this skylight."

"I'm not planning on going up there," I remind him.

The glass rattles as his foot taps it. "Flimsy. Branch falls on that, it's gonna take out the whole window." Another moment passes. "It's pretty incredible. Want me to take a picture?"

"No. Thanks. What do we do about the damp?"

One foot drops to the ladder, then the other as he descends. "We need a pro." He arrives at the floor, slots the ladder into place. "To seal the roof. But I can use a paint scraper to get rid of the mildew." He folds the trapdoor back into the ceiling. "Sand down the area. Then put on some stain block and some emulsion paint."

"Do you have all that?"

"I'll get the block and the paint. It'd help if we could ventilate in here."

I freeze. "What do you mean?"

"Open some windows. Doesn't have to be on this floor."

"I don't open windows. Anywhere."

He shrugs. "It'd help."

I turn to the stairs. He follows me. We go down in silence.

"Thank you for cleaning up the mess outside," I say, mostly to say something, once we're in the kitchen.

"Who did that?"

"Some kids."

"Do you know who?"

"No." I pause. "Why? Could you rough them up for me?"

He blinks. I press on.

"You're still comfortable downstairs, I hope?" He's been here two months, ever since Dr Fielding suggested that a tenant would be useful: someone to run errands, dispose of the trash, assist with general upkeep, et cetera, all in exchange for reduced rent. David was the first to answer my ad, posted on

Craigslist; I remember thinking his email was terse, even curt, until I met the man and realized he'd been downright chatty.

Just relocated from Boston, experienced handyman, nonsmoker, $7,000 in the bank. We agreed on a lease that afternoon.

"Yeah." He looks up, at the lights sunk in the ceiling. "There a reason you keep it so dark? A medical reason or something?"

I feel myself flush. "A lot of people in my..." What's the word here? "... position feel exposed if the light's too bright." I gesture to the windows. "And there's plenty of natural light in this house in any case."

David considers this, nods.

"Are you getting enough light in your apartment?" I ask.

"It's fine."

Now I nod. "If you find any more of Ed's blueprints down there, just let me know. I'm saving them."

I hear the snicker of Punch's door flap, see him slink into the kitchen.

"I really do appreciate all that you do for me," I continue, although I've mistimed it—he's moving toward the basement door. "With the... trash and the housework and everything. You're a lifesaver," I add, lamely.

"Sure."

"If you wouldn't mind calling someone to take care of the ceiling..."

"Sure."

Punch bounds onto the island between us and drops something from his mouth. I look at it.

A dead rat.

I recoil. I'm gratified to see that David does, too. It's a small one, with oily fur and a black worm of a tail; its body has been mauled.

Punch watches us proudly.

"No," I scold him. He cocks his head.

"He really did a number on it," David says.

I inspect the rat. "Did you do this?" I ask Punch, before I remember I'm interrogating a cat. He springs from the island.

"Look at that," David breathes. I glance up: On the opposite side of the island, he's bent forward, his dark eyes glittering.

"Do we bury it someplace?" I ask. "I don't want it rotting in the trash."

David clears his throat. "Tomorrow's Tuesday," he says. Trash day. "I'll take it all out now. You got a newspaper?"

"Does anyone anymore?" That came out more pointed than I intended. I follow up quickly. "I have a plastic bag."

I find one in a drawer. David extends his hand, but I can do this myself. I snap the bag inside out, tuck my hand inside, gingerly grasp the carcass. A little shiver jolts me.

I tug the bag over the rat and seal the band at the top. David takes it from me and slides open the trash receptacle beneath the island, dumps the dead rat inside. RIP.

Just as he's yanking the garbage bag from its container, there's a sound from downstairs; the pipes sing, the walls start talking to one another. The shower.

I look at David. He doesn't flinch; instead he knots the bag at the top and slings it over his shoulder. "I'll take this outside," he says, striding toward the front door.

It's not as though I was going to ask him her name.

## 15

"Guess who."

"Mom."

I let it slide. "How was Halloween, pumpkin?"

"Good." She's chewing on something. I hope Ed remembers to watch her weight.

"Did you get a lot of candy?"

"A *lot*. More than ever."

"What was your favorite?" Peanut M&M's, of course.

"Snickers."

I stand corrected.

"They're little," she explains. "They're like baby Snickers."

"So did you have Chinese for dinner or Snickers for dinner?"

"Both."

I'll have a word with Ed.

But when I do, he's defensive. "It's the one night of the year she gets to eat candy for dinner," he says.

"I don't want her getting into trouble."

Silence. "With the dentist?"

"With her *weight*."

He sighs. "I can take care of her."

I sigh back. "I'm not saying you can't."

"That's what it sounds like."

I bank a hand against my forehead. "It's just that she's eight years old, and a lot of kids experience significant weight gain at this age. Girls especially."

"I'll be careful."

"And remember she already went through a chubby phase."

"You want her to be a waif?"

"No, that would be just as bad. I want her to be healthy."

"Fine. I'll give her a low-calorie kiss tonight," he says. "A Diet Smooch."

I smile. Still, when we say goodbye, it's stiff.

## TUESDAY, NOVEMBER 2

# 16

In mid-February—after nearly six weeks shriveled inside my house, after I realized that I wasn't Getting Better—I contacted a psychiatrist whose lecture ("Atypical Antipsychotics and Post-Traumatic Stress Disorder") I'd attended at a conference in Baltimore five years back. He didn't know me then. He does now.

Those unfamiliar with therapy often assume that the therapist is by default soft-spoken and solicitous; you smear yourself along his sofa like butter on toast, and you melt. It ain't necessarily so, as the song goes. Exhibit A: Dr Julian Fielding.

For one thing, there's no sofa. We meet every Tuesday in Ed's library, Dr Fielding in the club chair beside the fireplace, me in a wingback by the window. And although he speaks softly, his voice creaking like an old door, he's precise, particular, as a good psychiatrist should be. "Kind of guy who steps out of the shower to piss," Ed has said, more than once.

"So," Dr Fielding rasps. An arrow of afternoon light has shot into his face, making tiny suns of his glasses. "You say that you and Ed argued about Olivia yesterday. Are these conversations helpful?"

I twist my head, glance at the Russell house. I wonder what Jane Russell is up to. I'd like a drink.

My fingers trace the line of my throat. I look back at Dr Fielding.

He watches me, the grooves in his forehead scored deep.

Maybe he's tired—I certainly am. It's been an eventful session: I caught him up on my panic attack (he seemed concerned), on my dealings with David (he seemed uninterested), on my chats with Ed and Olivia (concerned again).

Now I look away once more, unblinking, unthinking, at the books on Ed's shelves. A history of the Pinkerton detectives.

Two volumes on Napoléon. *Bay Area Architecture*. An eclectic reader, my husband. My estranged husband.

"It sounds to me as though these conversations are causing you some mixed feelings," Dr Fielding says. This is classic therapist argot: *It sounds to me*. *What I'm hearing*. *I think you're saying*. We're interpreters. We're translators.

"I keep..." I begin, the words forming in my mouth unbidden. Can I go here again? I can; I do. "I keep thinking—I can't stop thinking—about the trip. I hate that it was my idea."

Nothing from across the room, even though—or perhaps because—he knows this, knows all of it, has heard it over and over. And over.

"I keep wishing it wasn't. Weren't. I keep wishing it had been Ed's idea. Or no one's. That we'd never gone." I knot my fingers. "Obviously."

Gently: "But you did go."

I feel singed.

"You arranged a family vacation. No one should feel ashamed of that."

"In New England, in *winter*."

"Many people go to New England in winter."

"It was stupid."

"It was thoughtful."

"It was incredibly stupid," I insist.

Dr Fielding doesn't respond. The central heating clears its throat, exhales.

"If I hadn't done it, we'd still be together."

He shrugs. "Maybe."

"Definitely."

I can feel his gaze on me like a weight.

"I helped someone yesterday," I say. "A woman in Montana. A grandmother. She's been inside for a month."

He's accustomed to these abrupt swerves—"synaptic leaps," he calls them, even though we both know I'm willfully changing the subject. But I steam ahead, telling him about GrannyLizzie, how I shared my name with her.

"What made you do that?"

"I felt she was trying to connect." Isn't that what—yes, there it is: Isn't that what Forster exhorted us to do? "Only connect"? *Howards End*—July's official book club selection. "I wanted to help her. I wanted to be accessible."

"That was an act of generosity," he says. "I suppose so."

He shifts in his seat. "It sounds to me as though you're getting to a place where you can meet others on their terms, not just your own."

"That's possible."

"That's progress."

Punch has stolen into the room and is circling my feet, eyes on my lap. I hitch one leg beneath the other thigh.

"How is the physical therapy going?" Dr Fielding asks.

I scan my legs and torso with my hand, like I'm presenting a prize on a game show. *You too can win this disused thirty-eight-year-old body!* "I've looked better." And then, before he can correct me, I add, "I know it's not a fitness program."

He corrects me all the same: "It's not *only* a fitness program."

"No, I know."

"Is it going well, then?"

"I'm healed. All better."

He looks at me evenly.

"Really. My spine is fine, my ribs aren't cracked. I don't limp anymore."

"Yes, I noticed."

"But I need a little exercise. And I like Bina."

"She's become a friend."

"In a way," I admit. "A friend I pay."

"She's coming on Wednesdays these days, is that right?"

"Usually."

"Good," he says, as though Wednesday is a day particularly suitable for aerobic activity. He's never met Bina. I can't picture them together; they don't seem to occupy the same dimension.

It's quitting time. I know this without consulting the clock hunched on the mantel, just as Dr Fielding knows it—after years in practice, both of us can time fifty minutes almost to the second. "I want you to continue with the beta-blocker at the same dosage," he says. "You're on one-fifty Tofranil. We'll increase it to two-fifty." He frowns. "That's based on what we've discussed today. It should help with your moods."

"I get pretty blurry as is," I remind him.

"Blurry?"

"Or bleary, I guess. Or both."

"You mean your vision?"

"No, not my vision. It's more..." We've discussed this—doesn't he remember? Or have we discussed it? *Blurry. Bleary.* I could really use that drink. "Sometimes I've got too many thoughts at once. It's like there's a four-way intersection in my brain where everyone's trying to go at the same time." I chuckle, a bit uneasy.

Dr Fielding knits his brow, then sighs. "Well, it's not an exact science. As you know."

"I do. I know."

"You're on quite a few different medications. We'll adjust them one by one until we get it right."

I nod. I know what this means. He thinks I'm getting worse. My chest tightens.

"Try the two-fifty and see how you feel. If it gets problematic, we can look at something to help you focus."

"A nootropic?" Adderall. The number of times parents asked me whether Adderall would benefit their kids, the number of times I turned them down cold—and now I'm angling for it myself. *Plus ça change.*

"Let's discuss it as and when," he says. He slashes his pen across a prescription pad, peels away the top sheet, offers it to me. It twitches in his hand. Essential tremor or low blood sugar? Not, I hope, early-onset Parkinson's. Not my place to ask, either. I take the paper.

"Thank you," I say as he stands, smoothing his tie. "I'll put this to good use."

He nods. "Until next week, then." He turns toward the door. "Anna?" Turning back.

"Yes?"

He nods again. "Please get that prescription filled."

After Dr Fielding leaves, I log the prescription request online. They'll deliver by five P.M. That's enough time for a glass. Or even *deux*.

Not just yet, though. First I drag the mouse to a neglected corner of the desktop, hesitantly double-click on an Excel spreadsheet: meds.xlsx.

Here I've detailed all the drugs I'm on, all the dosages, all the directions... all the ingredients in my pharma-cocktail. I stopped updating it back in August, I see.

Dr Fielding is, as usual, correct: I'm on quite a few medications. I need two hands to count them all. And I know—I wince as I think it—I know I'm not taking them as or when I should, not always. The double doses, the skipped doses, the drunk doses... Dr Fielding would be furious. I need to do better. Don't want to lose my grip.

Command-Q, and I'm out of Excel. Time for that drink.

# 17

With a tumbler in one hand and the Nikon in the other, I settle down in the corner of my study, cupped between the south and west windows, and survey the neighborhood—inventory check, Ed likes to say. There's Rita Miller, returning from yoga, bright with sweat, a cell phone stuck to one ear. I adjust the lens and zoom in: She's smiling. I wonder if it's her contractor on the other end. Or her husband. Or neither.

Next door, outside 214, Mrs Wasserman and her Henry pick their way down the front steps. Off to spread sweetness and light.

I swing my camera west: Two pedestrians loiter outside the double-wide, one of them pointing at the shutters. "Good bones," I imagine him saying.

God. I'm inventing conversations now.

Cautiously, as though I don't want to be caught—and indeed I don't—I slide my sights across the park, over to the Russells'. The kitchen is dim and vacant, its blinds partly down, like half-shut eyes; but one floor up, in the parlour, captured neatly within the window, I spot Jane and Ethan on a candy-striped love seat. She wears a butter-yellow sweater that exposes a terse slit of cleavage; her locket dangles there, a mountaineer above a gorge.

I twist the lens; the image sharpens. She's speaking quickly, teeth bared in a grin, her hands a flurry. His eyes are on his lap, but that shy smile skews his lips.

I haven't mentioned the Russells to Dr Fielding. I know what he'll say; I can analyze myself: I've located in this nuclear unit—this mother, this father, their only child—an echo of my own. One house away, one door down, there's the family I had, the life that was mine—a life thought lost, irretrievably, except here it is, right across the park. *So what?* I think. Maybe I say it; these days I'm not sure.

I sip my wine, wipe my lip, raise the Nikon again. Look through the lens.

She's looking back at me.

I drop the camera in my lap.

No mistake: Even with my naked eye, I can clearly see her level gaze, her parted lips.

She raises a hand, waves it.

I want to hide.

Should I wave back? Do I look away? Can I blink at her, blankly, as though I'd been aiming the camera at something else, something near her? *Didn't see you there?*

No.

I shoot to my feet, the camera tumbling to the floor. "Leave it," I say—I definitely say it—and I flee the room, into the dark of the stairwell.

No one's ever caught me before. Not Dr and Rita Miller, not the Takedas, not the Wassermen, not the gaggle of Grays. Not the Lords before they moved, nor the Motts before they split. Not passing cabs, not passersby. Not even the postman, whom I used to photograph every day, at every door. And for months I'd pore over those pictures, reliving those moments, until at last I could no longer keep up with the world beyond my window. I still make the odd exception, of course—the Millers interest me. Or they did before the Russells arrived.

And that Opteka zoom is better than binoculars.

But now shame live-wires through my body. I think of everyone and everything I've caught on camera: the neighbors, the strangers, the kisses, the crises, the chewed nails, the dropped change, the strides, the stumbles. The Takeda boy, his eyes closed, fingers quaking on his cello strings. The Grays, wineglasses aloft in a giddy toast. Mrs Lord in her living room, lighting candles atop a cake. The young Motts, in the dying days of their marriage, bellowing at each other from opposite ends of their Valentine-red parlour, a vase in ruins on the floor between them.

I think of my hard drive, swollen with stolen images. I think of Jane Russell as she looked at me, unblinking, across the park. I'm not invisible. I'm not dead. I'm alive, and on display, and ashamed.

I think of Dr Brulov in *Spellbound:* "My dear girl, you cannot keep bumping your head against reality and saying it is not there."

Three minutes later, I step back into the study. The Russells' love seat is empty. I glance at Ethan's bedroom; he's in there, crouched over his computer.

Carefully, I pick up the camera. It's undamaged. Then the doorbell rings.

# 18

"You must be bored as hell," she says when I open the hall door. Then she folds me into a hug. I laugh, nervously. "Sick of all those black-and-white movies, I bet."

She surges past me. I still haven't said a word.

"I brought something for you." She smiles, dipping a hand into her bag. "It's cold, too." A sweaty bottle of Riesling. My mouth waters. It's been ages since I drank white.

"Oh, you shouldn't—"

But she's already chugging toward the kitchen.

Within ten minutes we're glugging the wine. Jane sparks a Virginia Slim, then another, and soon the air wobbles with smoke, rolling overhead, roiling beneath the ceiling lights. My Riesling tastes of it. I find I don't mind; reminds me of grad school, starless nights outside the taverns of New Haven, men with mouths like ash.

"You've got a lot of merlot over there," she says, eyeing the kitchen counter.

"I order it in bulk," I explain. "I like it."

"How often do you restock?"

"Just a few times a year." At least once a month.

She nods. "You've been like this—how long did you say?" she asks. "Six months?"

"Almost eleven."

"Eleven months." Pressing her lips into a tiny O. "I can't whistle. But pretend I just did." She jams her cigarette into a cereal bowl, steeples her fingers, leans forward, as though in prayer. "So what do you *do* all day?"

"I counsel people," I say, nobly.

"Who?"

"People online."

"Ah."

"And I take French lessons online. And I play chess," I add.

"Online?"

"Online."

She sweeps a finger along the tide line in her wineglass. "So the Internet," she says, "is sort of your... window to the world."

"Well, so is my actual window." I gesture to the expanse of glass behind her.

"Your spyglass," she says, and I blush. "I'm *kidding*."

"I'm so sorry about—"

She waves a hand, lights a fresh cigarette. "Oh, hush." Smoke leaks from her mouth. "Do you have a real chessboard?"

"Do you play?"

"I used to." She slants the cigarette against the bowl. "Show me what you got."

We're waist-deep in our first game when the doorbell rings. Five sharp—the pharmacy delivery. Jane does the honors. "Door-to-door drugs!" she squawks, shuttling back from the hall. "These any good?"

"They're uppers," I say, uncorking a second bottle. Merlot this time.

"Now it's a party."

As we drink, as we play, we chat. We're both mothers of only children, as I knew; we're both sailors, as I hadn't known. Jane prefers solo craft, I'm more into two-handers—or I was, anyway.

I tell her about my honeymoon with Ed: how we'd chartered an Alerion, a thirty-three-footer, and cruised the Greek Isles, pinballing between Santorini and Delos, Naxos and Mykonos. "Just the two of us," I remember, "scudding around the Aegean."

"That's just like *Dead Calm*," Jane says.

I swallow some wine. "I think in *Dead Calm* they were in the Pacific."

"Well, except for that, it's just like *Dead Calm*."

"Also, they went sailing to recover from an accident."

"Okay, right."

"And then they rescued a psychopath who tried to kill them."

"Are you going to let me make my point or not?"

While she frowns at the chessboard, I rummage through the fridge for a stick of Toblerone, chop it roughly with a kitchen knife. We sit at the table, chewing. Candy for dinner. Just like Olivia.

Later:

"Do you get a lot of visitors?" She strokes her bishop, slides him across the board.

I shake my head, shake the wine down my throat. "None. You and your son."

"Why? Or why not?"

"I don't know. My parents are gone, and I worked too much to have many friends."

"No one from work?"

I think of Wesley. "It was a two-person practice," I say. "So now he has a double load to keep him busy."

She looks at me. "That's sad."

"You're telling me."

"Do you even have a *phone*?"

I point to the landline, lurking in a corner on the kitchen counter, and pat my pocket. "Ancient, ancient iPhone, but it works. In case my psychiatrist calls. Or anyone else. My tenant."

"Your handsome tenant."

"My handsome tenant, yes." I take a sip, take her queen. "That was cold." She flicks a speck of ash from the table and roars with laughter.

After the second game, she requests a tour of the house. I hesitate, just for a moment; the last person to examine the place top to bottom was David, and before that... I truly can't recall. Bina's never been beyond the first story; Dr Fielding is confined to the library. The very idea feels intimate, as though I'm about to lead a new lover by the hand.

But I agree, and escort her room by room, floor by floor.

The red room: "I feel like I'm trapped in an artery." The library: "So many books! Have you read all of them?" I shake my head. "Have you read *any* of them?" I giggle.

Olivia's bedroom: "Maybe a little small? Too small. She needs a room she can grow into, like Ethan's." My study, on the other hand: "Ooh and aah," says Jane. "A girl could get stuff *done* in a place like this."

"Well, I mostly play chess and talk to shut-ins. If you call that getting stuff done."

"Look." She sets her glass on the windowsill, slides her hands into her back pockets. Leans into the window. "There's the house," she says, gazing at her home, her voice slung low, almost husky.

She's been so playful, so jolly, that to see her looking serious produces a kind of jolt, a needle skidding off the vinyl. "There's the house," I agree.

"Nice, isn't it? Quite a place."

"It is."

She peers outside a minute longer. Then we return to the kitchen.

Later still:

"Get much use out of that?" Jane asks, roaming the living room as I debate my next move. The sun is sinking fast; in her yellow sweater, in the frail light, she looks like a wraith, floating through my house.

She's pointing to the umbrella, leaning like a drunkard against a far wall.

"More than you'd think," I reply. I rock back in my chair and describe Dr Fielding's backyard therapy, the unsteady march through the door and down the steps, the bubble of nylon shielding me from oblivion; the clarity of outside air, the drift of wind.

"Interesting," says Jane.

"I believe it's pronounced 'ridiculous.'"

"But does it work?" she asks.

I shrug. "Sort of."

"Well," she says, patting the umbrella handle as you would a dog's head, "there you go."

"Hey, when's your birthday?"

"You going to buy me something?"

"Easy there."

"Coming up, actually," I say.

"So's mine."

"November eleventh."

She gawks. "That's my birthday, too."

"You're kidding."

"I am not. Eleven eleven."

I lift my glass. "To eleven eleven."

We toast.

"Got a pen and paper?"

I fetch both from a drawer, lay them before her. "Just sit there," Jane tells me. "Look pretty." I bat my lashes.

She whips the pen across the sheet, short, sharp strokes. I watch my face take form: the deep eyes, the soft cheekbones, the long jaw. "Make sure you get my underbite," I urge her, but she shushes me.

For three minutes she sketches, twice lifting her glass to her lips. "Voilà," she says, presenting the paper to me.

I study it. The likeness is astonishing. "Now *that* is a nifty trick."

"Isn't it?"

"Can you do others?"

"You mean, portraits besides yours? Believe it or not, I can."

"No, I mean—animals, you know, or still lifes. Lives."

"I don't know. I'm mostly interested in people. Same as you." With a flourish, she scribbles her signature in one corner. "*Ta-da*. A Jane Russell original."

I slip the sketch into a kitchen drawer, the one where I keep the good table linens. Otherwise it'd probably get stained.

"Look at all those." They're scattered like gems across the table. "What's that one do?"

"Which one?"

"The pink one. Octagon. No, six-agon."

"Hexagon."

"Fine."

"That's Inderal. Beta-blocker."

She squints at it. "That's for heart attacks."

"Also for panic attacks. It slows your heart rate."

"And what's that one? The little white oval?"

"Aripiprazole. Atypical antipsychotic."

"That sounds serious."

"Sounds and is, in some cases. For me it's just an add-on. Keeps me sane. Makes me fat."

She nods. "And what's that one?"

"Imipramine. Tofranil. For depression. Also bed-wetting."

"You're a bed wetter?"

"Tonight I might be." I sip my wine.

"And that one?"

"Temazepam. Sleeping pill. That's for later."

She nods. "Are you supposed to be taking any of these with alcohol?"

I swallow. "Nope."

It's only as the pills squeeze down my throat that I remember I already took them this morning.

Jane casts her head back, her mouth a fountain of smoke. "*Please* don't say checkmate." She giggles. "My ego can't take three in a row. Remember that I haven't played in *years*."

"It shows," I tell her. She snorts, laughs, exposing a trove of silver fillings.

I inspect my prisoners: both rooks, both bishops, a chain gang of pawns. Jane has captured a single pawn and a lonely knight. She sees me looking, swats the knight onto its side. "Horse down," she says. "Summon the vet."

"I love horses," I tell her.

"Look at that. Miracle recovery." She rights the knight, strokes its marble mane.

I smile, drain the last of my red. She eases more into my glass. I watch her. "I love your earrings, too."

She fingers one of them, then the other—a little choir of pearls in each ear. "Gift from an old boyfriend," she says.

"Does Alistair mind you wearing them?"

She thinks about it, then laughs. "I doubt Alistair knows." She spurs the wheel of her lighter with her thumb, kisses it to a cigarette.

"Knows you're wearing them or knows who they're from?"

Jane inhales, arrows smoke to one side. "Either. Both. He can be difficult." She taps her cigarette against the bowl. "Don't get me wrong—he's a good man, and a good father. But he's controlling."

"Why's that?"

"Dr Fox, are you analyzing me?" she asks. Her voice is light, but her eyes are cool.

"If anything, I'm analyzing your husband."

She inhales again, frowns. "He's always been like that. Not very trusting. At least not with me."

"And why's *that*?"

"Oh, I was a wild child," she says. "*Dis-so-lute*. That's the word. That's his—that's Alistair's word, anyway. Bad crowds, bad choices."

"Until you met Alistair?"

"Even then. It took me a little while to clean myself up." It couldn't have taken *that* long, I think—by the looks of her, she would've been early twenties when she became a mother.

Now she shakes her head. "I was with someone else for a time."

"Who was that?"

A grimace. "*Was* is right. Not worth mentioning. We've all made mistakes."

I say nothing.

"That ended, anyhow. But my family life is still"—her fingers strum the air—"challenging. That's the word."

"*Le mot juste*."

"Those French lessons are totally paying off." She grits her teeth in a grin, cocking the cigarette upward.

I press her. "What makes your family life challenging?"

She exhales. A perfect wreath of smoke wobbles through the air.

"Do it again," I say, in spite of myself. She does. I'm drunk, I realize.

"You know"—clearing her throat—"it isn't just one thing. It's complicated. Alistair is challenging. Families are challenging."

"But Ethan is a good kid. And I say this as someone who knows a good kid when she sees one," I add.

She looks me in the eye. "I'm glad you think so. I do, too." She bats her cigarette on the lip of the bowl again. "You must miss *your* family."

"Yes. Terribly. But I talk to them every day."

She nods. Her eyes are swimming a bit; she must be drunk, too. "It's not the same as them being here, though, is it?"

"No. Of course not."

She nods a second time. "So. Anna. You'll notice I'm not asking what made you this way."

"Overweight?" I say. "Prematurely gray?" I really am soused.

She sips her wine. "Agoraphobic."

"Well..." If we're trading confidences, then I suppose: "Trauma. Same as anyone." I fidget. "It got me depressed. Severely depressed. It isn't something I like to remember."

But she's shaking her head. "No, no, I understand—it's not my business. And I'm guessing you can't invite people over for a party. I just think we need to find you some more hobbies. Besides chess and your black-and-white movies."

"And espionage."

"And espionage."

I think about it. "I used to take photographs."

"Looks as though you still do."

That deserves a smirk. "Fair enough. But I mean outdoor photography. I enjoyed it."

"Sort of *Humans of New York* stuff?"

"More like nature photography."

"In New York City?"

"In New England. We used to go there sometimes."

Jane turns to the window. "Look at that," she says, pointing west, and I do: a pulpy sunset, the dregs of dusk, buildings paper-cut against the glow. A bird circles nearby. "That's nature, isn't it?"

"Technically. Some of it. But I mean—"

"The world is a beautiful place," she insists, and she's serious; her gaze is even, her voice level. Her eyes catch mine, hold them. "Don't forget that." She reclines, mashing her cigarette into the hollow of the bowl. "And don't miss it."

I fish my phone from my pocket, aim it at the glass, snap a shot. I look at Jane.

"Attagirl," she growls.

## 19

I pour her into the front hall a little past six. "I've got very important things to do," she informs me.

"So do I," I reply.

Two and a half hours. When did I last speak to someone, anyone, for two and a half hours? I cast my mind back, like a fishing line, across months, across seasons. Nothing. No one. Not since my first meeting with Dr Fielding, long ago in midwinter—and even then I could only talk for so long; my windpipe was still damaged.

I feel young again, almost giddy. Maybe it's the wine, but I suspect not. Dear diary, today I made a friend.

Later that evening, I'm drowsing through *Rebecca* when the buzzer rings.

I shed my blanket, straggle to the door. "Why don't you go?" Judith Anderson sneers behind me. "Why don't you leave Manderley?"

I check the intercom monitor. A tall man, broad-shouldered and slim-hipped, with a bold widow's peak. It takes me a moment—I'm used to seeing him in living colour—but then I recognize Alistair Russell.

"Now what might you be after?" I say, or think. I think I say it. Definitely still drunk. I shouldn't have popped those pills before, either.

I press the buzzer. The latch clacks; the door groans; I wait for it to shut.

When I open the hall door, he's standing there, pale and luminous in the dark. Smiling. Strong teeth bolting from strong gums. Clear eyes, crow's feet raking the edges.

"Alistair Russell," he says. "We live in two-oh-seven, across the park."

"Come in." I extend a hand. "I'm Anna Fox." He waves away my hand, stays put.

"I really don't want to intrude—and I'm sorry to disturb you in the middle of something. Movie night?"

I nod.

He smiles again, bright as a Christmas storefront. "I just wanted to know if you'd had any visitors this evening?"

I frown. Before I can answer, an explosion booms behind me—the shipwreck scene. "Ship ashore!" the coastliners wail. "Everybody down to the bay!" Much hubbub.

I return to the sofa, pause the film. When I face him again, Alistair has taken a step into the room. Bathed in white light, shadows pooled in the hollows of his cheeks, he looks like a cadaver. Behind him the door yawns in the wall, a dark mouth.

"Would you mind closing that?" He does so. "Thanks," I say, and the word slides off my tongue: I'm slurring.

"Have I caught you at a bad time?"

"No, it's fine. Can I get you a drink?"

"Oh, thanks, I'm all right."

"I meant water," I clarify.

He shakes his head politely. "Have you had any visitors tonight?" he repeats.

Well, Jane warned me. He doesn't look like the controlling type, all beady eyes and thin lips; he's more a jovial lion-in-autumn sort, with his peppery beard, his hairline in rapid retreat. I imagine him and Ed getting on, laddishly, hail-fellow-well-mettishly, slinging back whiskey and swapping war stories. But appearances, et cetera.

It's none of his business, of course. Still, I don't want to look defensive. "I've been alone all night," I tell him. "I'm in the middle of a movie marathon."

"What's that?"

"*Rebecca*. One of my favorites. Are you—"

Then I see that he's looking past me, dark brow furrowed. I turn.

The chess set.

I've filed the glasses neatly in the dishwasher, scrubbed the bowl in the sink, but the chessboard is still there, littered with the living and the dead, Jane's fallen king rolled to one side.

I turn back to Alistair.

"Oh, *that*. My tenant likes to play chess," I explain. Casual. He looks at me, squints. I can't tell what he's thinking. Usually this isn't a challenge for me, not after sixteen years spent living in other people's heads; but perhaps I'm out of practice. Or else it's the drink. And the drugs.

"Do you play?"

He doesn't answer for a moment. "Not in a long time," he says. "Is it just you and your tenant here?"

"No, I—yes. I'm separated from my husband. Our daughter is with him."

"Well." He throws one last look at the chess set, at the television; then he moves toward the door. "I appreciate your time. Sorry to bother you."

"Of course," I say as he steps into the hall. "And please thank your wife for the candle."

He pivots, looks at me.

"Ethan brought it over."

"When was that?" he asks.

"A few days ago. Sunday." Wait—what day is today? "Or Saturday." I feel annoyed; why should he care when it was? "Does it matter?"

He pauses, his mouth ajar. Then he flashes an absent smile and leaves without another word.

Before I tilt myself into bed, I peer through the window at number 207. There they are, the family Russell, collected in the parlour: Jane and Ethan on the sofa, Alistair seated in an armchair across from them, speaking intently. *A good man and a good father.*

Who knows what goes on in a family? I learned this as a grad student. "You can spend years with a patient and still they'll surprise you," Wesley told me after we'd shaken hands for the first time, his fingers yellow with nicotine.

"How so?" I asked.

He settled himself behind his desk, clawed his hair back. "You can hear someone's secrets and their fears and their wants, but remember that these exist alongside other people's secrets and fears, people living in the same rooms. You've heard that line about all happy families being the same?"

"*War and Peace*," I said.

"*Anna Karenina*, but that's not the point. The point is, it's untrue. No family, happy or unhappy, is quite like any other. Tolstoy was chock-full o' shit. Remember that."

I remember it now as I gently thumb the focusing ring, as I frame a photo. A family portrait.

But then I set the camera down.

## WEDNESDAY, NOVEMBER 3

# 20

I wake with Wesley in my head.

Wesley and a hard-earned hangover. I wade my way down to the study, as if through a fog, then run into the bathroom and vomit. Heavenly Rapture.

As I've discovered, I throw up with great accuracy. I could go pro, Ed says. One flush and the mess slides away; I rinse my mouth, pat some colour into my cheeks, return to the study.

Across the park, the Russells' windows are empty, their rooms dim. I stare at the house; it stares back. I find I miss them.

I look south, where a beat-up taxi drags itself down the street; a woman strides in its wake, coffee cup in hand, goldendoodle on a leash. I check the clock on my phone: 10:28. How am I up this early?

Right: I forgot my temazepam. Well, I keeled over before I could remember it. It keeps me unconscious, weighs me down like a rock.

And now last night swirls in my brain, strobe-light dazzly, like the carousel from *Strangers on a Train*. Did that even happen? Yes: We uncorked Jane's wine; we talked boats; we wolfed chocolate; I took a photo; we discussed our families; I arranged my pills across the table; we drank some more. Not in that order.

Three bottles of wine—or was it four? Even so, I can stomach more, *have* stomached more. "The pills," I say, the way a detective cries "Eureka!"—my dosage. I double-dosed yesterday, I remember. Must be the pills. "I bet those'll knock you on your behind," Jane giggled after I'd downed the lot, chased them with a slug of wine.

My head is quaking; my hands are shaking. I find a travel-size tube of Advil hidden in the back of my desk drawer, toss three capsules down my throat. The expiration date came and went nine months ago. Children have been conceived and born in that time, I reflect. Whole lives created.

I swallow a fourth, just in case.

And then... What then? Yes: Then Alistair arrived, asking after his wife.

Motion beyond the window. I look up. It's Dr Miller, leaving the house for work. "See you at three fifteen," I tell him. "Don't be late."

*Don't be late*—that was Wesley's golden rule. "For some people, this is the most important fifty minutes of their week," he would remind me. "So for Christ's sake, whatever else you do or fail to do, don't be late."

Wesley Brilliant. It's been three months since I checked up. I grip the mouse and visit Google. The cursor flashes in the search field like a pulse.

He still occupies the same endowed adjunct chair, I see; he's still publishing articles in the *Times* and assorted industry journals. And he's still in practice, of course, although I recall that the office moved to Yorkville over the summer. I say "the office," but really it would've been just Wesley and his receptionist, Phoebe, and her Square card reader. And that Eames lounge chair. He adores his Eames.

That Eames but not much else. Wesley never married; his lectureship was his love, his patients his children. "Don't you go feeling sorry for poor Dr Brill, Fox," he warned me.

I remember it perfectly: Central Park, swans with their question-mark necks, high noon beyond the lacy elms. He'd just asked me to join him as junior partner in the practice. "My life is *too* full," he said. "That's why I need you, or someone like you. There are more children we can help together."

He was, as ever, right.

I click on Google Images. The search yields a small gallery of photographs, none especially recent, none especially flattering. "I don't photograph well," he once observed, uncomplaining, a roily halo of cigar smoke churning overhead, his fingernails stained and split.

"You don't," I agreed.

He hitched one bristly brow. "True or false: You're this tough on your husband."

"Not strictly true."

He snorted. "Something can't be 'strictly true,'" he said. "It's either true or it isn't. It's either real or it's not."

"Quite true," I answered.

# 21

"Guess who," Ed says.

I shift in my chair. "That's my line."

"You sound like hell, slugger."

"Sound and feel."

"Are you sick?"

"I *was*," I reply. I shouldn't tell him about last night, I know, but I'm too weak. And I want to be honest with Ed. He deserves that.

He's displeased. "You can't *do* that, Anna. Not on medication."

"I know." Already I regret having said anything.

"But *really*."

"I know, I said."

When he speaks again, his voice is softer. "You've had a lot of visitors lately," he says. "A lot of stimulation." He pauses. "Maybe these people across the park—"

"The Russells."

"—maybe they can leave you alone for a little while."

"As long as I don't go fainting outside, I'm sure they will."

"You're none of their business." *And they're none of yours,* I bet he's thinking.

"What does Dr Fielding say?" he continues.

I've come to suspect that Ed asks this whenever he's at a loss. "He's more interested in my relationship with you."

"With me?"

"With both of you."

"Ah."

"Ed, I miss you."

I hadn't meant to say it—hadn't even realized I was thinking it. Unfiltered subconscious. "Sorry—that's just the id talking," I explain.

He's quiet for a moment.

Finally: "Well, now it's the Ed talking," he says.

I miss this, too—his stupid puns. He used to tell me I put the "Anna" in "psycho-anna-lyst."

"That's *terrible*," I'd say, gagging. "You know you love it," he'd reply, and I did.

He's quiet again.

Then:

"So what do you miss about me?"

I hadn't expected this. "I miss..." I begin, hoping the sentence will complete itself.

And it spouts from me in a torrent, water pluming from a drain, a burst dam. "I miss the way you bowl," I say, because these idiot words are first to my tongue. "I miss how you can never tie a bowline right. I miss your razor burn. I miss your eyebrows."

As I speak, I find myself climbing the stairs, past the landing, into the bedroom. "I miss your shoes. I miss you asking me for coffee in the morning. I miss that time you wore my mascara and everybody noticed. I miss that time you actually asked me to sew something. I miss how polite you are to waiters."

In my bed now, our bed. "I miss your eggs." Scrambled, even when sunny-side up. "I miss your bedtime stories." The heroines rejected the princes, opting instead to pursue their doctorates. "I miss your Nicolas Cage impression." It got shriller post-*Wicker Man*. "I miss how for the longest time you thought the word *misled* was pronounced 'mizzled.'"

"Misleading little word. It mizzled me."

I laugh wetly, and find I'm crying. "I miss your stupid, stupid jokes. I miss how you always break a piece off a chocolate bar before eating it instead of just biting into the fucking chocolate bar."

"Language."

"Sorry."

"Also, it tastes better that way."

"I miss your heart," I say.

A pause.

"I miss you so much."

Another pause.

"I love you so much." I catch my ragged breath. "Both of you."

No pattern here, not that I can see—and I'm trained to discern patterns. I just miss him. I miss him, I love him. I love them.

There's a silence, long and deep. I breathe.

"But, Anna," he tells me, gently, "if—"

A sound downstairs.

It's quiet, just a low roll. Possibly the house settling.

"Wait," I say to Ed.

Then, clearly, a dry cough, a grunt.

Someone is in my kitchen.

"I have to go," I say to Ed.

"What—"

But I'm already stealing toward the door, phone clutched in one hand; my fingers glance across the screen—911—and my thumb hovers over the Dial button. I remember the last time I called. Called more than once, in fact, or tried to. Someone will answer this time.

I stalk down the stairs, hand slick on the banister, the steps beneath my feet invisible in the dark.

Round the corner, and light swerves into the stairwell. I slink into the kitchen. The phone trembles in my hand.

There's a man by the dishwasher, his broad back to me.

He turns. I press Dial.

# 22

"Hi," David says.

For fuck's sake. I exhale, quickly cancel the call. Tuck the phone back into my pocket.

"Sorry," he adds. "I rang the bell about half an hour ago, but I think you were asleep."

"I must have been in the shower," I say.

He doesn't react. Probably embarrassed for me; my hair isn't even wet. "So I came up through the basement. Hope that's okay."

"Of course it's okay," I tell him. "You're welcome to anytime." I walk to the sink, fill a glass with water. My nerves are shot. "What did you need me for?"

"I'm looking for an X-Acto."

"An X-Acto?"

"X-Acto knife."

"Like a box cutter."

"Exactly."

"X-Acto-ly," I say. What is wrong with me?

"I checked under the sink," he continues, mercifully, "and in that drawer by the phone. Your phone's not plugged in, by the way. I think it's dead."

I can't even remember the last time I used the landline. "I'm sure it is."

"Might want to fix that."

*No need*, I think.

I move back toward the stairs. "I've got a box cutter in the utility closet up here," I say, but he's already trailing me.

At the landing I turn and open the closet door. Black as a spent match inside. I yank the string beside the bare bulb. It's a deep, narrow attic of a room, folded beach chairs slumped at the far end, tins of paint like flowerpots on the floor—and, improbably, toile wallpaper, shepherdesses and noblemen, the odd urchin. Ed's toolbox sits on a shelf, pristine. "So I'm not handy," he'd say. "With a body like mine, I don't need to be."

I unlatch the box, rummage.

"There." David points—a silver plastic sheath, the blade peeking out at one end. I grasp it. "Careful."

"I won't cut you." I hand it to him gently, the blade aimed toward myself.

"It's you I don't want cut," he says.

A little flicker of pleasure within me, like the bud of a flame. "What are you doing with this, anyway?" I tug the string again, and once more it's night in here. David doesn't move.

It occurs to me as we stand there in the dark, me in my robe and David with a knife, that this is the closest I've ever been to him. He could kiss me. He could kill me.

"The guy next door asked me to do some work. Open some boxes and put some stuff away."

"Which guy next door?"

"The one across the park. Russell." He walks out, heads for the stairs.

"How did he find you?" I ask, following him.

"I put up some flyers. He saw one in the coffee shop or someplace." He turns and looks at me. "You know him?"

"No," I say. "He came by yesterday, that's all."

We're back in the kitchen. "He's got some boxes that need unpacking and some furniture to assemble in the basement. I should be back sometime in the afternoon."

"I don't think they're there."

He squints at me. "How do you know?"

*Because I watch their house.* "It doesn't look like anybody's home." I point to number 207 through the kitchen window, and as I do, their living room flushes with light. Alistair stands there, a phone cradled between cheek and shoulder, his hair just out of bed.

"That's the guy," says David, heading toward the hall door. "I'll be back later. Thanks for the knife."

# 23

I mean to get back to Ed—"Guess who," I'll say; my turn this time—but there's a knock on the hall door a moment after David walks through it. I go to see what he needs.

A woman stands on the other side, wide-eyed and lissome: Bina. I glance at my phone—noon exactly. X-Acto-ly. God.

"David let me in," she explains. "He gets better-looking every time I see him. Where does it end?"

"Maybe you should do something about that," I tell her.

"Maybe you should shut your mouth and get ready to exercise. Go change into real clothes."

I do, and after I've unfurled my mat, we begin, right there on the living room floor. It's been almost ten months since Bina and I first met—almost ten months since I left the hospital, my spine bruised, my throat damaged—and in that time we've become fond of each other. Maybe even friends, as Dr Fielding said.

"Warm out today." She lays a weight in the hollow of my back; my elbows wobble. "You should open a window."

"Not happening," I grunt.

"You're missing out."

"I'm missing out on a lot."

An hour later, with my T-shirt sucking at my skin, she hauls me to my feet. "Do you want to try that umbrella trick?" she asks.

I shake my head. My hair clings to my neck. "Not today. And it's not a trick."

"It's a good day for it. Nice and mild outside."

"No—I'm... no."

"You're hungover."

"That, too."

A small sigh. "Did you try it with Dr Fielding this week?"

"Yes," I lie.

"And how was it?"

"Fine."

"How far did you make it?"

"Thirteen steps."

Bina studies me. "All right. Not bad for a lady your age."

"Getting older, too."

"Why, when's your birthday?"

"Next week. The eleventh. Eleven eleven."

"Gonna have to give you a seniors' discount." She bends down, packs her weights into their case. "Let's eat."

I never used to cook much—Ed was the chef—and these days FreshDirect delivers my groceries to the door: frozen dinners, microwave meals, ice cream, wine. (Wine in bulk.) Also a few portions of lean protein and fruit, for Bina's benefit. And my own, she'd argue.

Our lunches are off the clock—it seems Bina enjoys the pleasure of my company. "Shouldn't I be paying you for this?" I asked her once.

"You're already cooking for me," she replied.

I scraped a black chunk of chicken onto her plate. "Is that what this is?"

Today it's melon with honey and a few strips of dry bacon. "Definitely uncured?" Bina asks.

"Definitely."

"Thanks, lady." She spoons fruit into her mouth, brushes honey from her lip. "I was reading an article about how bees can travel six miles from their hive in search of pollen."

"Where'd you read that?"

"*The Economist.*"

"Ooh, *The Economist.*"

"Isn't that amazing?"

"It's depressing. I can't even leave my house."

"The article wasn't about you."

"Doesn't sound like it."

"And they dance, too. It's called a—"

"Waggle dance."

She snaps a bacon strip in two. "How did you know that?"

"There was an exhibit on honeybees at the Pitt Rivers in Oxford when I was there. That's their natural history museum."

"Ooh, Oxford."

"I remember the waggle dance in particular because we tried to imitate it. A lot of bumbling and thrashing. Much like the way I exercise."

"Were you drunk?"

"We were not sober."

"I've been dreaming about bees ever since I read the article," she says. "What do you think that means?"

"I'm not a Freudian. I don't interpret dreams."

"But if you did."

"If I did, I'd say that the bees represent your urgent need to stop asking me what your dreams mean."

She chews. "I'm going to make you suffer next time."

We eat in silence.

"Did you take your pills today?"

"Yes." I haven't. I'll do it after she leaves.

A moment later, water lunges through the pipes. Bina looks toward the stairs. "Was that a toilet?"

"It was."

"Is someone else here?"

I shake my head, swallow. "David's got a friend over, sounds like."

"What a slut."

"He's no angel."

"Do you know who it is?"

"I never do. Are you jealous?"

"Definitely not."

"You wouldn't like to waggle dance with David?"

She flicks a crumb of bacon at me. "I've got a conflict next Wednesday. Same as last week."

"Your sister."

"Yes. Back for more. Would Thursday work for you?"

"The odds are excellent."

"Hooray." She chews, swirls her water glass. "You look tired, Anna. Are you resting?"

I nod my head, then shake it. "No. I've—I mean, yes, but I've had a lot on my mind lately. This is hard for me, you know. All... this." My arm sweeps the room.

"I know it must be. I know it *is*."

"And exercise is hard for me."

"You're doing really great. I promise."

"And therapy is hard for me. It's hard to be on the other side of it."

"I can imagine."

I breathe. Don't want to get worked up.

One last thing: "And I miss Livvy and Ed."

Bina sets her fork down. "Of course you do," she says, and her smile is so warm I could cry.

# 24

GRANNYLIZZIE: Hello, Doctor Anna!

The message appears on my desktop screen with a chirp. I set my glass to one side, suspend my chess game. I'm 3-0 since Bina left. A banner day.

THEDOCTORISIN: Hello Lizzie! How are you feeling?

GRANNYLIZZIE: Doing better, thank you kindly.

THEDOCTORISIN: Great to hear.

GRANNYLIZZIE: I donated Richard's clothing to our church.

THEDOCTORISIN: I'm sure they appreciated that.

GRANNYLIZZIE: They did and it's what Richard would want .

GRANNYLIZZIE: And the students in my third grade class made a big get well card for me. It's enormous. Glitter and cotton balls everywhere.

THEDOCTORISIN: That's very sweet.

GRANNYLIZZIE: Honestly I would give it a C+, but it's the thought that counts.

I laugh. LOL, I type, but then I delete it.

THEDOCTORISIN: I worked with kids, too.

GRANNYLIZZIE: Did you?

THEDOCTORISIN: Child psychology.

GRANNYLIZZIE: Sometimes I feel like that was my job...

I laugh again.

GRANNYLIZZIE: Whoa whoa whoa! I almost forgot!

GRANNYLIZZIE: I was able to take a little walk outside this morning! One of my old students dropped by and got me out of the house.

GRANNYLIZZIE: Just for a minute, but it was worth it.

THEDOCTORISIN: What a terrific step. It will only get easier from here.

That might not be true, but for Lizzie's sake, I hope otherwise.

THEDOCTORISIN: And how wonderful that your students are so fond of you.

GRANNYLIZZIE: This is Sam. No artistic instincts at all, but he was a very nice child and now he's a very nice man.

GRANNYLIZZIE: Although I forgot my house key.

THEDOCTORISIN: Understandable!

GRANNYLIZZIE: Wasn't able to get back inside for a moment.

THEDOCTORISIN: I hope that wasn't too frightening.

GRANNYLIZZIE: A little freaky but I keep a spare in our flower pot. I have beautiful violets in bloom.

THEDOCTORISIN: We don't have that luxury in NYC!

GRANNYLIZZIE: Laughing Out Loud!

I smile. She hasn't quite mastered it.

GRANNYLIZZIE: I must go make lunch. Friend coming over.

THEDOCTORISIN: Go do that. I'm glad you have company.

GRANNYLIZZIE: Thanky ou!

GRANNYLIZZIE:)

She logs out, and I feel radiant. "I may do some good before I am dead."—*Jude*, Part Sixth, Chapter 1.

Five o'clock and all's well. I finish my match (4-0!), sip the last of my wine, and walk downstairs to the television. A Hitchcock doubleheader tonight, I think as I open the DVD cabinet; maybe *Rope* (underrated) and *Strangers on a Train* (criss-cross!). Both starring gay actors—I wonder if that's why I paired them. I'm still on my analyst's kick. "Criss-cross," I say to myself. I've been monologuing a lot lately. Stick a pin in that for Dr Fielding.

Or perhaps *North by Northwest.*

Or *The Lady Vanish*—

A scream, raw and horrorstruck, torn from the throat.

I spin toward the kitchen windows.

The room is silent. My heart drums.

Where did it come from?

Waves of honeyed evening light outside, wind shifting in the trees. Was it from the street or—

And then again, dredged from the deep, shredding the air, full-blooded and frenzied: that scream. Coming from number 207. The parlour windows gape, the curtains restless in the breeze. *Warm out today*, Bina had said. *You should open a window*.

I stare at the house, my eyes flicking between the kitchen and parlour, swerving up to Ethan's bedroom, back to the kitchen.

Is he attacking her? *Very controlling*.

I don't have their number. I wriggle my iPhone from my pocket, drop it on the floor—"Fuck."—and dial directory assistance.

"What address?" Sullen. I answer; a moment later an automated voice recites ten digits, offers to repeat them in Spanish. I hang up, punch the number into the phone.

A ring, purring in my ear.

Another ring.

A third.

A fo—

"Hello?"

Ethan. Shaky, quiet. I scan the side of the house, but can't find him.

"It's Anna. Across the park." A sniffle. "Hi."

"What's going on there? I heard a scream."

"Oh. No—no." He coughs.

"It's fine."

"I heard someone scream. Was that your mom?"

"It's fine," he repeats. "He just lost his temper."

"Do you need help?"

A pause. "No."

Two tones stutter in my ear. He's hung up.

His house looks at me neutrally.

David—David's over there today. Or has he returned? I rap on the basement door, call his name. For an instant I fear that a stranger will open the door, explain sleepily that David's due back in a little while and would you mind if I went back to bed, thanks so much.

Nothing.

Did he hear it? Did he *see* it? I ring his number.

Four tones, long and unhurried, then a generic recorded greeting: "We're sorry. The person you have called..." A woman's voice—always a woman. Maybe we sound more apologetic.

I press Cancel. Stroke the phone as though it's a magic lamp and a genie will spout forth, ready to dispense his wisdom, grant my wishes.

Jane screamed. Twice. Her son denied that anything was wrong. I can't summon the police; if he wouldn't come clean to me, he certainly won't say anything to men in uniform.

My nails carve sickles into my palm.

No. I need to speak to him again—or better still, to her. I jab the Recent button on my screen, press the Russells' number. It rings just once before it's picked up.

"Yes?" says Alistair in his pleasant tenor.

I catch my breath.

I look up: There he is, in the kitchen, phone at his ear. A hammer in his other hand. He doesn't see me.

"This is Anna Fox from number two-thirteen. We met last—"

"Yes, I remember. Hello."

"Hello," I say, then wish I hadn't. "I heard a scream just now, so I wanted to check on—"

Turning his back to me, he places the hammer on the counter—the hammer; was that what alarmed her?—and claps his hand to the nape of his neck, as if he's comforting himself. "Sorry—you heard a what?" he asks.

I hadn't expected this. "A scream?" I say. No: Make it authoritative. "A scream. A minute ago."

"A *scream*?" Like it's a foreign word. *Sprezzatura. Schadenfreude. Scream.*

"Yes."

"From *where*?"

"From your house." Turn around. I want to see your face. "That's... there's been no scream here, I can promise you that." I hear him chuckle, watch him lean against the wall.

"But I heard it." *And your son confirmed it,* I think, although I won't tell him that—it might aggravate him, might incense him.

"I think you must have heard something else. Or heard it from somewhere else."

"No, I distinctly heard it from your house."

"The only people here are myself and my son. I didn't scream, and I'm pretty sure he didn't, either."

"But I *heard*—"

"Mrs Fox, I'm so sorry, but I have to go—I've got another call coming in. Everything's fine here. No scream, I promise you!"

"You—"

"Have a good day. Enjoy the weather."

I watch him hang up, hear those two tones again. He lifts the hammer from the counter, leaves the room through a far door.

I gawk at my phone in disbelief, as if it might explain things to me.

And just then, as I look back toward the Russell house, I see her on her front stoop. She stands still for a moment, like a meerkat sensing a predator, before descending the steps. Twists her head that way, then this, then that way again; finally she walks west, toward the avenue, the crown of her head a halo in the sunset.

# 25

He leans in the doorway, shirt dark with sweat, hair matted. An earbud is plugged into one ear.

"What's that?"

"Did you hear that scream at the Russells'?" I repeat. I heard him return just now, barely thirty minutes after Jane appeared on the stoop. In the meantime my Nikon has veered from window to window at the Russell house, like a dog snouting out foxholes.

"No, I left about a half hour ago," David says. "Went down to the coffee shop for a sandwich." He lifts his shirt to his face, mops up the sweat. His stomach is corrugated. "You heard a scream?"

"Two of them. Loud and clear. Around six o'clock?"

He eyes his watch. "I might've been there, only I didn't hear much," he says, pointing to the earbud; the other swings against his thigh. "Except for Springsteen."

It's practically the first personal preference he's ever expressed, but the timing is off. I steam ahead. "Mr Russell didn't say you were there. He said it was just him and his son."

"Then I'd probably left."

"I called you." It sounds like a plea.

He frowns, takes his phone from his pocket, looks at it, frowns deeper, as though the phone has let him down. "Oh. You need something?"

"So you didn't hear anyone scream."

"I didn't hear anyone scream."

I turn. "You need something?" he says again, but I'm already moving toward the window, camera in hand.

I see him as he sets out. The door opens, and when it closes, there he is. He trips quickly down the steps, turns left, marches along the sidewalk. Toward my house.

When the bell rings a moment later, I'm already waiting by the buzzer. I press it, hear him enter the hall, hear the front door crack shut behind him. I open the hall door to find him standing there in the dark, eyes red and raw, the blood vessels frayed within them.

"I'm sorry," Ethan says, hovering on the threshold.

"Don't be. Come in."

He moves like a kite, feinting first toward the sofa, then to the kitchen. "Do you want something to eat?" I ask him.

"No, I can't stay." Shaking his head, tears skittering down his face. Twice this child has set foot in my house, and twice he's cried.

Of course, I'm accustomed to children in distress: weeping, shouting, pummeling dolls, flaying books. It used to be that Olivia was the only one I could hug. Now I open my arms to

Ethan, spread them wide like wings, and he walks into them awkwardly, as though bumping into me.

For an instant, and then for a moment, I'm holding my daughter again—holding her before her first day of school, holding her in the swimming pool on our vacation in Barbados, clutching her amid the silent snowfall. Her heart beating against my own, a beat apart, a continuous drumline, blood surging through us both.

He mutters something indistinct against my shoulder. "What's that?"

"I said I'm really sorry," he repeats, prying himself free, skidding his sleeve beneath his nose. "I'm really sorry."

"It's fine. Stop saying that. It's fine." I brush a lock of hair from my eye, do the same for him. "What's going on?"

"My dad..." He stops, glances through the window at his house. In the dark it glowers like a skull. "My dad was yelling, and I needed to get out of the house."

"Where's your mom?"

He sniffles, swipes at his nose again. "I don't know." A couple of deep breaths and he looks me in the eye. "Sorry. I don't know where she is. She's fine, though."

"Is she?"

He sneezes, looks down. Punch has slipped between his feet, grating his body against Ethan's shins. Ethan sneezes again.

"Sorry." Another sniffle. "Cat." He looks around, as if surprised to find himself in my kitchen. "I should go back. My dad'll be angry."

"Sounds as though he's already angry." I tug a chair back from the table, gesture to it.

He considers the chair, then darts his eyes back to the window. "I've gotta go. I shouldn't have come over. I just..."

"You needed to get out of the house," I finish. "I understand. But is it safe to go back?"

To my surprise, he laughs, short and spiky. "He talks big. That's all. I'm not afraid of him."

"But your mom is."

He says nothing.

As far as I can see, Ethan doesn't display any of the more obvious hallmarks of child abuse: His face and forearms are unmarked, his demeanor bright and outgoing (although he *has* cried twice, let's not forget that), his hygiene satisfactory. But this is just an impression, just a glance. And he is, after all, standing here in my kitchen, slinging nervous looks at his home across the park.

I push the chair back into place. "I want you to have my cell number," I tell him.

He nods—grudgingly, I think, but it'll do. "Could you write it down for me?" he asks.

"You don't have a phone?"

A shake of the head. "He—my dad won't let me." He sniffles. "I don't have email, either."

Not surprising. I fetch an old receipt from a kitchen drawer, scribble on it. Four digits in, I realize I'm writing out my old work number, the emergency line I reserved for my patients. "1-800-ANNA-NOW," Ed used to joke.

"Sorry. Wrong number." I slash a line through it, then jot down the correct one. When I look up again, he's standing by the kitchen door, looking across the park at his house.

"You don't have to go back there," I say.

He turns. Hesitates. Shakes his head. "I've gotta head home."

I nod, offer him the paper. He pockets it.

"You can call me anytime," I say. "And share that number with your mom too, please."

"Okay." He's moving toward the door, shoulders back, back straight. Bracing for battle, I think.

"Ethan?"

He turns, one hand on the doorknob.

"I mean it. Anytime."

He nods. Then he opens the door and walks out.

I return to the window, watch him walk past the park, climb the steps, push his key into the lock. He pauses, draws a breath. Then he disappears inside.

# 26

Two hours later, I sluice the last of the wine down my throat, stand the bottle on the coffee table. I prop myself up, slowly, then tip to the other side, like the second hand of a clock.

No. Haul yourself to your bedroom. To your bathroom. With the shower gushing, the last few days flood my brain, filling the fissures there, welling up in the hollows: Ethan, crying on the couch; Dr Fielding and his high-voltage glasses; Bina, her leg braced against my spine; that whirlpool of a night when Jane visited. Ed's voice in my ear. David with the knife. Alistair—a good man, a good father. Those screams.

I squeeze a slug of shampoo into one hand, smear it absently into my hair. The tide rises at my feet.

And the pills—God, the pills. "These are powerful psychotropics, Anna," Dr Fielding advised me at the very beginning, back when I was woolly on painkillers. "Use them responsibly."

I press my palms against the wall, hang my head beneath the faucet, my face lurking within a dark cave of hair. Something's happening to me, through me, something dangerous and new. It's taken root, a poison tree; it's grown, fanning out, vines winding round my gut, my lungs, my heart. "The pills," I say, my voice soft and low amid the roar, like I'm speaking underwater.

My hand sketches hieroglyphs on the glass. I clear my eyes and read them. Over and over, across the door, I've written Jane Russell's name.

# THURSDAY, NOVEMBER 4

## 27

He lies on his back. I run a finger along the fence of dark hair that partitions his torso from navel to chest. "I like your body," I tell him.

He sighs and smiles. "Don't," he says; and then, with my hand idling in the shallows of his neck, he catalogues his every flaw: the dry skin that makes terrazzo of his back; the single mole between his shoulder blades, like an Eskimo marooned on an expanse of flaggy ice; his warped thumbnail; his knobbed wrists; the tiny white scar that hyphenates his nostrils.

I finger the wound. My pinkie dips into his nose; he snorts. "How did it happen?" I ask.

He twists my hair around his thumb. "My cousin."

"I didn't know you had a cousin."

"Two. This was my cousin Robin. He held a razor against my nose and said he'd slit my nostrils so that I only had one. And when I shook my head no, the blade sliced me."

"God."

He exhales. "I know. If I'd only nodded okay, it would've been fine."

I smile. "How old were you?"

"Oh, this was last Tuesday." Now I laugh, and so does he.

As I surface, the dream drains away like water. The memory, really. I try to scoop it up in my palms, but it's gone.

I press a hand against my forehead, hoping to smooth away the hangover. Cast the sheets to one side, ditch my nightclothes as I walk to the dresser, check the clock on the wall: 10:10, a waxed mustache on its face. I slept for twelve hours.

Yesterday has faded like a flower, yellow and wilted. A domestic dispute, unpleasant but not uncommon—that's what I heard. *Over*heard, really; it's none of my business. Perhaps Ed is right, I think as I clop down to my study.

Of course he's right. A *lot of stimulation:* yes, indeed. Too much. I'm sleeping too much, drinking too much, thinking too much; too much, too much. *De trop*. Did I involve myself like this with the Millers when they arrived back in August? They never visited me, no, but still I studied their routines, tracked their movements, tagged them like sharks in the wild. So it isn't that the Russells are particularly interesting. They're just particularly nearby.

I'm concerned for Jane, naturally. And especially for Ethan. *He just lost his temper*—that must be a pretty ferocious temper. But I can't approach, say, Child Protective Services; there's nothing to go on. At this point it would do more harm than good. That I know.

My phone rings.

This happens so infrequently that for a moment I'm confused. I look outside, as though it's a birdcall. The phone isn't in the pockets of my robe; I hear it buzzing somewhere above me. By the time I've reached my bedroom and found it in the trough of the sheets, it's gone mute.

The screen reads Julian Fielding. I hit Redial.

"Hello?"

"Hi, Dr Fielding. I missed you just now."

"Anna. Hello."

"Hello, hi." Many benedictions all round. My head throbs.

"I'm calling—one minute..." His voice shrinks, then returns, hard in my ear. "I'm in an elevator. I'm calling to make sure you filled your prescription."

*What prescript*—ah, yes; the pills Jane collected for me at the door. "I did, in fact."

"Good. I hope you don't think this patronizing, me checking in on you."

I do, in fact. "Not at all."

"You should experience the effects quite quickly."

The rattan on the stairs scratches at my soles. "Swift results."

"Well, I'd call them effects rather than results."

No shower-pisser, he. "I'll keep you posted," I assure him, descending to the study.

"I felt concerned after our last session."

I pause. "I—" No. I don't know what to say.

"My hope is that this adjustment in your medication will help."

Still I say nothing.

"Anna?"

"Yes. I hope so, too."

His voice shrivels again.

"Sorry?"

A second later he's at full volume. "These pills," he says, "are not to be taken with alcohol."

# 28

In the kitchen, I chase the pills with merlot. I understand Dr Fielding's concern, I do; I recognize that alcohol is a depressant, and as such, ill-suited to a depressive. I get it. I've *written* about it—"Juvenile Depression and Alcohol Abuse,"

*Journal of Pediatric Psychology* (volume 37, number 4), Wesley Brill, coauthor. I can quote our conclusions, if necessary. As Bernard Shaw said, I often quote myself; it adds spice to my conversation. As Shaw also said, alcohol is the anesthesia by which we endure the operation of life. Good old Shaw.

So come on, Julian: These aren't antibiotics. Besides, I've been mixing my medicines for almost a year, and take a look at me now.

My laptop sits in a pane of sunlight on the kitchen table. I pry it open, visit the Agora, walk two new recruits through the drill, weigh in on yet another drug debate. (None of them are to be taken with alcohol, I preach.) Once—only once—I cast a quick look at the Russell house. There's Ethan, tapping away at his desk—playing a game, I suppose, or writing a paper; not surfing the Internet, anyway—and in the parlour Alistair sits with a tablet propped in his lap. A twenty-first-century family. No Jane, but that's fine. None of my business. Too much stimulation.

"Goodbye, Russells," I say, and turn my attention to the television. *Gaslight*—Ingrid Bergman, never more luscious, slowly going insane.

# 29

Sometime after lunch, I'm back at the laptop when I see GrannyLizzie enter the Agora, the little icon beside her name morphing into a smiley face, as though to be present on this forum is a pleasure and a joy. I decide to beat her to the punch.

THEDOCTORISIN: Hello, Lizzie!

GRANNYLIZZIE: Hello Doctor Anna!

THEDOCTORISIN: How's the weather in Montana?

GRANNYLIZZIE: Rainy outside. Which is OK for an indoor gal like me!

GRANNYLIZZIE: How's the weather in New York City?

GRANNYLIZZIE: Do I sound like a hillbilly saying that? Should I just say NYC??

THEDOCTORISIN: Both work! It's sunny here. How are you doing?

GRANNYLIZZIE: Today has been tougher than yesterday, to be honest. So far.

I sip, roll the wine around my tongue.

THEDOCTORISIN: That happens. Progress isn't always smooth.

GRANNYLIZZIE: I can tell that ! My neighbors are bringing groceries to me at home.

THEDOCTORISIN: How terrific that yo've got such suportive people around you.

Two typos. More than two glasses of wine. That's a pretty decent batting average, I think. "Pretty damn decent," I say to myself, sipping again.

GRANNYLIZZIE: BUT: The big news is that... my sons will be visiting me this weekend. Really want to be able to go outside with them. Really really!

THEDOCTORISIN: Don't be hard on yourself if its not meant to be this time around.

A pause.

GRANNYLIZZIE: I know this is a harsh word, but it's difficult for me not to feel like "a freak".

Harsh indeed, and it needles my heart. I drain my glass, pull back the sleeves of my robe, rush my fingers over the keyboard.

THEDOCTORISIN: You are NOT a freak. You are a victim of circumstance. What you're going through is hard as hell. I've been housebound for ten months and I know as well as anyone how difficult this is. PLEASE don't ever think of yourself as a freak or aloser or anything other than a tough and resourceful person who's been bravev enough to ask for help. Your sons should be proud of you and you should be proud of yourself.

*Fin.* Not poetry. Not even decent English—my fingers slipped on and off the keys—but every word was true. Strictly true.

GRANNYLIZZIE: That's wonderful.

GRANNYLIZZIE: Thank you.

GRANNYLIZZIE: No wonder you're a psychologist. You know just what to say and how to say it.

I feel the smile spreading across my lips.

GRANNYLIZZIE: Do you have a family of your own?

The smile freezes.

Before answering, I pour myself more wine. It brims at the lip of the glass; I bow my head, slurp it down to high tide. A drop rolls off my lip, down my chin, onto my robe. I smear it into the terry cloth. Good thing Ed isn't watching. Good thing nobody's watching.

THEDOCTORISIN: I do, but we don't live together.

GRANNYLIZZIE: Why not?

Why not, indeed? Why don't you live together, Anna? I lift the glass to my mouth, set it down again. The scene unfolds before me like a Japanese fan: the vast flats of snow, the chocolate-box hotel, the ancient ice machine.

And to my surprise, I begin to tell her.

# 30

We'd decided ten days earlier to separate. That's the starting point, the once-upon-a-time. Or rather—to be entirely fair, to be strictly true—Ed had decided, and I had agreed, in principle. I admit I didn't think it would happen, not even when he summoned the broker. Could've fooled me.

Why, I reason, isn't for Lizzie to concern herself with. With which it is not for Lizzie to concern herself, as Wesley might insist; he was a stickler for dangling prepositions. I assume he still is. But no: The why isn't important, not here. The where and the when I can provide.

Vermont and last December, respectively, when we packed Olivia into the Audi and revved onto 9A, over the Henry Hudson Bridge, and out of Manhattan. Two hours later, wending through upstate New York, we'd hit what Ed liked to call the back roads—"with lots of diners and pancake places for us," he promised Olivia.

"Mom doesn't like pancakes," she said.

"She can go to a crafts store."

"Mom doesn't like crafts," I said.

As it turned out, the back roads of the region are remarkably fallow when it comes to pancake places and crafts stores. We found a single lonely IHOP in easternmost New York, where Olivia dredged her waffles in maple syrup (locally sourced, claimed the menu) and Ed and I arrowed glances at each other across the table. Outside, a light snow began to shake down, frail little kamikaze flakes smiting themselves against the windows. Olivia pointed with her fork and squealed.

I jousted her fork with my own. "There'll be a lot more of that at Blue River," I told her. This was our final destination, a ski resort in central Vermont that Olivia's friend had visited. Classmate, not friend.

Back to the car, back on the road. The ride was quiet, on the whole. We hadn't said anything to Olivia; no sense spoiling her vacation, I'd argued, and Ed nodded. We'd forge ahead for her.

So in silence we swept past broad fields and little streams lacquered with ice, through forgotten villages and into a feeble snowstorm near the Vermont border. At one point Olivia burst into "Over the Meadow and Through the Woods," and I piled on, trying and failing to harmonize.

"Daddy, will you sing?" Olivia pleaded. She's always done that: asked rather than ordered. Unusual in a child. Unusual in anyone, I sometimes think.

Ed cleared his throat and sang.

It was only as we reached the Green Mountains, bulging like shoulders from the earth, that he began to thaw. Olivia had gone breathless. "I've never *seen* such things," she wheezed, and I wondered where she'd heard those words in that order.

"Do you like the mountains?" I asked.

"They look like a rumpled blanket."

"They do."

"Like a giant's bed."

"A giant's bed?" Ed repeated.

"Yes—like a giant is sleeping under a blanket. That's why it's all lumpy."

"You'll be skiing on some of these mountains tomorrow," Ed promised as we hugged a tight turn. "We'll go up, up, up in the ski lift, and then down, down, down the mountain."

"Up, up, up," she repeated. The words popped from her lips.

"You got it."

"Down, down, down."

"You got it again."

"That one looks like a horse. Those are his ears." She pointed at a pair of spindly peaks in the distance. Olivia was at that age when everything reminded her of a horse.

Ed smiled. "What would you call a horse if you had one, Liv?"

"We are *not* getting a horse," I added.

"I'd call him Vixen."

"A vixen is a fox," Ed told her. "A girl fox."

"He would be fast like a fox."

We considered this.

"What would you call a horse, Mom?"

"Don't you want to call me Mommy?"

"Okay."

"Okay?"

"Okay, Mommy."

"I'd call a horse Of Course, Of Course." I looked at Ed. Nothing.

"Why?" asked Olivia.

"It's from a song on TV."

"What song?"

"From an old show about a talking horse."

"A talking horse?" She wrinkled her nose. "That's dumb."

"I agree."

"Daddy, what would you call a horse?"

Ed glanced in the rearview. "I like Vixen, too."

"Whoa," Olivia breathed. I turned.

Space had opened up beside us, beneath us, a vast chasm gutted from the land below, a huge bowl of nothing; thatched evergreens at the bottom of the void, rags of mist caught in midair. We were so close to the edge of the road that it felt like floating. We could peer into the well of the world.

"How far down is that?" she asked.

"Far," I answered, turning to Ed. "Can we slow up a bit?"

"Slow up?"

"Slow down, whatever? Just—can we go slower?"

He decelerated slightly.

"Can we slow *down* more?"

"We're fine," he said.

"It's scary," said Olivia, her voice curled up at the edges, hands edging toward her eyes, and Ed eased up on the gas.

"Don't look down, pumpkin," I said, twisting in my seat. "Look at Mommy."

She did so, her eyes wide. I took her hand, gathered her fingers in my own. "Everything's fine," I told her. "Just look at Mommy."

We'd arranged to lodge outside Two Pines, about half an hour from the resort—"Central Vermont's finest historic inn," bragged the Fisher Arms on its website, a slick collage of hearths in full bloom and windows frilly with snow.

We parked in the small lot. Icicles hung like fangs from the eaves above the front door. Rustic New England decor within: steeply pitched ceiling, shabby-genteel furniture, flames playing in one of those photo-friendly fireplaces. The receptionist, a plump young blonde whose name tag read MARIE, invited us to sign the guest registry, primped the irises on the desk as we did so. I wondered if she was going to address us as "folks."

"You folks here to ski?"

"We are," I said. "Blue River."

"Glad you made it." Marie beamed at Olivia. "Storm's coming in."

"Nor'easter?" suggested Ed, trying to sound local.

She trained her laser smile on him. "A nor'easter is more of a coastal storm, sir."

He nearly flinched. "Oh."

"This is just a storm-storm. But it'll be a whopper. You folks be sure to lock your windows tonight."

I wanted to ask why the windows would be unlocked the week before Christmas, but Marie dropped the keys into my palm and wished us folks a pleasant evening.

We trundled our luggage down the hall—the Fisher Arms' "many amenities" did not include bellhop service—and entered our suite. Paintings of pheasant flanked the fireplace; layer cakes of blankets sat on the edges of the beds. Olivia made straight for the toilet, leaving the door ajar; she was afraid of strange bathrooms.

"It's nice," I murmured.

"Liv," Ed called, "what's the bathroom like?"

"Cold."

"Which bed do you want?" Ed asked me. On holidays, he and I always slept separately, so that Olivia wouldn't crowd the bed when she inevitably climbed in. Some nights she ferried herself from Ed's bed to my own and back again; he called her Pong, after that Atari game with a four-bit ball bouncing between two bars.

"You take the one by the window." I sat on the edge of the other bed, unzipped my suitcase. "Better make sure it's locked."

Ed swung his bag onto the mattress. We began to unpack in silence. Beyond the window, curtains of snow shifted, gray and white in the creeping dusk.

After a moment, he rolled up one sleeve and scratched at his forearm. "You know..." he said. I turned to him.

The toilet flushed and Olivia burst into the room, hopping from one foot to the other. "When can we get up to ski?"

Dinner was to be prepacked PB&Js and assorted juice boxes, although I'd stowed a bottle of sauvignon blanc amid my sweaters. By now the wine was room temperature, and Ed liked his whites "really dry and really cold," as he always notified waiters. I rang the front desk, asked for ice. "There's a machine in the hallway just past your room," Marie told me. "Make sure to give the lid a real hard push."

I took the ice bucket from the minibar beneath the television, walked into the corridor, spotted an old Luma Comfort model humming in an alcove a few steps away. "You sound like a mattress," I informed it. I gave the lid a real hard push and back it slid, the machine exhaling into my face, frosty cold, the way people's breath looks in spearmint-gum commercials.

There was no trowel. I rummaged within, the cold scorching my hands, and shook the cubes into the bucket. They clung to my skin. So much for Luma Comfort.

That's where Ed found me, wrist-deep in ice.

He appeared suddenly at my side, leaning against the wall. For a moment I pretended not to see him; I stared into the basin of the machine, as though its contents fascinated me, and continued to scoop ice, wishing he'd leave, wishing he'd hold me.

"Interesting?"

I turned to him, didn't bother feigning surprise.

"Look," he said, and in my head I completed the sentence for him. *Let's rethink this*, maybe. *I've overreacted*, even.

Instead, he coughed—he'd been battling a cold in recent days, ever since the night of the party. I waited.

Then he spoke. "I don't want to do it this way."

I squeezed a fistful of ice cubes. "Do what?" My heart felt faint. "Do what?" I repeated.

"*This*," he answered, almost hissing, sweeping one arm through the air. "A whole happy-family holiday, and then the day after Christmas we..."

My heart slowed; my fingers burned. "What do you want to do? Tell her now?"

He didn't say anything.

I withdrew my hand from the machine, slid the lid shut. Not "real hard" enough: It jammed halfway down. I propped the bucket of ice on my hip, tugged at the lid. Ed gripped it and yanked it.

The bucket rolled away from me, clattering to the carpet, spattering cubes across the floor.

"Shit."

"Forget it," he said. "I don't want anything to drink."

"I do." I knelt to rake the cubes back into the bucket. Ed watched me.

"What are you going to do with those?" he asked.

"Should I just let them melt?"

"Yes."

I stood and set the bucket atop the machine. "You seriously want to do this now?"

He sighed. "I don't see why we—"

"Because we're already *here*. We're already..." I pointed to the door of our suite.

He nodded. "I thought about that."

"You've been thinking a lot lately."

"I thought," he continued, "that..."

He went quiet, and I heard the click of a door behind me. I twisted my head to see a middle-aged woman moving down the corridor toward us. She smiled shyly, eyes averted; picked her way through the ice cubes on the floor, walked on to the lobby.

"I thought that you'd want to start healing right away. That's what you'd say to one of your patients."

"Don't—please don't tell me what I would or wouldn't say."

He said nothing.

"And I wouldn't talk that way to a child."

"You'd talk that way to their parents."

"Don't *tell* me how I'd *talk*."

More nothing.

"And as far as she knows, there's nothing to heal."

He sighed again, rubbed at a spot on the bucket. "The fact is, Anna," he told me, and I could see the weight in his eyes, that broad cliff of his brow near collapse, "I just can't take this any longer."

I looked down, stared at the ice cubes already softening on the ground.

Neither of us spoke. Neither of us moved. I didn't know what to say.

Then I heard my voice, soft and low. "Don't blame me when she's upset."

A pause. And then his voice, softer still. "I do blame you." He breathed in. Breathed out. "I thought of you as the girl next door," he said.

I braced myself for more.

"But right now I can barely look at you."

I screwed my eyes shut, inhaled the cold tang of ice. And I thought not of our wedding day, nor of the night Olivia was born, but of the morning we harvested cranberries in New Jersey—Olivia shrieking and laughing in her waders, buttery with sunblock; slow skies above, the September sun drenching us; a vast sea of rose-red fruit all around. Ed with his hands full, his eyes bright; me clutching our daughter's sticky fingers. I remembered the bog waters risen to our hips, felt them flood my heart, surge into my veins, rise within my eyes.

I looked up, gazed into Ed's eyes, those dark-brown eyes; "Completely ordinary eyes," he assured me on our second date, but to me they were beautiful. They still are.

He looked back at me. The ice machine thrummed between us.

Then we went to tell Olivia.

# 31

THEDOCTORISIN: Then we went to tell Olivia.

I pause. How much more would she want to know? How much more can I bear to tell her? My heart already hurts, aching within my chest.

A minute later, there's still no response. I wonder if all this is hitting too close to home for Lizzie; here I am talking about a separation from my husband when she's lost hers irrevocably. I wonder if—

GRANNYLIZZIE HAS LEFT THE CHAT.

I stare at the screen.

Now I have to remember the rest of the story on my own.

# 32

"Don't you get lonely up here by yourself?"

I wriggle from sleep as a voice questions me, male, flat. I unpaste my eyelids.

"I was born lonely, I guess." A woman now. Creamy contralto.

Light and shadow flicker in my vision. It's *Dark Passage*—Bogie and Bacall making bedroom eyes across a coffee table.

"Is that why you visit murder trials?"

On my own coffee table stand the remnants of my dinner: two drained-hollow bottles of merlot and four canisters of pills.

"No. I went because your case was like my father's."

I swat at the remote beside me. Swat again.

"I know he didn't kill my stepmoth—" The TV goes dark, and the living room with it.

How much have I drunk? Right: two bottles' worth. Plus lunchtime. That's... a lot of wine. I can admit it.

And the drugs: Did I take the right quantity this morning? Did I take the right *pills*? I've been sloppy lately, I know. No wonder Dr Fielding thinks I'm getting worse. "You've been *bad*," I chide myself.

I peek into the canisters. One of them is almost depleted; twin tablets crouch within it, little white pellets, at either side of the bottle.

God, I'm very drunk.

I look up, look at the window. Dark outside, deep night. I cast about for my phone, can't find it. The grandfather clock, looming in the corner, ticks as though trying to get my attention. Nine fifty. "Nine fiffy," I say. Not great. Try ten to ten. "Ten to ten." Better. I nod to the clock. "Thanks," I tell him. He gazes at me, all solemn-like.

Lurching toward the kitchen now. *Lurching*—isn't that how Jane Russell described me, that day at the door? Those little shits with their eggs? *Lurch*. From *The Addams Family*. The gangly butler. Olivia loves that theme song. Snap, snap.

I grasp the faucet, duck my head beneath it, jerk the handle toward the ceiling. A whip of white water. Plunge my mouth forth, gulp deeply.

Drag one hand along my face, totter back to the living room. My eyes wander across the Russells' house: There's the ghost-glow of Ethan's computer, with the kid bent over the desk; there's the empty kitchen. There's their parlour, merry and bright. And there's Jane, in a snow-white blouse, sitting on that striped love seat. I wave. She doesn't see me. I wave again.

She doesn't see me.

One foot, then the other, then the first foot. Then the other—don't forget the other. I melt into the sofa, loll my head on my shoulder. Shut my eyes.

What happened to Lizzie? Did I say something wrong? I feel myself frown.

The cranberry bog stretches before me, shimmery, shifting. Olivia's hand takes my own.

The ice bucket smashes on the floor.

I'll watch the rest of the movie.

I open my eyes, unearth the remote from beneath me. The speakers exhale organ music, and there's Bacall, playing peekaboo over her shoulder. "You'll be all right," she vows. "Hold your breath, cross your fingers." The surgery scene—Bogie doped up, specters revolving before him, an unholy carousel. "It's in your bloodstream now." The organ drones. "Let me in." Agnes Moorehead, rapping at the camera lens. "Let me in." A flame wavers—"Light?" suggests the cabbie.

Light. I turn my head, look into the Russell house. Jane is still in her living room, on her feet now, shouting silently.

I swivel in my seat. Strings, a fleet of them, the organ shrilling beneath. I can't see who she's shouting at, or at whom she's shouting—the wall of the house blocks my view of the rest of the room.

"Hold your breath, cross your fingers."

She's really bellowing, her face gone scarlet. I spy my Nikon on the kitchen counter.

"It's in your bloodstream now."

I rise from the sofa, cross to the kitchen, paw the camera with one hand. Move to the window.

"Let me in. Let me in. *Let me in.*"

I lean into the glass, lift the camera to my eye. A blur of black, and then Jane jumps into view, soft around the edges; a twist of the lens and now she's clear, crisp—I can even see her locket winking. Her eyes are narrowed, her mouth wide. She jabs the air with one finger—"Light?"—jabs again. A lock of hair has swung from her head, flopping against her cheek.

Just as I zoom in further, she storms to the left, out of sight.

"Hold your breath." I turn to the television. Bacall again, almost purring. "Cross your fingers," I say along with her. I face the window again, Nikon at my eye.

Once more Jane enters the frame—but walking slowly, strangely. Staggering. A dark patch of crimson has stained the top of her blouse; even as I watch, it spreads to her stomach. Her hands scrabble at her chest. Something slender and silver has lodged there, like a hilt.

It is a hilt.

Now the blood surges up to her throat, washes it with red. Her mouth has gone slack; her brow is creased, as though she's confused. She grips the hilt with one hand, limply. With the other she reaches out, her finger aimed toward the window.

She's pointing straight at me.

I drop the camera, feel it rappel down my leg, the strap snagging in my fingers.

Jane's arm folds against the window. Her eyes are wide, pleading. She mouths something I can't hear, can't read. And then, as time slows to a near halt, she presses her hand to the window and keels to one side, wiping a bold smear of blood across the glass.

I'm stricken where I stand.

I can't move.

The room is still. The world is still.

And then, as time lurches forward, I move.

I spin, shake the camera strap loose, lunge across the room, my hip butting into the kitchen table. I stumble, reach the counter, wrench the landline from its dock. Press the power button.

Nothing. Dead.

Somewhere I remember David telling me as much. *It isn't even plugged—*

David.

I drop the phone and race to the basement door, yell his name, yell it, yell it. Seize the doorknob, pull hard.

Nothing.

Run to the stairs. Up, up—crashing against the wall—once—twice—round the landing, trip on the final step, half crawl to the study.

Check the desk. No phone. I swear I left it here.

Skype.

My hands jumping, I reach for the mouse, streak it over the desk. Double-click on Skype, double-click again, hear the sweep of the welcome tone, bash 911 into the dial pad.

A red triangle flashes on the screen. NO EMERGENCY CALLS. SKYPE IS NOT A TELEPHONE REPLACEMENT SERVICE.

"Fuck you, Skype," I shout.

Flee the study, rush the steps, whip around the landing, crash through the bedroom door.

Near bedside table: wineglass, picture frame. Far bedside table: two books, reading glasses.

My bed—is it in my bed again? I grab the duvet with both hands, snap it hard.

The phone launches into the air like a missile.

I pounce before it lands, knock it beneath the armchair, reach for it, grip it tight in my hand, swipe it on. Tap in the passcode. It trembles. Wrong code. Tap it in again, my fingers slipping.

The home screen appears. I stab the Phone icon, stab the Keypad icon, dial 911.

"911, what is your emergency?"

"My neighbor," I say, braking, motionless for the first time in ninety seconds. "She's—stabbed. Oh, God. Help her."

"Ma'am, slow down." He's speaking slowly, as if by example, in a languid Georgia drawl. It's jarring. "What's your address?"

I squeeze it from my brain, from my throat, stammering. Through the window I can see the Russells' cheery parlour, that arc of blood smeared across their window like war paint.

He repeats the address.

"Yes. Yes."

"And you say your neighbor was stabbed?"

"*Yes*. Help. She's bleeding."

"What?"

"I said *help*." Why isn't he helping? I gulp air, cough, gulp once more.

"Help is on the way, ma'am. I need you to calm down. Could you give me your name?"

"Anna Fox."

"All right, Anna. What's your neighbor's name?"

"Jane Russell. Oh, God."

"Are you with her now?"

"No. She's across—she's in the house across the park from me."

"Anna, did..."

He's pouring words in my ear like syrup—what kind of emergency dispatch service hires a slow talker?—when I feel a brush at my ankle. I look down to find Punch rubbing his flank against me.

"What?"

"Did you stab your neighbor?"

In the dark of the window I can see my mouth drop open. "*No*."

"All right."

"I looked through the window and *saw her get stabbed*."

"All right. Do you know who stabbed her?"

I'm squinting through the glass, peering into the Russells' parlour—it's a story below me now, but I see nothing on the floor except a floral-print rug. I brace myself on my toes, strain my neck.

Still nothing.

And then it appears: a hand at the windowsill.

Creeping upward, like a soldier edging his head above the trench. I watch the fingers swipe at the glass, drag lines through the blood.

She's still alive.

"Ma'am? Do you know who—"

But already I'm bolting from the room, the phone dropped, the cat mewling behind me.

# 33

The umbrella stands in its corner, cowering against the wall, as if afraid of some approaching threat. I grip the handle by the crook, cool and smooth in my damp palm.

The ambulance isn't here, but I am, just steps away from her. Beyond these walls, outside those two doors, she helped me, came to my aid—and now there's a blade in her chest. My psychotherapist's oath: *I must first do no harm. I will promote healing and well-being and place others' interests above my own.*

Jane is across the park, her hand trawling through blood.

I push the hall door open.

It's thick with dark in here as I cross to the door. I snap the latch and flick the umbrella spring, feel it huff air as it blossoms in the blackness; the tips of its spokes catch against the wall, drag there, tiny claws.

One. Two.

I set my hand on the knob.

Three.

I twist.

*Four.*

I stand there, the brass cold in my fist.

I can't move.

I can feel the outside trying to get in—isn't that how Lizzie put it? It's swelling against the door, bulging its muscles, battering the wood; I hear its breath, its nostrils steaming, its teeth grinding. It will trample me; it will tear me; it will devour me.

I press my head to the door, exhale. One. Two. Three. Four.

The street is a canyon, deep and broad. It's too exposed. I'll never make it.

She's steps away. Across the park.

Across the park.

I retreat from the hall, towing the umbrella in my wake, and move into the kitchen. There it is, right by the dishwasher: the side door, leading directly to the park. Locked for almost a year now. I've placed a recycling bin in front of it, bottle necks poking from its mouth like broken teeth.

I push the bin aside—a chorus of chinking glass from within—and flip the lock.

But what if the door closes behind me? What if I can't get back in? I glance at the key dangling on the hook beside the jamb. Slip it off, drop it into the pocket of my robe.

I swivel the umbrella ahead of me—my secret weapon; my sword and my shield—and lean over to press my hand to the knob. I turn it.

I push.

Air breaks against me, cold and sharp. I close my eyes.

Stillness. Darkness.

One. Two.

Three.

Four.

I step outside.

# 34

My foot misses the first step altogether, falling hard on the second, so that I wobble into the dark, the umbrella wobbling before me. The other foot trips after it, skitters down, the back of my calf scraping the steps, until I spill onto the grass.

I crush my eyes shut. My head brushes against the canopy of the umbrella. It's encasing me like a tent.

Huddled there, I stretch my arm back along the steps, up, up, up, tiptoeing one finger ahead of the other, until I can feel the top step. I peek. There's the door flung open, the kitchen glowing gold. I reach for it, as though I could snag my fingers in the light, tug it toward me.

She's dying over there.

I turn my head back to the umbrella. Four squares of black, four lines of white.

Pressing my hand against the rough brick of the steps, I haul myself to my feet, up, up, up.

I hear branches creaking overhead, take tiny sips of cold air. I'd forgotten cold air.

And—one, two, three, four—I begin to walk. I'm unsteady, like a drunk. I *am* drunk, I remember.

One, two, three, four.

During the third year of my residency, I met a child who, following surgery for epilepsy, manifested a curious set of behaviors. Prior to her lobectomy, she was by all accounts a happy ten-year-old, albeit one prone to severe epileptic episodes ("epilepisodes," someone quipped); afterward, she withdrew from her family, ignored her younger brother, shriveled at her parents' touch.

Initially her teachers suspected abuse, but then someone observed how much friendlier the girl had become toward people she barely knew, people she *didn't* know—she would fling her arms around her doctors, take the hands of passersby, chat with saleswomen as though they were old pals. And all the while her loved ones—her former loved ones—shivered in the cold.

We never determined the cause. But we termed the result *selective emotional detachment*. I wonder where she is now; I wonder what her family is doing.

I think of that little girl, her warmth toward strangers, her affinity for the unknown, as I ford the park, to the rescue of a woman I've met twice.

And even as I think it, the umbrella bumps against something, and I stop in my tracks.

It's a bench.

It's *the* bench, the only one in the park, a shabby little wooden rig with curlicue arms and an in-memoriam plaque bolted to the back. I used to watch Ed and Olivia sit here, from my aerie atop the house; he'd idle over a tablet, she'd thumb through a book, and then they'd swap. "Are you enjoying your children's literature?" I'd ask him later.

"*Expelliarmus*," he'd say.

The tip of the umbrella has caught between the planks of the seat. Gently I pry it loose—and then I realize, or rather remember:

The Russell house doesn't have a door leading to the park. There's no way to enter except by the street.

I haven't thought this through.

One. Two. Three. Four.

I'm in the middle of a quarter-acre park, with only nylon and cotton for armor, travelling to the home of a woman who's been stabbed.

I hear the night growl. I feel it circle my lungs, lick its lips.

I can do this, I think as my knees go slack. Come on: up, up, up. One, two, three, four.

I falter forward—a tiny step, but a step. I watch my feet, the grass springing up around my slippers. *I will promote healing and well-being.*

Now the night has my heart in its claws. It's squeezing. I'll burst. I'm going to burst.

*And I will place others' interests above my own.*

*Jane, I'm coming.* I drag my other foot ahead, my body sinking, sinking. One, two, three, four.

Sirens whine in the distance, like mourners at a wake. Blood-red light floods the bowl of the umbrella. Before I can stop myself, I twist toward the noise.

Wind howls. Headlights blind me.

One-two-three—

## FRIDAY, NOVEMBER 5

# 35

"I guess we should have locked the door," Ed mumbled after she fled into the hall.

I turned to him. "What were you expecting?"

"I didn't—"

"What did you think would happen? What did I *say* would happen?"

Without waiting for an answer, I left the room. Ed's footsteps followed me, soft on the carpet.

In the lobby, Marie had emerged from behind her desk. "You folks okay?" she asked, frowning.

"No," I replied, just as Ed said, "Fine."

Olivia was lodged in an armchair beside the hearth, her face rinsed with tears, filmy in the firelight. Ed and I crouched on either side of her. The flames snapped at my back.

"Livvy," Ed began.

"No," she answered, rattling her head back and forth. He tried again, softer. "Livvy."

"*Fuck you,*" she shrieked.

We both recoiled; I nearly edged into the grate. Marie had retreated behind her desk and was doing her best to ignore us folks.

"Where did you hear that word?" I asked.

"Anna," said Ed.

"It wasn't from *me*."

"That's not the point."

He was right. "Pumpkin," I said, smoothing her hair; she shook her head again, buried her face in a cushion. "Pumpkin."

Ed placed his hand on hers. She swatted it away.

He looked at me, helpless.

*A child is crying in your office. What do you do?* First pediatric psych course, first day, first ten minutes. Answer: You let them cry it out. You listen, of course, and you seek to understand, and you offer consolation, and you encourage them to breathe deeply—but you let them cry it out.

"Take a breath, pumpkin," I murmured, cupping her scalp in my palm.

She choked, spluttered.

A moment drifted past. The room felt cold; the flames shivered in the fireplace behind me. Then she spoke into the cushion.

"What?" Ed asked.

Lifting her head, her cheeks smeared, Olivia addressed the window. "I want to go home."

I watched her face, her quaking lip, her streaming nose; and then I watched Ed, the creases in his forehead, the hollows beneath his eyes.

Did I do this to us?

Snow beyond the window. I watched it fall, saw the three of us collected in the glass: my husband and my daughter and me, huddled by the fire together.

A brief silence.

I stood, walked over to the desk. Marie looked up and shaped her lips into a tight smile. I smiled back.

"The storm," I began.

"Yes, ma'am."

"Is it... how close is it? Is it safe to drive?"

She frowned, rattled her fingers over her keyboard. "Heavy snowfall isn't due for another couple of hours," she said. "But—"

"Then could we—" I interrupted her. "Sorry."

"I was just saying that winter storms are tough to predict." She glanced over my shoulder. "Are you folks wanting to leave?"

I turned, looked at Olivia in the armchair, Ed crouching beside her. "I think we are."

"In that case," said Marie, "I'd say now's the time to go." I nodded. "Could we get the bill, please?"

She said something in reply, but all I heard was the skirling wind, the crackle of flames.

# 36

The crackle of an overstarched pillowcase.

Footfalls nearby.

Then quiet—but a strange quiet, a different quality of quiet.

My eyes spring open.

I'm on my side, looking at a radiator.

And above the radiator, a window.

And outside the window, brickwork, the zigzag of a fire escape, the boxy rumps of AC units.

Another building.

I'm in a twin bed, sheathed in tucked-tight sheets. I twist, sit up.

I back into the pillow, telescope the room. It's small, plainly furnished—barely furnished, really: a plastic chair against one wall, a walnut table beside the bed, a pale-pink tissue box on the table. A table lamp. A slim vase, empty. Dull linoleum floor. A door across from me, closed, frosted panel. Overhead, a quilt of stucco and fluorescents—

My fingers crumple the bedding.

Now it begins.

The far wall slides away, receding; the door within it shrinks. I look to the walls on either side of me, watch them ebb from each other. The ceiling shudders, creaks, peels off like a sardine tin, like a roof rent by a hurricane. The air goes with it, whipping from my lungs. The floor rumbles. The bed trembles.

Here I lie, on this heaving mattress, in this scalped room, with nothing to breathe. I'm drowning in the bed, dying in the bed.

"Help," I shout, only it's a whisper, creeping through my throat on tiptoe, smearing itself across my tongue. "He-*elp*," I try again; this time my teeth bite into it, sparks raining from my mouth as though I've chewed a live wire, and my voice catches like a fuse, explodes.

I scream.

I hear voices rumble, watch as a scrimmage of shadows crowds through that distant door, lunges toward me, bounding in impossible strides across the endless, endless room.

I scream again. The shadows scatter in a flock, flare around my bed.

"*Help*," I plead, with the last gasp of air in my body.

Then a needle slips into my arm. It's deftly done—I hardly feel a thing.

A wave rolls above me, soundless and smooth. I'm floating, suspended, in some radiant abyss, deep, cool. Words dart around me like fish.

"Coming back now," someone murmurs.

"... stable," says someone else.

And then, clearly, as though I've just surfaced, just drained water from my ear: "Just in time."

I swivel my head. It bobs lazily against the pillow.

"I was about to leave."

Now I see him, or most of him—it takes me a moment to scan him from one side to the other, because I'm high on drugs (I know enough to know that) and because he's holy-shit vast, a mountain of a man: blue-black skin, boulder shoulders, a broad range of chest, a scrub of thick dark hair. His suit clings to him with a sort of desperation, unequal to the task but trying its damnedest.

"Hello there," he says, his voice sweet and low. "I'm Detective Little."

I blink. At his elbow—practically *on* his elbow—hovers a pigeon of a woman in a yellow nurse's smock.

"Can you understand what we're saying?" she asks.

I blink again, then nod. I feel the air shift around me, like it's almost viscous, like I'm still underwater.

"This is Morningside," the nurse explains. "The police have been waiting for you to come around all morning." The way you'd chide someone for failing to answer the doorbell.

"What's your name? Can you tell us your name?" asks Detective Little.

I open my mouth, squeak. My throat has gone dry. I feel as if I've just coughed up a puff of dust.

The nurse rounds the bed, zeroes in on the side table. I follow her, my head slowly revolving, and watch as she places a cup in my hands. I sip. Tepid water. "You're under sedation," she tells me, almost apologetic now. "You were fussing a little bit earlier."

The detective's question hangs in the air, unanswered. I turn my eyes back to Mount Little.

"Anna," I say, the syllables stumbling in my mouth, as though my tongue is a speed bump. What the hell did they pump into me?

"You got a last name, Anna?" he asks.

I take another sip. "Fox." It sounds elongated in my ears.

"Uh-huh." He tugs a notepad from his breast pocket, eyes it. "And can you tell me where you live?"

I recite my address.

Little, nodding: "Do you know where you were picked up last night, Ms Fox?"

"Doctor," I say.

The nurse twitches beside me. "The doctor will be here soon."

"No." Shaking my head. "I'm a doctor."

Little stares at me.

"I'm Dr Fox."

A smile breaks like dawn across his face. His teeth are almost phosphorescently white. "*Doctor* Fox," he continues, tapping the pad with his finger. "Do you know where they picked you up last night?"

I sip my water, study him. The nurse flutters near me. "Who?" I say. That's right: I'll ask questions, too. I'll slur them, at any rate.

"The EMTs." Then, before I can reply: "They picked you up in Hanover Park. You were unconscious."

"Unconscious," echoes the nurse, in case I missed it the first time.

"You'd placed a phone call a little after ten thirty. They found you in your bathrobe with this in your pocket." He unfolds one massive hand, and I see the house key glinting in his palm. "And this beside you." Across his knees he lays my umbrella, its body cinched.

It starts somewhere in my gut, then rushes past my lungs, across my heart, into my throat, shreds itself against my teeth:

Jane.

"What's that?" Little is frowning at me.

"Jane," I repeat.

The nurse looks at Little. "She said 'Jane,'" she translates, ever helpful.

"My neighbor. I saw her get stabbed." It takes an ice age, the words thawing in my mouth before I can spit them out.

"Yes. I heard the 911 call," Little tells me.

911. That's right: that southern dispatcher. And then the trek out the side door, into the park, the branches shifting overhead, the lights swirling like some unholy potion in the bowl of the umbrella. My vision swims. I breathe hard.

"Try to stay calm," the nurse orders me.

I breathe again, choke.

"Easy," frets the nurse. I lock eyes with Little.

"She's okay," he says.

I bleat at him, wheeze at him, lift my head from the pillow, neck straining, drag shallow breaths through my mouth. And with my lungs shrinking, I bristle—how would *he* know how I am? He's a cop I've just met. A *cop*—have I ever even met a cop before? The odd traffic ticket, I suppose.

The light strobes before my eyes, faintly, tiger stripes of dark clawed across my vision. His own eyes never leave mine, even as my gaze climbs his face and slips, like a struggling hiker. His pupils are almost absurdly huge. His lips are full, kind.

And as I stare at Little, as my fingers rake the blankets, I find my body relaxing, my chest expanding, my vision clearing. Whatever they put into me has won. I am indeed okay.

"She's okay," Little says again. The nurse pats my knuckles. Good girl.

I roll my head back, close my eyes. I feel exhausted. I feel embalmed.

"My neighbor was stabbed," I whisper. "Her name is Jane Russell."

I hear Little's chair complain as he leans toward me. "Did you see who attacked her?"

"No." I work my eyelids open, like rusty garage doors. Little is hunched over his notepad, his brow grooved with wrinkles. He frowns and nods at the same time. Mixed messages.

"But you saw her bleeding?"

"Yes." I wish I'd stop slurring. I wish he'd stop interrogating me.

"Had you been drinking?"

A lot. "A little," I admit. "But that's..." I inhale, and now I feel fresh panic volt through me. "You need to help her. She's—she could be dead."

"I'll get the doctor," says the nurse, moving toward the door.

As she leaves, Little nods again. "Do you know who would want to hurt your neighbor?"

I swallow. "Her husband."

He nods some more, frowns some more, shakes his wrist, flips the notepad shut. "Here's the thing, Anna Fox," he says, suddenly brisk, all business. "I went to visit the Russells this morning."

"Is she okay?"

"I'd like you to go back with me to make a statement."

The doctor is a youngish Hispanic woman so beautiful that I lose my breath again, although that isn't why she injects me with lorazepam.

"Is there anyone we should contact for you?" she asks. I'm about to give Ed's name, then check myself. No point. "No point," I say.

"What's that?"

"No one," I tell her. "I don't have—I'm fine." Carefully sculpting each word, as though it's origami. "But—"

"No family member?" She looks at my wedding ring.

"No," I say, my right hand stealing over my left. "My husband—I'm not—we're not together. Anymore."

"A friend?" I shake my head. Whom could she possibly call? Not David, certainly not Wesley; Bina, maybe, except I really am fine. Jane isn't.

"What about a doctor?"

"Julian Fielding," I answer automatically, before I interrupt myself. "No. Not him."

I watch her exchange glances with the nurse, who then exchanges glances with Little, who forwards the glance to the doctor. It's a Mexican standoff. I want to giggle. I don't. Jane.

"As you know, you were unconscious in a park," the doctor continues, "and the EMTs couldn't identify you, so they brought you to Morningside. When you came around, you had a panic attack."

"A big one," pipes up the nurse.

The doctor nods. "A big one." She inspects her clipboard. "And it happened again this morning. I understand you're a doctor?"

"Not a medical doctor," I tell her.

"What sort of doctor?"

"A psychologist. I work with children."

"Do you have—"

"A woman's been stabbed," I say, my voice surging. The nurse steps back as though I've swung a fist. "Why isn't anyone doing anything?"

The doctor snaps a glance at Little. "Do you have a history of panic attacks?" she asks me.

And so, with Little attending amiably from his chair and the nurse trembling like a hummingbird, I tell the doctor—tell all of them—about my agoraphobia, my depression, and, yes, my panic disorder; I tell them about my drug regimen, about my ten months indoors, about Dr Fielding and his aversion therapy. It takes a while, with my voice still swathed in wool; every minute I tip more water down my throat, trickling past my words as they bubble up from within, spill over my lips.

Once I've finished, once I've sagged back into the pillow, the doctor consults her clipboard for a moment. Nods slowly. "All right," she says. A brisker nod. "All right." She looks up.

"Let me speak with the detective. Detective, would you—" She gestures toward the door.

Little rises, the chair creaking as he stands. He smiles at me, follows the doctor from the room.

His absence leaves a void. It's just me and the nurse now. "Have some more water," she suggests.

They return some minutes later. Or maybe it's longer than that; there's no clock in here.

"The detective has offered to escort you back home," says the doctor. I look at Little; he beams back. "And I'm giving you some Ativan to take later. But we need to make sure that you don't have an attack before you get there. So the fastest way to do this..."

I know the fastest way to do this. And the nurse is already brandishing her needle.

# 37

"We thought it was a prank," he explains. "Well, they did. I'm supposed to say *we*—or I guess *we're* supposed to say *we*—because *we* are all working together. You know, 'as a team.' For the common good. Or something. Words to that effect." He accelerates. "But I wasn't there. So I didn't think it was a prank. I didn't know about it. If you follow me."

I don't.

We're sliding down the avenue in his unmarked sedan; hazy afternoon sun blinks through the windows like a stone skipping across a pond. My head bumps against the glass, my face twinned beside me, my robe frothy at my neck. Little overflows in his seat, his elbow brushing mine.

I feel decelerated, body and brain.

"Of course, then they saw you all crumpled on the grass. That's what they said, that's how they described it. And they saw the door to your house open, and so they thought that's where the incident occurred, but when they looked inside the place was empty. They had to look inside, you know. Because of what they'd heard on the phone."

I nod. I can't remember exactly what I said on that call.

"You got kids?" I nod again. "How many?" I extend a single finger. "Only child, huh? I've got four. Well, I'll have four in January. We've got one on order." He laughs; I don't. I can barely move my lips. "Forty-four years old and a fourth kid on the way. I guess four is my lucky number."

*One, two, three, four,* I think. *In and out. Feel the lorazepam flying through your veins, like a flock of birds.*

Little taps on the horn and the car in front of us scoots ahead. "Lunch rush," he says.

I lift my eyes to the window. It's been nearly ten months since I found myself on the streets, or in a car, or in a car on the streets. Ten months since I've seen the city from anywhere besides my house; it feels otherworldly, as though I'm exploring alien terrain, as though I'm coasting through some future civilization. The buildings loom impossibly tall, thrusting like fingers into a rinsed-blue sky above. Signs and shops streak past, blaring colour: 99¢ FRESH PIZZA!!!, Starbucks, Whole Foods (when did *that* set up shop?), an old fire station refitted as a condo building (UNITS FROM $1.99M). Cool dark alleys; windows blank with sunlight. Sirens keen behind us, and Little shrugs the car to one side as an ambulance pushes past.

We approach an intersection, slow to a stop. I study the traffic light, glowing like an evil eye, and watch the stream of pedestrians flow along the crosswalk: two blue-jeaned mothers pushing strollers, a bent-double old man leaning on a cane, teenagers hunched under hot-pink backpacks, a woman in a turquoise burka. A green balloon, loosed from a pretzel stand, dizzies upward. Sounds invade the car: a giddy shriek, the seafloor rumble of traffic, a bicycle bell trilling. A rage of colours, a riot of sounds. I feel as though I'm in a coral reef.

"Off we go," murmurs Little, and the car surges forward.

Is this what's become of me? A woman who gawks like a guppy at an everyday lunch hour? A visitor from another world, awed by the miracle of a new grocery store? Deep within my dry-iced brain, something throbs, something angry and vanquished. A flush sunrises in my cheeks. This is what's become of me. This is who I am.

If it weren't for the drugs, I'd scream until the windows shattered.

# 38

"Now," says Little, "here's our turn."

We ease right onto our street. My street.

My street as I haven't seen it in almost a year. The coffee shop on the corner: still there, presumably still slinging the same too-bitter brew. The house beside it: fire-red as ever, its flower boxes crowded with chrysanthemums. The antique shop just across: dark and sulky now, a COMMERCIAL SPACE FOR RENT sign pasted in the storefront. St. Dymphna's, permanently forlorn.

And as the street opens before us, as we drive west beneath a vault of bare branches, I feel tears brimming in my eyes. My street, four seasons later. *Strange*, I think.

"What's strange?" says Little.

I must have thought it out loud.

As the car nears the far end of the road, I catch my breath. There's our house—my house: the black front door, the numbers 2-1-3 wrought in brass above the knocker; the panes of leaded glass on either side, the twin lanterns next to them with their orange electric light; four stories of windows staring dully straight ahead. The stone is less lustrous than I remember, with waterfalls of stains beneath the windows, like they're weeping, and on the roof, I see a fragment of the rotted trellis. All the glass could stand to be washed—even from the street I can pick out the grime. "Best-looking house on the block," Ed used to say, and I used to agree.

We've aged, the house and I. We've decayed.

We roll past it, past the park.

"It's there," I say to Little, wagging a hand toward the backseat. "My house."

"I'd like to take you to speak to your neighbors with me," he explains, parking the car at the curb and cutting the engine.

"I can't." I shake my head. Doesn't he get it? "I need to go home." I fumble with the seat belt, then realize that this isn't likely to lead anywhere.

Little looks at me. Strokes the steering wheel. "How are we going to do this?" he asks, himself more than me.

I don't care. I don't care. I want to go home. You can bring them to my house. Cram them all in. Throw a fucking block party. But take me home now. Please.

He's still eyeing me, and I realize I've spoken to him again. I huddle into myself.

A rap on the glass, quick and crisp. I look up; it's a woman, sharp-nosed, olive-skinned, in a turtleneck and long coat. "Hold on," says Little. He starts to lower my window, but I cringe, I whine, and he rolls it back up before unpacking himself from the driver's seat and stepping into the street, shutting the door gently behind him.

He and the woman speak to each other across the roof of the car. My ears sieve their words—*stabbing, confused, doctor*—as I sink underwater, close my eyes, nestle into the crook of the passenger seat; the air goes calm and still. Shoals flicker past—*psychologist, house, family, alone*—and I drift away. With one hand I idly stroke the other sleeve; my fingers swim into my robe, pinch a roll of skin bulging from my stomach.

I'm trapped in a police car fondling my fat. This is a new low.

After a minute—or is it an hour?—the voices subside. I crack one eye open, see the woman gazing down at me, glaring down at me. I screw my eye shut again.

The crunch of the driver's door as Little opens it. Cool air wafts in, licks my legs, wanders around the cabin, makes itself at home.

"Detective Norelli is my partner," I hear him tell me, a little flint in that dark-soil voice of his. "I've told her what's happening with you. She's going to bring some people into your house. That okay?"

I dip my chin, lift it.

"Okay." The car gasps as he settles into his seat. I wonder how much he weighs. I wonder how much *I* weigh.

"You want to open your eyes?" he suggests. "Or are you good?"

I dip my chin again.

The door clacks shut and he revives the engine, knocks the gearshift into reverse, backs up—back, back, back—the vehicle catching its breath as it rolls over a seam in the pavement, until we brake. I hear Little switch the ignition again.

"Here we are," he announces as I open my eyes, peek out the window.

Here we are. The house towers above me, the black mouth of the front door, the front steps like a tongue unspooled; the cornices form even brows above the windows. Olivia always speaks of brownstones as though they have faces, and from this angle, I see why.

"Nice place," Little comments. "*Big* place. Four stories? Is that a basement?"

I incline my head.

"So *five* stories." A pause. A leaf throws itself against my window, skitters away. "And you're all alone in there?"

"Tenant," I say.

"Where does he live? Basement or on top?"

"Basement."

"Is your tenant here?"

I shift my shoulders into a shrug. "Sometimes."

Silence. Little's fingers tap-dance on the dash. I turn to him. He catches me looking, grins.

"That's where they picked you up," he reminds me, jutting his jaw toward the park.

"I know," I mumble.

"Nice little park."

"I guess."

"Nice street."

"Yes. All nice."

He grins again. "Okay," he says, then looks past me, past my shoulder, into the eyes of the house. "Does this work for the front door, or just the door the EMTs came in last night?" He dangles my house key from one finger, the key ring noosed at his knuckle.

"Both," I tell him.

"Okay, then." He whirls the key around his finger. "You need me to carry you?"

# 39

He doesn't carry me, but he does hoist me out of the car, usher me through the gate, propel me up the stairs, my arm flung across his football-field back, my feet half dragged behind me, the crook of the umbrella jaunting over one wrist, as if we're out for a stroll. A drugged-stupid stroll.

The sun nearly caves in my eyelids. At the landing Little slides the key into the lock, pushes; the door sails wide, slamming so hard that the glass shivers.

I wonder if the neighbors are watching. I wonder if Mrs Wasserman has just seen an economy-size black man drag me into my house. I bet she's calling the cops right now.

There's scarcely room for both of us in the hall—I'm squeezed to one side, pinned there, my shoulder pressed into the wall. Little kicks the door shut, and suddenly it's dusk. I close my eyes, roll my head against his arm. The key scrapes into the second lock.

And then I feel it: the warmth of the living room.

And I smell it: the stale air of my home.

And I hear it: the squeal of the cat.

The cat. I'd completely forgotten about Punch.

I open my eyes. Everything is as it was when I plunged outside: the dishwasher yawning open; the skein of blankets tangled on the sofa; TV glowing, the *Dark Passage* DVD menu frozen on the screen; and on the coffee table, the two depleted bottles of wine, incandescent in the sunlight, and the four pill canisters, one of them toppled, as though drunk.

Home. My heart nearly detonates in my chest. I could sob with relief.

The umbrella slides from my arm, drops to the floor.

Little steers me to the kitchen table, but I wave my hand left, like a motorist, and we veer off-course toward the sofa, where Punch has wedged himself behind a pillow.

"There you go," Little breathes, easing me onto the cushions. The cat observes us. When Little steps back, he sidewinds toward me, picking his way among the blankets, before turning his head to hiss at my escort.

"Hello to you, too," Little greets him.

I ebb into the sofa, feel my heart slow, hear the blood singing softly in my veins. A moment passes; I grip my robe in my hands, regain myself. Home. Safe. Safe. Home.

The panic seeps from me like water.

"Why were people in my house?" I ask Little.

"What's that?"

"You said that EMTs came into my house."

His eyebrows lift. "They found you in the park. They saw your kitchen door open. They needed to see what was going on."

Before I can respond, he turns to the photograph of Livvy on the side table. "Daughter?"

I nod.

"She here?"

I shake my head. "With her father," I mutter.

His turn to nod.

He turns, stops, sizes up the spread on the coffee table. "Someone having a party?"

I inhale, exhale. "It was the cat," I say. What's that from? *Goodness me! Why, what was that? Silent be, It was the cat.* Shakespeare? I frown. Not Shakespeare. Too cutesy.

Apparently, I'm also too cutesy, because Little isn't even smirking. "All this yours?" he asks, inspecting the wine bottles. "Nice merlot."

I shift in my seat. I feel like a naughty child. "Yes," I admit. "But..." It looks worse than it is? It's actually worse than it looks?

Little fishes in his pocket for the tube of Ativan capsules that the lovely young doctor prescribed. He sets it on the coffee table. I mumble a thank-you.

And then, deep in the riverbed of my brain, something detaches itself, tumbles in the undertow, rises to the surface.

It's a body.

It's Jane.

I open my mouth.

For the first time, I notice the gun holstered at Little's hip. I remember Olivia once gawking at a mounted policeman in Midtown; she ogled him for a solid ten seconds before I realized she was staring at his weapon, not his horse. I smiled then, teased her, but here it is, within arm's reach, and I'm not smiling.

Little catches me. He tugs his coat over the gun, as though I'd been peeking down his shirt.

"What about my neighbor?" I ask.

He digs his phone from his pocket, brings it close to his eyes. I wonder if he's nearsighted. Then he swipes it, drops his hand to his side.

"This whole house is just you, huh?" He walks toward the kitchen. "And your tenant," he adds before I can do so. "That go downstairs?" He jabs a thumb toward the basement door.

"Yes. What about my neighbor?"

He checks his phone again—then stops, stoops. When he stands up, unfolding his hundred-yard body, he's got the cat's water bowl in his right hand and, in the left, the landline phone. He looks at one, then the other, as though weighing them. "Guy's probably thirsty," he says, stepping over to the sink.

I watch his reflection in the television screen, hear the gush of the faucet. There's a shallow puddle of merlot left in one of the bottles. I wonder if I could knock it back without him seeing.

The water bowl rings against the floor, and now Little sets the phone in its dock, squints at the readout. "Battery's dead," he says.

"I know."

"Just saying." He approaches the basement door. "Can I bang on this?" he asks me. I nod.

He plays his knuckles against the wood—shave-and-a-haircut—and waits. "What's your tenant's name?"

"David."

Little knocks again. Nothing.

He turns to me. "So where's your phone, Dr Fox?"

I blink. "My phone?"

"Your cell phone." He waves his own at me. "You got one?" I nod.

"Well, they didn't find it on you. Most people would go straight for their phone if they'd been away all night."

"I don't know." Where *is* it? "I don't use it much."

He says nothing.

I've had enough. I brace my feet against the carpet, haul myself upright. The room wobbles around me, a spinning plate; but after a moment it steadies, and I lock eyes with Little.

Punch congratulates me with a tiny meow.

"You all right?" Little asks, stepping toward me. "You good?"

"Yes." My robe has flapped open; I gather it to my body, knot the sash tight. "What is happening with my neighbor?" But he's stopped short, his eyes on his phone.

I repeat myself: "What—"

"Okay," he says, "okay. They're on their way over." And now suddenly he's surging through the kitchen like a great wave, his gaze revolving around the room. "Is that the window you saw your neighbor from?" He points.

"Yes."

He strides to the sink, one long lunge of his long legs, props his palms on the counter, peers outside. I study his back, filling the window. Then I look at the coffee table, start to clear it up.

He turns. "Leave all that there," he says. "Leave the TV on, too. What movie is that?"

"An old thriller."

"You like thrillers?"

I fidget. The lorazepam must be running dry. "Sure. Why can't I clean up?"

"Because we'll want to see exactly what was going on with you when you witnessed the attack on your neighbor."

"Doesn't it matter more what was going on with *her*?"

Little ignores me. "Maybe put that cat somewhere," he tells me. "Seems like he's got an attitude. Don't want him scratching anybody." He pivots back to the sink, fills a glass with water. "Drink this. You need to stay hydrated. You've had a shock." He crosses the room, puts it in my hand. There's something almost tender about it. I half expect him to caress my cheek.

I bring the glass to my lips. The buzzer rings.

# 40

"I've got Mr Russell with me," Detective Norelli announces, unnecessarily.

Her voice is slight, girlish, a bad fit for the high-rise sweater, the bitch-on-wheels leather coat. She sweeps the room with a single glance, then trains a glass-cutting gaze on me. Doesn't introduce herself. She is Bad Cop, no doubt about it, and with disappointment I realize that Little's aw-shucks shtick must be just smoke.

Alistair trails her, fresh and crisp in khakis and sweater, although there's a ridge of flesh drawn bowstring-taut at his throat. Maybe it's always there. He looks at me, smiles. "Hi," he says, with faint surprise.

I wasn't expecting that.

I sway. I'm uneasy. My system is still sluggish, like an engine clotted with sugar; and now my neighbor has just back-footed me with a grin.

"You okay?" Little closes the hall door behind Alistair, moves to my side.

I swirl my head. Yes. No.

He hooks a finger beneath my elbow. "Let's get you—"

"Ma'am, are you all right?" Norelli's frowning.

Little raises a hand. "She's good—she's good. She's under sedation."

My cheeks simmer.

He guides me toward the kitchen alcove, sits me down at the table—the same table where Jane blew through an entire matchbox, where we played sloppy chess and talked about our kids, where she told me to photograph the sunset. The same table where she spoke of Alistair and her past.

Norelli moves to the kitchen window, phone in hand. "Ms. Fox," she says.

Little interrupts her: "Dr Fox."

She glitches, then reboots. "Dr Fox, I understand from Detective Little that you saw something last night."

I flick a glance at Alistair, still wallflowered by the hall door. "I saw my neighbor get stabbed."

"Who's your neighbor?" Norelli asks.

"Jane Russell."

"And you saw this through the window?"

"Yes."

"Which window?"

I point past her. "That one."

Norelli follows my finger. She's got moonless eyes, flat and dark; I watch them scope the Russell house, left to right, as though she's reading lines of text.

"Did you see who stabbed your neighbor?" Still looking outside.

"No, but I saw her bleeding, and I saw something in her chest."

"What was in her chest?"

I shift in the chair. "Something silver." *What does it matter?*

"Something silver?"

I nod.

Norelli nods, too; turns, looks at me, then past me, into the living room. "Who was with you last night?"

"No one."

"So that whole setup on the table is yours?"

I shift again. "Yes."

"Okay, Dr Fox." But she's watching Little. "I'm going to—"

"His wife—" I begin, raising a hand, as Alistair moves toward us.

"Wait a moment." Norelli steps forward, places her phone on the table in front me. "I'm going to play for you the 911 call you placed at ten thirty-three last night."

"His *wife*—"

"I think it answers a lot of questions." She slashes the screen with one long finger, and a voice blasts my ears, speakerphone-tinny: "911, what is—"

Norelli starts, thumbs the volume control, dials it down.

"—your emergency?"

"My neighbor." Shrill. "She's—stabbed. Oh, God. Help her." It's me, I know—my words, anyway—but not my voice; I sound slurred, melted.

"Ma'am, slow down." That drawl. Maddening even now. "What's your address?"

I look at Alistair, at Little. They're watching Norelli's phone. Norelli is watching me.

"And you say your neighbor was stabbed?"

"*Yes*. Help. She's bleeding." I wince. Almost unintelligible.

"What?"

"I said *help*." A cough, wet, spluttery. Near tears.

"Help is on the way, ma'am. I need you to calm down. Could you give me your name?"

"Anna Fox."

"All right, Anna. What's your neighbor's name?"

"Jane Russell. Oh, God." A croak.

"Are you with her now?"

"No. She's across—she's in the house across the park from me."

I feel Alistair's gaze on me. I return it, level.

"Anna, did you stab your neighbor?"

A pause. "What?"

"Did you stab your neighbor?"

"No."

Now Little is watching me, too. All three of them, staring me down. I lean forward, look at Norelli's cell. The screen fades to black as the voices continue.

"All right."

"I looked through the window and *saw her get stabbed*."

"All right. Do you know who stabbed her?"

Another pause, longer.

"Ma'am? Do you know who—"

A rasp and a rumble. The dropped phone. Up there on the study carpet—that's where it must remain, like an abandoned body.

"Ma'am?" Silence.

I crane my neck, look at Little. He isn't watching me anymore.

Norelli bends over the table, drags a finger across her screen. "The dispatcher stayed on the line for six minutes," she says, "until the EMTs confirmed they were on the scene."

*The scene.* And what did they find at *the scene*? What's happened to Jane?

"I don't understand." Suddenly I feel tired, hollowed-out tired. I cast a slow glance around the kitchen, at the cutlery bristling in the dishwasher, at the ruined bottles in the bin. "What's happened to—"

"Nothing's happened, Dr Fox," says Little, softly. "To anyone."

I look at him. "What do you mean?"

He hitches his trousers at the thighs, squats beside me. "I think," he tells me, "that with all that nice merlot you were drinking and the medication you were taking and the movie you were watching, you maybe got a little excited and saw something that wasn't there."

I stare at him.

He blinks at me.

"You think I imagined this?" My voice sounds pinched.

Shaking his massive head now: "No, ma'am, I think you were just overstimulated, and it all went to your head a little."

My mouth has swung open.

"Does your medication have any side effects?" he presses me.

"Yes," I say. "But—"

"Hallucinations, maybe?"

"I don't know." Even though I *do* know, I know it does.

"The doctor at the hospital said that hallucinations can be a side effect of the medication you're taking."

"I wasn't hallucinating. I saw what I saw." I struggle to my feet. The cat bolts from beneath the chair, streaks into the living room.

Little raises his hands, his worn palms broad and flat. "Now, you heard the phone call just now. You were having a pretty tough time talking."

Norelli steps forward. "When the hospital checked, you had a blood-alcohol level of point two-two," she tells me. "That's almost three times the legal limit."

"So?"

Behind her, Alistair's eyes are ping-ponging between us. "I wasn't *hallucinating*," I hiss. My words tumble as they flee my mouth, land on their sides. "I wasn't *imagining* things. I'm not *insane*."

"I understand your family doesn't live here, ma'am?" Norelli says.

"Is that a question?"

"That's a question."

Alistair: "My son says you're divorced."

"Separated," I correct him, automatically.

"And from what Mr Russell tells us," says Norelli, "no one in the neighborhood ever sees you. Seems you don't go outside very often."

I say nothing. I do nothing.

"So here's another theory," she continues. "You were looking for some attention."

I step back, bump into the kitchen counter. My robe flaps open.

"No friends, family's wherever, you have too much to drink and decide to raise a little ruckus."

"You think I *made this up*?" I pitch forward, bellowing.

"That's what I think," she confirms.

Little clears his throat. "I think," he says, his voice soft, "that you were maybe going a little stir-crazy in here, and—we're not saying you did this on purpose..."

"You're the ones imagining things." I point a wobbly finger at them, wave it like a wand. "You're the ones *making things up*. I saw her *covered in blood* through *that window*."

Norelli closes her eyes, sighs. "Ma'am, Mr Russell says his wife has been out of town. He says you've never met her."

Silence. The room feels electrified.

"She was in here," I say, slowly and clearly, "*twice*."

"There's—"

"First she helped me off the street. Then she visited again. And"—glaring at Alistair now—"he came *looking* for her."

He nods. "I was looking for my son, not my wife." He swallows. "And you said no one had been here."

"I lied. She sat at that table. We played chess."

He looks at Norelli, helpless.

"And you made her scream," I say.

Now Norelli turns to Alistair.

"She says she heard a scream," he explains.

"I *did* hear a scream. Three days ago." Is that accurate? Maybe not. "And Ethan told me it was her." Not strictly true, but close.

"Let's leave Ethan out of it," Little says.

I stare at them, ranged around me, like those three kids hurling eggs, those three little shits.

I'm going to lay them out flat.

"So where is she?" I ask, snapping my arms across my chest. "Where's Jane? If she's fine, bring her over here."

They share a glance.

"Come on." I gather my robe around me, yank the sash, cross my arms again. "Go get her."

Norelli turns to Alistair. "Will you..." she murmurs, and he nods, recedes into the living room, pulling his phone from his pocket.

"And then," I say to Little, "I want all of you out of my house. *You* think I'm delusional." He flinches. "And *you* think I'm lying." Norelli doesn't react. "And *he's* saying I never met a woman I met *twice*." Alistair mutters into the phone. "And I want to know exactly who went where in here when where—" Snarling myself in my words. I pause, recover. "I want to know who else has been in here."

Alistair walks back toward us. "It'll just take a moment," he says, slipping the phone into his pocket.

I lock eyes with him. "I bet this'll be a long moment."

No one speaks. My eyes roam the room: Alistair, inspecting his watch; Norelli, placidly observing the cat. Only Little watches me.

Twenty seconds pass.

Twenty more.

I sigh, unfold my arms.

This is ridiculous. The woman was—

The buzzer stutters.

My head swerves toward Norelli, then Little.

"Let me get that," says Alistair, as he turns toward the door.

I watch, stock-still, as he presses the buzzer button, twists the knob, opens the hall door, stands to one side.

A second later, Ethan slopes into the room, eyes cast low.

"You've met my son," Alistair says. "And this is my wife," he adds, shutting the door after her.

I look at him. I look at her.

I've never seen this woman in my life.

# 41

She's tall but fine-boned, with sleek dark hair framing a sculpted face. Her brows are slender, sharp, arched above a pair of gray-green eyes. She regards me coolly, then crosses the kitchen and extends a hand.

"I don't believe we've met," she says.

Her voice is low and lush, very Bacall. It clots in my ears.

I don't move. I can't.

Her hand stays there, thrust toward my chest. After a moment I wave it away.

"Who is this?"

"This is your neighbor." Little sounds almost sad.

"Jane Russell," says Norelli.

I look at her, then at him. Then at the woman.

"No, you're not," I tell her.

She withdraws her hand.

Back to the detectives: "No, she isn't. What are you *saying*? She isn't Jane."

"I promise you," Alistair begins, "she is—"

"You don't need to promise anything, Mr Russell," Norelli tells him.

"Does it make a difference if *I* promise?" asks the woman.

I round on her, step forward. "Who *are* you?" I sound raw, jagged, and I'm pleased to see her and Alistair scuttle back together, as though they're cuffed at the ankle.

"Dr Fox," Little says, "let's calm down." He places a hand on my arm.

It jolts me. I spin away from him, away from Norelli, and now I'm in the center of the kitchen, the detectives looming by the window, Alistair and the woman backed into the living room.

I turn to them, advance. "I have met Jane Russell twice," I say slowly, simply. "You are not Jane Russell."

This time she stands her ground. "I can show you my driver's license," she offers, dipping a hand into her pocket.

I shake my head, simply, slowly. "I don't want to see your driver's license."

"Ma'am," calls Norelli, and I twist my head over my shoulder. She approaches, steps between us. "That's enough."

Alistair is watching me with wide eyes. The woman's hand is still burrowed in her pocket. Behind them, Ethan has retreated to the chaise, Punch coiled at his feet.

"Ethan," I say, and his gaze glides up to me, like he was waiting to be summoned. "Ethan." I push between Alistair and the woman. "What's happening?"

He looks at me. Looks away.

"She is not your mother." I touch his shoulder. "Tell them that."

He cocks his head, swerves his eyes left. Clenches his jaw and swallows. Picks at a fingernail. "You've never met my mother," he mumbles.

I remove my hand.

Turn around, slowly, dazed.

Then they speak at once, a little chorus: "Can we—" asks Alistair, nodding toward the hall door just as Norelli says, "We're finished here," and Little invites me to "get some rest."

I blink at them.

"Can we—" Alistair tries again.

"Thank you, Mr Russell," says Norelli. "And Mrs Russell."

He and the woman eye me warily, as though I'm an animal that's just been tranquilized, then walk to the door.

"Come on," says Alistair, sharply. Ethan rises, his eyes fixed on the floor, and steps over the cat.

As they file out the door, Norelli lines up after them. "Dr Fox, it's a criminal offense to make false police reports," she informs me. "Do you understand?"

I stare at her. I think I bob my head.

"Good." She tugs at her collar. "That's all I've got."

The door closes behind her. I hear the outer door unlatch.

It's just me and Little. I look at his wingtips, black and spade-sharp, and remember (how? why?) that I've missed my French lesson with Yves today.

Just me and Little. *Les deux.*

The crack of the front door as it shuts.

"Am I okay to leave you alone?" he asks.

I nod, vacant.

"Is there someone you can talk to?"

I nod again.

"Here," he says, thumbing a card from his breast pocket, pressing it into my hand. I examine it. Flimsy stock. DETECTIVE CONRAD LITTLE, NYPD. Two phone numbers. An email address.

"You need anything, you can call me. Hey." I look up. "You can call me. Okay?"

I nod.

"Okay?"

The word barrels down my tongue, elbows other words aside. "Okay."

"Good. Day or night." He slings his phone from one hand to the other. "I got those kids. I don't sleep." To the first hand again. He catches me watching, goes still.

We look at each other.

"Be well, Dr Fox." Little moves to the hall door, opens it, gently draws it closed behind him.

Again the front door clacks open. Again it slams shut.

# 42

Sudden, intense quiet. The world has braked to a halt.

I'm alone, for the first time all day.

I survey the room. The wine bottles, radiant in the slanting sun. The chair angled beside the kitchen table. The cat, patrolling the sofa.

Flecks of dust amble through the light.

I drift to the hall door, lock it.

Turn to face the room again.

Did that just happen?

*What* just happened?

I wander to the kitchen, excavate a bottle of wine. Plunge the screw in, wedge the cork out. Glug the stuff into a glass. Bring it to my lips.

I think of Jane.

I drain the glass, then press the bottle to my mouth, tilt it hard. Drink, long and deep.

I think of that woman.

Weave my way to the living room now, gaining speed; rattle two pills into my palm. They dance down my throat.

I think of Alistair. *And this is my wife.*

Stand there, swigging, gulping, until I choke.

And when I set the bottle down again, I think of Ethan, and how he looked away from me, how he turned his head. How he swallowed before answering me. How he scratched at his fingernail. How he muttered.

How he lied.

Because he *did* lie. The averted gaze, the leftward glance, the delayed response, the fidgeting—all the tells of a liar. I knew it before he opened his mouth.

The clenched jaw, though: That's a sign of something else.

That's a sign of fear.

# 43

The phone is on the floor in the study, just where I dropped it. I tap at the screen as I return the pill bottles to the medicine cabinet in my bathroom. Dr Fielding, I'm well aware, is the one equipped with an MD and a prescription pad, but he won't be able to help me here.

"Can you come over?" I say as soon as she picks up.

A pause. "What?" She sounds bewildered.

"Can you come over?" I cross to my bed, climb in.

"Right now? I'm not—"

"Please, Bina?"

Another pause. "I can make it to you by... nine, nine thirty. I have dinner plans," she adds.

I don't care. "Fine." I lie back, the pillow foaming in my ear. Beyond the window branches stir, shedding leaves like embers; they spark against the glass, fly away.

"Iz evitingaite?"

"What?" The temazepam is clogging my brain. I can feel the circuits shorting.

"Is everything all right, I said?"

"No. Yes. I'll explain when you're here." My eyelids droop, drop.

"Okay. Seeyoutonight."

But I'm already disintegrating into sleep.

It's dark and dreamless, a little oblivion, and when the buzzer brays downstairs, I awake exhausted.

## 44

Bina stares at me, her mouth unhinged.

Finally she closes it, slowly but firmly, like a flytrap. Says nothing.

We're in Ed's library, me balled into the wingback, Bina draped along the club chair, the one where Dr Fielding parks. Her drainpipe legs are folded beneath the seat, and Punch churns around her ankles like smoke.

In the grate, a low tide of fire.

Now she shifts her gaze, watches the little wave of flames. "How much *did* you have to drink?" she asks, wincing, as though I might strike her.

"Not enough to *hallucinate*."

She nods. "Okay. And the pills..."

I grip the blanket on my lap, wring it. "I met Jane. Two times. Different days."

"Right."

"I saw her with her family in their house. Repeatedly."

"Right."

"I saw Jane bleeding. With a knife in her chest."

"It was definitely a knife?"

"Well, it wasn't a fucking *brooch*."

"I'm just—Okay, right."

"I saw it through my camera. Very clearly."

"But you didn't take a photo."

"No, I didn't take a photo. I was trying to help her, not... document it."

"Okay." She idly strokes a strand of hair. "And now they're saying that no one was stabbed."

"*And* they're trying to say that Jane is someone else. Or someone else is Jane."

She coils her hair around one long finger.

"You're sure..." she begins, and I tense, because I know what's coming. "You're definitely sure there's no way this is all a misunderst—"

I lean forward. "I know what I saw."

Bina drops her hand. "I don't... know what to say."

Speaking slowly, as though I'm picking my way through ground glass. "They're not going to believe that anything happened to Jane," I say, as much to her as to myself, "until they believe that the woman they think is Jane—isn't."

It's a knot, but she nods.

"Only—wouldn't the police just ask this person for, like, ID?"

"No. No. They'd just take her husband's—they'd just take her 'husband's' word. Wouldn't they? Why wouldn't they?" The cat trots across the carpet, slinks beneath my chair. "And no one's seen her before. They've barely been here a week.

She could be anyone. She could be a relative. She could be a mistress. She could be a mail-order bride." I go for my drink, then remember I haven't got one. "But I saw Jane *with her family*. I saw her locket with Ethan's picture in it. I saw—she sent him over here with a candle, for Christ's sake."

Bina nods again.

"And her husband wasn't acting—?"

"As though he'd just stabbed somebody? No."

"It was definitely him who..."

"Who what?"

She twists. "Did it."

"Who else could it be? Their kid is an angel. If he was—*were* going to stab anyone, it'd be his father." I reach for my glass once more, swipe at air. "And I saw him at his computer right beforehand, so unless he just sprinted downstairs to cut up his mom, I think he's in the clear."

"Have you told anyone else about this?"

"Not yet."

"Your doctor?"

"I will." Ed, too. Talk to him later.

Now, quiet—just the ripple of flames in the hearth.

Watching her, watching her skin glow copper in the firelight, I wonder if she's humoring me, if she doubts me. It's an impossible story, isn't it? *My neighbor killed his wife and now an impostor is posing as her. And their son is too frightened to tell the truth.*

"Where do you think Jane is?" Bina asks softly.

Quiet.

"I had no idea she was even a thing," says Bina, leaning over my shoulder, her hair a curtain between me and the table lamp.

"Major pinup in the fifties," I murmur. "Then a hard-core pro-lifer."

"Ah."

"Botched abortion."

"Oh."

We're at my desk, scrolling through twenty-two pages of Jane Russell photographs—pendulous with jewels (*Gentlemen Prefer Blondes*), dishabille in a haystack (*The Outlaw*), swirling a gypsy skirt (*Hot Blood*). We consulted Pinterest. We scraped the trenches of Instagram. We scoured Boston-based newspapers and websites. We visited Patrick McMullan's photography gallery. Nothing.

"Isn't it amazing," Bina says, "how according to the Internet, some people might as well not exist?"

Alistair is easier. There he is, sausage-cased in a too-tight suit, from a *Consulting Magazine* article two years old; RUSSELL MOVES TO ATKINSON, the headline explains. His LinkedIn profile features the same photograph. A portrait in a Dartmouth alumni newsletter, hoisting a glass at a fundraiser.

But no Jane.

Even stranger: no Ethan. He isn't on Facebook—or Foursquare, or anywhere—and Google yields nothing beyond assorted links to a photographer by the same name.

"Aren't most kids on Facebook?" Bina asks.

"His dad won't let him. He doesn't even have a cell phone." I roll one sagging sleeve up my arm. "And he's homeschooled. He probably doesn't know many people here. Probably doesn't know *anyone*."

"Someone must know his *mother*, though," she says. "Someone in Boston, or... just *someone*." She walks to the window. "Wouldn't there be photographs? Weren't the police at their house today?"

I consider this. "For all we know, they could have photographs of this other woman. Alistair could've just shown them anything, told them anything. They're not going to search their house. They made that very clear."

She nods, turns, looks at the Russell house. "The blinds are down," she says.

"What?" I join her at the window and see it for myself: the kitchen, the parlour, Ethan's bedroom—each one shuttered.

The house has closed its eyes. Screwed them shut.

"See?" I tell her. "They don't want me looking in anymore."

"I don't blame them."

"They're being careful. Doesn't that prove it?"

"It's suspicious, yes." She tilts her head. "Do they close the blinds often?"

"Never. Never. It's been like a goldfish bowl."

She hesitates. "Do you think... do you think you might be, you know—in danger?"

This hadn't occurred me. "Why?" I ask slowly.

"Because if what you saw really happened—"

I flinch. "It did."

"—then you're, you know, a witness."

I draw a breath, then another.

"Will you please stay the night?"

Her brows lift. "This *is* a come-on."

"I'll pay you."

She looks at me half-lidded. "It's not *that*. I've got an early day tomorrow, and all my things are back—"

"Please." I gaze deep into her eyes. "Please."

She sighs.

# 45

Darkness—dense, thick. Bomb-shelter dark. Deep-space dark.

Then, far away, a remote star, a prick of light.

Move closer.

The light trembles, bulges, pulses.

A heart. A tiny heart. Beating. Beaming.

Flushing the dark around it, dawning on a silk-fine loop of chain. A blouse, white as a ghost. A pair of shoulders, gilt with light. A line of neck. A hand, the fingers playing at the throbbing little heart.

And above it, a face: Jane. The real Jane, radiant. Watching me. Smiling.

I smile back.

And now a pane of glass slides in front of her. She presses a hand to it, prints it with tiny maps of her fingertips.

And behind her, suddenly, the darkness lifts on a scene: the love seat, raked with white and red lines; twin lamps, now bursting into light; the carpet, a garden in bloom.

Jane looks down at the locket, fingers it tenderly. At her luminous shirt. At the inkblot of blood spreading, swelling, lapping at her collar, flaming against her skin.

And when she looks up again, looks at me, it's the other woman.

## SATURDAY, NOVEMBER 6

# 46

Bina leaves a little past seven, just as light is wrapping its fingers around the curtains. She snores, I've learned, light little snuffles, like distant waves. Unexpected.

I thank her, sink my head into the pillow, drop back into sleep. When I wake, I check my phone. Almost eleven o'clock.

I stare at the screen for a moment. A minute later I'm talking to Ed. No "guess who" this time.

"That's unbelievable," he says after a pause.

"Yet it happened."

He pauses again. "I'm not saying it didn't. But"—I brace myself—"you've been *really* heavily medicated lately. So—"

"So *you* don't believe me, either."

A sigh. "No, it's not that I don't believe you. Only—"

"Do you know how *frustrating* this is?" I shout.

He goes quiet. I continue.

"I saw it happen. Yes, I was medicated, and I—yes. But I didn't *imagine* it. You don't take a bunch of pills and *imagine* something like that." I suck in a breath. "I'm not some high schooler who plays violent video games and shoots up his school. *I know what I saw.*"

Ed's still quiet.

Then:

"Well, for one thing, just to be academic, are you sure it was him?"

"Him who?"

"The husband. Who... did it."

"Bina said the same thing. Of course I'm sure."

"Couldn't have been this other woman?"

I go still.

Ed's voice perks, the way it does when he's thinking out loud. "Say she's the mistress, as you say. Down from Boston or wherever. They fight. Out comes the knife. Or whatever. In goes the knife. No husband involved."

I think. I resist it, but—maybe. Except: "Who did it is beside the point," I insist. "For now. The fact is, it was done, and the *problem* is that no one believes me. I don't even think Bina believes me. I don't think *you* believe me."

Silence. I find I've drifted up the stairs, entered Olivia's bedroom.

"Don't tell Livvy about this," I add.

Ed laughs, an actual *Ha!*, bright as tin. "I'm not going to." He coughs. "What does Dr Fielding say?"

"I haven't talked to him." I should.

"You should."

"I will."

A pause.

"And what's going on with the rest of the block?"

I realize I have no idea. The Takedas, the Millers, even the Wassermen—they haven't so much as pinged my radar this last week. A curtain has fallen on the street; the homes across the road are veiled, vanished; all that exists are my house and the Russells' house and the park between us. I wonder what's become of Rita's contractor. I wonder which book Mrs Gray has selected for her reading group. I used to log their every activity, my neighbors, used to chronicle each entrance and exit. I've got whole chapters of their lives stored on my memory card. But now...

"I don't know," I admit.

"Well," he says, "maybe that's for the best."

After we've spoken, I check the phone clock again. Eleven eleven. My birthday. Jane's, too.

# 47

I've avoided the kitchen since yesterday, avoided the first floor altogether. Now, though, I'm once more at the window, staring down the house across the park. I pour a ribbon of wine into a glass.

I know what I saw. Bleeding. Pleading.

This isn't nearly over.

I drink.

# 48

The blinds, I see, are up.

The house gawks at me, wide-eyed, as though surprised to find me looking back. I zoom in, pan the windows with my gaze, focus on the parlour.

Spotless. Nothing. The love seat. The lamps like guardsmen.

Shifting in the window seat, I swerve the lens up toward Ethan's room. He's gargoyle-perched at his desk, in front of his computer.

I zoom further. I can practically make out the text on the screen.

Movement on the street. A car, glossy as a shark, cruises into a spot in front of the Russells' walk, parks. The driver's door fans out like a fin, and Alistair emerges in a winter coat.

He strides toward the house.

I snap a photo.

When he reaches the door, I snap another.

I don't have a plan. (Do I ever have a plan anymore, I wonder?) It's not as though I'll see his hands rinsed in blood. He won't knock on my door and confess.

But I can watch.

He enters the house. My lens jumps to the kitchen, and sure enough, he appears there a moment later. Slaps the keys on the counter, shrugs off his coat. Leaves the room.

Doesn't return.

I move the camera one floor up, to the parlour.

And as I do, she appears, light and bright in a spring-green pullover: "Jane."

I adjust the lens. She goes crisp, sharp, as she moves first to one lamp, then the other, switching them on. I watch her fine hands, her long neck, the sweep of her hair against her cheek.

The liar.

Then she leaves, slim hips shifting as she walks out the door.

Nothing. The parlour is empty. The kitchen is empty.

Upstairs, Ethan's chair sits vacant, the computer screen a black box.

The phone rings.

My head swivels, almost back to front, like an owl, and the camera drops to my lap.

The sound is behind me, but my phone is by my hand.

It's the landline.

Not the kitchen landline, rotting downstairs in its dock, but the one in Ed's library. I'd forgotten it entirely.

It rings again, distant, insistent. I don't move.

I don't breathe.

Who's calling me? No one's called the house phone in... I can't remember. Who would even have this number? I can barely remember it myself.

Another ring.

And another.

I shrivel against the glass, wilt there in the cold. I imagine the rooms of my house, one by one, throbbing with that noise.

Another ring.

I look across the park.

She's there, in the parlour window, a phone at her ear.

Looking right at me, hard.

I scuttle from my seat, grip the camera in one hand, retreat to my desk. She holds her gaze, her mouth a terse line.

How did she get this number?

But then how did I get hers? Directory assistance. I think of her dialing, speaking my name, asking to be connected. To me.

Invading my house, my head.

The *liar*.

I watch her. I glare.

She glares back.

One more ring.

And then another sound—Ed's voice.

"You've reached Anna and Ed," he says, low and rough, like a movie-trailer announcer. I remember him recording the message; "You sound like Vin Diesel," I told him, and he laughed, and pitched his voice lower still.

"We're away right now, but leave us a message and we'll get right back to you." And I remember how as soon as he'd finished, as soon as he'd pressed the Stop button, he'd added, in a god-awful Cockney accent, "When we bloody feel like it."

For an instant, I close my eyes, picture him calling to me. But it's her voice that fills the air, fills the house.

"I think you know who I am." A pause. I open my eyes, find her looking at me, watch her mouth shape the words boring into my ears. The effect is uncanny. "Stop photographing our house or I'll call the police."

She removes the phone from her ear, slips it into her pocket.

Stares at me. I stare back.

All is silent.

Then I leave the room.

# 49

GIRLPOOL has challenged you!

It's my chess program. I give the screen the finger and press the phone to my ear. Dr Fielding's voicemail greeting, brittle as a dead leaf, invites me to leave a message. I do so, enunciating carefully.

I'm in Ed's library, laptop warming my thighs, midday sun puddled on the carpet. A glass of merlot stands on the table beside me. A glass and a bottle.

I don't want to drink. I want to stay clear; I want to think. I want to *analyze*. Already the past thirty-six hours are receding, evaporating, like a bank of fog. Already I can feel the house squaring its shoulders, shrugging the outside world away.

I need a drink.

Girlpool. What a stupid name. Girlpool. *Whirlpool.* Tierney. Bacall. *It's in your bloodstream now.*

It certainly is. I tip the glass to my lips, feel the flood of wine rushing down my throat, the fizz in my veins.

*Hold your breath, cross your fingers.*

*Let me in!*

*You'll be all right.*

You'll be all right. I snort.

My mind is a swamp, deep and brackish, the true and the false mingling and mixing. What are those trees that grow in heavily sedimented swampland? The ones with their roots exposed? Man... mandrake? Man-something, definitely.

David.

The glass wobbles in my hand.

In the rush, in the rumble, I've forgotten about David.

Who worked at the Russells'. Who could have—*must* have—met Jane.

I set the glass on the table, bring myself to my feet. Sway into the hall. Down the stairs, emerging into the kitchen. I lob a glance at the Russell house—no one on display, no one watching me—then knock on the basement door, gently at first, again with force. I call his name.

No response. I wonder if he's asleep. But it's midafternoon.

An idea flares in my brain.

It's wrong, I know, but this *is* my house. And it's urgent. It's very urgent.

I move to the desk in the living room, slide open the drawer, and find it there, dull silver and jagged with teeth: the key.

I return to the basement door. Knock once more—nothing—then push the key into the lock. Twist it.

Pull the door open.

It whines. I wince.

But all is quiet as I peer down the stairs. I descend into darkness, softly in my slipper feet, grazing one hand along the rough plaster of the wall.

I reach the floor. The blackouts are drawn; it's night down here. My fingers brush the switch on the wall, flip it. The room bursts into light.

It's been two months since I last visited, two months since David arrived for a tour. He scanned it all with his licorice-dark eyes—the living area, with Ed's drafting table front and center; the narrow sleeping alcove; the chrome-and-walnut kitchenette; the bathroom—and nodded once.

He hasn't done much with the place. He's scarcely done *anything* with the place. Ed's sofa is where it was; the drafting table has stayed put, although it's now level. A plate rests on its surface, plastic fork and knife X-ed across it like a coat of arms. Toolboxes are stacked against the far wall, next to the outside door. On the topmost box I spot the borrowed box cutter, its little tongue of blade glittering beneath the overheads. Beside it a book, spine broken. *Siddhartha*.

A photograph in a slim black frame hangs on the wall opposite. Me and Olivia, age five, on our front steps, my arms wreathed around her. Grinning, both of us, Olivia with her summer teeth—"summer here, summer there," Ed liked to say.

I'd forgotten about that picture. My heart twitches a little. I wonder why it's still hanging.

I tread to the alcove. "David?" I ask quietly, even though I'm certain he's not here.

The sheets are roiled at the foot of the mattress. Deep dents in the pillows, like they've been scissor-kicked. I catalogue the inventory of the bed: filigree of brittle ramen noodle coiling upon pillowcase; prophylactic, wilted and greasy, snagged upon the newel; aspirin bottle lodged between bedstead and wall; hieroglyphs of dried sweat, or semen, inscribed across top sheet; a slender laptop at the foot of the mattress. A belt of condom packets is looped around a floor lamp. An earring beams on the nightstand.

I peek into the bathroom. The sink is brindled with whiskers, the toilet yawning wide. Within the shower, a gaunt bottle of store-brand shampoo and a shard of soap.

I retreat, return to the main room. Run a hand along the drafting table.

Something nibbles at my brain. I grasp at it, lose it.

I scan the room once more. No photo albums, although I suppose no one keeps photo albums anymore (*Jane did,*

I remember); no CD wallet or DVD tower, but I guess those are extinct as well. *Isn't it amazing how according to the Internet, some people might as well not exist?* Bina had asked. All David's memories, all his music, everything that might unlock the man—it's gone. Or, rather, it's all around me, floating in the ether, but invisible, files and icons, ones and zeros.

Nothing left on display in the real world, not a sign, not a clue.

*Isn't it amazing?*

I look again at the picture on the wall. I think of my cabinet in the living room, packed with DVD slipcases. I'm a relic.

I've been left behind.

I turn to go.

And as I do, I hear a scratch behind me. It's the outside door.

And as I watch, it opens, and David stands before me, staring.

# 50

"What the fuck are you doing?"

I flinch. I've never heard him swear. I've barely ever heard him speak.

"What the *fuck* are you doing?"

I back up, open my mouth.

"I was just—"

"What makes you think you can just come down here?"

I take another step back, stumble. "I'm so sorry—"

He's advancing, the door behind him wide open. My vision rolls.

"I'm so sorry." I breathe deep. "I was looking for something."

"For what?"

Breathe again. "I was looking for you."

He lifts his hands, drops them to his sides, the keys flailing in his fingers. "Here I am." He shakes his head. "Why?"

"Because—"

"You could have called me."

"I didn't think—"

"No, you thought you'd just come down here."

I start to nod, then stop. This is almost the longest conversation we've ever had.

"Could you close the door?" I ask.

He stares, turns, pushes it. It shuts with a crack.

When he looks back at me, his features have softened. But his voice is still hard: "What is it you need?"

I feel dizzy. "Can I sit?" He doesn't move.

I drift to the sofa, sink into it. He stands statue-still for a moment, the keys jumbled in one palm; then he jams them in his pocket, tugs off his jacket, tosses it into the bedroom. I hear it land on the bed, slither onto the floor.

"This isn't cool."

I shake my head. "No, I know."

"You wouldn't like it if I went into your space. Uninvited."

"No. I know."

"You'd be fuck—You'd be pissed off."

"Yes."

"What if I'd been here with someone?"

"I knocked."

"Is that supposed to make it better?" I say nothing.

He watches me for another moment, then walks to the kitchen, kicking his boots off. Opens the refrigerator door, grabs a Rolling Rock from the shelf. Chinks it against the edge of the counter, and off pops the cap. It hits the floor, rolls beneath the radiator.

When I was younger, that would have impressed me.

He presses the bottle to his mouth, sips, slowly walks back to me. Slanting his long body against the drafting table, he sips again.

"Well?" he says. "I'm here."

I nod, gazing up at him. "Have you met the woman across the park?"

His brow creases. "Who?".

"Jane Russell. Across the park. Number—"

"No."

Flat as a horizon.

"But you did work there."

"Yeah."

"So—"

"I worked for Mr Russell. I never met his wife. I didn't even know he had a wife."

"He has a son."

"Single guys can have kids." He swigs his beer. "Not that I thought about it that far. That was your question?"

I nod. I feel tiny. Study my hands.

"That's what you came down here for?"

I nod again.

"Well, you've got your answer."

I sit there.

"Why do you want to know, anyway?"

I look up at him. He's not going to believe me.

"No reason," I say. I push my fist against the armrest, try to stand.

He offers me his hand. I take it, his palm rough against my own, and he pulls me to my feet, smooth and swift. I watch the bands of muscle shift in his forearm.

"I'm really sorry for coming down here," I tell him.

He nods.

"It won't happen again."

He nods.

I move toward the stairs. I feel his eyes on my back.

Three steps up, I remember something.

"Did you—didn't you hear a scream the day you were working there?" I ask, turning, my shoulder pressed against the wall.

"You already asked me that. Remember? No scream? Springsteen."

Did I? I feel as though I'm falling through my own mind.

# 51

As I enter the kitchen, the basement door clicking shut behind me, Dr Fielding calls.

"I received your voicemail," he tells me. "You sounded concerned."

I part my lips. I'd been prepared to share the whole story, to decant myself, but there's no point, is there? *He's* the one who sounds concerned, always, about everything; he's the one magicking my medication to the point where... well. "It was nothing," I say.

He's quiet. "Nothing?"

"No. I mean, I had a question about"—I gulp—"going generic."

Still quiet.

I forge ahead: "I wondered if I could go generic on some of them. The drugs."

"Medications," he corrects me, automatically.

"Medications, I mean."

"Well, yes." He sounds unconvinced.

"That'd be great. Just because it's getting expensive."

"Has this been a problem?"

"No, no. But I don't want it to *become* a problem."

"I see." He doesn't.

Silence. I open a cabinet by the fridge.

"Well," he continues, "let's discuss this on Tuesday."

"All right," I say, selecting a bottle of merlot.

"It can wait that long, I assume?"

"Yes, absolutely." I twist the cap off the bottle.

"And you're sure you're feeling all right?"

"Completely." I fetch a glass from the sink.

"You're not mixing with alcohol?"

"No." Pouring.

"Good. Well, I'll see you then."

"See you then."

The line goes dead, and I sip.

# 52

I travel upstairs. In Ed's library, I find the glass and bottle I abandoned twenty minutes ago, brimming with sun. I collect them, ferry the whole lot to my study.

At the desk I sit. And think.

Spread across the screen before me is a chessboard, pieces already in place, night-and-day armies braced for battle. The white queen: I remember claiming Jane's. Jane, in her snowy blouse, saturated with blood.

Jane. The white queen.

The computer chirps.

I look toward the Russell house. No signs of life.

GRANNYLIZZIE: Hello, Doctor Anna.

I start, stare.

Where had we left things? *When* had we left things? I expand the chat box, scroll up. GRANNYLIZZIE HAS LEFT THE CHAT at 4:46 P.M. on Thursday, November 4.

That's right: just as Ed and I had broken the news to Olivia. I remember how my heart thrummed.

And six hours later I dialed 911.

And since then... the journey outside. The night in the hospital. The interview with Little, with the doctor. The injection. The ride through Harlem, sun aching in my eyes. The hustle inside. Punch, snaking into my lap. Norelli, circling me. Alistair in my house. Ethan in my house.

That woman in my house.

And Bina, and our Internet searches, and her prim snores in the night. And today: Ed, disbelieving; that phone call from "Jane"; David's apartment, David's anger; Dr Fielding's voice croaking in my ear.

Has it only been two days?

THEDOCTORISIN: Hello! How are you?

She cut me off cold, but I'm taking the high road.

GRANNYLIZZIE: I'm fine, but more importantly I am SO sorry for leaving so abruptly the last time we spoke.

Good.

THEDOCTORISIN That's all right! We've all got things to do!

GRANNYLIZZIE: It wasn't that, I PROMISE. My internet gave up on life! Rest in peace internet!

GRANNYLIZZIE: This happens every couple of months but this time it was on a Thursday and the company couldn't get anyone out here until the weekend.

GRANNYLIZZIE: I'm SO sorry, I can't imagine what you must think of me.

I put the glass to my mouth, drink. Set it down and sip from the other glass. I'd assumed that Lizzie didn't want to hear my sob story. Me of little faith.

THEDOCTORISIN: Please don't apologize! These things happen!

GRANNYLIZZIE: Well I feel like a real rhymes with witch!!

THEDOCTORISIN: Not at all.

GRANNYLIZZIE: Forgive me?

THEDOCTORISIN: Nothing to forgive! I hope you're doing well.

GRANNYLIZZIE: Yes I am well. My sons are visiting :-)

THEDOCTORISIN :-) indeed! How nice for you!

GRANNYLIZZIE: Wonderful to have them here.

THEDOCTORISIN: What are your sons' names?

GRANNYLIZZIE: Beau

GRANNYLIZZIE: And William.

THEDOCTORISIN: Great names.

GRANNYLIZZIE: Great guys. They've always been a huge help. Especially when Richard was ill. We raised them right!

THEDOCTORISIN: Sounds like it!

GRANNYLIZZIE: William calls me every day from Florida. He says HELLO THERE in his biggest voice and I smile. Gets me every time.

I smile too.

THEDOCTORISIN: My family always says "Guess who" when I talk to them!

GRANNYLIZZIE: Oh I like that!

I think of Livvy and Ed, hear their voices in my head. My throat swells. I swallow some more wine.

THEDOCTORISIN: It must be very nice to have your sons with you.

GRANNYLIZZIE: Anna, it is SO nice. They are back in their old bedrooms and it feels like "old times".

For the first time in days, I feel relaxed, in charge. Useful, even. Almost like I'm back on East Eighty-Eighth, in my office, helping a patient. *Only connect.*

I might need this more than Lizzie does.

And so, as the light dims outside and the shadows fade across my ceiling, I chat with a lonely grandmother thousands of miles away. Lizzie loves to cook, she tells me; the boys' favorite meal is my famous pot roast (not really famous), and she bakes cream cheese brownies every year for the fire department.

There used to be a cat—here I tell her about Punch—but now she has a rabbit, a brown girl named Petunia. Though not a film buff, Lizzie likes cooking shows and Game of Thrones. The latter surprises me—pretty gritty.

She talks about Richard, of course. We all miss him very much. He was a teacher, a Methodist deacon, a lover of trains (with a big model set in our cellar), an affectionate parent—a good man.

*A good man and a good father.* Suddenly Alistair steps into my mind. I shudder, wade deeper into my wineglass.

GRANNYLIZZIE: Hope I'm not boring you...

THEDOCTORISIN: Not at all.

I learn that Richard was not only decent but responsible, and managed all the house work: maintenance, electronics (William brought me an "apple TV" I cannot work, Lizzie frets), landscaping, bills. In his absence, explains his widow, I feel overwhelmed. I feel like an old lady.

I drum my fingers atop the mouse. It isn't exactly the Cotard delusion, but I can propose some quick fixes. Let's solve this, I tell her—and instantly my blood runs warm, the way it does when I'm walking a patient through a problem.

I take a pencil from the drawer, slash a few words onto a Post-it. At the office I used a Moleskine notebook and a fountain pen. Makes no difference.

*Maintenance:* See if there's a local handyman who can visit weekly—can she do that?

GRANNYLIZZIE: There is Martin who works at my church.

THEDOCTORISIN: Great!

*Electronics:* Most young people are good with computers and TVs. I'm not sure how many teenagers Lizzie knows, but—

GRANNYLIZZIE: The Roberts on my street have a son with an ipad.

THEDOCTORISIN: He's your man!

*Bills* (a particular challenge for her, it seems; paying on line is difficult, too many different user names and pass words): She should Choose consistent and easy-to-remember logins for both—her own name, I suggest, or a child's, or a loved one's birthday—but switch out some of the letters for numbers and symbols. W1LL1@M, for example.

A pause.

GRANNYLIZZIE: My name would be L1221E

I smile again.

THEDOCTORISIN: That's catchy!

GRANNYLIZZIE: Laughing Out Loud.

GRANNYLIZZIE: The news said I could be "hacked", is that something I should worry about??

THEDOCTORISIN: I don't think anyone will crack your code!

I should hope nobody would, anyway. She's a septuagenarian in Montana.

Finally, *outdoor work:* Winters are really really cold here, Lizzie notes, so she'll need someone to clear snow off the roof, spread rock salt on the front walk, shear icicles from the gutters... Even if I am able to go outside, it's a heck of a lot of work to get ready for winter.

THEDOCTORISIN: Well, let's hope you're back in the world by then. But either way, maybe Martin from church could help you. Or kids from the neighborhood. Your students, even. Don't underestimate the power of $10 an hour!

GRANNYLIZZIE: Yes. Good ideas.

GRANNYLIZZIE: Thank you so much, Doctor Anna. I feel SO much better.

Problem solved. Patient helped. I feel as though I'm glowing. I sip my wine.

And then it's back to pot roast, and rabbits, and William and Beau.

A light in the Russell parlour. I peek around the side of the desktop screen and see that woman walk into the room. I haven't thought about her for more than an hour, I realize. My session with Lizzie is doing me good.

GRANNYLIZZIE: William is back with shopping. He better have bought the donuts I asked for!

GRANNYLIZZIE: I have to go stop him from eating them.

THEDOCTORISIN: Please do!

GRANNYLIZZIE: Have you been able to go outside yet, btw?

btw. She's learning Internet slang.

I splay my fingers, fan them over the keyboard. Yes, I've been able to go outside. Twice, in fact.

THEDOCTORISIN: No luck, I'm afraid.

No need to go into it, either.

GRANNYLIZZIE: I hope you will be able to soon...

THEDOCTORISIN: That makes two of us!

She signs off, and I drain my glass. Set it on the desk.

I push one foot against the floor, set the chair slowly spinning. The walls revolve before me.

*I will promote healing and well-being.* I did that today.

I close my eyes. I've helped Lizzie prepare for life, helped her live it a little more fully. Helped her find relief.

*I will place others' interests above my own.* Well, yes—but I benefited, too: For nearly ninety minutes, the Russells retreated from my brain. Alistair, that woman, even Ethan.

Even Jane.

The chair drifts to a halt. When I open my eyes, I'm looking through the doorway, into the hall, into Ed's library.

And I think about what I haven't told Lizzie, what I didn't get to tell her.

## 53

Olivia refused to return to the room, so Ed remained with her while I packed, my heart booming. I trudged back to the lobby, where the flames were simmering low in the grate, and Marie dragged my credit card through a reader. She wished us folks a pleasant evening, her smile absurdly broad, her eyes wide.

Olivia reached for me. I looked at Ed; he took the bags, slung one over each shoulder. I gripped our daughter's hot little hand in my own.

We'd parked in the far corner of the lot; by the time we reached the car, we were starchy with flakes. Ed popped the trunk, stuffed the luggage inside, while I swept my arm across the windshield. Olivia clambered into the backseat, slamming the door after herself.

Ed and I stood there, at opposite ends of the car, as the snow fell on us, between us.

I saw his mouth move. "What?" I asked.

He spoke again, louder. "You're driving."

I drove.

I drove out of the lot, tires squealing on the frost. I drove into the road, snowflakes thrilling against the windows. I drove onto the highway, into the night, into the white.

All was silent, just the hum of the engine. Beside me, Ed gazed dead ahead. I checked the mirror. Olivia was slumped in her seat, head bobbing against her shoulder—not asleep, but eyes half-shuttered.

We coasted around a bend. I gripped the wheel harder.

And suddenly the chasm opened up next to us, that vast pit gouged from the earth; now, under the moon, the trees below glowed like ghosts. Flakes of snow, silver and dark, tumbled into the gorge, down, down, lost forever, mariners drowned in the deep.

I lifted my foot from the gas.

In the rearview I watched Olivia as she peered through the window. Her face was shiny; she'd been crying again, in silence.

My heart cracked.

My phone buzzed.

Two weeks earlier we'd attended a party, Ed and I, at the house across the park, the Lord place—holiday cocktails, all glossy drinks and mistletoe sprigs. The Takedas were there, and the Grays (the Wassermen, our host told me, declined to RSVP); one of the grown Lord children put in a cameo, girlfriend in tow. And Bert's colleagues from the bank, legions of them. The house was a war zone, a minefield, air-kisses popping at every step, cannon-fire laughter, backslaps like bombs.

Midway through the evening, midway through my fourth glass, Josie Lord approached.

"Anna!"

"Josie!"

We embraced. Her hands fluttered over my back.

"Look at your gown," I said.

"Isn't it?"

I didn't know how to respond. "It *is*."

"But look at you in slacks!"

I gestured to my pants. "Look at me."

"I had to retire my shawl just a moment ago—Bert spilled his... oh, thank you, Anna," as I tweezed a length of hair from her glove. "Spilled his wine all over my shoulder."

"Bad Bert!" I sipped.

"I told him he's in a lot of trouble later. This is the second time... oh, thank you, Anna," as I pinched another filament from her dress. Ed always said I was a hands-on drunk. "Second time he's done that to my shawl."

"The same shawl?"

"No, no."

Her teeth were round and off-white; I was reminded of the Weddell seal, which, I'd recently learned from a nature program, uses its fangs to clear holes in Antarctic ice fields. "Its teeth," the narrator had pointed out, "become badly worn down." Cue shot of seal thrashing its jaws against the snow. "Weddell seals die young," added the narrator, ominously.

"Now, who's been calling you all night?" asked the Weddell seal before me.

I went still. My phone had buzzed steadily throughout the evening, humming against my hip. I would slip it into my palm, drop my eyes to the screen, tap a reply with my thumb. I'd been discreet, I thought.

"It's a work thing," I explained.

"But what could a child possibly need at this hour?" Josie asked.

I smiled. "That's confidential. You understand."

"Oh, of course, of course. You're very professional, dear."

Yet amid the roar, even as I skimmed the surface of my brain, mouthed questions and answers, even as the wine flowed and the carols droned—even then I could think only of him.

The phone buzzed again.

My hands jumped from the wheel for an instant. I'd stowed the phone in the cup well between the front seats, where now it rattled against the plastic.

I looked at Ed. He was watching the phone.

Another buzz. I flicked my eyes to the mirror. Olivia was staring out the window.

Quiet. We drove on. Buzz.

"Guess who," Ed said.

I didn't respond.

"Bet it's him."

I didn't argue.

Ed took the phone in his hand, inspected the screen. Sighed. We cruised down the road. We hugged a turn.

"You want to answer it?"

I couldn't look at him. My gaze bore through the windshield. I shook my head.

"I'll answer it, then."

"No." I snatched at the phone. Ed held it from me.

It kept buzzing. "I want to answer it," Ed said. "I want to have a word with him."

"No." I knocked the phone from his hand. It clattered beneath my feet.

"Stop it," cried Olivia.

I looked down, saw the screen trembling on the floor, saw his name on it.

"Anna," Ed breathed.

I looked up. The road had vanished.

We were rocketing over the edge of the gorge. We were sailing into the dark.

# 54

A knock.

I've drifted off. I sit up, groggy. The room has gone dark; night beyond the windows.

The knock again. Downstairs. It isn't the front door; it's the basement.

I walk to the stairs. David almost always uses the front door when he visits. I wonder if this is one of his houseguests.

But when I flick the kitchen lights and open the basement door, it's the man himself on the other side, looking up at me from two steps below.

"I thought maybe now I should start coming in this way," he says.

I pause, then realize he's trying to joke. "Fair enough." I step aside, and he moves past me into the kitchen.

I shut the door. We eye each other. I think I know what he's going to say. I think he's going to tell me about Jane.

"I wanted—I want to apologize," he begins.

I freeze.

"For earlier," he says.

I twitch my head, my hair loose around my shoulders. "I'm the one who should apologize."

"You *did* apologize."

"I'm happy to apologize again."

"No, I don't want that. I want to say I'm sorry. For shouting." He nods. "And for leaving the door open. I know that bothers you."

An understatement, but I owe him at least that. "It's fine." I want to hear about Jane. Can I ask him again?

"I just—" He strokes the kitchen island with one hand, props himself against it. "I get territorial. Probably this is something I should've told you before, but."

The sentence ends there. He swings one foot in front of the other.

"But?" I say.

He lifts his eyes from beneath those dark brows. Rough and ready. "You got any beer?"

"I've got wine." I think of the two bottles on my desk upstairs, the two glasses. I should probably empty them. "Should I open a bottle?"

"Sure."

I move past him to the cabinet—he smells of Ivory—and remove a bottle of red. "Merlot okay?"

"I don't even know what that is."

"It's a nice red."

"Sounds good."

I open another cabinet door. Bare. Over to the dishwasher. A pair of glasses clash in my hand; I set them on the island, pry the cork out of the bottle, and pour.

He slides a glass toward himself, tips it toward me.

"Cheers," I say, and sip.

"The thing is," he says, rolling the glass in his hand, "I did some time."

I nod, then feel my eyes widen. I don't think I've ever heard anyone use that expression. No one outside movies, anyway.

"Jail?" I hear myself say, stupidly.

He smiles. "Jail."

I nod again. "What did you—were you in jail for?"

He looks at me evenly. "Assault." Then: "Against a man." I stare at him.

"That makes you nervous," he says.

"No."

The lie hangs in the air.

"I'm just surprised," I tell him.

"I should have said something." He scratches his jaw. "Before moving in, I mean. I understand if you want me to clear out."

I don't know if he means it. Do I want him to clear out? "What... happened?" I ask.

He sighs, faintly. "Fight in a bar. Nothing fancy." A shrug. "Except I had a prior. Same thing. Two strikes."

"I thought it was three."

"Depends who you are."

"Mm," I say, as though this is wisdom not to be questioned. "And my PD was a drunk."

"Mm," I repeat, working it out. *Public defender.*

"So I did fourteen months."

"Where was this?"

"The fight or the prison?"

"Both."

"Both in Massachusetts."

"Oh."

"Do you want to know, like, details?" I do. "Oh, no."

"It was just stupid stuff. Drunk stuff."

"I see."

"But that's where I learned to—you know. Watch out for my... space."

"I see."

We stand there, eyes downcast, like two teenagers at a dance.

I shift my weight. "When were you—when did you do time?" *Where appropriate, use the patient's vocabulary.*

"Got out in April. Stayed in Boston over the summer, then came down here."

"I see."

"You keep saying that," he says, but it's friendly.

I smile. "Well." Clearing my throat. "I invaded your space, and I shouldn't have. Of course you can stay." Do I mean that? I think I do.

He sips his wine. "I just wanted you to know. Also," he adds, nodding his glass toward me, "this stuff is pretty good."

"I haven't forgotten about the ceiling, you know."

We're on the sofa, three glasses deep—well, three for him, four for me, so seven glasses deep, if we're counting, which we're not—and it takes me a second to catch up.

"Which ceiling?"

He points. "The roof."

"Right." I look up, as though I can gaze through the bones of the house to the roof. "Oh, right. What made you think of that?"

"You just said that once you can go outside you're going to get up there. Check it out."

Did I? "That's not happening for a while," I tell him crisply. Crispishly. "I can't even walk across the garden."

A slight grin, a tilt of the head. "Someday, then." He places his glass on the coffee table, stands. "Where's the bathroom?"

I twist in my seat. "Over there."

"Thanks." He pads away to the red room.

I keel back into the sofa. The cushion whispers in my ears as I rock my head side to side. *I saw my neighbor get stabbed. That woman you never met. That woman nobody has ever met. Please believe me.*

I can hear urine drilling into the bowl. Ed used to do that, pee so forcibly that it was audible even with the door closed, like he was boring a hole through the porcelain.

The flush of the toilet. The hiss of the tap.

*There's someone in her house. Someone pretending to be her.*

The bathroom door opens, closes.

*The son and the husband are lying. They're all lying.* I sink deeper into the cushion.

I stare at the ceiling, at the lights like dimples. Shut my eyes.

*Help me find her.*

A creak. A hinge, someplace. David might have gone back downstairs. I tip to one side.

*Help me find her.*

But when I open my eyes a moment later, he's returned, flopping onto the sofa. I straighten up, smile. He smiles back, looks past me. "Cute kid."

I swivel. It's Olivia, beaming within a silver frame. "You've got her picture downstairs," I remember. "On the wall."

"Yeah."

"Why?"

He shrugs. "Don't know. Didn't have anything to replace it with." He drains his glass. "Where is she, anyway?"

"With her dad." Swallowing wine.

A pause. "You miss her?"

"Yes."

"You miss him?"

"I do, in fact."

"Talk to them a lot?"

"All the time. Just yesterday, actually."

"When do you see them next?"

"Probably not for a while. But soon, I hope."

I don't want to talk about this, about them. I want to talk about the woman across the park. "Should we check out that ceiling?"

The steps coil up into blackness. I lead; David follows.

As we pass the study, something ripples beside my leg. Punch, stealing downstairs. "Was that the cat?" David asks.

"That was the cat," I answer.

We ascend past the bedrooms, both dark, and onto the uppermost landing. I slap my hand to the wall, find the switch. In the sudden light, I see David's eyes on mine.

"It doesn't look any worse," I say, pointing to the stain overhead, spread across the trapdoor like a bruise.

"No," he agrees. "But it'll get there. I'll take care of it this week."

Silence.

"Are you very busy? Finding a lot of work?"

Nothing.

I wonder if I might *tell* him about Jane. I wonder what he'd say.

But before I can decide, he's kissed me.

## 55

We're on the floor of the landing, the carpet rough against my skin; then he hoists me up, carries me to the nearest bed.

His mouth is on my mouth; stubble sandpapers my cheeks and chin. One hand rakes my hair hard, while the other tugs at my sash. I suck in my gut as the robe spreads wide, but he only kisses me harder, my throat, my shoulders.

*Out flew the web, and floated wide;*
*The mirror crack'd from side to side;*
*"I am half-sick of shadows," cried*
*The Lady of Shalott.*

Why Tennyson? Why now?

I haven't felt this in so long. I haven't *felt* in so long.

I want to feel this. I want to feel. I am so sick of shadows.

Later, in the dark, my fingers brush his chest, his stomach, the line of hair trailing down from his navel like a fuse.

He breathes quietly. And then I drift away. And I half dream of sunsets, and of Jane; and at some point I hear a soft tread on the landing, and to my surprise, I hope he comes back to bed.

## SUNDAY, NOVEMBER 7

# 56

When I awake, my head swollen, David is gone. His pillow feels cool. I press my face to it; it smells of sweat.

I roll to my side, away from the window, from the light.

What the hell happened?

We were drinking—of course we were drinking; I pinch my eyes shut—and then we made our way to the top story. Stood beneath the trapdoor. And so to bed. Or, no: First we hit the landing floor. Then bed.

Olivia's bed.

My eyes bolt open.

I'm in my daughter's bed, her blankets wrapped around my naked body, her pillow dry with the sweat of a man I barely know. God, Livvy, I'm sorry.

I squint at the doorway, into the dim of the hall; then I sit up, the sheets clasped to my breasts—Olivia's sheets, printed with little ponies. Her favorite. She refused to sleep on anything else.

I turn toward the window. Gray outside, November drizzle, rain leaking from the leaves, from the eaves.

I cast a glance across the park. From here I can gaze directly into Ethan's bedroom. He isn't there.

I shiver.

My robe is smeared across the floor like a skid mark. I step from the bed, gather it in my hands—why are they shaking?—and swaddle myself. One slipper lies abandoned beneath the bed; I find the other on the landing.

At the top of the stairs, I take a breath. The air is stale.

David's right: I should ventilate. I won't, but I should.

I walk down the stairs. At the next landing, I look one way, then the other, as though I'm about to cross a street; the bedrooms are quiet, my sheets still disarranged from my night with Bina. *My Night with Bina.* Sounds filthy.

I'm hungover.

One flight down and I peer into the library, into the study. The Russell place peers back at me. I feel as though it's tracking me as I move through my house.

I hear him before I see him.

And when I see him, he's in the kitchen, sucking water from a tumbler. The room is shadows and glass, as dim as the world beyond the window.

I study his Adam's apple as it bobs in his throat. His hair is scruffy at the nape; a slim hip peeks from beneath the fold of his shirt. For an instant I close my eyes and recall that hip in my hand, that throat against my mouth.

When I open them again, he's looking at me, eyes dark and full in the gray light. "Quite an apology, huh?" he says.

I feel myself blush.

"Hope I didn't wake you up." He raises his glass. "Just needed a refill. Got to head out in a minute." He gulps the rest of it, sets the glass in the sink. Drags a hand across his lips.

I don't know what to say.

He seems to sense this. "I'm gonna get out of your hair," he says, and comes toward me. I tense, but he's making for the basement door; I move aside to let him pass. When we're shoulder to shoulder, he turns his head, speaks low.

"Not sure if I should be saying thanks or sorry."

I look him in the eye, summon the words. "It was nothing." My voice is throaty in my ears. "Don't worry about it."

He considers, nods. "Sounds like I should be saying sorry."

I drop my gaze. He steps past me and opens the door. "I'm heading out tonight. Job in Connecticut. Should be back tomorrow."

I say nothing.

When I hear the door shut behind me, I exhale. At the sink I fill his glass with water and bring it to my lips. I think I can taste him all over again.

# 57

So: That happened.

I never liked that expression. Too flip. But here I am and there it is:

That happened.

Glass in hand, I drift to the sofa, where I find Punch curled on the cushion, his tail switching back and forth. I sit beside him, stow the glass between my thighs, and tilt my head back.

Ethics aside—though it isn't really an ethical issue, is it? Sex with a tenant, I mean?—I can't believe we did what we did in my daughter's bed. What would Ed say? I cringe. He's not going to find out, of course, but still. But still. I want to torch the sheets. Ponies and all.

The house breathes around me, the steady tick of the grandfather clock a faint pulse. The whole room is in shadow, a blur of shades. I see myself, my phantom self, reflected in the television screen.

What would I do if I were on that screen, a character in one of my films? I would leave the house to investigate, like Teresa Wright in *Shadow of a Doubt*. I would summon a friend, like Jimmy Stewart in *Rear Window*. I wouldn't sit here, in a puddle of robe, wondering where next to turn.

Locked-in syndrome. Causes include stroke, brain stem injury, MS, even poison. It's a neurological condition, in other words, not a psychological one. Yet here I am, utterly, literally locked in—doors closed, windows shut, while I shy and shrink from the light, and a woman is stabbed across the park, and no one notices, no one knows. Except me—me, swollen with booze, parted from her family, *fucking her tenant*. A freak to the neighbors. A joke to the cops. A special case to her doctor. A pity case to her physical therapist. A shut-in. No hero. No sleuth.

I am locked in. I am locked out.

At some point I rise, move to the stairs, put one foot in front of the other. I'm on the landing, about to step into my study, when I notice it. The closet door is ajar. Just slightly, but ajar.

My heart stops for an instant.

But why should it? It's just an open door. I opened it myself the other day. For David.

...Except I closed it again. I would have noticed if it had been left open—because I *did* just notice it had been left open.

I stand there, wavering like a flame. Do I trust myself? Despite everything, I do.

I walk toward the closet. I place my hand on the knob, gingerly, as though it might twist away from me. I pull it.

Dark inside, deeply dark. I wave my hand overhead, find the frayed string, tug. The room flares with light, blind white, like the inside of a bulb.

I look around. Nothing new, nothing gone. The paint tins, the beach chairs.

And there on the shelf sits Ed's toolbox.

And I know, somehow, what's inside.

I approach, reach for it. Unbuckle one latch, then the other. Lift the lid, slowly.

It's the first thing I see. The box cutter, back in place, its blade gleaming in the glare.

# 58

Wedged in the library wingback, thoughts tumble-drying in my brain. Had settled myself in the study a moment earlier, but then that woman appeared in Jane's kitchen; my body jolted, and I fled the room. There are now forbidden zones in my own house.

I watch the clock on the mantel. Nearly twelve. I haven't had a drink today. I suppose that's A Good Thing.

I might not be mobile—I'm *not* mobile—but I can think my way through this. It's a chessboard. I'm good at chess. Concentrate; think. Move.

My shadow stretches along the carpet, as though trying to detach itself from me.

David said he hadn't met Jane. And Jane never mentioned having met David—but then maybe she didn't, not until later, not until after our four-bottle throttle. When did David borrow the box cutter? Was it the same day I heard Jane scream? *Wasn't* it? Did he threaten her with it? Did he end up doing more than that?

I chew on a thumbnail. My head was once a filing cabinet. Now it's a flurry of papers, floating on a draft.

No. Stop. You've spun this out of control.

Still, though.

What do I know about David? He "did time" for assault. Serial offender. Acquired a box cutter.

And I saw what I saw. No matter what the police say. Or Bina. Or Ed, even.

I hear a door close downstairs. I dislodge myself, pad to the landing, then into the study. No one visible at the Russells'.

I approach the window, cast my eyes down: There he is, on the sidewalk, that indolent walk, the jeans tugged below his waistline, a backpack slung over one shoulder. He heads east. I watch him vanish.

I retreat from the sill and stand there, washed in dim noonday light. Again I look across the park. Nothing. Empty rooms. But I'm tense, waiting for her to appear, waiting for her to look back at me.

My robe has come loose. Come undone. *She's come undone.* That was a book, I believe. I never read it.

God, my mind is swirling. I grasp my skull with both hands, squeeze. Think.

Then, like a jack-in-the-box, it springs at me, with such a pop that I step back: the earring.

That's what had gnawed at my mind yesterday—the earring, glowing on David's bedside table, luminous against the dark wood.

Three tiny pearls. I'm sure of it.

I'm almost sure of it.

Did it belong to Jane?

That night, that quicksand night. *Gift from an old boyfriend.* Touching fingertips to earlobe. *I doubt Alistair knows.* Red wine ebbing down my throat. Those three tiny pearls.

*Didn't* it belong to Jane?

Or is this the stuff of a hothouse brain? It could be another earring. It could be someone else's. But already I'm shaking my head, my hair scratching at my cheeks: It *must* be Jane's.

In which case.

I dip my hand into my robe pocket, feel the rub of paper against my skin. I pull out the card: DETECTIVE CONRAD LITTLE, NYPD.

No. Tuck it away.

I turn, leave the room. Fumble downstairs in the dark, two stories, unsteady on my feet even though I'm sober. In the kitchen I approach the basement door. The bolt whines as I slide it home.

I step back, inspect the door. Then I return to the stairwell. One floor up I open the closet, pull the string beside the lightbulb. I find it leaning against the far wall: a stepladder.

Back in the kitchen, I prop the ladder against the basement door, jam it firmly beneath the knob. Kick its legs with one slippered foot until it won't budge. Kick it some more. I stub my toe. I kick again.

Once more I step back. The door is barricaded. That's one less way in.

Of course, it's also one less way out.

# 59

My veins are flammably dry. I need a drink.

I pivot from the door and stumble over Punch's bowl; it skids across the floor, slopping water over the brim. I swear, then catch myself. I need to focus. I need to think. A slug of merlot will help.

It's velvet in my throat, plush and pure, and I feel it cool my blood as I set the tumbler down. I survey the room, my vision clear, my brain oiled. I'm a machine. A thinking machine. That was the nickname, wasn't it, of a character in some century-old detective novel by Jacques someone-or-other—a ruthlessly logical PhD who could solve any mystery by application of reason. The author, as I recall, died on the *Titanic* after ushering his wife into a lifeboat. Witnesses saw him sharing a cigarette with Jack Astor as the ship sank, breathing smoke against the waning moon. I suppose that's one scenario you can't think your way out of.

I too am a PhD. I too can be ruthlessly logical. Next move.

*Someone* must be able to confirm what happened. Or at least to whom. If I can't start with Jane, then I'll start with Alistair. He's the one with the deepest footprint. He's the one with a history.

I walk up to the study, the plan evolving in my mind with each step. By the time I slant a glance across the park—there she is again, in the parlour, silver cell pressed to one ear; I flinch before settling myself at my desk—I've got a script, I've got a strategy. Besides, I'm good on my feet (I tell myself, sitting).

Mouse. Keyboard. Google. Phone. My tools. I throw one more look at the Russell place. Now her back is to me, a cashmere wall. Good. Keep it that way. This is my house; this is my view.

I enter the password on my desktop screen; a minute later, I find what I'm looking for online. But before I tap the code into my phone, I pause: Could they trace the number?

I frown. I set the phone down. I grasp the mouse; the cursor stirs on the desktop screen, then travels down to the Skype icon.

A moment later, a crisp alto greets me. "Atkinson."

"Hi," I say, then clear my throat.

"Hi. I'm looking for Alistair Russell's office. Only," I add, "I'd like to speak to his assistant, not to Alistair." A pause at the other end of the line. "It's a surprise," I explain.

Another pause. I hear the rattle of a keyboard. Then: "Alistair Russell's employment was terminated last month."

"Terminated?"

"Yes. Ma'am." She's been trained to say that. It sounds grudging.

"Why?" Stupid question.

"I have no idea. Ma'am."

"Could you transfer me to his office?"

"As I said, his—"

"His former office, I mean?"

"That would be the Boston office." She's got one of those young-woman voices that frills upward at the end of a sentence. I can't tell if it's a question or a statement.

"Yes, the Boston—"

"I'm transferring you now." Cue the music—a Chopin nocturne. A year ago I could have told you which one. No: Don't get distracted. Think. This would be easier with a drink.

Across the park, she moves out of sight. I wonder if she's speaking to him. I wish I could lip-read. I wish—

"Atkinson." A man this time.

"I'm looking for Alistair Russell's office."

Instantly: "I'm afraid Mr Russell—"

"I know he's no longer there, but I'd like to speak to his assistant. Or his former assistant. It's a personal matter."

After a moment, he speaks again. "I can put you through to his desk."

"That would be—" Once more with the piano, a rill of notes. Number 17, I think, B major. Or is it number 3? Or number 9? I used to *know* this.

*Concentrate*. I shake my head, my shoulders, like a wet dog.

"Hello, this is Alex." Another man, I think, although the voice is so light and glassy that I'm not entirely sure, and the name's no help.

"This is—" I need a name. Missed a step. "Alex. I'm another Alex." Jesus. Best I could do.

If there's a secret handshake among Alexes, this Alex does not extend it. "How can I help you?"

"Well, I'm an old friend of Alistair's—Mr Russell's—and I just tried him at his New York office, but it seems he's left the company."

"That's right." Alex sniffs.

"Are you his..." Assistant? Secretary?

"I was his assistant."

"Oh. Well, I was wondering—a couple of things, actually. When did he leave?"

Another sniff. "Four weeks ago. No, five."

"That's so strange," I say. "We were so excited for him to come down to New York."

"You know," says Alex, and I hear in his or her voice the warmth of a revving motor: There's gossip to be shared. "He still went down to New York, but he didn't transfer. He was all set to stay within the company. They bought a house and everything."

"Did they?"

"Yes. A big one in Harlem. I found it online. A little Internet stalking." Would a man relish behind-the-back talk this much? Maybe Alex is a woman. What a sexist I am. "But I don't know what happened. I don't think he went anywhere else. He can tell you more than I can." Sniff. "Sorry. Head cold. How do you know him?"

"Alistair?"

"Yes."

"Oh, we're old college friends."

"From Dartmouth?"

"That's right." I hadn't remembered that. "So did he—I'm sorry to phrase it this way, but did he jump or was he pushed?"

"I don't know. You'll *have* to find out what went down. It's all *super*-mysterious."

"I'll ask him."

"He was so *well-liked* here," Alex says. "*Such* a good guy. I can't believe they'd fire him or anything."

I make a sympathetic noise. "I do have one other question for you, about his wife."

Sniff. "Jane."

"I've never met her. Alistair tends to compartmentalize." I sound like a shrink. I hope Alex doesn't notice. "I'd like to get her a little 'welcome to New York' present, but I'm not sure what she likes."

Sniff.

"I was thinking a scarf, except I don't know what her colouring is." I gulp. It sounds lame. "It sounds lame, I know."

"Actually," says Alex, voice dropped low, "I've never met her, either."

Well, then. Maybe Alistair really *does* compartmentalize. Such a good shrink I am.

"Because he *totally* compartmentalizes!" Alex continues. "That's the exact word."

"I *know*!" I agree.

"I worked for him for almost six months and never met her. Jane. I only met their kid once."

"Ethan."

"Nice boy. A little shy. Have you met him?"

"Yes. Ages ago."

"Nice boy. He came in once so they could go to a Bruins game together."

"So you can't tell me anything about Jane," I remind Alex.

"No. Oh—but you wanted to know what she looks like, right?"

"Right."

"I think there's a photo in his office."

"A photo?"

"We had a box of stuff to send down to New York. Still have it. We're not sure what to do with it." Sniff and cough. "Let me go check."

I hear the phone scuff the desk as Alex sets it down—no Chopin this time. Chew my lip, peek at the window. The woman is in the kitchen, staring into the depths of the freezer. For a lunatic moment I imagine Jane packed in there, her body glazed with frost, her eyes bright and rimy.

The scratch of the receiver. "I've got her in front of me," says Alex. "The photo, I mean."

My breath catches in my throat.

"She's got dark hair and light skin."

I exhale. They're both dark-haired and light-skinned, Jane and the impostor. Not helpful. But I can't ask about her weight. "Right—okay," I say. "Anything else? You know what—could you maybe scan the photo? And send it to me?"

A pause. I watch the woman across the park slide the freezer door shut, leave the room.

"I'll give you my email address," I say.

Nothing. Then:

"Did you say you're a friend of..."

"Of Alistair's. Yes."

"You know, I don't think I should be sharing his personal materials with anyone. You'll have to ask him about this." No sniff this time. "You said your name was Alex?"

"Yes."

"Alex what?"

I open my mouth, then click the End Call button.

The room is silent. From across the hall, I can hear the tick of the clock in Ed's library. I'm holding my breath.

Is Alex calling Alistair right now? Would he or she describe my voice? Could he dial my landline, even my cell phone? I stare at the cell on the desk, watch it for a moment, as though it's a sleeping animal; I wait for it to stir, my heart thrumming against my ribs.

The phone lies there immobile. An immobile mobile. Ha. Focus.

# 60

Down in the kitchen, drops of rain popping against the window, I pour more merlot into a tumbler. A long swig. I needed that.

Focus.

What do I know now that I didn't know before? Alistair kept his work and home lives separate. Consistent with the profile of many violent offenders, but otherwise not useful. Moving on: He was prepared to relocate to his firm's New York branch, even bought property, shipped the whole family south... but then something went wrong, and he hasn't landed anywhere.

What happened?

My flesh creeps. It's cool in here. I shuffle to the fireplace, twist the knob by the grate. A little garden of flame blooms.

I ease myself onto the sofa, into the cushions, the wine tilting in the glass, my robe swirled around me. It could use a wash. *I* could use a wash.

My fingers slip into my pocket. Again they brush Little's card. Again they release it.

And again I watch myself, my shadow self, in the television screen. Sunk in the pillows, in my dull robe, I look like a ghost. I *feel* like a ghost.

No. Focus. Next move. I place the glass on the coffee table, prop my elbows on my knees.

And realize I have no next move. I can't even prove the existence, present or past, of Jane—my Jane, the real Jane—much less her disappearance. Or death.

Or death.

I think of Ethan, trapped in that house. *Nice boy.*

My fingers push their way through my hair, as though they're plowing a field. I feel like a mouse in a maze. It's experimental psych all over again: those tiny creatures, with their pinprick eyes and balloon-string tails, scurrying into first one dead end, then another. "Come on," we'd urge them from overhead as we laughed, placed bets.

I'm not laughing now. I wonder once more if I should talk to Little.

But instead I talk to Ed.

"So you're going a little stir-crazy, are you, slugger?"

I sigh, drag my feet across the study carpet. I've tugged the blinds down so that that woman can't watch me; the room is striped with dim light, like a cage.

"I feel completely useless. I feel as though I'm at a movie and the film is over and the lights are up and everyone's filed out of the theater and I'm still sitting there, trying to work out what happened."

He snickers.

"What? What's funny?"

"It's just that it's very you to liken this to a movie."

"Is it?"

"It is."

"Well, my points of reference are somewhat limited these days."

"Okay, okay."

I've said nothing about last night. Even as I think of it, I wince. But the rest unspools like a celluloid reel: the message from the impostor, the earring in David's apartment, the box cutter, the phone call with Alex.

"It feels like something out of a film," I repeat. "And I'd think you'd be more alarmed."

"About what?"

"For one thing, about the fact that my tenant has a dead woman's jewelry in his bedroom."

"You don't know that it's hers."

"I do. I'm sure of it."

"You can't be. You're not even sure that she's..."

"What?"

"You know."

"What?"

Now he sighs. "Alive."

"I *don't* think she's alive."

"I mean that you're not even sure that she exists, or ever—"

*"Yes, I am. I am sure. I am not delusional."*

Silence. I listen to him breathe.

"You don't think you're being paranoid?"

And before he's finished, I'm on top of him: "It isn't paranoia if it's really happening."

Silence. This time he doesn't follow up.

When I speak again, my voice jangles. "It's very frustrating to be questioned like this. It's very, *very* frustrating to be stuck here." I gulp. "In this house, and in this..." I want to say *loop*, but by the time I've found the word, he's talking.

"I know."

"You *don't* know."

"I imagine, then. Look, Anna," he continues before I can jump in. "You've been going at warp speed for two straight days. All weekend. Now you're saying David might have something to do with... whatever." He coughs. "You're winding yourself up. Maybe tonight you can just watch a movie or read or something. Go to bed early." Cough. "Are you taking your meds properly?"

No. "Yes."

"And you're keeping off the booze?"

Of course not. "Of course."

A pause. I can't tell if he believes me.

"Got anything to say to Livvy?"

I exhale in relief. "I do." I listen to the rain drumming its fingers against the glass. And a moment later I hear her voice, soft and breathy.

"Mommy?"

I beam. "Hi, pumpkin."

"Hi."

"You doing well?"

"Yes."

"I miss you."

"Mm."

"What's that?"

"I said 'mm.'"

"Does that mean 'I miss you too, Mommy'?"

"Yes. What's *happening* there?"

"Where?"

"In New York City." That's how she's always referred to it. So formal.

"You mean at home?" My heart swells: *home*. "Yes, at home."

"Just something with the new neighbors. Our new neighbors."

"What is it?"

"It's nothing really, pumpkin. Just a misunderstanding." Then I hear Ed again. "Look, Anna—sorry to interrupt, kiddo: If you're worried about David, you ought to get in touch with the police. *Not* because he's, you know... necessarily involved in whatever's going on, but—he's got a record, and you shouldn't be afraid of your own tenant."

I nod. "Yes."

"Okay?"

I nod again.

"You've got that cop's number?"

"Little. I've got it."

I peek through the blinds. There's a flicker of movement across the park. The Russells' front door has swung open, a bright flap of white in the gray drizzle.

"Okay," says Ed, but I'm not listening anymore.

When the door closes, the woman has appeared on the stoop. She's in a knee-length red coat, like the flame of a torch, and above her head bobs a translucent half-moon umbrella. I reach for my camera on the desk, lift it to my eye.

"What was that?" I ask Ed.

"I said I want you to take care of yourself."

I'm peering through the viewfinder. Streaks of rainwater like varicose veins slide down the umbrella. I lower the lens, zoom in on her face: the tip-tilt nose, the milky skin. Dark clouds brew under her eyes. She hasn't been sleeping.

By the time I say goodbye to Ed, she's slowly descending the front steps in her high boots. She stops, withdraws her phone from her pocket, studies it; then she tucks it away and turns east, toward me. Her face is blurry behind the bowl of the umbrella.

I've got to speak to her.

# 61

Now, while she's alone. Now, while Alistair can't interfere. Now, while the blood is roaring in my temples.

Now.

I fly into the hall, whirl down the stairs. If I don't think, I can do it. If I don't think. *Don't think.* Thinking hasn't gotten me anywhere so far. "The definition of insanity, Fox," Wesley used to remind me, paraphrasing Einstein, "is doing the same thing again and again and expecting a different result." So stop thinking and start acting.

Of course, it was only three days ago that I acted—acted in this very same way—and I wound up in a hospital bed. To try *that* again is insane.

Either way, I'm crazy. Fine. I need to know. And I'm no longer sure my house is safe.

My slippers skid on the kitchen floor as I rush across it, swerve around the sofa. That tube of Ativan on the coffee table. I upend it, shake three into my palm, clap my hand to my mouth. Down the hatch. I feel like Alice swigging the DRINK ME potion.

Run to the door. Kneel to retrieve the umbrella. Stand, twist the lock, yank the door open. Now I'm in the hall, watery light leaking through the leaded glass. I breathe—one, two—and thumb the umbrella spring. With a sound like a sudden breath, the canopy spreads in the gloom. I bring it to eye level, fumble for the lock with my other hand. The trick is to keep breathing. The trick is to not stop.

I don't stop.

The lock turns in my hand. The knob turns next. I crush my eyelids shut and pull. A gasp of cool air. The door dents the umbrella; I maneuver myself through the doorway.

Now the cold encloses me, hugs me. I scurry down the steps. *One, two, three, four.* The umbrella pushes against the air, plows through it, like the prow of a ship; with my eyes buttoned tight, I feel it flowing in sharp currents on either side of me.

My shins brake. Metal. The gate. I wave my hand until I've grasped it and draw it open, step through. The soles of my slippers slap concrete. I'm on the sidewalk. I feel needles of rain pricking my hair, my skin.

It's strange: In all the months we've been experimenting with this ludicrous umbrella technique, it never occurred to me or (I assume) to Dr Fielding that I might simply close my eyes. No sense in wandering around sightless, I suppose. I can feel the shift in barometric pressure, and my senses prickle; I know the skies are vast and deep, an upside-down ocean... but I screw my eyelids tighter still and think of my house: my study, my kitchen, my sofa. My cat. My computer. My pictures.

I pivot left. East.

I'm walking blind down a sidewalk. I need to orient myself.

I need to look. Slowly I unshutter one eye. Light dribbles in through the thicket of my lashes.

For an instant I slow, almost stop. I'm squinting at the crosshatched innards of the umbrella. Four blocks of black, four lines of white. I imagine those lines surging with energy, bulging like a heartbeat monitor, spiking and sinking with the rhythm of my blood. *Focus*. One, two, three, four.

I tilt the umbrella up a few degrees, then a few more. There she is, bright as a spotlight, red as a stoplight: that scarlet coat, those dark boots, the clear plastic half-moon nodding above her. Between us stretches a tunnel of rain and pavement.

What will I do if she turns around?

But she doesn't. I drop the umbrella and cram my eyelid shut once more. Step forward.

A second step. A third. A fourth. By the time I've stumbled over a crack in the sidewalk, my slippers sopping, my body shaking, sweat sliding down my back, I've decided to hazard a second look. This time I open the other eye, lift the umbrella until she flares within my view again, a streaking flame. I flick a glance left—St. Dymphna's, and now the fire-red house, its window boxes throbbing with mums. I flick a glance right: the beady eyes of a pickup staring down the street, headlights livid in the gloom. I freeze. The car swims past. I squeeze my eyes shut.

When I open them again, it's gone. And when I look down the sidewalk, I see that she is, too.

Gone. The sidewalk is empty. In the distance, through the haze, I can make out a knot of traffic at the intersection.

The haze thickens, and I realize it's my vision thickening, quickening.

My knees buck, then buckle. I start to sink to the ground. And as I do, even with my eyes reeling in my skull, I picture myself from overhead, shivering in my sodden robe, my hair pasted against my back, an umbrella dipped uselessly in front of me. A lone figure on a lonely sidewalk.

I sink further, melting into the concrete.

But—

—she can't be *gone*. She hadn't reached the end of the block. I shut my eyes, picture her back, the hair brushing her neck; then I think of Jane as she stood at my sink, one long braid plunging between her shoulder blades.

And as Jane turns to face me, my knees brace themselves against each other. I feel the robe dragging along the sidewalk, but I haven't collapsed yet.

I stand still, my legs locked.

She must have disappeared into... I review the map in my brain. What's beyond that red house? The antique shop sits across the street—vacant now, I remember—and beside the house is—

The coffee shop, of course. She must be in the coffee shop.

I lift my head back, raise my chin to the sky, as though I might fling myself upright. My elbows piston. My splayed feet press against the sidewalk. The umbrella handle wobbles in my fist. I swing one arm out for balance. And with the rain misting around me and the hiss of traffic in the distance, I build myself back up—up, up, up—until I'm once again standing.

My nerves crackle. My heart ignites. I can feel the Ativan in my blood vessels, clearing them like clean water gushing through a disused hose.

One. Two. Three. Four.

I scrape one foot forward. A moment later, the other follows. I shuffle. I can't believe I'm doing this. I'm doing this.

Now I hear the traffic squalling closer, louder. Keep walking. I peek at the umbrella; it fills my vision, surrounds me. There's nothing outside it.

Until it jolts to the right.

"Oh—sorry."

I flinch. Something—someone—has bumped into me, knocked the umbrella aside; it rushes past, a blue blur of jeans and coat, and as I turn to watch, I see myself in a pane of glass: my hair in weeds, my skin damp, a tattersall umbrella protruding from my hand like an enormous flower.

And behind my reflection, on the other side of the window, I see the woman.

I'm at the coffee shop.

I stare. My vision bends. The awning overhead droops toward me. I shut my eyes, then open them again.

The entrance is within reach. I extend my arm, fingers trembling. Before they can grasp the handle, the door jerks open and a young man emerges. I recognize him. The Takeda boy.

It's been more than a year since I saw him up close—in person, I mean, not through a lens. He's taller now, his chin and cheeks a scrubland of blunt dark hair, but he still radiates that same ineffable Good Kid-ness I've learned to spot in young people, a secret halo orbiting their heads. Livvy's got one. Ethan's got one.

The boy—young man, I suppose (and why can't I remember his name?)—props the door open with one elbow, beckons me in. I notice his hands, those fine-boned cellist's hands. I must look derelict, yet still he's treating me this way. His parents raised him right, as GrannyLizzie would say. I wonder if he recognizes me. I suppose I'd scarcely recognize myself.

As I drift past him, entering the shop, my memory thaws. I used to drop in here a few times a week, on those mornings when I was too rushed to brew coffee at home. The store blend tasted pretty bitter—I assume it still does—but I liked the ambience of the place: the cracked mirror with the day's specials scrawled on it in Magic Marker, the countertops with their Olympic-ring stains, the speaker system piping oldies.

"Unpretentious mise-en-scène," Ed remarked the first time I brought him there.

"You can't say those words in the same sentence," I told him.

"Just unpretentious, then."

And unchanged. The hospital room crushed me, but this is different—this is terra cognita. My eyelashes flutter. I loft my gaze over the gaggle of customers, study the menu tacked above the cash register. A cup now costs $2.95. That's a fifty-cent hike since I was last here. Inflation is a bitch.

The umbrella swings low, grazes my ankles.

So much I haven't seen in so long. So much I haven't felt, haven't heard, haven't *smelled*—the radiant warmth of human bodies, pop music from decades past, the punch of ground beans. The whole scene unreels in slow motion, in golden light. For a moment I shut my eyes, inhale, remember.

I remember moving through the world the way you move through air. I remember striding into this coffee shop, a winter coat wrapped tight around me or a sundress billowing at the knees; I remember brushing against people, smiling at them, talking to them.

When I open my eyes again, the gilt light fades. I'm in a dim room, next to windows rinsed with rain. My heart speeds.

A bolt of red flames by the pastry counter. It's her, inspecting Danishes. She lifts her chin, catches sight of herself in the mirror. Tugs a hand through her hair.

I edge closer. I can feel eyes on me—not hers, but other customers', sizing me up, this woman in a bathrobe with a mushroomed umbrella wagging before her. I clear a channel through the crowd, through the noise, as I chug toward the counter. Then the chatter resumes, like water closing over me while I sink.

She's a few feet away from me. One more step and I could reach out and touch her. Catch her hair in my fingers. Pull.

At that moment, she turns slightly and drops a hand into her pocket, wiggles loose her oversize iPhone. In the mirror I watch her fingers dance across the screen, watch her face flicker. I imagine her writing to Alistair.

"Excuse me?" the barista asks.

The woman taps on her phone.

"Excuse me?"

And now—what am I doing?—I clear my throat. "You're up," I mutter.

She stops, nods in my direction. "Oh," she says, then turns to the man behind the counter. "Skim latte, medium."

She didn't even look at me. I look at myself, in the mirror, see me standing in back of her like a specter, an avenging angel. I've come for her.

"Skim latte, medium. Did you want something to eat with that?"

I watch the mirror, watch her mouth—small, precision-cut, so unlike Jane's. A little wave of anger wells within me, swells within me, crests against the base of my brain. "No," she says after a second. Then, with a bright sickle smile: "No, I'd better not."

Behind us, a chorus of chairs scrapes across the floor. I glance over my shoulder; a party of four is heading for the door. I turn back.

The barista, his voice ringing above the din: "Name?"

Then the woman and I lock eyes in the mirror. Her shoulders hop. Her smile melts.

For an instant, time freezes, that breathless moment when you're sailing off the road, into the gorge.

And without turning around, without averting her gaze, she replies, in the same clear tone, "Jane."

*Jane.*

The name bubbles to my lips before I can swallow it down. The woman pivots, spears me with a stare.

"I'm surprised to see you here." Her tone as flat as her eyes. Shark eyes, I think, cold, hard. I want to point out that I'm surprised to be here myself, but the words skid on my tongue.

"I thought you were... impaired," she continues. Withering.

I shake my head. She says nothing further.

I clear my throat again. *Where is she and who are you?* I want to ask. *Who are you and where is she?* Voices swirl around me, mingle with the words inside my head.

"What?"

"Who are you?" There.

"Jane." It isn't her voice, but the barista's, floating across the counter, tapping Jane on the shoulder. "Skim latte for Jane."

She keeps looking at me, *watching* me, as though I might strike. *I'm a well-regarded psychologist,* I could say to her, should say to her. *And you're a liar and a fraud.*

"Jane?" The barista, trying a third time. "Your latte?"

She swivels, accepts the cup in its snug cardboard jacket. "You know who I am," she tells me.

I shake my head once more. "I know Jane. I met her. I saw her in her house." My voice is quaky but clear.

"It's my house, and you didn't see anyone."

"I did."

"You *didn't,*" says the woman.

"I—"

"I hear you're a drunk. I hear you're on pills." She's moving now, circling me, the way a lioness does. Slowly I revolve with her, trying to keep up. I feel like a child. The conversations around us have stalled, stilled; there's a brittle silence. In the corner of my eye, in a corner of the coffee shop, I can see the Takeda boy, still stationed by the door.

"You're watching my house. You're *following* me."

I shake my head, drag it back and forth, slow, stupid.

"This has got to stop. We can't live like this. Maybe *you* can, but we can't."

"Just tell me where she is," I whisper.

We've come full circle.

"I don't know who or what you're talking about. And I'm calling the police." She pushes past me, knocks my shoulder with her own. In the mirror I watch her leave, maneuvering between the tables as though they're buoys.

The bell cries as she opens the door, again when it slams behind her.

I stand there. The room is quiet. My gaze sinks to my umbrella. My eyes close. *It's like the outside is trying to get in.* I feel harrowed, hollowed. And once again, I've learned nothing.

Except this: She wasn't arguing with me—not *only* arguing with me, anyway.

I think she was pleading.

# 62

"Dr Fox?"

A voice, hushed, right behind me. A hand, gentle, on my elbow. I turn, crack an eyelid.

It's the Takeda boy.

Still can't remember his name. I close my eye.

"Do you need some help?"

Do I need some help? I'm a couple hundred yards from my home, swaying in my bathrobe with my eyes screwed shut in the middle of a coffee shop. Yes, I need some help. I dip my head.

His grip tightens. "Let's go this way," he says.

He steers me through the café, the umbrella slapping against chairs and knees as though it's a white cane. A low rumble of coffee-talk surrounds us.

Then the bell chimes and a draft rushes toward me, and his hand drops to the small of my back; he nudges me out the door.

Outside the air is still—no drizzle. I feel him move to take the umbrella from me, but I tug it away from him.

His hand returns to my elbow. "Let me walk you home," he says.

As we walk, he keeps a hand clasped firmly around my arm, like a blood-pressure strap. I imagine he can feel my arteries humming. It's strange, being escorted like this; makes me feel old. I want to open my eyes, look at his face. I don't.

We proceed fitfully, the Takeda boy matching my pace; we break the backs of leaves beneath us. I hear the sweep of a car as it coasts past on the left, sighing. Somewhere above, a tree sheds raindrops onto my head, my shoulders. I wonder if the woman is on the sidewalk ahead of us. I imagine her turning her head, watching me trail her.

Then:

"My parents told me what happened," he says. "I'm really sorry."

I nod, eyes still shut. We move on.

"It's been a while since you got out of the house, I guess?"

Surprisingly often of late, I think, but I nod again.

"Well, we're almost home. I can see it."

My heart fills.

Something clacks against my knee—his own umbrella, I realize, hooked over his arm. "Sorry," he says. I don't bother to reply.

Last time I spoke to him—when was that? Halloween, I think, more than a year ago. That's right: He answered the door when we knocked, Ed and I in our weekend clothes,

Olivia dressed as a fire truck. He complimented her costume, ladled candy into her backpack. Wished us happy trick-or-treating. Such a nice boy.

And now, twelve months later, he's guiding me down the block as I shuffle in my bathrobe, eyes sealed against the world.

Such a nice boy.

Which reminds me:

"Do you know the Russells?" My voice sounds bent but unbroken.

He pauses. Perhaps he's surprised I've spoken. "The Russells?"

I suppose that answers my question, but I try again: "Across the street."

"Oh," he says. "The new—no. My mom keeps meaning to visit them, but I don't think she's done it yet."

Another strike.

"Here we are," he says, softly turning me to the right.

I raise the umbrella and, unpeeling my eyelids, find myself before the gate, the house looming above me. I shiver.

He speaks again. "Your door is open."

He's right, of course: I can look straight into the lamp-lit living room, glinting like a gold tooth in the face of the house. The umbrella wobbles in my hand. I close my eyes again.

"Did you leave it open?"

I nod.

"Okay." His hand glides up to my shoulder, gently presses me forward.

"What are you doing?"

It isn't his voice. His grip jostles; my eyes spring open before I can stop them.

Standing beside us, shrunken in an oversize sweatshirt and pale in the gloom, is Ethan. A stealth pimple deranges one eyebrow. His fingers worry at his pockets.

I hear myself murmur his name.

The Takeda boy turns to me. "Do you know each other?"

"What are you doing?" Ethan repeats, stepping forward. "You shouldn't be out of the house."

*Your "mother" can tell you all about it,* I think.

"Is she okay?" he asks.

"I think so," answers the Takeda boy. Somehow, suddenly, I remember he's called Nick.

Slowly I swing my gaze between them. They must be almost the same age, but my escort is already a young man, fully formed, finished in marble; Ethan—gawky, narrow, with his slender shoulders and riven brow—looks like a child next to him. He *is* a child, I remind myself.

"I can—can I take her inside?" he says, looking at me.

Nick does the same. I nod again. "I guess so," he agrees.

Ethan takes another step toward us, lays a hand on my back. For a moment I'm flanked by the two of them, fastened like wings to my shoulder blades. "Only if you want me to," Ethan adds.

I look him in the eyes, those liquid blue eyes. "Yes," I breathe.

Nick releases me, moves back. I mouth the words before I can say them.

"You're welcome," he replies. To Ethan: "I think she's had a shock. Maybe give her some water." He retreats to the street. "Want me to check in on you later?"

I shake my head. Ethan shrugs. "Maybe. Let's see how it goes."

"Okay." Nick raises a hand, twitches it in a tiny wave. "Bye, Dr Fox."

As he walks away, a shiver of rain falls on us, wetting our heads, splattering against my umbrella. "Let's go inside," Ethan says.

# 63

The fire is still spurting in the grate, as though freshly laid. I've left it burning all this time. So irresponsible.

Still, the house feels warm, even with November gusting through the door. Once we're in the living room, Ethan slips the umbrella from my hand, collapses it, tucks it in the corner, while I sway toward the hearth, the flames waving at me, beckoning me. I slump to my knees.

For a moment, I hear the lapping of the fire. I hear myself breathe.

I feel his eyes on my back.

The grandfather clock gathers itself, tolls three times.

Then he moves to the kitchen. Fills a glass at the sink. Walks it back to me.

By now my breath is deep and even. He sets the glass on the floor beside me; it cracks gently on the stone.

"Why did you lie?" I say.

There's a pause. I gaze into the flames and wait for him to respond.

Instead I hear him shift where he stands. I swivel toward him, still on my knees. He towers over me, rail-thin, face flushed in the firelight.

"About what?" he asks at last, looking at his feet.

Already I'm shaking my head. "You know what."

Another pause. He shuts his eyes, his lashes fanning out over his cheeks. Suddenly he looks very young, even younger than before.

"Who is that woman?" I press him.

"My mother," he says in a low voice.

"I met your mother."

"No, you—you're confused." Now he's shaking his head. "You don't know what you're talking about. That's what..." He stops. "That's what my dad says," he finishes.

*My dad.* I spread my hands on the floor, push myself up until I'm standing. "That's what everyone's been telling me. Even my friends." I swallow. "Even my husband. But I know what I saw."

"My dad says you're crazy."

I say nothing.

He retreats a step. "I have to leave. I shouldn't be here."

I take a step forward. "Where is your mother?"

He says nothing, just looks at me, eyes wide. *Use a light touch,* Wesley always advised us, only I'm past that point.

"Is your mother dead?"

Nothing. I see the firelight reflected in his eyes. His pupils are tiny sparks.

Then he mouths something I can't hear.

"What?" I lean in, hear him whisper a pair of words:

"I'm scared."

And before I can reply, he bolts to the door, flings it open. It swings there as the front door groans, slams shut.

I'm left standing by the fireplace, heat at my back, the chill of the hall before me.

# 64

After pressing the door shut, I lift the glass of water from the floor and dump its contents down the sink. The merlot bottle chimes against the rim as I pour wine into it. Chimes again. My hands are trembling.

I drink deep, think deep. I feel exhausted, exhilarated. I ventured outside—*walked* outside—and survived. I wonder what Dr Fielding will say. I wonder what I should tell him. Maybe nothing. I frown.

I know more now, too. The woman is panicking. Ethan is frightened. Jane is... well. I don't know about Jane. But it's more than I knew before. I feel as though I've captured a pawn. I'm the Thinking Machine.

I drink deeper still. I'm the Drinking Machine.

I drink until my nerves stop twitching—an hour, by the grandfather clock. I watch the minute hand sweep its face, imagine my veins filling with wine, bold and thick, cooling me, strengthening me. Then I float upstairs. I spy the cat on the landing; he notices me, slinks into the study. I follow him.

On the desk, my phone lights up. I don't recognize the number. I set the glass down on the desk. After the third ring, I swipe the screen.

"Dr Fox." The voice is trench-deep. "Detective Little here. We met on Friday, if you remember."

I pause, then sit at the desk. Push the glass out of reach. "Yes, I remember."

"Good, good." He sounds pleased; I imagine him stretching back in his seat, folding one arm behind his head. "How is the good doctor?"

"Fine, thanks."

"I was wondering if I'd hear from you before now."

I say nothing.

"Got your number from Morningside and wanted to check in. You doing okay?"

I just told him I was. "Fine, thanks."

"Good, good. Family okay?"

"Fine. All fine."

"Good, good." Where is this going?

Then his voice shifts gears. "Here's the thing: We had a call from your neighbor a little while ago."

Of course. Bitch. Well, she warned me. Reliable bitch. I extend my arm, grasp the glass of wine.

"She says that you followed her to a coffee place down the block." He waits for me to respond. I don't. "Now, I'm assuming you didn't choose today to go get yourself a flat white. I'm assuming you didn't run into her there by coincidence."

In spite of myself, I nearly grin.

"I know it's been a tough time for you. You've had a bad week." I find myself nodding. He's very agreeable. Would make a good shrink. "But doing stuff like this isn't going to help anybody, including you."

He hasn't said her name yet. Will he? "What you said on Friday really upset some people. Just between you and me, Mrs Russell"—there it is—"seems pretty high-strung."

*I bet she's high-strung,* I think. *She's impersonating a dead woman.*

"And I don't think her kid was too happy about it, either." I open my mouth. "I spoke—"

"So I—" He stops. "What was that?"

I purse my lips. "Nothing."

"You sure?"

"Yes."

He grunts. "I wanted to ask you to just take it easy for a while. Good to hear you're getting outside." Is that a joke? "How's that cat? He still got an attitude?"

I don't respond. He doesn't seem to notice.

"And your tenant?"

I chew my lip. Downstairs, there's that stepladder braced against the basement door; belowground, I saw a dead woman's earring at David's bedside.

"Detective." I grip the phone. I need to hear it once more. "You really don't believe me?"

A long silence, then he sighs, deep and rumbly. "I'm sorry, Dr Fox. I think you believe what you say you saw. I just—I don't."

I wasn't expecting otherwise. Fine. All fine.

"You know, if you want to talk to someone ever, we've got good counselors here who can help you out. Or just listen."

"Thank you, Detective." I sound stiff.

Another silence. "Just—take it easy, okay? I'll let Mrs Russell know that we've talked."

I wince. And hang up before he can.

# 65

I sip my wine, grab my phone, stalk into the hall. I want to forget about Little. I want to forget about the Russells.

The Agora. I'll check my messages. I walk downstairs, place the glass in the kitchen sink. Moving to the living room, I tap my passcode onto the phone screen.

Passcode incorrect.

I furrow my brow. Clumsy fingers. I peck at the screen a second time.

Passcode incorrect.

"What?" I ask. The living room has gone dark with dusk; I reach for the lamp, switch it on. Once more, carefully, eyes on hands: 0-2-1-4.

Passcode incorrect.

The phone twitches. I'm locked out. I don't understand.

When was the last time I tapped in my passcode? I didn't need it to answer Little's call just now; I used Skype to dial Boston earlier. My mind is foggy.

Annoyed, I march back up to the study, to the desktop. Surely I'm not locked out of email as well? I enter the computer password, visit the Gmail home page. My screen name is preloaded into the address field. I type the password slowly.

Yes—I'm in. The restore-access process for my phone is simple enough; within sixty seconds, a replacement code pings in my inbox. I enter it onto the phone screen, switch it back to 0214.

Still, what the hell? Maybe the code expired—does that happen? Did I *change* it? Or was it just fumbling fingers? I chew a nail. My memory isn't what it used to be. Nor are my motor skills. I eye the wineglass.

A little batch of messages awaits me in my inbox, one a plea from a Nigerian prince, the remainder dispatches from my Agora crew. I spend an hour replying. Mitzi from Manchester recently switched anxiety medications. Kala88 is engaged. And GrannyLizzie, it seems, squired by her sons, managed to take a few steps outside this afternoon. *Me too*, I think.

Past six, and suddenly fatigue avalanches me, buries me. I slump forward, like a beat-up pillow, and rest my forehead against the desk. I need to sleep. I'll double-dose on temazepam tonight. And tomorrow I can work on Ethan.

One of my more precocious patients used to begin every session with the words "It's the strangest thing, but..."—and then proceed to describe experiences that were perfectly ordinary. But I feel that way now. It's the strangest thing. It's the strangest thing, but what seemed urgent just a moment ago—what's seemed urgent since Thursday—has shrunk, dwindled, like a flame in the cold. Jane. Ethan. That woman. Even Alistair.

I'm running on fumes. *Grape fumes*, I hear Ed crack. Ha-ha. I'll talk to them, too. Tomorrow. Ed. Livvy.

## MONDAY, NOVEMBER 8

# 66

"Ed."

Then a moment later—or maybe an hour:
"Livvy."
My voice was a puff of breath. I could see it, a little spirit floating before my face, ghostly white in the frozen air.

Somewhere nearby, a chirp, over and over, ceaselessly—a single tone, like the call of a demented bird.

Then it stopped.

My vision swam in a low tide of red. My head throbbed. My ribs ached. My back felt broken. My throat felt seared.

The airbag was crumpled against the side of my face. The dashboard glowed crimson. The windshield sagged toward me, cracked and slack.

I frowned. Some process behind my eyes kept rebooting itself, some system glitch, a buzz in the machine.

I breathed, choked. Heard myself croak with pain. Swiveled my head, felt the top of my skull twist on the ceiling. That was unusual, wasn't it? And I could taste saliva welling in the roof of my mouth. How was—

The buzz ceased.

We were upside down.

I choked again. My hands flew down, buried themselves in the fabric around my head, as though they could upend the car, push me upright. I heard myself whine, splutter.

Turned my head farther. And saw Ed, facing away from me, still. Blood seeped from his ear.

I said his name, or tried to, one breathy syllable in the chill, a little cloud of smoke. My windpipe was sore. The seat belt had drawn tight around my throat.

I licked my lips. My tongue dipped into a hollow in the upper gum. I'd lost a tooth.

The seat belt was slicing against my waist, wire-taut. With my right hand I pressed the buckle, pressed harder, gasped as it clicked. The belt slithered from my body and I slumped toward the roof.

That chirp. The seat-belt alert, stuttering. Then silent.

Breath fountained from my mouth, red in the dashboard light, as I splayed my hands on the ceiling. Braced them. Pivoted my head.

Olivia was strapped into the backseat, suspended there, her ponytail dangling. I crooked my neck, squared my shoulder against the ceiling, reached for her cheek. My fingers rattled.

Her skin was ice.

My elbow folded; my legs dropped to one side, landed hard on the spider-webbed glass of the sunroof. It crunched beneath me. I scrambled to right myself, knees scuffling, and crawled toward her as my heart knocked against my chest. Seized her shoulders in my hands. Shook.

Screamed.

I thrashed. She thrashed with me, her hair swinging.

"Livvy," I shouted, my throat flaming, and tasted blood in my mouth, on my lips.

"Livvy," I called, and tears shot down my cheeks. "Livvy," I breathed, and her eyes opened.

My heart failed for an instant.

She looked at me, inside me, mouthed a single word:

"Mommy."

I jammed my thumb into her seat-belt buckle. The belt released with a hiss, and I cradled her head as she descended, caught her body in my arms, her limbs spilling, jangling against each other like wind chimes. One of her arms felt loose within its sleeve.

I unrolled her along the sunroof. "Shh," I told her, even though she hadn't made a sound, even though her eyes were shut again. She looked like a princess.

"Hey." I shook her shoulder. She looked at me once more. "Hey," I repeated. I tried to smile. My face felt numb.

I scuttled toward the door, grasped the handle, yanked. Yanked again. Heard the snap of the latch. I pushed against the window, strained my fingers upon the glass. The door swung wide without a sound, gliding into the dark.

I stretched forward and pressed my hands to the ground outside, felt the burning snow against my palms. Dug my elbows in, steadied my knees, and pulled. Dragged my torso out of the car, flopping onto the frost. It squeaked beneath me. I kept dragging. My hips. My thighs. Knees. Shins. Feet. The cuff around my ankle snagged on a coat hook; I hitched it loose, slid free of the car.

And rolled onto my back. My spine went electric with pain. I sucked in air. Winced. My head rolled, as though my neck had quit.

No time. No time. I gathered myself, collected my legs, reassembled them into working order, and knelt by the car. Looked around.

Looked up. My vision wheeled, reeled.

The sky was a bowl of stars and space. The moon loomed planet-huge, solar-bright, and the canyon below blazed with shadow and light, crisp as a woodcut. The snowfall had nearly ceased, just a spray of stray flakes floating through the air. It looked like a new world.

And the sound...

Quiet. Utter, final quiet. Not a breath of wind, not a shift of branches. A silent film, a still photograph. I turned on my knees, heard snow crumpling beneath them.

Back to earth. The car was pitched forward, its nose bashed against the ground, its rear seesawed slightly upward. I saw its chassis exposed, like the underside of an insect. I shuddered. My spine twitched.

I dove back through the doorway, hooked my fingers in the down of Olivia's jacket. And hauled. Hauled her across the sunroof, hauled her past the headrest, hauled her out of the car. Wrapped my arms around her, her little body rag-limp in my arms. Spoke her name. Spoke it again. She opened her eyes.

"Hi," I said.

Her eyelids fluttered shut.

I laid her beside the car, then tugged her back in case it should capsize. Her head drifted toward her shoulder; I held it—gently, gently—and turned her face toward the sky again.

I paused, my lungs working like a bellows. Looked at my baby, an angel in the snow. Touched her wounded arm. She didn't react. I touched it again, more firmly, and saw a wince warp her face.

Ed next.

I crawled inside once more before realizing that there was no way to yank him out through the backseat. I reversed, shuffling my shins backward; cleared the car; reached for the front-door handle. Squeezed. Squeezed again. The lock caught, clicked. The door flapped open.

There he was, his skin warm red in the woozy ambulance light of the dashboard. I wondered about that light, how the battery had survived the impact, as I released his seat belt. He slouched toward me, unspooling, like a tugged knot. I gripped him under the armpits.

And dragged him, my head knocking against the gearshift, his body trawling along the ceiling. When we emerged from the car, I saw his face was rinsed in blood.

I stood, pulled, staggered backward until we were next to Olivia, then rested him beside her. She stirred. He didn't. I seized his hand, peeled his sleeve back from the wrist, pressed my fingers into the skin. His pulse was flickering.

We were out of the car, all of us, beneath the sprawl of stars, at the floor of the universe. I heard a steady locomotive chug—my own breath. I was panting. Sweat slid down my sides, slicked my neck.

I bent an arm behind my back, felt carefully, fingers climbing my spine like a ladder. Between my shoulder blades the vertebrae flamed with pain.

I inhaled, exhaled. Watched breath spout feebly from Olivia's mouth, from Ed's.

I turned around.

My eyes scaled what looked like a hundred yards of sheer cliff, blasted fluorescent white in the moonlight. The road lay unseen somewhere overhead, but there was no climbing toward it, no climbing anywhere. We'd crash-landed on a small shelf, a little ledge of rock jutting from the side of the mountain; beyond and below, oblivion. Stars, snow, space. Silence.

My phone.

I slapped my pockets—front, back, coat—and then remembered how Ed had clutched it, waved it away from me; how it had spun to the floor, danced there, rattling between my feet, that name blaring on the screen.

I plunged into the car for the third time, swept the ceiling with my hands, finally found it lodged against the windshield, screen intact. It was a shock to see it so pristine; my husband was bleeding, my daughter was injured, my body was damaged, our SUV was destroyed—but the phone had survived unmarked. A relic from another era, another earth. 10:27 p.m., it read. We'd been off the road for almost a half hour.

Crouching in the cabin of the car, I slid my thumb across the screen—911—and lifted the phone to my ear, felt it tremble against my cheek.

Nothing. I frowned.

I ended the call, retreated from the car, inspected the screen. No Signal. I knelt in the snow. Dialed again.

Nothing.

I dialed twice more.

Nothing. Nothing.

I stood, stabbed the speakerphone button, thrust my arm into the air. Nothing.

I circled the car, stumbling in the snow. Dialed again. And again. Four times, eight times, thirteen times. I lost count.

Nothing. Nothing. Nothing.

I screamed. It burst from me, scouring my throat, cracking the night like a pane of ice, fading away in a flock of echoes. I screamed until my tongue burned, until my voice gave out.

Whirled around. Dizzied myself. Hurled the phone to the ground. It sank into the snow. Picked it up, its screen dewy, and flung it down again, farther away. Panic surged through me. I lunged, dug through the frost. My hand closed on it. Shook off the snow, dialed again.

Nothing.

I was back with Olivia and Ed; they lay there, side by side, still, luminous beneath the moon.

A sob kicked its way to my mouth, desperate for air, thrashed past my lips. My knees buckled beneath me, folded like switchblades. I melted to the ground. I crawled between my husband and my daughter. I cried.

When I awoke, my fingers were cool and blue, curled around the phone. 12:58 a.m. Its battery was drained, just 11 percent remaining. Didn't matter, I reasoned; I couldn't call 911, couldn't call anyone.

I tried to all the same. Nothing.

I rotated my head to the left, to the right: Ed and Livvy, on either side of me, their breathing shallow but steady, Ed's face spackled with dried blood, Olivia's cheeks plastered with streaks of hair. I cupped her forehead in my hand. Cold. Were we better off sheltering in the car? But what if... I didn't know; what if it rolled? What if it *exploded*?

I sat up. Stood up. Looked at the hulk of the car. Surveyed the sky—that ripe moon, that bath of stars. Turned, slowly, toward the mountain.

As I approached it, I brandished my phone and held it in front of me, like a wand. Drew my thumb up the screen, tapped the flashlight button. Hard light, a tiny star in my hand.

The rock face, in the glare, was flat and faultless. Nowhere to jam my fingers, nothing to seize, not a weed or a branch, not a lip of rock—just soil and scree, forbidding as a wall. I walked the width of our little cliff, scanned every inch. I aimed the light upward until the night smothered it.

Nothing. Everything had become nothing.

10 percent power. 1:11 a.m.

As a girl I'd loved constellations, made a study of them, mapped whole skies across scrolls of butcher paper in the backyard on summer evenings, bluebottles drowsing around me, the grass soft beneath my elbows. Now they paraded overhead, the winter heroes, spangled against the night: Orion, bright and belted; Canis Major, loping after him; the Pleiades, strung out like jewels along Taurus's shoulder. Gemini. Perseus. Cetus.

In my wounded voice I murmured their names like a spell to Livvy and Ed, their heads on my chest, rising and falling with my breath. My fingers stroked their hair, his lips, her cheek.

All those stars, smoking cold. We shivered beneath them. We slept.

4:34 a.m. I shuddered myself awake. Inspected both of them—Olivia first, then Ed. I applied some snow to his face. He didn't flinch. I rubbed it against his skin, sloughing off the blood; he twitched. "Ed," I said, jostling his shoulder. No response. I checked his pulse again. Faster, fainter.

My stomach complained. We never ate dinner, I remembered. They must be famished.

I ducked into the car, where the dashboard light had dimmed, almost died. There it was, squashed against the rear passenger window: the duffel bag I'd packed with PB&Js and juice boxes. As I gripped the strap in my fist, the light went out completely.

Back outside, I peeled the plastic wrap from a sandwich, shook it to one side; a strand of wind caught it, and I watched as it floated up and away, gossamer, like a fairy, a will-o'-the-wisp. I tore off a corner of bread, brought it to Olivia. "Hey," I murmured, my fingers playing against her cheek, and her eyes drew open. "Here," I offered, tucking the bread into her mouth. Her lips parted; the bread bobbed there, like a drowning swimmer, before sinking to her tongue. I picked the straw off the juice box, stabbed it in. Lemonade bubbled through it, dribbled onto the snow. I pushed an arm beneath Olivia's head and lifted her face to the straw, squeezed the box. It overflowed her mouth. She spluttered.

I lifted her head farther, and she sipped, hummingbird gulps. After a moment, her skull lolled into my hand, and her eyes slipped shut. I laid her softly on the ground.

Ed next.

I knelt beside him, but he wouldn't open his mouth, wouldn't even open his eyes. I tapped the pinch of bread against his lips, stroked his cheek as though it might unhinge his jaw, yet still he didn't move. Panic rose inside me. I put my head to his face. A current of breath, weak but insistent, warmed my skin. I exhaled.

If he couldn't eat, he could still drink, surely. I rubbed his dry lips with a bit of snow, then slid the straw into his mouth. Clenched my fingers around the box. The juice ran down either side of his chin, clotted in his stubble. "Come on," I pleaded, but liquid kept hurrying down his jaw.

I withdrew the straw and placed another dollop of frost on his lips, then on his tongue. Let it melt down his throat.

I sat on the snow again, sucked on the straw. The lemonade was too sweet. I drained the box anyway.

From the car I pulled a duffel bag stuffed with down parkas and ski pants. I yanked them out, laid them across Livvy and Ed.

Looked up at the sky. It was impossibly huge.

Light settled on my lids like a weight. I opened them.

And squinted. Above us stretched the sky, unbroken, unending, a deep sea of clouds. Snow sifted down in dandelion flakes, burst against my skin. I checked the phone. 7:28 a.m. 5 percent power.

Olivia had shifted slightly in her sleep, banked herself upon her left arm, the right trailing loose along her side. Her cheek was pressed into the ground. I tipped her onto her back, mopped the snow from her skin. Gently thumbed her ear.

Ed hadn't moved. I leaned into his face. He was still breathing.

I'd pushed the phone into my jeans pocket. Now I fished it out, squeezed it for luck, dialed 911 again. For a breathless second I imagined it ringing, could almost hear it, trilling in my ear.

Nothing. I stared at the screen.

Stared at the car, turtled on its back, helpless, like a wounded animal. It looked unnatural, even embarrassed.

Stared at the valley beneath us, spiky with trees, a thin silver ribbon of river unfurled in the distance.

I stood up. I turned around.

The mountain reared over me. In the daylight, I could see that I'd misjudged how far we'd dropped—we were at least two hundred yards from the road above, and the stone face looked even more impassable, more impossible, than it had the night before. Up, up, up my gaze climbed, until it reached the summit.

My hand wandered to my throat. We'd plunged all that way.

We'd survived.

I tilted my head back farther still, to take in the sky. And squinted. It all seemed too vast, somehow, too massive. I felt like a miniature in a dollhouse. I could see myself from without, from afar, tiny, a speck. I spun around, wobbled.

My vision swam. Something twinged in my legs.

I shook my head, rubbed my eyes. The world subsided, retreated to its boundaries.

For a few hours I dozed beside Ed and Olivia. When I awoke—11:10 a.m.—the snow was crashing on us in waves, wind cracking like whips overhead. A low growl of thunder sounded nearby. I swept flakes from my face, jolted to my feet.

That same flutter in my vision, like ripples in water, and this time my knees snapped toward each other, magnet-jerked. I started to slump toward the ground. "No," I said, my voice raw and chapped. I swung a hand to the snow, propped myself up.

What was wrong with me?

No time. No time. I pushed against the ground, stood. Saw Ed and Olivia at my feet, half-submerged.

And I began dragging them into the car.

How did the time creep by? It seemed, during the following year, that the months were passing more quickly than those hours with Ed and Livvy on that inverted ceiling, the snow rising against the windows like a tide, the windshield creaking and popping under the weight of white.

I sang to her, pop songs, nursery rhymes, tunes I invented, as the noise outside grew louder and the light within got dimmer. I studied the whorls of her ear, traced them with my finger, hummed into them. I wrapped my arms around his, braided my legs with his, twined my hands with his. I wolfed a sandwich, guzzled a juice box. I unscrewed a bottle of wine before remembering that it would dehydrate me. But I wanted it. I wanted it.

We were underground, it felt; we had burrowed someplace secret and dark, someplace sheltered from the world. I didn't know when we would emerge. How we would emerge. If.

At some point my phone died. I fell asleep at 3:40 p.m., 2 percent power, and when I awoke, the screen had gone dark.

The world was silent, except for the scream of wind, and Livvy, tugging breaths from the air, and Ed, a faint crackle in his throat. And me, sobs guttering somewhere in my body.

Quiet. Absolute quiet.

I came to in that womb of a cabin, my eyes bleary. But then I saw light leaking into the car, saw the dim glow behind the windshield, and heard the silence the way I'd heard the noise. It inhabited the car like a living thing.

I uncoiled myself and reached for the door handle. It clacked reassuringly, but the door wouldn't budge.

No.

I scuttled on my knees, rolled onto my aching back, crammed my feet against the door and pushed. It budged against the snow, then stopped. I kicked the window, clopped it with my heels. The door stuttered open. A little avalanche piled into the car.

I slithered outside on my stomach, crushing my eyes shut against the light. When I opened them again, I could see dawn boiling over the distant mountains. I rose to my knees, surveyed the new world around me: the valley, drenched in white; that faraway river; the plush snowfall beneath my feet.

I swayed on my knees. And then I heard a crack, and I knew it was the windshield collapsing.

I sank one foot then the other into the snow, stumbled to the front of the car, saw the glass staved in. Back to the passenger door, back inside. Once more I pulled them from the wreckage, Livvy first, then Ed; once more I arranged them side by side on the ground.

And as I stood above them, my breath steaming before me, my vision went fuzzy yet again. The sky seemed to bulge toward me, pressing upon me; I crumpled, eyelids clenched, heart hammering.

I howled, a wild thing. I turned onto my stomach, flung my arms around Olivia and Ed, clutched them to myself as I whimpered into the snow.

That was how they found us.

# 67

When I wake on Monday morning, I want to speak to Wesley.

I've twisted myself in the sheets, have to peel them from my body, like apple skin. Sun is pouring through the windows, lighting up the bedclothes. My skin glows with heat. I feel oddly beautiful.

My phone is on the pillow beside me. For an instant, as the ring purrs in my ear, I wonder if he might have changed his number, but then I hear his voice boom, unstoppably loud as ever: "Leave a message," he commands.

I don't. Instead I try his office.

"This is Anna Fox," I tell the woman who answers the phone. She sounds young.

"Dr Fox. It's Phoebe."

I was wrong. "I'm sorry," I say. Phoebe—I worked with her for almost a year. Definitely not young. "I didn't recognize you. Your voice."

"That's all right. I think I've got a cold, so I probably sound different." She's being polite. Typical Phoebe. "How are you?"

"I'm fine, thanks. Is Wesley available?" Of course, Phoebe's quite formal, and will probably call him—

"Dr Brill," she says, "has sessions all morning, but I can ask him to give you a buzz later."

I thank her, offer my number—"Yes, that's what I have on file"—and hang up.

I wonder if he'll call back.

# 68

I head downstairs. No wine today, I've decided, or at least not this morning; I need to keep a clear head for Wesley. Dr Brill.

First things first: I visit the kitchen, find the stepladder as I left it, leaning against the basement door. In the morning light, almost combustibly bright, it looks flimsy, preposterous; David could knock it down with a smash of his shoulder. For an instant, doubt tiptoes into my brain: So he's got a woman's earring on his bedside table; so what? *You don't know that it's hers*, Ed said, and that's true. Three small pearls—I think I've got a similar pair myself.

I watch the ladder as though it might walk toward me on its spindly aluminum legs. I eye the bottle of merlot gleaming on the counter, next to the house key on its hook. No, no booze. Besides, the place must be littered with wineglasses by this point. (Where have I seen something like that? Yes: that thriller *Signs*—middling film, splendid Bernard Herrmann-esque score. Precocious daughter strews half-drunk cups of water everywhere, and they end up deterring the space invaders. "Why would aliens come to *Earth* if they're allergic to *water*?" Ed ranted. It was our third date.)

I'm getting distracted. Up to the study with me.

I park at my desk, slap my phone next to the mouse pad, plug it into the computer to charge. Check the clock on the computer: just past eleven. Later than I thought. That temazepam really put me under. Those temazepams, technically. Plural.

I look out the window. On the other side of the street, right on schedule, Mrs Miller emerges from her front door, soundlessly shutting it behind herself. She's in a dark winter coat this morning, I see, and white breath flows from her mouth. I tap my phone's weather app. Twelve degrees outside. I stand, pad to the thermostat on the landing.

I wonder what Rita's husband is up to. It's been ages since I saw him, since I looked for him.

Back at my desk, I gaze across the room, across the park, at the Russell house. Its windows loom empty. *Ethan,* I think. *I've got to get to Ethan.* I felt him waver last night; "I'm scared," he'd said, his eyes gone wide, almost wild. A child in distress. It's my duty to help him. Whatever has happened to Jane, whatever has become of her, I must protect her son.

What's the next move?

I chew my lip. I log on to the chess forum. I start to play.

An hour later, past noon, and nothing has occurred to me.

I've just kissed the bottle to the wineglass—again, it's past noon—and think. The problem has been droning in the back of my mind like ambient noise: How to reach Ethan? Every few minutes I glance across the park, as though the answer might be scrawled on the wall of the house. I can't call his landline; he doesn't have his own phone; if I were somehow to attempt to signal to him, his father—or that woman—might see me first. No email address, he told me, no Facebook account. *Might as well not exist.*

He's almost as isolated as I am.

I sit back in the chair, sip. Set the glass down. Watch the noonday light crawl over the windowsill. The computer pings. I move a knight, hook him around the chessboard. Await another move.

The clock on-screen reads 12:12. Nothing from Wesley—surely he'll call? Or should I try again? I reach for my phone, swipe it to life.

A chime on the desktop—Gmail. I grasp my mouse, guide the cursor away from the chessboard. Click on the browser. With my other hand, I bring the wineglass to my lips. It glows in the sun.

I peer over the lip of the glass at the inbox, empty except for a single message, the subject line blank, the sender's name in bold.

Jane Russell.

My teeth chink on the glass.

I stare at the screen. The air around me is suddenly thin.

My hand quakes as I place the glass on the desk, the wine trembling within. The mouse bulges against my palm as I grip it. I've stopped breathing.

The cursor travels to her name. Jane Russell.

I click.

The message opens, a field of white. There's no text, just an attachment icon, a tiny paper clip. I double-click on it.

The screen goes black.

Then an image begins to load, slowly, band by band. Grainy bars of dark gray.

I'm transfixed. I still can't breathe.

Line upon line of darkness on-screen, like a curtain slowly falling. A moment passes. Another.

Then—

—then a tangle of... branches? No: hair, dark and knotty, in close-up.

A curve of fair skin.

An eye, closed, running vertical, edged with a frill of lashes.

It's someone on their side. I'm looking at a sleeping face.

I'm looking at *my* sleeping face.

The picture suddenly expands, the bottom half bursting into view—and there I am, my head, in full. A strand of hair trailing across my brow. My eyes clasped shut, my mouth slightly open. My cheek submerged in the pillow.

I bolt to my feet. The chair topples behind me.

Jane has sent a photograph of me asleep. The idea downloads slowly in my brain, the way that picture did, stuttering line by line.

Jane has been in my house at night.

Jane has been in my bedroom.

Jane has watched me sleep.

I stand there, stunned, in deafening silence. And then I see the ghostly figures in the lower-right corner. A time stamp—today's date, 02:02 a.m.

This morning. Two o'clock. How is it possible? I look at the email address bracketed beside the sender's name: guesswhoanna@gmail.com

# 69

So not Jane, then. Someone hiding behind her name. Someone mocking me.

My thoughts aim like an arrow straight downstairs. David, behind that door.

I clutch myself through my robe. Think. Don't panic. Stay calm.

Has he forced the door? No—I found the stepladder as I'd left it.

So—my hands are shivering against my body; I lean forward, splay them on the desk—so did he make a copy of my key? I heard sounds on the landing that night I led him to bed; had he roamed the house, stolen the key from the kitchen?

Except I saw it on its hook just an hour ago, and I barred the basement door shortly after he left—there was no way back in.

Unless—but of course, of course there was a way back in: He could have just entered the house whenever he liked, using a copied key. Replaced the original.

But he left yesterday. For Connecticut.

At least that's what he told me.

I look at myself on the screen, at the half-moon of my eyelashes, at the line of teeth peeking from behind my upper lip: utterly oblivious, utterly unarmed. I shudder. Acid roils somewhere in my throat.

GUESSWHOANNA. Who, if not David? And why tell me? Not only has someone trespassed in my house, entered my bedroom, recorded me sleeping—but someone wants me to know it.

Someone who knows about Jane.

I reach for my glass with both hands. Drink it, drink deep. Set it down and pick up my phone.

Little's voice is crinkly and soft, like a pillowcase. Maybe he was sleeping. Doesn't matter.

"Someone's been in my house," I tell him. I'm in the kitchen now, phone in one hand, glass in the other, staring at the basement door; as I say them out loud, those impossible words, they sound flat, unconvincing. Unreal.

"Dr Fox," he says, jolly. "That you?"

"Someone came into my house at two o'clock this morning."

"Hold on." I hear him pass the phone across his face. "Someone was in your house?"

"At two this morning."

"Why didn't you report it earlier?"

"Because I was asleep at the time."

His voice warms. He thinks he's got me. "Then how do you know someone was in your house?"

"Because he took a picture and emailed it to me."

A pause. "A picture of what?"

"A picture of me. Sleeping."

When he speaks again, he sounds closer. "Are you sure about this?"

"Yes."

"And—now, I don't want to scare you..."

"I'm already scared."

"Are you sure the house is empty now?"

I go still. This hadn't occurred to me.

"Dr Fox? Anna?"

"Yes." Surely there's no one here. Surely I would know by now.

"Can you—are you able to go outside?"

I nearly laugh. Instead I just breathe "No."

"Okay. Just—stay there. Don't—just stay there. Do you want me to stay on the line with you?"

"I want you to come here."

"We're coming." *We're.* So Norelli will be with him. Good—I want her here for this. Because this is real. This is undeniable.

Little is still talking, his breath billowing into the phone. "What I'd like for you to do, Anna? Is get to the front door. In case you need to leave. We can be there real soon, just a few minutes, but in case you need to leave..."

I look at the hall door, move toward it.

"We're in the car now. There real soon."

I nod, slowly, watching the door draw closer.

"You seen any movies lately, Dr Fox?"

I can't bring myself to open it. Can't set foot in that twilight zone. I shake my head. My hair brushes against my cheeks.

"Any of your old thrillers?"

I shake my head again, start to tell him no, when I realize I'm still cradling the wineglass in my fingers. Intruder or not—and I don't think there is—I won't answer the door like this. I need to get rid of it.

But my hand is shaking, and now wine slops onto the front of my robe, staining it blood-red, right above the heart. It looks like a wound.

Little is still chattering in my ear—"Anna? You okay there?"—as I return to the kitchen, phone pressed to my temple, and place the glass in the sink.

"... everything okay?" Little asks.

"Fine," I tell him. I flip the tap, shed my robe, push it under running water as I stand there in my T-shirt and sweatpants. The wine stain boils beneath the flow, bleeding, thinning, going a soft pink. I squeeze it, my fingers blanching in the cold.

"You able to get to the front door?"

"Yes."

Off with the tap. I pull the robe from the sink and wring it.

"Okay. Stay there."

Shaking the robe dry, I see that I'm out of paper towels—the spindle stands naked. I reach for the linen drawer, slide it open. And inside, atop a stack of folded napkins, I see myself again.

Not deep asleep in close-up, not half-baked into a pillow, but upright, beaming, my hair swept back, my eyes bright and keen—a likeness in paper and ink.

A *nifty trick*, I'd said.

A *Jane Russell original*, she'd said.

And then she'd signed it.

# 70

The paper twitches in my hand. I look at the signature slashed in the corner.

I'd almost doubted it. I'd almost doubted her. Yet here it is, a souvenir from that vanished night. A memento. Memento mori. *Remember that you have to die*.

Remember.

And I do: I remember the chess and the chocolate; I remember the cigarettes, the wine, the tour of the house. Most of all, I remember Jane, braying and boozing, in living colour; her silver fillings; the way she leaned into the window as she took in her house—*Quite a place*, she'd murmured.

She was here.

"We're almost with you," Little is saying.

"I've got—"

I clear my throat. "I've got—"

He interrupts me. "We're turning onto..."

But I don't hear where they are, because through the window I'm watching Ethan exit his front door. He must have been inside the whole time. I'd thrown skipping-stone glances at his house for an hour, my eyes leaping from kitchen to parlour to bedroom; I don't know how I missed him.

"Anna?" Little's voice sounds tiny, shrunken. I look down, see the phone in my hand, by my hip; see the robe pooled at my feet. Then I clap the phone onto the counter and set the picture next to the sink. I rap on the glass, hard.

"Anna?" Little calls again. I ignore him.

I rap harder still. Ethan has swerved onto the sidewalk now, heading toward my house. Yes.

I know what I have to do.

My fingers grip the window sash. I tense them, drum them, flex them. Screw my eyes shut. And lift.

Frigid air seizes my body, so raw that my heart feels faint; storms my clothes, sets them trembling around me. My ears brim with the sound of wind. I'm filling up with cold, running over with cold.

But I scream his name all the same, a single roar, two syllables, springing from my tongue, cannonballing into the outside world: *E-than!*

I can hear the silence splinter. I imagine flocks of birds mounting, passersby stopping in their tracks.

And then, with my next breath, last breath:

*I know.*

I know your mother was the woman I said she was; I know she was here; I know you're lying.

I slam the window shut, lean my forehead against the glass. Open my eyes.

He's there on the sidewalk, frozen, wearing a too-big down coat and not-big-enough jeans, his flap of hair fanning in the breeze. He looks at me, breath clouding before his face. I look back, my chest heaving, my heart going ninety miles an hour.

He shakes his head. He keeps walking.

# 71

I watch him until he's out of sight, my lungs deflating, my shoulders slumped, the chill air haunting the kitchen. That was my best shot. At least he didn't run home.

But still. But still. The detectives will be here any moment. I've got the portrait—there, facedown on the floor, blown by the draft. I stoop to collect it, to grab my robe, damp in my hand.

The doorbell rings. Little. I straighten, seize the phone, drop it into my pocket; hurry toward the door, bash the buzzer with my fist, wrench the lock. Watch the frosted glass. A shadow rises, resolves itself into a figure.

The scrap of paper shakes in my hand. I can't wait. I reach for the knob, twist it, yank the door open.

It's Ethan.

I'm too surprised to greet him. I stand there, the paper pinched between my fingers, the robe dripping onto my feet.

His cheeks are red from the cold. His hair needs cutting; it skims his brows, curls around his ears. His eyes have gone wide.

We look at each other.

"You can't just scream at me, you know," he says quietly.

This is unexpected. Before I can stop myself: "I didn't know how else to reach you," I say.

Drops of water tap on my feet, on the floor. I shift the robe beneath my arm.

Punch trots into the room from the stairwell, heads straight for Ethan's shins.

"What do you want?" he asks, looking down. I can't tell if he's talking to me or to the cat.

"I know your mother was here," I tell him.

He sighs, shakes his head. "You're—delusional." The word steps off his tongue on stilts, as though unfamiliar to him. I don't need to wonder where he heard it. Or about whom.

I shake my head in turn. "No," I say, and I feel my lips bending into a smile. "No. I found this." I hold the portrait in front of him.

He looks at it.

The house is silent, except for the shuffle of Punch's fur against Ethan's jeans.

I watch him. He's just gawking at the picture.

"What is this?" he asks.

"It's me."

"Who drew it?"

I incline my head, step forward. "You can read the signature."

He takes the paper. His eyes narrow. "But—"

The buzzer jolts us both. Our heads snap toward the door.

Punch streaks toward the sofa.

With Ethan watching, I reach for the intercom, press it. Footsteps clop in the hall, and Little enters the room, a tidal wave of a man, Norelli trailing in his wake.

They see Ethan first.

"What's going on here?" Norelli asks, her eyes swerving hard from him to me.

"You said that someone had been in your house," says Little.

Ethan looks at me, slides a glance toward the door. "You stay here," I say.

"You can go," Norelli tells him.

"Stay," I bark, and he doesn't move.

"Have you checked the house?" Little asks. I shake my head.

He nods at Norelli, who walks across the kitchen, pausing by the basement door. She eyes the stepladder, eyes me. "Tenant," I say.

She proceeds to the stairwell without a word.

I turn back to Little. His hands are plunged into his pockets; his eyes are locked on mine. I take a breath.

"So much—so much has happened," I say. "First I got this..." My fingers dip into the pocket of the robe and dig out my phone. "... this message." The robe lands on the floor with a splat.

I click on the email, expand the picture. Little takes the phone from me, holds it in his massive hand.

As he inspects the screen, I shiver—it's chilly in here, and I'm barely dressed. My hair, I know, is snarly, bed-headed. I feel self-conscious.

So does Ethan, it seems, shifting his weight from one foot to the other. Next to Little, he looks impossibly delicate, almost breakable. I want to hold him.

The detective thumbs the phone screen. "Jane Russell."

"But it's not," I tell him. "Look at the email address."

Little squints. "Guesswhoanna@gmail.com," he recites carefully.

I nod.

"Taken at two oh two in the morning." He looks at me. "And this was sent at twelve eleven this afternoon."

I nod again.

"Have you ever received a message from this address before?"

"No. But can't you... track it?"

Behind me, Ethan speaks. "What is it?"

"It's a picture," I start to say, but Little continues: "How would someone get into your house? Don't you have an alarm?"

"No. I'm always here. Why would I need..." I trail off. The answer is in Little's hand. "No," I repeat.

"What's it a picture of?" Ethan asks.

This time Little looks at him, pins him with a stare. "Enough questions," he says, and Ethan flinches. "You go over there." Ethan moves to the sofa, sits beside Punch.

Little steps into the kitchen, toward the side door. "So someone could have come in here." He sounds sharp. He flips the lock, opens the door, shuts it. A puff of cold air wafts across the room.

"Someone *did* come in here," I point out.

"Without setting off an alarm, I mean."

"Yes."

"Has anything been taken from the house?"

This hadn't occurred to me. "I don't know," I admit. "My desktop and my phone are still here, but maybe—I don't know. I haven't looked. I was scared," I add.

His expression thaws. "I bet." Softer now. "Do you have any idea who could have photographed you?"

I pause. "The only person with a key—the only person who might have a key is my tenant. David."

"And where is he?"

"I don't know. He said he was going out of town, but—"

"So he has a key, or he might have a key?"

I cross my arms. "Might. His apartment—the apartment has a different key, but he could have... stolen mine."

Little nods. "You having any problems with David?"

"No. I mean—no."

Little nods again. "Anything else?"

"There—he—there was a razor that he borrowed. A box cutter, I mean. And then he put it back without telling me."

"And no one else could have come in?"

"No one."

"Just thinking out loud." Now he gulps a mouthful of air, bellows so loud my nerves throb: "Hey, Val?"

"Still upstairs," Norelli calls.

"Anything to see up there?" Quiet. We wait.

"Nothing," she shouts.

"Any mess?"

"No mess."

"Anyone in the closet?"

"No one in the closet." I hear her footsteps on the stairs. "Coming down."

Little returns to me. "So we've got someone coming in—we don't know how—and taking a picture of you, but not taking anything else."

"Yes." Is he doubting me? I point to the phone in his hand again, as though it can answer his questions. It *can* answer his questions.

"Sorry," he says, and passes it back to me.

Norelli walks into the kitchen, coat whipping behind her. "We good?" asks Little.

"We're all good."

He smiles at me. "Coast is clear," he says. I don't respond. Norelli steps toward us. "What's the story with our B&E?"

I extend the phone to her. She doesn't take it, but looks at the screen.

"Jane Russell?" she asks.

I point to the email address beside Jane's name. A glare ripples across Norelli's face.

"Have they sent you anything before?"

"No. I was saying to—No."

"It's a Gmail address," she points out. I see her exchange a look with Little.

"Yes." I wrap my arms around myself. "Can't you track it? Or trace it?"

"Well," she says, rocking back, "that's a problem."

"Why?"

She tilts her head toward her partner. "It's Gmail," he says.

"Yes. So?"

"So Gmail hides IP addresses."

"I don't know what that means."

"It means there's no way to trace a Gmail account," he continues.

I stare at him.

"For all we know," Norelli explains, "you could have sent this to yourself."

I swivel to look at her. Her arms are folded across her chest.

A laugh escapes me. "*What?*" I say—because what else can be said?

"You could have sent that email from that phone and we wouldn't be able to prove it."

"Why—*why*?" I'm spluttering. Norelli glances down at the soggy robe. I bend over to pick it up, just to do something, just to restore some sense of order.

"This photo looks to me like a little midnight selfie."

"I'm asleep," I argue.

"Your eyes are shut."

"Because I'm asleep."

"Or because you wanted to look asleep." I turn to Little.

"Look at it this way, Dr Fox," he says. "We can't find any sign of anyone in here. It doesn't look like anything's missing.

Front door looks okay, that looks okay"—he jabs a finger at the side door—"and you said that no one else has a key."

"No, I said that my tenant *could* have made a key." Didn't I say that? My mind is churning. I shiver again; the air feels drugged with cold.

Norelli points to the ladder. "What's the story there?"

"Dispute with the tenant," Little replies before I can speak. "You ask her about—you know, the husband?" There's something in her tone I can't place, some minor chord. She raises an eyebrow.

Then she faces me. "Ms Fox"—this time I don't correct her—"I warned you about wasting—"

"I'm not the one wasting time," I growl. "You are. *You* are. Someone was in my house, and I've given you proof, and you're standing there telling me that I made it up. Just like last time. I saw someone get *stabbed* and you didn't believe me. What do I have to do to get you—"

The portrait.

I spin, find Ethan bolted to the sofa, Punch in his lap. "Come here," I say. "Bring that drawing."

"Let's leave him out of it," interrupts Norelli, but Ethan is already walking toward me, the cat scooped in one hand, the scrap of paper held in the other. He offers it to me almost ceremoniously, the way you'd present a communion wafer.

"You see this?" I ask, thrusting it in front of Norelli, so that she takes a step back. "Look at the signature," I add.

Her forehead furrows.

And for the third time today, the doorbell rings.

# 72

Little looks at me, then walks toward the door and studies the intercom. He pushes the buzzer.

"Who is it?" I ask, but he's already pulling the door open. A crisp march of footsteps and Alistair Russell walks in, packed into a cardigan, his face florid with the cold. He seems older than when I last saw him.

His eyes swoop the room, hawklike. They alight on Ethan. "You're going home," he tells his son. Ethan doesn't move. "Put the cat down and leave."

"I want you to see this," I start, swinging the picture toward him, but he ignores me, addresses Little.

"I'm glad you're here," he says, looking less than glad. "My wife says she heard this woman *scream* out the window at my son, and then I saw your car pull up." On his previous visit, I remember, he'd been polite, even bemused. No more.

Little approaches. "Mr Russell—"

"She's been calling my house—did you know that?" Little doesn't answer. "And my old office. She called my old *office*."

So Alex turned me in. "Why were you fired?" I ask, but already he's charging ahead, furious, leaning into his words.

"She followed my wife yesterday—did she mention that? I don't suppose she did. Followed her to a coffee shop."

"We know that, sir."

"Tried to... *confront* her." I peek at Ethan. It seems he didn't tell his father he saw me afterward.

"This is the second time we've all been here." Alistair's voice has run raw. "First she claims she saw an attack in my house. Now she's luring my son into her home. This has to stop. Where does it stop?" He looks directly at me. "She's a menace."

I stab the picture with my finger. "I know your *wife*—"

"You don't know my wife!" he shouts.

I go silent.

"You don't know *anyone*! You stay here in your house and you *watch* people."

A flush stalks the length of my neck. My hand drops to my side.

He isn't finished. "You've invented some... *encounters* with some woman who isn't my wife and isn't even—" I wait for the next word, the way you brace for a blow. "Isn't even *real*," he says. "And now you're harassing my son. You're harassing *all* of us."

The room is quiet.

Finally Little speaks. "All right."

"She's delusional," adds Alistair. There it is. I glance at Ethan; he's staring at the floor.

"All right, all right," Little repeats. "Ethan, I think it's time for you to head home. Mr Russell, if you could stay here—"

But now it's my turn.

"Stay here," I agree. "Maybe you can explain this." I lift my arm again, up above my head, level with Alistair's eyes.

He reaches for the paper, takes it. "What is this?"

"It's a picture your wife drew."

His face goes blank.

"When she was here. At that table."

"What is it?" asks Little, moving to Alistair's side.

"Jane drew it for me."

"It's you," Little says.

I nod. "She was here. This proves it."

Alistair has collected himself. "It doesn't prove anything," he snaps. "No—it proves you're so crazy that you're actually trying to... fabricate evidence." He snorts. "You're out of your mind."

*Ka-pow, out of your mind*, I think. *Rosemary's Baby*. I feel myself frown. "What do you mean, fabricate evidence?"

"You drew this yourself."

Between us, Norelli speaks. "Just like you could've taken that photo and sent it to yourself and we wouldn't be able to prove it."

I reel back, as though I've been punched. "I—"

"You okay there, Dr Fox?" Little, stepping toward me.

The robe drops from my hand again, slithers to the floor.

I'm swaying. The room revolves around me like a carousel. Alistair glowers; Norelli's eyes have gone dark; Little's hand hovers over my shoulder. Ethan hangs back, the cat still draped over his arm. They whirl past me, all of them; no one to cling to, no ground to stand on. "I didn't draw this picture. *Jane* drew it. Right here." I wag my fingers toward the kitchen. "And I didn't take that photo. I *couldn't* have taken it. I'm—

Something is happening, and you're not *helping*." I can't put it any other way. I try to seize the room; it slips from my grip. I fumble toward Ethan, reach for him, clasp his shoulder with my shaking hand.

"Stay away from him," Alistair explodes, but I look into Ethan's eyes, raise my voice: "Something is *happening*."

"What's happening?"

We all turn as one.

"Front door was open," says David.

# 73

He stands framed in the doorway, hands thrust in his pockets, a battered bag slung over one shoulder. "What's going on?" he asks again as I release my grip on Ethan.

Norelli uncrosses her arms. "Who are you?"

David crosses his in turn. "I live downstairs."

"So," says Little, "you're the famous David."

"Don't know about that."

"You got a last name, David?"

"Most people do."

"Winters," I say, dredging it up from the depths of my brain.

David ignores me. "Who are you people?"

"Police," Norelli answers. "I'm Detective Norelli, this is Detective Little."

David angles his jaw toward Alistair. "Him I know."

Alistair nods. "Maybe you can explain what's wrong with this woman."

"Who says there's anything wrong with her?"

Gratitude wells within me. I feel my lungs fill. Someone's on my side.

Then I remember who that someone is.

"Where were you last night, Mr Winters?" asks Little.

"Connecticut. On a job." He cracks his jaw. "Why are you asking?"

"Someone took a picture of Dr Fox in her sleep. Around two A.M. Then emailed it to her."

David's eyes flicker. "That's messed up." He looks at me. "Someone broke in?"

Little doesn't let me answer. "Can anyone confirm you were in Connecticut last night?"

David swings one foot in front of the other. "Lady I was with."

"Who might that have been?"

"Didn't get her last name."

"She have a phone number?"

"Don't most people?"

"We're going to need that number," says Little.

"He's the only one who could have taken that picture," I insist.

A beat. David's brow creases. "What?"

Looking at him, into those depthless eyes, I feel myself waver. "Did you take that picture?"

He sneers. "You think I came up here and—"

"No one thinks that," Norelli says.

"I do," I tell her.

"I don't know what the fuck you're talking about." David sounds almost bored. He offers his phone to Norelli. "Here. Call her. Name's Elizabeth." Norelli steps toward the living room.

I can't take another word without a drink. I leave Little's side, head for the kitchen; behind me I hear his voice.

"Dr Fox says she saw a woman get assaulted across the way. In Mr Russell's house. Do you know anything about this?"

"No. That why she asked me about a scream that time?" I don't turn around; I'm already tipping wine into a tumbler. "Like I said, I didn't hear anything."

"Of course you didn't," says Alistair.

I spin to face them, the glass in my hand. "But Ethan said—"

"Ethan, get the *hell* out of here," Alistair shouts. "How many times—"

"Calm down, Mr Russell. Dr Fox, I really don't recommend that right now," says Little, waving a finger at me. I set the tumbler on the counter, but keep my hand wrapped around it. I feel defiant.

He turns back to David. "Have you seen anything unusual in the house across the park?"

"His house?" asks David, glancing at Alistair, who bristles.

"This is—" he begins.

"No, I haven't seen anything." David's bag is slipping down his shoulder; he straightens, jostles it back in place. "Haven't been looking."

Little nods. "Uh-huh. And have you met Mrs Russell?"

"No."

"How do you know Mr Russell?"

"I hired him—" Alistair tries, but Little shows him his palm.

"He hired me to do some work," David says. "Didn't meet the wife."

"But you had her earring in your bedroom."

All eyes on me.

"I saw an earring in your bedroom," I say, clutching my glass. "On your nightstand. Three pearls. That's Jane Russell's earring."

David sighs. "No, it's Katherine's."

"Katherine?" I say.

He nods. "Woman I was seeing. Wasn't even seeing her. Woman who spent the night here a few times."

"When was this?" asks Little.

"Last week. What does it matter?"

"It doesn't," Norelli assures him, returning to David's side. She puts his phone in his hand. "Elizabeth Hughes says she was with him in Darien last night from midnight until ten."

"Then I came straight here," David says.

"So why were you in his bedroom?" Norelli asks me.

"She was snooping around," answers David.

I blush, fire back. "You took a box cutter from me."

He steps forward. I see Little tense. "You gave it to me."

"Yes, but then you replaced it without saying anything."

"Yeah, I had it in my pocket when I was going for a piss and I put it back where I got it. You're welcome."

"It just so happens that you put it back right after Jane—"

"That's *enough*," hisses Norelli.

I lift the glass to my lips, wine sloshing against the sides. As they watch, I swig it.

The portrait. The photograph. The earring. The box cutter. All of them knocked down, all of them burst like bubbles. There's nothing left.

There's almost nothing left.

I swallow, breathe.

"He was in prison, you know."

Even as the words leave my mouth, I can't believe I'm saying them, can't believe I'm hearing them.

"He was in prison," I repeat. I feel disembodied. I go on. "For assault."

David's jaw tightens. Alistair is glaring at him; Norelli and Ethan are staring at me. And Little—Little looks inexpressibly sad.

"So why aren't you giving him a hard time?" I ask. "I watch a woman get killed"—I flourish my phone—"and you say I'm imagining it. You say I'm *lying*." I slap the phone onto the island. "I show you a picture that she drew and signed"—I point at Alistair, at the portrait in his hand—"and you say I did it myself. There's a woman in that house who is *not* who she says she is, but you haven't even bothered to check. You haven't even *tried*."

I move forward, just a small step, but everyone else retreats, as though I'm an approaching storm, as though I'm a predator. Good. "Someone comes into my house when I'm asleep and photographs me and sends me the photo—and you blame me." I hear the catch in my throat, the crack in my voice. Tears are rolling down my cheeks. I keep going.

"I'm *not* crazy, I'm *not* making any of this up." I point a jittering finger at Alistair and Ethan. "I'm not seeing things that aren't there. All this started when I saw *his* wife and *his* mother get *stabbed*. That's what you should be looking into. Those are the questions you should be asking. And don't tell me I didn't see it, because *I know what I saw*."

Silence. They're frozen, a tableau. Even Punch has gone still, his tail curled into a question mark.

I wipe my face with the back of my hand, drag it across my nose. Push my hair out of my eyes. Raise the glass to my mouth, drain it.

Little comes to life. He steps toward me, one long, slow stride, clearing half the kitchen, his eyes fastened on mine. I set the empty glass on the counter. We look at each other across the island.

He places his hand over the top of the glass. Slides it away, as though it's a weapon.

"The thing is, Anna," he says, speaking low, speaking slow, "I talked to your doctor yesterday, after you and I had our phone call."

My mouth goes dry.

"Dr Fielding," he continues. "You mentioned him at the hospital. I just wanted to follow up with someone who knew you."

My heart goes weak.

"He's someone who cares about you a lot. I told him I was pretty concerned about what you'd been saying to me. To us. And I was worried about you all alone in this big house, because you told me that your family was far away and you had no one here to talk to. And—"

—and. And. And I know what he's about to say; and I'm so grateful that he's the one to say it, because he's kind, and his voice is warm, and I couldn't bear it otherwise, I couldn't bear it—

But instead Norelli cuts him off. "It turns out your husband and your daughter are dead."

# 74

No one's ever put it like that, said those words in that order.

Not the emergency-room doctor, who told me that *Your husband didn't make it* while they tended to my bruised back, my damaged windpipe.

Not the head RN, who forty minutes later said, *I'm so sorry, Mrs Fox*—she didn't even finish the sentence, didn't need to.

Not the friends—Ed's, as it happened; I learned the hard way that Livvy and I didn't have many friends of our own—who expressed condolences, attended the funerals, followed up sparingly as the months dragged by: *They're gone*, they'd say, or *They're no longer with us*, or (from the brusque ones) *They died*.

Not even Bina. Not even Dr Fielding.

Yet Norelli has done it, broken the spell, said the unsayable: *Your husband and your daughter are dead.*

They are. Yes. They didn't make it, they're gone, they've died—they're dead. I don't deny it.

"But don't you see, Anna"—now I hear Dr Fielding speaking, almost pleading—"that's what this *is*. Denial."

Strictly true.

Still:

How can I explain? To anyone—to Little or Norelli, or to Alistair or Ethan, or to David, or even to Jane? I *hear* them; their voices echo inside me, outside me. I hear them when I'm overwhelmed by the pain of their absence, their loss—I can say it: their deaths. I hear them when I need someone to talk to. I hear them when I least expect it. "Guess who," they'll say, and I beam, and my heart sings.

And I respond.

# 75

The words hang in the air, float there, like smoke.

Behind Little's shoulders, I see Alistair and Ethan, their eyes wide; I see David, his jaw dropped. Norelli, for some reason, turns her gaze to the floor.

"Dr Fox?"

Little. I bring him into focus, standing across the island from me, his face bathed in full afternoon light.

"Anna," he says.

I don't move, can't move.

He takes a breath, holds it. Expels. "Dr Fielding told me the story."

I screw my eyes shut. All I see is darkness. All I hear is Little's voice.

"He said a state trooper found you at the bottom of a cliff."

Yes. I remember his voice, that deep cry, rappelling down the face of the mountain.

"And by that point you'd spent two nights outside. In a snowstorm. In the middle of winter."

Thirty-three hours, from the instant we dove off the road to the moment the chopper appeared, its rotors swirling overhead like a whirlpool.

"He said that Olivia was still alive when they got down to you."

*Mommy,* she'd whispered as they loaded her onto the stretcher, sheathed her little body in a blanket.

"But your husband was already gone."

No, he wasn't gone. He was there, very much there, all too much there, his body cooling in the snow. *Internal damage,* they told me. *Compounded by exposure. There was nothing you could have done differently.*

There's so much I could have done differently.

"That's when your troubles started. Your problems going outside. Post-traumatic stress. Which I—I mean, I can't imagine."

God, how I cowered beneath the hospital fluorescents; how I panicked in the squad car. How I collapsed, those first times leaving the house, once and twice and twice more, until at last I dragged myself back inside.

And locked my doors.

And shut my windows.

And swore I'd keep myself hidden.

"You wanted someplace safe. I get that. They found you half-frozen. You'd been through hell."

My fingernails gouge my palms.

"Dr Fielding said that you sometimes... hear them."

I squeeze my eyes tighter, straining for more dark. *They aren't—you know, hallucinations,* I'd told him; *I just like pretending they're here every now and then. As a coping mechanism. I know that too much contact isn't healthy.*

"And that you sometimes talk back."

Feel the sun on my neck. *It's best you don't indulge in these conversations too often,* he'd warned me. *We wouldn't want them to become a crutch.*

"See, I was a little confused, because from what you were saying it sounded like they were just someplace else." I don't point out that this is technically true. There's no fight left in me. I'm hollow as a bottle.

"You told me that you were separated. That your daughter was with your husband." Another technicality. I'm so tired.

"You told me the same thing." I open my eyes. Light douses the room now, draining the shadows. The five of them are ranged before me like chess pieces. I look at Alistair.

"You told me that they lived somewhere else," he says, curling his lip. He looks repulsed. I didn't, of course—I never said they lived anywhere. I'm careful. But it doesn't matter anymore. Nothing matters.

Little reaches across the island, presses his hand onto mine. "I think that you've had a hell of a time. I think that you really believe you met with this lady, just like you believe you're talking to Olivia and Ed." There's a tiny pause before that last word, as though he isn't sure of Ed's name, although maybe he's just pacing himself. I peer into his eyes. Bottomless.

"But what you're thinking here isn't real," he says, his voice snow-soft. "And I need you to let this one go."

I find myself nodding. Because he's right. I've gone too far. *This has to stop,* Alistair said.

"You know, you've got people who care about you." Little's hand bunches my fingers together. The knuckles crackle. "Dr Fielding. And your physical therapist." *And?* I want to say. *And?* "And..." For an instant my heart leaps; who else cares about me? "... they want to help you."

I drop my gaze to the island, to my hand, nestled in his. Study the dull gold of his wedding band. Study mine.

Quieter still now. "The doctor said—he told me that the medication you're on can cause hallucinations."

And depression. And insomnia. And spontaneous combustion. But these *aren't* hallucinations. They're—

"And maybe that's okay by you. I know it'd be okay by me."

Norelli breaks in. "Jane Russell—"

But Little lifts his other hand, without looking away from me, and Norelli stops talking.

"She checks out," he says. "The lady in two-oh-seven. She is who she says she is." I don't ask how they know. I don't care anymore. So, so tired. "And this lady you thought you met—I think you... didn't."

To my surprise, I feel myself nod. *But then how...*

Except he's already there: "You said she helped you in off the street. But maybe that was you. Maybe you... I don't know, dreamed it."

*If I dream things when I'm awake...* Where have I heard that?

And I can picture it, like it's a film, in living colour: me, hauling my body off the stoop, rock-climbing those front steps. Dragging myself into the hall, into the house. I can almost *remember* it.

"And you said she was here playing chess with you and drawing pictures. But again..."

Yes, again. Oh, God. Again I see it: the bottles; the pill canisters; the pawns, the queens, the advancing two-tone armies—my hands reaching across the chessboard, hovering like helicopters. My fingers, stained with ink, a pen pinched between them. I'd practiced that signature, hadn't I, scrawling her name on the shower door, amid the steam and the spray, the letters bleeding down the glass, vanishing before my eyes.

"Your doctor said he hadn't heard about any of this." He pauses. "I was thinking that maybe you didn't tell him because you didn't want him to... talk you out of it."

My head shakes, nods.

"I don't know what that scream you heard was..."

I do. Ethan. He never claimed otherwise. And that afternoon I saw him with her in the parlour—he wasn't even looking at her. He was looking into his lap, not at the empty seat beside him.

I glance at him now, see him gently deposit Punch on the floor. His eyes never leave mine.

"I'm not sure about this photo business. Dr Fielding said that sometimes you act out, and maybe this is how you ask for help."

Did I do that? I *did* do that, didn't I? I did it. Of course: guess who—that's how I greet Ed and Livvy. Greeted.

guesswhoanna.

"But as for what you saw that night..."

I know what I saw that night.

I saw a movie. I saw an old thriller resurrected, brought to bloody Technicolour life. I saw *Rear Window*; I saw *Body Double*; I saw *Blow-Up*. I saw a showreel, archive footage from a hundred peeping-Tom thrillers.

I saw a killing without a killer, without a victim. I saw an empty sitting room, a vacant sofa. I saw what I wanted to see, what I needed to see. *Don't you get lonely up here?* Bogey had asked Bacall, asked me.

*I was born lonely*, she'd answered.

I wasn't. I was made lonely.

If I'm deranged enough to talk to Ed and Livvy, I can certainly stage a murder in my mind. Especially with some chemical help. And haven't I been resisting the truth all along? Didn't I bend and bash and break the facts?

Jane—the real Jane, flesh-and-blood Jane: Of course she is who she says she is.

And of course the earring in David's room belongs to Katherine, or whomever.

And of course no one came into my house last night. It crashes through me like a wave. Slams my shores, cleanses them; leaves behind only streaks of silt, pointing like fingers toward the sea.

I was wrong.

More than that: I was deluded.

More than *that*: I was responsible. Am responsible.

*If I dream things when I'm awake, I'm going out of my mind.* That was it. *Gaslight.*

Silence. I can't even hear Little breathe.

Then:

"So that's what's going on." Alistair is shaking his head, his lips parted. "I—wow. Christ." He looks at me hard. "I mean, *Christ.*"

I swallow.

He stares a moment longer, opens his mouth again, closes it. One more shake of the head.

At last he motions to his son, heads for the door. "We're leaving."

As Ethan follows him into the hall, he glances up, eyes shining. "I'm so sorry," he says, his voice small. I want to cry.

Then he's gone. The door cracks shut behind them.

Just the four of us now.

David steps forward, speaking to his toes. "So the kid in that picture downstairs—she's dead?"

I don't answer.

"And when you wanted me to save those blueprints, those were for a dead guy?"

I don't answer.

"And..." He points to the stepladder braked against the basement door.

I say nothing.

He nods, as though I've spoken. Then he hitches his bag farther up his shoulder, turns, and walks out the door.

Norelli watches him leave. "Do we need to talk to him?"

"He bothering you?" Little asks me.

I shake my head.

"Okay," he says, releasing my hand. "Now. I'm not really... qualified to deal with what happens next. My job is to shut all this down and make it safe for everyone to move ahead. Including you. I know that this has been hard for you. Today,

I mean. So I want you to give Dr Fielding a call. I think it's important."

I haven't uttered a word since Norelli's announcement. *Your husband and your daughter are dead.* I can't imagine what my voice might sound like, must sound like, in this new world where that sentence has been spoken, been heard.

Little's still talking. "I know you're struggling, and—" He stops for a moment. When he speaks again, he's hushed. "I know you're struggling."

I nod. So does he.

"Seems like I ask this every time we're here, but are you okay to be left alone?"

I nod again, slowly.

"Anna?" He eyes me. "Dr Fox?"

We've reverted to Dr Fox. I open my mouth. "Yes." I hear myself the way you do when you've got headphones on—remote, somehow. Muffled.

"In light of—" Norelli begins, but again Little raises a hand, and again she stops. I wonder what she was about to say.

"You've got my number," he reminds me. "Like I said, give Dr Fielding a call. Please. He'll want to hear from you. Don't make us worry. Either one of us." He gestures to his partner. "That includes Val here. She's a worrier at heart."

Norelli watches me.

Little's walking backward now, as though reluctant to turn away. "And like I said, we've got a lot of good people for you to talk to, if you want." Norelli turns, disappears into the hall. I hear her boots click on the tile. I hear the front door open.

It's just me and Little now. He's looking past me, out the window.

"You know," he says, after a moment, "I don't know what I'd do if anything happened to my girls." His eyes are on mine now. "Don't know what I'd do."

He clears his throat, raises a hand. "Bye." He steps into the hall, draws the door closed behind him.

A moment later I hear the front door shut.

I stand in my kitchen, watch little galaxies of dust form and dissolve in the sunlight.

My hand creeps to my glass. I pick it up gingerly, rotate it in my hand. Lift it to my face. Inhale.

Then I throw the fucking thing against the wall and scream louder than I've ever screamed in my life.

# 76

I sit at the edge of the bed, staring straight ahead. Shadows play on the wall before me.

I've lit a candle, a little potted Diptyque, fresh out of the box, a Christmas present from Livvy two years back. *Figuier*. She loves figs.

Loved.

A ghost of a draft haunts the room. The flame shifts, clings to the wick.

An hour passes. Then another.

The candle is burning fast, wick half-drowned in a soft pool of wax. I'm slumped over where I sit. My fingers are cradled between my thighs.

The phone lights up, shivers. Julian Fielding. He's supposed to see me tomorrow. He won't.

Night falls like a curtain.

*That's when your troubles started,* Little said. *Your problems going outside.*

At the hospital, they told me I was in shock. Then shock became fear. Fear mutated, became panic. And by the time Dr Fielding arrived on the scene, I was—well, he said it simplest, said it best: "A severe case of agoraphobia."

I need the familiar confines of my home—because I spent two nights in that alien wilderness, beneath those huge skies.

I need an environment I can control—because I watched my family as they slowly died.

*You'll notice I'm not asking what made you this way*, she said to me. Or, rather, I said it to myself.

Life made me this way.

"Guess who?"

I shake my head. I don't want to talk to Ed right now.

"How you feeling, slugger?"

But I shake my head again. I can't speak, won't speak. "Mom?"

No.

"Mommy?"

I flinch.

No.

At some point I keel to one side, sleep. When I wake, my neck sore, the candle flame has dwindled to a tiny blot of blue, shimmying in the cool air. The room is plunged in darkness.

I sit up, stand up, creaking, a rusty ladder. Drift to the bathroom.

As I return, I see the Russell place lit up like a dollhouse. Upstairs, Ethan sits at his computer; in the kitchen, Alistair seesaws a knife across a cutting board. Carrots, neon-bright beneath the kitchen glare. A glass of wine stands on the counter. My mouth goes dry.

And in the parlour, on the striped love seat, is that woman. I suppose I should call her Jane.

Jane's got a phone in her hand, and with the other she slashes and stabs at it. Scrolling through family photos, maybe. Playing solitaire, or something—games these days all seem to involve fruit.

Or else she's updating her friends. *Remember that freak neighbor... ?*

My throat hardens. I walk to the windows and tug the curtains shut.

And I stand there in the dark: cold, utterly alone, full of fear and something that feels like longing.

## TUESDAY, NOVEMBER 9

# 77

I spend the morning in bed. Sometime before noon, bleary with sleep, I find my fingers tapping out a message to Dr Fielding: Not today.

He calls me five minutes later, leaves a voicemail. I don't listen to it.

Midday ticks past; by three P.M. my stomach is cramping. I ferry myself downstairs and pluck a bruised tomato from the fridge.

As I bite into it, Ed tries to speak to me. Then Olivia. I turn away from them, pulp dribbling down my chin.

I feed the cat. I swallow a temazepam. Then a second. Then a third. Fold myself into sleep. All I want is sleep.

## WEDNESDAY, NOVEMBER 10

# 78

Hunger wakes me. In the kitchen I tilt a box of Grape Nuts into a bowl, chase it with some milk, expiration date today. I don't even much like Grape Nuts; Ed does. Did. They pebble-dash my throat, scour the insides of my cheeks. I don't know why I keep buying them.

Except of course I do.

I want to retreat to bed, but instead I aim my feet toward the living room, tread slowly to the television console, drag the drawer open. *Vertigo*, I think. Mistaken identity—or rather, taken identity. I know the dialogue by heart; strangely, it'll soothe me.

"What's the matter with you?" the policeman bellows at Jimmy Stewart, at me. "Give me your hand!" Then he loses his footing, plummets from the rooftop.

Strangely soothing.

Midway through the film, I pour myself a second bowl of cereal. Ed murmurs at me when I close the refrigerator door; Olivia says something indistinct. I return to the sofa, dial up the volume on the TV.

"His wife?" asks the woman in the jade-green Jag. "The poor thing. I didn't know her. Tell me: Is it true she really believed..."

I sink deeper into the cushions. Sleep overtakes me.

Sometime later, during the makeover sequence ("I don't want to be dressed like someone dead!"), my phone shakes, a little seizure, rattling the glass of the coffee table. Dr Fielding, I presume. I reach for it.

"Is that what I'm here for?" Kim Novak cries. "To make you feel that you're with someone that's dead?"

The phone screen reads Wesley Brill.

I go still for an instant.

Then I mute the film, press my thumb to the phone, and swipe. Lift it to my ear.

I find I can't speak. But I don't need to. After a moment's silence, he greets me: "I hear you breathing there, Fox."

It's been almost eleven months, but his voice is as thunderous as ever.

"Phoebe said you called," he goes on. "I meant to get back to you yesterday, but it's been busy. Very busy."

I say nothing. Nor, for a minute, does he.

"You *are* there, aren't you, Fox?"

"I'm here." I haven't heard my own voice in days. It sounds unfamiliar, frail, as though someone else is ventriloquizing through me.

"Good. I suspected as much." He's chewing on his words; I know there's a cigarette speared between his teeth. "My hypothesis was correct." A rush of white noise. He's blowing smoke across the mouthpiece.

"I wanted to speak to you," I begin.

He goes quiet. I can sense him shifting gears; I can practically *hear* it—something in his breathing. He's in psychologist mode.

"I wanted to tell you..."

A long pause. He clears his throat. He's nervous, I realize, and it's something of a jolt. Wesley Brilliant, on edge.

"I've been having a hard time." There.

"With anything in particular?" he asks.

*With the death of my husband and daughter,* I want to shout. "With..."

"Mm-hm." Is he stalling, or waiting for more?

"That night..." I don't know how to complete the sentence. I feel like the needle on a compass, spinning, seeking some place to settle.

"What are you thinking, Fox?" Very Brill, prompting me like this. My own practice is to let the patient proceed at her own pace; Wesley moves faster.

"That night..."

That night, right before our car dove off that cliff, you called me. I'm not blaming you. I'm not involving you. I just want you to know.

That night, it was already over—four months of lies: to Phoebe, who might have discovered us; to Ed, who *did* discover us, that December afternoon I sent him a text meant for you.

That night, I regretted every moment we spent together: the mornings in the hotel around the corner, shy light peeking through the curtains; the evenings we'd swap messages on our phones for hours. The day it all began, with that glass of wine in your office.

That night, we'd had the house on the market for a week, as the broker slotted tours and I pleaded with Ed and he struggled to look at me. *I thought you were the girl next door.*

That night—

But he interrupts me.

"To be very frank, Anna"—and I stiffen, because although he's seldom anything but frank, it's rare indeed for him to call me by my first name—"I've been trying to put that behind me." He pauses. "Trying and succeeding, largely."

Oh.

"You didn't want to see me afterward. In the hospital. I wanted—I offered to come see you at home, remember, but you wouldn't—you didn't get back to me." He's slipping on his words, stumbling, like a man striding through snow. Like a woman circling her wrecked car.

"I didn't—I don't know if you're seeing anyone. A professional, I mean. I'm happy to recommend someone." He pauses. "Or if you're set, then... well." Another pause, longer this time.

Finally: "I'm not sure what you want from me."

I was wrong. He isn't playing psychologist; he's not hoping to help me. He took two days to call me back. He's looking for an escape.

And what *do* I want from him? Fair question. I don't blame him, truly. I don't hate him. I don't miss him.

When I called his office—was it only two days ago?—I must have wanted something. But then Norelli spoke those magic words, and the world changed. And now it doesn't matter.

I must have said this out loud. "What doesn't matter?" he asks.

*You*, I think. I don't say it.

Instead I hang up.

## THURSDAY, NOVEMBER 11

# 79

At eleven sharp the doorbell rings. I wrest myself from bed, peer out the front windows. It's Bina at the door, her black hair brilliant in the morning sun. I'd forgotten about her visiting today. I'd forgotten about her altogether.

I step back, survey the houses across the street, scanning them east-west: the Gray Sisters, the Millers, the Takedas, that abandoned double-wide. My southern empire.

The doorbell again.

I slope downstairs, cross to the hall door, see her framed within the intercom screen. Press the speaker. "I'm not feeling well today," I say.

I watch her speak. "Should I come in?"

"No, I'm fine."

"*May* I come in?"

"No. Thanks. I really need to be alone." She chews her lip. "Is everything okay?"

"I just need to be alone," I repeat.

She nods. "Okay."

I wait for her to leave.

"Dr Fielding told me about what happened. He heard from the police."

I say nothing, just close my eyes. A long pause.

"Well—so I'm going to see you next week," she says.

"Wednesday, like usual."

Maybe not. "Yes."

"And will you call me if you need anything?" I won't. "I will."

I open my eyes, see her nod again. She turns, walks down the steps.

That's done. First Dr. Fielding, now Bina. Anyone else?

Oui: Yves tomorrow. I'll write him to cancel. Je ne peux pas...

I'll do it in English.

Before returning to the stairwell, I fill Punch's food and water bowls. He trots over, dips his tongue into his Fancy Feast, then pricks his ears—the pipes are gurgling.

David, downstairs. I haven't thought about him in a while.

I pause by the basement door, grasp the stepladder, move it to one side. I knock on the door, call his name.

Nothing. I call it again.

This time I hear footsteps. I flip the lock and raise my voice. "I've unlocked the door. You can come up. If you want," I add.

Before I've finished, the door opens, and he stands before me, two steps down, in a snug T-shirt and balding jeans. We look at each other.

I speak first. "I wanted to—" "I'm clearing out," he says.

I blink.

"Things got . . . weird." I nod.

He rummages in his back pocket, pulls out a slip of paper.

Hands it to me.

I accept it wordlessly, unfold it.

Not working out. Sorry I upset you. Left key under door.

I nod again. I hear the tick of the grandfather clock across the room.

"Well," I say.

"Here's the key," he says, offering it to me. "Door'll lock behind me."

I take it from him. Another pause.

He looks me in the eye. "That earring."

"Oh, you don't need—"

"It belonged to a lady named Katherine. Like I said. I don't know that Russell guy's wife."

"I know," I say. "I'm sorry."

Now he nods. And closes the door. I leave it unlocked.

Back in my bedroom, I send Dr Fielding a terse text: I'm fine. See you Tuesday. He calls me immediately. The phone rings on, rings out.

Bina, David, Dr Fielding. I'm clearing house.

I pause in the doorway of the master bath, eyeing the shower the way one might appraise a painting at a gallery; not for me, I decide, or at least not today. I select a robe (must wash the stained one, I remind myself, although by now that splash of wine will be tattooed into the fabric) and wander down to the study.

It's been three days since I sat at my computer. I grip the mouse, slide it to one side. The screen lights up, prompts me for the password. I enter it.

Once again I see my sleeping face.

I rock back in the chair. All this time it's been lurking behind the dark of the screen, an ugly secret. My hand strikes the mouse like a snake: I whip the cursor to the corner, click the picture shut.

Now I'm looking at the email it was smuggled in.

guesswhoanna.

*Guess who*. I don't recall doing this, this—what was it Norelli said? "Little midnight selfie"? Hand to heart, I've no memory. Yet those are my words, *our* words; and David has an alibi (an *alibi*—I've never before known anyone with, or for that matter without, an alibi); and no one else could have accessed the bedroom. No one's *Gaslight*-ing me.

...Only wouldn't the photograph still be in my camera roll?

I frown.

Yes, it would. Unless I thought to delete it, but... well.

But.

My Nikon is perched on the edge of my desk, strap dangling off the side. I reach for it, drag it toward me. Switch it on and inspect the photo cache.

The most recent picture: Alistair Russell, wrapped in a winter coat, hopping up the front steps of his house. Dated Saturday, November 6. Nothing since. I switch the camera off, set it on the desk.

But then the Nikon is too bulky for selfies, in any case. I pull my phone from the pocket of my robe, enter the passcode, tap the Photos icon.

And there it is, first up: that same shot, shrunk within the iPhone screen. The open mouth, the loose hair, the bulging pillow—and the time stamp: 02:02 a.m.

No one else has the passcode.

There's one more test, but already I know the answer.

I open the web browser, type in gmail.com. It loads instantly, the username field filled in: guesswhoanna.

I really did this to myself. Guess who. Anna.

And it had to be me. No one else knows the computer password. Even if someone else was in the house—even if David had made his way in here—I'm the only one with the code.

My head lists toward my lap.

I swear I don't remember any of it.

# 80

I slide the phone back into my pocket, draw a breath, and log on to the Agora.

A trove of messages awaits me. I sift through them. Mostly regulars, checking in: DiscoMickey, Pedro from Bolivia, Bay Area Talia. Even Sally4th—preggers!!! she writes. due in april!!!

I stare at the screen for a moment. My heart aches.

On to the newbies. Four of them, seeking help. My fingers hover over the keyboard, then drop to my lap. Who am I to tell anyone else how to manage their disorder?

I select all the messages. Hit Delete.

I'm signing out when a chat box appears.

GRANNYLIZZIE: How are you, Doctor Anna?

Why not? I've said goodbye to everyone else.

THEDOCTORISIN: Hello Lizzie! Are your sons still with you?

GRANNYLIZZIE: William is!

THEDOCTORISIN: Great! And how is your progress?

GRANNYLIZZIE: : Really pretty amazing. I have been getting outside regularly. How are you?

THEDOCTORISIN: All good! It's my birthday.

Jesus, I think—that's true. I'd completely forgotten. My birthday. I hadn't thought of it once this past week.

GRANNYLIZZIE: Happy birthday! Is it a big one??

THEDOCTORISIN: Not at all. Unless you think 39 is big!

GRANNYLIZZIE: : What I wouldn't give...

GRANNYLIZZIE: Have you heard from your family?

I squeeze the mouse.

THEDOCTORISIN:I need to be honest with you.

GRANNYLIZZIE: ??

THEDOCTORISIN:My family died last December.

The cursor blinks.

THEDOCTORISIN: In a car accident.

THEDOCTORISIN: I had an affair. My husband and I were fighting about it and we drove off the road.

THEDOCTORISIN: I drove off the road.

THEDOCTORISIN: I see a psychiatrist to help me deal with the guilt as well as the agoraphobia.

THEDOCTORISIN: I want you to know the truth.

Must end this.

THEDOCTORISIN: I've got to go now. Glad you're doing well.

GRANNYLIZZIE: Oh my dear girl

I see that she's typing another message, but I don't wait. I close the chat box and sign out.

So much for the Agora.

# 81

I've gone three days without a drink.

This occurs to me as I swipe a toothbrush across my teeth. (My body can wait to be cleaned; my mouth can't.) Three days —when did I last hold off that long? I've scarcely even thought about it.

I bow my head, spit.

Tubes and canisters and pots of pills crowd the medicine cabinet. I remove four.

I walk downstairs, the skylight shedding gray evening light overhead.

Sitting on the sofa, I select a canister, tip it over, drag it across the coffee table. A trail of pills follows it like bread crumbs.

I study them. Count them. Brush them into my cupped hand. Scatter them upon the tabletop.

Bring one to my lips.

No—not yet.

Night falls fast.

I turn to the windows and cast a long look across the park.

That house. A theater for my unquiet mind. *How poetic,* I think.

Its windows are blazing, birthday-candle-bright; its rooms are empty.

I feel as though a madness has released me. I shiver.

I lift myself up the stairs, up to my room. Tomorrow I'll revisit some favorite films. *Midnight Lace. Foreign Correspondent*—the windmill scene, at least. *23 Paces to Baker Street.* Maybe *Vertigo* again; I napped through my last viewing.

And the day after...

Lying in bed, sleep filling my head, I listen to the pulse of the house—the grandfather clock downstairs, tolling nine; the settling of the floors.

"Happy birthday," Ed and Livvy chorus. I roll over, roll away.

It's Jane's birthday too, I remember. The birthday I gave her. Eleven eleven.

And later still, in the dead of night, when I've surfaced for a moment, I hear the cat, prowling the ink-dark well of the staircase.

## FRIDAY, NOVEMBER 12

# 82

Sun cascades through the skylight, whitewashing the stairs, pooling in the landing outside the kitchen. When I step into it, I feel spotlit.

Otherwise, the house is dark. I've drawn every curtain, closed every blind. The darkness is smoke-thick; I can almost smell it.

The final scene of *Rope* plays on the television. Two handsome young men, a murdered classmate, a corpse packed into an antique chest in the center of the parlour, and Jimmy Stewart again, all staged in what appears to be a single take (actually eight ten-minute segments stitched together, but the effect is pretty seamless, especially for 1948). "Cat and mouse, cat and mouse," fumes Farley Granger, the net drawing tight around him, "but which is the cat and which is the mouse?" I say the words out loud.

My own cat is stretched along the back of the sofa, his tail switching like a charmed snake. He's sprained his rear left paw; I found him limping this morning, badly. I've filled his bowl with a few days' worth of food, just so he doesn't—

The doorbell rings.

I jolt back into the cushions. My head twists toward the door.

Who the hell?

Not David; not Bina. Not Dr Fielding, surely—he's left several voicemails, but I doubt he'd show up unannounced. Unless he announced it in a voicemail I ignored.

The bell rings again. I pause the film, swing my feet to the floor, stand up. Walk to the intercom screen.

It's Ethan. His hands are jammed in his pockets; a scarf is looped around his neck. His hair flames in the sunlight.

I push the speaker button. "Do your parents know you're here?" I ask.

"It's okay," he says.

I pause.

"It's really cold," he adds. I press the buzzer.

A moment later he enters the living room, frigid air chasing him. "Thanks," he huffs, his breath short. "So freezing out there." He looks around. "It's really dark in here."

"That's just because it's so bright outside," I say, but he's right. I switch on the floor lamp.

"Should I open the blinds?"

"Sure. Actually, no, this is fine. Isn't it?"

"Okay," he says.

I perch on the chaise. "Should I sit here?" asks Ethan, pointing to the sofa. *Should I, should I.* Very deferential, for a teenage boy.

"Sure." He sits. Punch drops down the back of the sofa, quickly crawls beneath it.

Ethan scans the room. "Does that fireplace work?"

"It's gas, but yes. Do you want me to turn it on?"

"No, just wondering."

Silence.

"What are all these pills for?"

I snap my gaze to the coffee table, studded with pills; four canisters, one empty, stand together in a little plastic glade.

"I'm just counting them," I explain. "Refills."

"Oh, okay."

More silence.

"I came over—" he begins, just as I say his name.

I steam ahead. "I'm so sorry."

He cocks his head.

"I'm just so sorry." Now he's peering into his lap, but I press on. "For all the trouble, and for involving you. I—was so... *sure*. I was *so sure* that something was happening."

He nods at the floor.

"I've had... it's been a very hard year." I close my eyes; when I open them again, I see that he's looking at me, his eyes bright, searching.

"I lost my child and my husband." Swallow. Say it. "They died. They're dead." Breathe. Breathe. One, two, three, four.

"And I started drinking. More than usual. And I self-medicated. Which is dangerous and wrong." He's watching me intently.

"It isn't like—it's not that I believed they were actually communicating with me—you know, from..."

"The other side," he says, his voice low.

"Exactly." I shift in my seat, lean forward. "I knew they were gone. Dead. But I liked hearing them. And feeling... It's very tough to explain."

"Like, connected?"

I nod. He's such an unusual teenager.

"As for the rest—I don't... I can't even remember a lot of it. I guess I wanted to connect with other people. Or needed to." My hair brushes my cheeks as I shake my head. "I don't understand it." I look directly at him. "But I'm very sorry." I clear my throat, straighten up. "I know you didn't come over here to see an adult cry."

"I've cried in front of you," he points out.

I smile. "Fair enough."

"I borrowed your movie, remember?" He slides a slipcase from his coat pocket, places it on the coffee table. *Night Must Fall*. I'd forgotten about that.

"Were you able to watch it?" I ask.

"Yeah."

"What did you think?"

"Creepy. That guy."

"Robert Montgomery."

"Was he Danny?"

"Yes."

"Really creepy. I like the part where he asks the girl—uh..."

"Rosalind Russell."

"Was she Olivia?"

"Yes."

"Where he asks her if she likes him, and she's like, no, and he's like, 'Everybody else does.'" He giggles. I grin.

"I'm glad you liked it."

"Yeah."

"Black-and-white's not so bad."

"No, it was fine."

"You're welcome to borrow anything you like."

"Thanks."

"But I don't want to get you in trouble with your parents." Now he looks away, studies the grate. "I know they're furious," I continue.

A quiet snort. "They've got their own issues." Eyes back on me. "They're really difficult to live with. Like, super-difficult."

"I think a lot of young people feel that way about their parents."

"No, but they really are."

I nod.

"I can't wait to go to college," he says. "Two more years. Not even."

"Do you know where you want to go?"

He shakes his head. "Not really. Someplace far away." He hooks his arm behind himself, scratches his back. "It's not like I have friends here anyway."

"Do you have a girlfriend?" I ask.

He shakes his head.

"Boyfriend?"

He looks at me, surprised. Shrugs. "I'm figuring things out," he explains.

"Fair enough." I wonder if his parents know.

The grandfather clock booms once, twice, three times, four. "You know," I say, "the apartment downstairs is empty." Ethan frowns. "What happened to that guy?"

"He left." I clear my throat again. "But—so if you want, you can use it. The space. I know what it's like to need your own space."

Am I trying to get back at Alistair and Jane? I don't think so. I don't *think* so. But it might be nice—it *would* be nice, I'm sure—to have someone else here. A young person, no less, even if he's a lonely teenager.

I go on, as though it's a sales pitch: "There's no TV, but I can give you the Wi-Fi password. And there's a couch in there." I'm talking brightly, convincing myself. "It could just be a place for you to get away to if things are hard at home."

He stares. "That'd be awesome."

I'm on my feet before he can change his mind. David's key is on the kitchen counter, a little shard of silver in the dim light. I palm it, present it to Ethan, who stands.

"Awesome," he repeats, tucking it into his pocket.

"Come over anytime," I tell him.

He glances at the door. "I should probably get home."

"Of course."

"Thanks for—" He pats his pocket. "And for the movie."

"You're welcome." I follow him to the hall.

Before leaving, he turns, waves at the sofa—"Little guy's shy today," he says—and gazes at me. "I got a phone," he announces proudly.

"Congratulations."

"Want to see it?"

"Sure."

He produces a scuffed iPhone. "It's secondhand, but still."

"It's awesome."

"What generation is yours?"

"I have no idea. What's yours?"

"Six. Almost the newest."

"Well, it's awesome. I'm glad you have a phone."

"I put your number in. Do you want mine?"

"Your number?"

"Yeah."

"Sure." He taps the screen, and I feel my phone buzz in the depths of my robe. "Now you've got it," he explains, hanging up.

"Thank you."

He reaches for the doorknob, then drops his hand, looks at me, suddenly serious.

"I'm sorry for everything that's happened to you," he says, and his voice is so soft that my throat constricts.

I nod.

He leaves. I lock the door behind him.

I float back to the sofa and look at the coffee table, at the pills dotting it like stars. I reach out, clasp the remote in my hand. Resume the film.

"To tell you the truth," says Jimmy Stewart, "it really scares me a little."

## SATURDAY, NOVEMBER 13

# 83

Half past ten, and I feel different.

Perhaps it was the sleep (two temazepams, twelve hours); perhaps it's my stomach—after Ethan left, after the movie ended, I made myself a sandwich. Closest thing I've had to a proper meal all week.

Whatever the case, whatever the cause, I feel different.

I feel better.

I shower. Stand beneath the spray; the water soaks my hair, pounds my shoulders. Fifteen minutes pass. Twenty. Half an hour. When I emerge, scrubbed and shampooed, my skin feels new. I wriggle into jeans and a sweater. (Jeans! When did I last wear jeans?)

I walk across the bedroom to the window, part the curtains; light blasts the room. I close my eyes, let it warm me.

I feel fit for fight, ready to face the day. Ready for a glass of wine. Just one.

I journey downstairs, visiting each room I pass, hiking up the blinds, pulling back the curtains. The house is flooded with light.

In the kitchen I pour myself a few fingers of merlot. ("Only Scotch is measured in fingers," I can hear Ed say. I push him away, pour another finger.)

Now: *Vertigo*, round two. I settle into the sofa, skip back to the beginning, to that lethal lunge-and-plunge rooftop sequence. Jimmy Stewart rises into frame, scaling a ladder. I've spent a lot of time with him lately.

An hour later, during my third glass:

"He was prepared to take his wife to an institution," intones the court official, presiding over the inquest, "where her mental health would have been in the hands of qualified specialists." I fidget, get up to refresh my drink.

This afternoon, I've decided, I'll play some chess, check in on my classic-film website, maybe clean the house—the upstairs rooms are powdery with dust. Under no circumstances will I watch my neighbors.

Not even the Russells.

Especially not the Russells.

Standing at the kitchen window, I don't even look at their house. I turn my back on it, return to the sofa, lie down.

A few moments pass.

"It is a pity that knowing her suicidal tendencies..."

I slide a glance at the buffet of pills on the tabletop. Then I sit up, plant my feet on the rug, and sweep them into one hand. A little mound in my fist.

"The jury finds that Madeleine Elster committed suicide while of unsound mind."

*You're wrong*, I think. *That's not what happened.*

I drop the pills, one by one, into their canisters. Screw the lids tight.

As I sit back, I find myself wondering when Ethan will arrive. Maybe he'll want to chat some more.

"This was as far as I could get," says Jimmy mournfully.

"As far as I could get," I echo.

Another hour has passed; western light slants into the kitchen. By now I'm pretty buzzed. The cat limps into the room; he whines when I inspect his paw.

I frown. Have I thought about the veterinarian even once this year? "Irresponsible of me," I tell Punch.

He blinks, nestles between my legs.

On-screen, Jimmy is forcing Kim Novak up the bell tower. "I couldn't follow her—God knows I tried," he cries, clutching Kim by the shoulders. "One doesn't often get a second chance. *I want to stop being haunted*."

"I want to stop being haunted," I say. I close my eyes, say it again. Stroke the cat. Reach for my glass.

"And she was the one who died, not you. The real wife," shouts Jimmy. His hands are on her throat. "You were the copy. You were the counterfeit."

Something chimes in my brain, like a radar ping. A gentle tone, high and remote, soft, but it distracts me.

Only briefly, though. I lean back, sip my wine.

A nun, a scream, a tolling bell, and the film ends. "That's how I wanna go," I inform the cat.

I scrape myself off the sofa, deposit Punch on the floor; he complains. Bring my glass to the sink. Must start keeping the house orderly. Ethan might want to spend time here—I can't go all Havisham. (Another Christine Gray book-club pick. I should find out what they're reading these days. No harm in *that*, surely.)

Upstairs, in the study, I visit my chess forum. Two hours go by, and night drops outside; I win three straight matches. Time to celebrate. I fetch a bottle of merlot from the kitchen—I play best when well oiled—and pour as I ascend the stairs, blotting the rattan with wine. I'll sponge it down later.

Two more hours, two more victories. Unstoppable me. I drain the last of the bottle into my glass. I've drunk more than I meant to, but I'll be better tomorrow.

As my sixth game kicks off, I think about the past two weeks, the fever that seized me. It felt like hypnosis, like Gene Tierney in *Whirlpool;* it felt like insanity, like Ingrid Bergman in *Gaslight.* I did things I can't remember. I *didn't* do things I *can* remember. The clinician in me rubs her hands together: A genuine dissociative episode? Dr Fielding will—

Dammit.

I've sacrificed the queen by accident—mistook it for a bishop. I swear, detonate an F-bomb. It's been days since I last cursed. I chew on the word, savor it.

Still, though. That queen. Rook & Roll pounces, of course, claims her.

WTF??? he messages me. Bad move lol!!!

Thought it was another piece, I explain, and lift the glass to my mouth.

And then I freeze.

# 84

What if...

*Think.*

It curls away from me, like blood in water. I grip the glass.

What if...

No.

Yes.

What if:

Jane—the woman I knew as Jane—was never Jane at all?

... No.

... Yes.

What if:

What if she had been someone else altogether?

This is what Little told me. No—it's *half* of what Little told me. He said that the woman in number 207, the woman with the sleek haircut and slender hips, was definitely, demonstrably Jane Russell. Fine. Accepted.

But what if the woman I met, or thought I met, was in fact real—just another person posing as Jane? A piece I mistook for another piece? A bishop I confused with a queen?

What if *she* was the copy—the one who died? What if *she* was the counterfeit?

The glass has drifted to my lips again. I set it on the desk, push it away.

Why, though?

Think. Assume she was real. Yes: Overrule Little, overrule logic, and assume I was right all along—or mostly right. She was real. She was here. She was *there*, in their house. Why would the Russells—why *did* they—deny her existence? They could have plausibly maintained that she wasn't Jane, but they went a step further.

And how could she know so much about them? And why did she pretend to be someone else, pretend to be Jane?

"Who could she have been?" asks Ed.

No. Stop it.

I stand, walk toward the window. Lift my eyes to the Russell house—*that house.* Alistair and Jane stand in the kitchen, talking; he clasps a laptop in one hand, her arms are folded across her chest. Let them look back, I think. In the dark of the study, I feel safe. I feel secret.

Movement in the corner of my eye. I flick a glance upstairs, to Ethan's bedroom.

He's at his window, just a narrow shadow against the lamplight behind him. Both hands are pressed against the glass, as though he's straining to see through it. After a moment, he raises one hand. Waves at me.

My pulse quickens. I wave back, slowly.

Next move.

# 85

Bina answers on the first ring.

"Are you okay?"

"I'm—"

"Your doctor called me. He's really worried about you."

"I know." I'm seated on the stairs, in a weak bath of moonlight. There's a damp patch by my foot where I spilled wine earlier. Must sponge that.

"He says he's been trying to reach you."

"He has. I'm fine. Tell him I'm fine. Listen—"

"Have you been drinking?"

"No."

"You sound—you're slurring."

"No. I was just asleep. Listen, I was thinking—"

"I thought you were asleep."

I ignore this. "I've been thinking about things."

"What things?" she asks, warily.

"The people across the park. That woman."

"Oh, Anna." She sighs. "This—I wanted to talk to you about it on Thursday, but you wouldn't even let me in."

"I know. I'm sorry. But—"

"That woman didn't even *exist*."

"No, I just can't *prove* that she exists. Existed."

"Anna. This is insane. It's over."

I'm silent.

"There's nothing to prove." Forceful, almost angry—I've never heard her sound like this. "I don't know what you were thinking, or what was... happening to you, but it's *over*. You're making a mess of your life."

I listen to her breathe.

"The longer you keep this up, the longer it'll take to heal."

Silence.

"You're right."

"Do you mean that?"

I sigh. "Yes."

"Please tell me you're not going to do anything crazy."

"I'm not."

"I need you to promise."

"I promise."

"I need you to say that this was all in your head."

"This was all in my head."

Quiet.

"Bina, you're right. I'm sorry. It was just—an aftershock, or something. Like when neurons continue firing after death."

"Well," she says, her voice warming, "I don't know about *that*."

"Sorry. The point is, I'm not going to do anything crazy."

"And you *promise*."

"I promise."

"So when I'm training you next week, I won't hear anything—you know. Disturbing."

"Nothing except the disturbing sounds I usually make."

I listen to her smile. "Dr Fielding said that you left the house again. Went down to the coffee shop."

An eternity ago. "I did."

"How was that?"

"Oh, horrific."

"Still."

"Still."

Another pause. "One last time..." she says.

"I promise. This was all in my head."

We say our goodbyes. We end the call.

My hand is rubbing the back of my neck, the way it often does when I lie.

# 86

I need to think before proceeding. There's no margin for error. I have no allies.

Or perhaps one ally. I won't reach out to him yet, though. Can't.

Think. I need to think. And first I need to sleep. Maybe it's the wine—it's probably the wine—but suddenly I feel very tired. I check my phone. Almost ten thirty. Time flies.

I return to the living room, switch off the lamp. Up to the study, power down the desktop (message from Rook&Roll: Where did u go???). Up again to the bedroom. Punch follows me, tripping. Must do something about that paw. Maybe Ethan can take him to the vet.

I glance into the bathroom. Too exhausted to wash my face, to brush my teeth. Besides, I did both this morning—will catch up tomorrow. I shed my clothes, scoop up the cat, climb into bed.

Punch tours the sheets, settling in a far corner. I listen to him breathe.

And again, perhaps it's the wine—it's almost certainly the wine—but I can't sleep. I lie on my back, staring at the ceiling, at the ripple of crown molding along the edges; I roll to one side, peer into the dark of the hall. I turn onto my stomach, press my face against the pillow.

The temazepam. Still in its bottle on the coffee table. I should swing myself upright, head downstairs. Instead I thrash onto my other side.

Now I can see across the park. The Russell house has put itself to bed: The kitchen is dark; the curtains are drawn in the parlour; Ethan's room is lit only by the phantom glow of the computer monitor.

I stare at it until my eyes go weak.

"What are you going to do, Mommy?"

I flip over, bury my face in the pillow, crush my eyelids shut. Not now. Not now. Focus on something else, anything else.

Focus on Jane.

I rewind. I replay the conversation with Bina; I picture Ethan at the window, backlit, fingers splayed against the glass. I switch reels, zip through *Vertigo*, through Ethan's visit. The lonely hours of the week rush by in reverse; my kitchen fills with visitors—first the detectives, then David, then Alistair and Ethan. Accelerating now, blurring, past the coffee shop, past the hospital, past the night I watched her die, the camera leaping from the floor to my hands—back, back, back to the moment she turned from the sink and faced me.

Stop. I twist onto my back, open my eyes. The ceiling spreads above me, a projection screen.

And filling the frame is Jane—the woman I knew as Jane. She stands at the kitchen window, that braid dangling between her shoulders.

The scene replays in slow motion.

Jane revolves toward me, and I zoom in on her bright face, the electric eyes, the gleaming silver pendant. Pull out now, go wide: a glass of water in one hand, a tumbler of brandy in the other. "No idea if brandy actually *works*!" she trills, in surround sound.

I freeze the frame.

What would Wesley say? *Let's refine our inquiry, Fox.*

Question one: Why does she introduce herself to me as Jane Russell?

... Question one, addendum: *Does* she? Aren't I the one who speaks first, calls her by that name?

I rewind again, to the moment I first heard her voice. She pivots back toward the sink. Play: "I was just headed next door..."

Yes. That was it—that was the moment I decided who she was. The moment I read the board wrong.

So, second question: How does she respond? I fast-forward, squint at the ceiling, zero in on her mouth as I hear myself speak: "You're the woman from across the park," I say. "You're Jane Russell."

She flushes. Her lips part. She says—

And now I hear something else, something off-screen.

Something downstairs.

The sound of breaking glass.

## 87

If I dial 911, how fast can they get here? If I call Little, will he pick up?

My hand springs to my side.

No phone.

I slap the pillow beside me, the blankets. Nothing. The phone isn't here.

Think. *Think*. When did I last use it? On the stairs, when I was talking to Bina. And then—and then I went into the living room to turn off the lights. What did I do with the phone? Bring it up to the study? Leave it there?

Doesn't matter, I realize. I don't have it.

That sound splits the silence again. A crash of glass.

I step out of bed, one leg before the other, press my feet into the carpet. Push myself upright. Find my robe draped on a chair, tug it on. Tread toward the door.

Outside, gray falls from the skylight. I steal through the doorway, flatten my back against the wall. Down the coiling staircase, my breath shallow, my heart a cannon.

I alight on the next landing. All is quiet below.

Slowly—slowly—I heel-toe into the study, feel rattan beneath my feet, then carpet. From the doorway I scan the desk. The phone isn't there.

I turn around. I'm one floor away. I'm unarmed. I can't call for help.

Glass shatters downstairs.

I shudder, knock my hip against the knob of the closet door.

The closet door.

I seize the knob. Twist. Hear the catch, pull the door open.

Charcoal darkness yawns before me. I step forward.

Inside, I wave my hand to the right, brush my fingers against a shelf. The lightbulb string bats against my forehead. Can I risk it? No—it's too bright; it would spill into the stairwell.

I move ahead in the dark, both hands fanning out now, like I'm playing blindman's bluff. Until one of them touches it: the cool metal of the toolbox. I feel for the latch, flick it, reach inside.

The box cutter.

I retreat from the closet, weapon in my fist, and slide the switch; the blade peeps out, glinting in a stray moonbeam. I walk to the top of the stairs, elbow tucked tight against my body, the box cutter aimed straight ahead. With my other hand I grip the banister. I put one foot forward.

And then I remember the phone in the library. The landline. Just a few yards away. I turn.

But before I can take a step, I hear another sound from downstairs:

"Mrs Fox," someone calls. "Come join me in the kitchen."

# 88

I know the voice.

The blade trembles in my hand as I make my way down the stairs, carefully, the banister smooth beneath my palm. I hear my breath. I hear my footsteps.

"That's right. Quicker, please."

I reach the floor, hover just outside the doorway. Inhale so deep that I cough, splutter. I try to muffle it, even though he knows I'm here.

"Come on in."

I come on in.

Moonlight floods the kitchen, paving the countertops silver, filling the empty bottles by the window. The faucet gleams; the sink is a bright basin. Even the hardwood shines.

He's leaning against the island, a silhouette in the white light, shadow-flat. Rubble glitters at his feet: shards and curls of glass sprayed across the floor. On the countertop beside him stands a skyline of bottles and glasses, brimming with the moon.

"Sorry for..."—he sweeps his arm around the room—"the mess. I didn't want to have to go upstairs."

I say nothing, but flex my fingers around the handle of the box cutter.

"I've been patient, Mrs Fox." Alistair sighs, turning his head to the side, so that I can see his profile edged with light: the high forehead, the steep nose. "*Dr* Fox. Whatever you... call yourself." His words drip with booze. He's very drunk, I realize.

"I've been patient," he repeats. "I've put up with a lot." He sniffs, selects a tumbler, rolls it between his palms. "We all have, but especially me." Now I can see him more clearly; his jacket is zippered to the collar, and he's wearing dark gloves. My throat tightens.

Still I don't respond. Instead I move to the light switch, reach for it.

Glass explodes inches from my outstretched hand. I jump back. "Keep the fucking lights off," he barks.

I stand still, my fingers wrapped around the doorframe. "Someone should've warned us about you." He's shaking his head, laughing.

I swallow. His laugh gutters, dies.

"You gave my son the key to your apartment." He holds it up. "I'm returning it." The key chinks as he drops it on the island. "Even if you weren't out of your... *goddamn* mind, I wouldn't want him spending time with a grown woman."

"I'll call the police," I whisper.

He snorts. "Go ahead. Here's your phone." He picks it up off the counter, tosses it in his hand, once, twice.

Yes—I left it in the kitchen. And for an instant I wait for him to dash it to the floor, to hurl it against the wall; but instead he sets it back down beside the key. "The police think you're a joke," he says, taking a step toward me. I raise the box cutter.

"Oh!" He's grinning. "*Oh!* What do you want to do with *that*?" Again he steps forward.

This time so do I.

"Get out of my house," I tell him. My arm wobbles; my hand is shaking. The blade gleams in the light, a little slice of silver.

He's stopped moving, stopped breathing.

"Who was that woman?" I ask.

And suddenly his hand lunges for my throat, seizes it. Drives me backward, so that I thud against the wall, my head cracking hard. I cry out. His fingers press into my skin.

"You're delusional." His breath, hot with liquor, flames against my face, stings my eyes. "Stay away from my son. Stay away from my wife."

I'm gagging, rasping. With one hand I claw at his fingers, rake my nails across his wrist.

With the other I swing the blade toward his side.

But my aim sails wide, and the box cutter clatters to the floor. He steps on it, squeezes my throat. I croak.

"Stay the *fuck* away from all of us," he breathes.

A moment passes.

Another.

My vision runs. Tears are leaking down my cheeks.

I'm losing conscious—

He releases my neck. I slide to the floor, gasping.

Now he towers above me. He drags his foot back sharply, sends the box cutter skidding into a corner.

"Remember this," he says, panting, his voice ragged. I can't look up at him.

But I hear him say one more word, small, breakably soft: "Please."

Silence. I watch his booted feet turn, step away.

As he passes the island, he sweeps his arm across it. A wave of glass crashes to the floor, splintering, smashing. I try to scream. My throat whistles.

He walks to the hall door, rips it open. I hear the front door unlatch, slam shut.

I hold myself, one hand touching my neck, the other clutching my body. I'm sobbing.

And when Punch limps through the doorway and gingerly licks my hand, I only sob harder.

## SUNDAY, NOVEMBER 14

# 89

I inspect my throat in the bathroom mirror. Five bruises, jewel-blue, a dark clasp around my neck.

I glance down at Punch, curled on the tile floor, nursing his lame paw. What a pair.

I won't report last night to the police. Won't and can't.

There's proof, of course, actual fingerprints on my skin, but they'll want to know why Alistair was here in the first place, and the truth is... well. *I invited a teenager whose family I stalked and harassed to hang out in my basement. You know, as a replacement for my dead child and my dead husband.* It wouldn't look good.

"Wouldn't look good," I say, testing my voice. It sounds weak, withered.

I leave the bathroom and descend the stairs. Deep in the pocket of my robe, my phone bumps against my thigh.

I sweep up the glass, the broken bodies of bottles and goblets; pluck splinters and slivers of the stuff from the floor, dump them into a trash bag. Try not to think about him seizing me, squeezing me. Standing over me. Stalking through the bright ruins underfoot.

Beneath my slippers, the white birch sparkles like a beach.

At the kitchen table I fiddle with the box cutter, listen to the snick of the blade as it glides out and in.

I look across the park. The Russell house looks back at me, its windows vacant. I wonder where they are. I wonder where he is.

I should have aimed better. Should have swung harder. I imagine the razor slicing through his jacket, ripping his skin.

*And then you would have had a wounded man in your house.*

I set the box cutter down and bring a mug to my lips.

There's no tea in the cupboard—Ed never cared for it, and I preferred drinking other things—so I sip warm water spiked with salt. It burns my throat. I wince.

I look across the park again. Then I get up, draw the blinds tight across the window.

Last night seems like a fever dream, a curl of smoke. The movie screen on my ceiling. The bright cry of glass. The void of the closet. The coiling staircase. And him, standing there, calling for me, waiting for me.

I touch my throat. *Don't tell me that it was a dream, that he never came here.* Where—yes: *Gaslight* again.

Because it was no dream. (*This is no dream! This is really happening!*—Mia Farrow, *Rosemary's Baby*.) My home was invaded. My property was destroyed. I was threatened. I was assaulted. And I can't do anything about it.

I can't do anything about *anything*. Now I know Alistair to be violent; now I know what he's capable of. But he's right: The police won't listen. Dr Fielding thinks I'm delusional. I told Bina, promised her, that I'd moved on. Ethan is out of reach. Wesley is gone. There's no one.

"Guess who?"

Her this time, faint but clear.

No. I shake my head.

*Who was that woman?* I'd asked Alistair.

If she existed.

I don't know. I'll never know.

# 90

I spend the rest of the morning in bed, then the afternoon, trying not to cry, trying not to think—about last night, about today, about tomorrow, about Jane.

Beyond the window, clouds are brewing, their bellies low and dark. I tap the weather app on my phone. Thunderstorms later tonight.

A somber dusk falls. I draw the curtains and unfold my laptop, place it beside me; it warms the sheets as I stream *Charade*.

"What do I have to do to satisfy you?" demands Cary Grant. "Become the next victim?"

I shudder.

By the time the films ends I'm half-asleep. The exit music swells; I flap a hand at the laptop, bat it shut.

Sometime later I awake to the buzzing of my phone.

Emergency Alert

Flood warning this area till 3:00 a.m. EDT. Avoid flood areas. Check local media.—NWS

Vigilant, that National Weather Service. I do plan to avoid flood areas. I unstopper a yawn, haul myself out of bed, shuffle to the curtains.

Darkness outside. No rain yet, but the sky has sunk, clouds dropped lower; the sycamore branches are stirring. I can hear the wind. I wrap one arm around myself.

Across the park, a light sparks in the Russells' kitchen: him, crossing to the refrigerator. He opens it, removes a bottle—beer, I think. I wonder if he's getting drunk again.

My fingers idle at my throat. My bruises ache.

I slide the curtain shut and return to bed. Clear the message from my phone, check the time: 9:29 p.m. I could watch another film. I could get a drink.

My hand strums the screen, absently. A drink, I think. Just one—it hurts to swallow.

A flare of colour at my fingertips. I glance at the phone; I've opened the photo roll. My heart slows: There's that picture of me, sleeping. The picture I allegedly took.

I recoil. After a moment, I delete it.

Instantly, the previous photo appears.

For a moment I don't recognize it. Then I remember: I snapped the shot from the kitchen window. A sunset, sherbet-orange, distant buildings biting into it like teeth. The street golden with light. A single bird frozen in the sky, wings flung wide.

And reflected in the glass is the woman I knew as Jane.

## 91

Translucent, soft at the edges—but Jane, unmistakably, haunting the lower-right corner like a ghost. She looks at the camera, eyes level, lips parted. One arm stretches out of frame—grinding a cigarette into a bowl, I remember. Above her head rises a thick whorl of smoke. The time stamp reads 06:04 p.m., the date almost two weeks ago.

Jane. I'm hunched over the screen, barely breathing.

Jane.

*The world is a beautiful place,* she said.

*Don't forget that, and don't miss it,* she said.

*Attagirl,* she said.

She *did* say these things, all of them, because she *was* real.

*Jane.*

I tumble from the bed, sheets trailing after me, laptop sliding to the floor. Spring to the window, rip back the curtains.

Now the lights are on in the Russells' parlour—that room where it all began. And there they sit, the two of them, on that striped love seat: Alistair and his wife. He slouches, beer bottle in his fist; her legs are cinched beneath her as she rakes a hand through her glossy hair.

The *liars*.

I look at the phone in my hand.

What do I do with this?

I know what Little would say, will say: The photo doesn't prove anything beyond its own existence—and that of an anonymous woman.

"Dr Fielding isn't going to listen to you, either," Ed tells me.

*Shut up.*

But he's right.

Think. Think.

"What about Bina, Mommy?"

*Stop it.*

Think.

There's only one move. My eyes travel from the parlour to the dark bedroom upstairs.

Take the pawn.

"Hello?"

A baby-bird voice, fragile and faint. I peer through the dark into his window. No sign of him.

"It's Anna," I say.

"I know." Almost a whisper.

"Where are you?"

"In my room."

"I don't see you."

A moment later he appears in the window like a phantom, slim and pale in a white T-shirt. I put a hand to the glass.

"Can you see me?" I ask.

"Yes."

"I need you to come over."

"I can't." He shakes his head. "I'm not allowed."

I drop my gaze to the parlour. Alistair and Jane haven't moved.

"I know, but it's very important. It's *very* important."

"My dad took the key away."

"I know."

A pause. "If I can see you..." He trails off.

"What?"

"If I can see you, they can see you."

I rock back on one foot, tug at the curtains, leaving a slit between them. Check the parlour. As they were.

"Just come," I say. "Please. You're not..."

"What?"

"You're—When can you leave your house?"

Another pause. I see him inspect his phone, press it to his ear again. "My parents watch *The Good Wife* at ten. I can maybe go out then."

Now I check my phone. Twenty minutes. "All right. Good."

"Is everything okay?"

"Yes." Don't alarm him. *You're not safe.* "But there's something I need to talk to you about."

"It'd be easier for me to come over tomorrow."

"It can't wait. Really—"

I glance downstairs. Jane is gazing at her lap, clutching a bottle of beer.

Alistair is gone.

"Hang up the phone," I say, my voice leaping.

"Why?"

"*Hang up.*"

His mouth falls open.

His room bursts into light.

Behind him stands Alistair, his hand on the switch.

Ethan spins, arm dropping to one side. I hear the line go dead.

And I watch the scene in silence.

Alistair looms in the doorway, speaking. Ethan steps forward, raises his hand, wags the phone.

For a moment they stand still.

Then Alistair strides toward his son. Takes the phone from him. Looks at it.

Looks at Ethan.

Moves past him, to the window, glaring. I withdraw farther into my bedroom.

He spreads his arms, folds a shutter over either half of the glass. Presses them tight.

The room is sealed shut.

Checkmate.

# 92

I turn from the curtains and stare into my bedroom.

I can't imagine what's happening over there. Because of me.

I drag my feet to the stairwell. With each step I think of Ethan, behind those windows, alone with his father.

Down, down, down.

I reach the kitchen. As I rinse a glass at the sink, a low burr of thunder sounds, and I peep through the blinds. The clouds are scudding faster now, the tree branches flailing. The wind is picking up. The storm is coming.

I sit at the table, nursing a merlot. SILVER BAY, NEW ZEALAND, the label reads, below a little etching of a sea-tossed ship. Maybe I can move to New Zealand, start fresh there. I like the sound of Silver Bay. I'd love to sail again.

If I ever leave this house.

I walk to the window and lift a slat; rain is prickling the glass. I look across the park. His shutters are still closed.

As soon as I return to the table, the doorbell rings.

It rips through the silence like an alarm. My hand jolts; wine slops over the brim of the glass. I look at the door.

It's him. It's Alistair.

Panic ambushes me. My fingers dive into my pocket, clutch the phone. And with the other hand I reach for the box cutter.

I stand and cross the kitchen slowly. Approach the intercom.

Brace myself, look at the screen.

Ethan.

My lungs relax.

Ethan, rocking on his heels, arms wrapped around himself. I press the buzzer and turn the lock. An instant later he's inside, his hair sparkling with raindrops.

"What are you doing here?"

He stares. "You told me to come."

"I thought your father..."

He closes the door, moves past me into the living room. "I said it was a friend from swimming."

"Didn't he check your phone?" I ask, following him. "I saved your number under a different name."

"What if he'd called me back?"

Ethan shrugs. "He didn't. What's that?" He's looking at the box cutter.

"Nothing." I drop it into my pocket.

"Can I use your bathroom?"

I nod.

While he's in the red room, I tap at my phone, ready my move.

The toilet flushes, the faucet gushes, and he's walking toward me again. "Where's Punch?"

"I don't know."

"How's his paw?"

"Fine." Right now, I don't care. "I want to show you something." I press the phone into his hand. "Hit the Photos app."

He looks at me, brow furrowed. "Just open the app," I repeat.

As he does, I watch his face. The grandfather clock starts to toll ten o'clock. I'm holding my breath.

For a moment, nothing. He's impassive. "Our street. At sunrise," he says. "Or—wait, that's west. So it's sunse—"

He stops.

There it is.

A moment passes.

He lifts his wide eyes to me.

Six tolls, seven.

He opens his mouth.

Eight. Nine.

"What—" he begins.

Ten.

"I think it's time for the truth," I tell him.

# 93

As the last deep bell rings, he stands before me, barely breathing, until I grasp his shoulder and steer him toward the sofa. We sit, Ethan still holding the phone in his hand.

I say nothing, merely gaze at him. My heart is going wild, like a trapped fly. I fold my hands in my lap to keep them from trembling.

He whispers.

"What?"

Clears his throat. "When did you find that?"

"Tonight, right before I called you."

A nod.

"Who is she?"

He's still looking at the phone. For a moment I think he hasn't heard me.

"Who is—"

"She's my mother."

I frown. "No, the detective said that your mother—"

"My *real* mother. Biological."

I stare. "You're adopted?"

He says nothing, just nods again, eyes cast low.

"So..." I lean forward, rake my hands through my hair. "So..."

"She—I don't even know how to begin."

I close my eyes, push my confusion aside. He needs to be guided. This I can do.

I angle my body toward him, smooth the robe along my thighs, look at him. "When were you adopted?" I ask.

He sighs, sits back, the cushions exhaling beneath his weight. "When I was five."

"Why so late?"

"Because she was an—she was on drugs." Halting, like a foal taking its first steps. I wonder how many times he's said it before. "She was on drugs and really young."

That explains why Jane looked so youthful.

"So I went to live with my mom and dad." I study his face, the tip of tongue glossing his lips, the shimmer of rain at his temples.

"Where did you grow up?" I ask.

"Before Boston?"

"Yes."

"San Francisco. That's where my parents got me."

I resist the impulse to touch him. Instead I take the phone from his hand, set it on the table.

"She found me once," he continues. "When I was twelve. She found us in Boston. She showed up at the house and asked my dad if she could see me. He said no."

"So you didn't get to talk to her?"

"No." He pauses, breathes deep, his eyes bright. "My parents were so mad. They told me that if she ever tried to see me again—that I should tell them."

I nod, sit back. He's speaking freely now.

"And then we moved here."

"But your father lost his job."

"Yeah." Wary.

"Why was that?"

He fidgets. "Something with his boss's wife. I don't know.

They were screaming about it a lot."

*It's all* super-*mysterious,* Alex had gloated. Now I know. A little affair. Nothing special. I wonder if it was worth it.

"Right after we moved in, my mom went back to Boston to take care of some stuff. And to get away from my dad, I think. And then he went up. They left me alone, just for the night. They'd done it before. And she showed up."

"Your birth mother?"

"Yes."

"What's her name?"

He sniffles. Swipes at his nose. "Katie."

"And she came to your house."

"Yeah." Another sniffle. "When? Exactly?"

"I don't remember." Shaking his head. "No, wait—it was Halloween."

The night I met her.

"She told me she was... 'clean,'" he says, pinching the word like it's a wet towel. "She wasn't doing drugs anymore."

I nod.

"She said she'd read about my dad's transfer online and found out we were moving to New York. So she followed us here. And she was waiting to decide what to do when my parents left for Boston." He pauses, scratches one hand with the other.

"And what happened then?"

"And then..." His eyes are shut now. "Then she came to the house."

"And you spoke to her?"

"Yeah. I let her in."

"This was Halloween?"

"Yeah. During the day."

"I met her that afternoon," I say.

He nods into his lap. "She went to get a photo album at her hotel. She wanted to show me some old pictures. Baby pictures and stuff. And then on her way back to the house she saw you."

I think of her arms around my waist, her hair brushing my cheek. "But she introduced herself to me as your mother. Your—as Jane Russell."

Again he nods.

"You knew this."

"Yeah."

"Why? Why would she tell me she was someone she wasn't?"

Finally he looks at me. "She said she didn't. She said that *you* called her by my mom's name, and she couldn't think of an excuse fast enough. She wasn't supposed to be there, remember." He gestures around the room. "She wasn't supposed to be *here*." Pauses, scratching his hand again. "Plus I think she liked pretending she was—you know. My mom."

A crack of thunder, as though the sky is breaking. We both start.

After a moment I press him. "So what happened next? After she helped me?"

He turns his gaze to his fingers. "She came back to the house and we talked some more. About what I was like as a baby. About what she'd been doing since she gave me up. She showed me photos."

"And then?"

"She left."

"She went back to her hotel?"

Another shake of the head, slower.

"Where did she go?"

"Well, I didn't know then."

My stomach twinges. "Where did she go?"

Again he lifts his eyes to me. "She went here."

The tick of the clock.

"What do you mean?"

"She met that guy who lives downstairs. Or used to live."

I stare. "David?"

Now a nod.

I think of the morning after Halloween, how I'd heard water pushing through the pipes as David and I examined the dead rat. I think of the earring on his bedside table. *It belonged to a lady named Katherine*. Katie.

"She was in my basement," I say.

"I didn't know until after," he insists.

"How long was she here?"

"Until..." His voice shrivels in his throat.

"Until what?"

Now he knots his fingers. "She came back the day after Halloween and we talked a little, and I said I'd tell my parents that I wanted to see her, like, officially. Because I'm almost seventeen and when I'm eighteen I can do whatever I want. So the next day I called my mom and dad and told them.

"My dad blew up," he continues. "Like, my mom was mad, but my dad was *furious*. He came straight back and wanted to know where she was, and when I wouldn't tell him, he..." A tear rolls from his eye.

I place a hand on his shoulder. "Did he hit you?" I ask. He nods soundlessly. We sit in silence.

Ethan pulls a breath from the air, then another. "I knew she was with you," he says shakily. "I saw you over there"—he looks at the kitchen—"from my room. I finally told him. I'm sorry. I'm really sorry." He's crying now.

"Oh..." I say, my hand hovering over his back.

"I just had to get him away from me."

"I understand."

"I mean..." He drags a finger beneath his nose. "I saw that she'd left your house. So I knew he wouldn't find her. That's when he came over here."

"Yes."

"I was watching you. I was praying he wouldn't get mad at you."

"No, he didn't." *I just wanted to know if you'd had any visitors this evening,* he'd explained. And later: *I was looking for my son, not my wife*. Lies.

"Then right after he got back home, she... she showed up again. She didn't know he was there already. He was supposed to come back the next day. She rang the doorbell and he made me answer it and invite her in. I was so scared."

I say nothing, just listen.

"We tried to talk to him. Both of us did."

"In your parlour," I murmur.

He blinks. "Did you see?"

"I saw." I remember them there, Ethan and Jane—Katie—on the love seat, Alistair in a chair across from them. *Who knows what goes on in a family?*

"It didn't go very well." His breath is choppy now. He hiccups. "Dad told her that if she ever came back, he would call the police and have her arrested for harassing us."

I'm still thinking of that tableau in the window: child, father, "mother." *Who knows what goes on...*

And then I recall something else.

"The next day..." I begin.

He nods, stares at the floor. His fingers writhe in his lap. "She came back. And Dad said he would kill her. He grabbed her throat."

Silence. The words almost echo. *He would kill her. He grabbed her throat.* I remember Alistair pinning me to the wall, his hand gripping my neck.

"And she screamed." I sound quiet.

"Yeah."

"That's when I called your house."

He nods again.

"Why didn't you tell me what was happening?"

"He was there. And I was *scared*," he says, his voice rising, his cheeks wet. "I *wanted* to. I came here after she left."

"I know. I know you did."

"I tried."

"I know."

"And then my mom came back from Boston the next day." He sniffles. "And so did she. Katie. That night. I think she thought Mom might be easier to talk to." He plants his face in his palms, wipes.

"So what happened?"

He says nothing for a moment, merely looks at me out of the corner of his eye, almost suspicious.

"You really didn't see?"

"No. I only saw your—I only saw her shouting at someone, and then I saw her with..." My hand flutters at my chest.

"... with something in..." I trail off. "I didn't see anyone else there."

When he speaks again, his voice is lower, steadier. "They went upstairs to talk. My dad and my mom and her. I was in my room, but I could hear everything. My dad wanted to call the police. She—my—she kept saying that I was her son, and that we should be able to see each other, and that my parents shouldn't stop us. And Mom was screaming at her, saying she'd make sure she never saw me again. And then everything got quiet. And a minute later I went downstairs and she was—"

His face crumples and he splutters, sobs bubbling deep in his chest and bursting at the surface. He looks to the left, fidgets where he sits.

"She was on the floor. She'd stabbed her." Now Ethan's the one pointing at his chest. "With a letter opener."

I nod, then stop. "Wait—who stabbed her?"

He chokes. "My mom."

I stare.

"She said she didn't want someone else to take me"—a hiccup—"take me away." He sags forward, his hands making a visor over his brow. His shoulders jump and shake as he cries.

*My mom.* I had it wrong. I had it all wrong.

"She said she'd waited so long to have a child, and..."

I close my eyes.

"... and she said she wouldn't let her hurt me again."

I hear him weeping softly.

A minute passes, then another. I think of Jane, the real Jane; I think of that mother-lion instinct, the same impulse that possessed me in the gorge. *She'd waited so long to have a child. She didn't want someone else to take me.*

When I open my eyes, his tears have subsided. Ethan is gasping now, as though he's just sprinted. "She did it for me," he says. "To protect me."

Another minute passes.

He clears his throat. "They took her—they took her to our house upstate and buried her there." He puts his hands in his lap.

"That's where she is?" I say.

Deep, dense breaths. "Yes."

"And what happened when the police came the next day to ask about it?"

"That was so scary," he says. "I was in the kitchen, but I heard them talking in the living room. They said that someone had reported a disturbance the night before. My parents just denied it. And then when they found out it was you, they realized it was your word against theirs. Ours. No one else had seen her."

"But David saw her. He spent..." I riffle through dates in my head. "Four nights with her."

"We didn't know that until after. When we went through her phone to see who she might have been talking to. And my dad said that no one was going to listen to a guy who lived in a basement, anyway. So it was them against you. And Dad said that you—" He stops.

"That I what?"

He swallows. "That you were unstable and you drank too much."

I don't respond. I can hear rain, a fusillade against the windows.

"We didn't know about your family then."

I close my eyes and begin to count. One. Two.

By three, Ethan is speaking again, his voice tight. "I feel like I've been keeping all these secrets from all these people. I can't do it anymore."

I open my eyes. In the dusk of the living room, in the fragile light of the lamp, he looks like an angel.

"We have to tell the police."

Ethan bends forward, hugging his knees. Then he straightens up, looks at me for a moment, looks away.

"Ethan."

"I know." Barely audible.

A cry behind me. I twist in my seat. Punch sits behind us, head tilted to one side. He mews again.

"There he is." Ethan reaches over the back of the sofa, but the cat pulls away. "I guess he doesn't like me anymore," says Ethan, softly.

"Look." I clear my throat. "This is very, very serious. I'm going to call Detective Little and have him come here so that you can tell him what you've told me."

"Can I tell them? First?"

I frown. "Tell who? Your—"

"My mom. And my dad."

"No," I say, shaking my head. "We—"

"Oh, please. *Please*." His voice breaks like a dam.

"Ethan, we—"

"*Please. Please*." Almost screaming now. I stare at him: His eyes are streaming, his skin is blotched. Half-wild with panic. Do I let him cry it out?

But already he's talking again, a wet flood of words: "She did it for *me*." His eyes are brimming. "She did it for *me*. I can't—I can't do that to her. After what she did for *me*."

My breath is shallow. "I—"

"And won't it be better for them if they turn themselves in?" he asks.

I consider this. Better for them, so better for him. Yet—"They've been freaking out ever since it happened. They're really going crazy." His upper lip glistens—sweat and snot. He swipes at it. "My dad told my mom they should go to the police. They'll listen to me."

"I don't—"

"They will." Nodding firmly, breathing deeply. "If I say I talked to you and you're going to tell the police if they don't."

"Are you sure..." *That you can trust your mother? That Alistair won't attack you? That neither one of them will come for me?*

"Can you just wait to let me talk to them? I can't—If I let the police come and get them now, I don't..." His gaze travels to his hands. "I just can't do that. I don't know how I'd... *live* with myself." His voice is swollen again. "Without giving them a chance first. To help themselves." He can barely speak. "She's my *mother*."

He means Jane.

Nothing in my experience has prepared me for this. I think of Wesley, of what he'd advise. *Think for yourself, Fox.*

Can I let him go back to that house? To those people?

But could I doom him to lifelong regret? I know how it feels; I know the ceaseless ache, the constant drone of it. I don't want him to feel that way.

"All right," I say.

He blinks. "All right?"

"Yes. Tell them."

He's gawking now, as though in disbelief. After a moment he recovers. "Thank you."

"Please be *very* careful."

"I will." He starts to stand.

"What are you going to say?"

He sits again, sighs wetly. "I guess—I'll say that... you know. That you have evidence." He nods. "I'll tell the truth. I told you what happened, and you said we need to go to the police." His voice quavers. "Before you do." Rubbing his eyes. "What do you think will happen to them?"

I pause, pick my way through a response. "It's... I think—the police will understand that your parents were being harassed, that she—that Katie was in effect stalking you. And was probably in violation of what was agreed when you were adopted." He nods slowly. "And," I add, "they'll take into account that it happened during an argument."

He chews his lip.

"It won't be easy."

His eyes drop. "No," he breathes. Then he looks at me with such force that I shift where I sit. "Thank you."

"Well, I..."

"Really." He swallows. "Thank you."

I nod. "You have your phone, right?"

He taps his coat pocket. "Yeah."

"Call me if—just let me know that everything's okay."

"Okay." He stands again; I stand with him. He turns toward the door.

"Ethan—"

He pivots.

"I need to know: your father."

He watches me.

"Does he—did he come to my house at night?"

He frowns. "Yeah. Last night. I thought—"

"No, I mean last week."

Ethan says nothing.

"Because I was told that I imagined something happening in your house, and now I know that I didn't. And I was told that I had drawn a picture that I hadn't drawn. And I want—I need to know who took that photograph of me. Because"—I hear my voice tremble—"I really don't want it to have been me."

A hush.

"I don't know," says Ethan. "How would he have gotten in?"

That I can't answer.

We walk to the door together. As he reaches for the knob, I catch him in my arms, bring him close, hold him tight.

"Please be safe," I whisper.

We stand there for a moment as rain spits on the windows and wind hisses outside.

He steps away from me, smiles sadly. Then he leaves.

## 94

I part the blinds, watch him climb his front steps, jab the key into the lock. He opens the door; when it closes, he's disappeared.

Was I right to let him go? Should we have warned Little first? Should we have summoned Alistair and Jane to my house?

Too late.

I gaze across the park, at the empty windows, the vacant rooms. Somewhere in the depths of that place, he's talking to his parents, taking a claw hammer to their world. I feel as I did every day of Olivia's life: *Please be safe.*

If there's one thing I've learned in all my time working with children, if I could whittle those years down to a single revelation, it's this: They are extraordinarily resilient. They can withstand neglect; they can survive abuse; they can endure, even thrive, where adults would collapse like umbrellas. My heart beats for Ethan. He'll need that resilience. He must endure.

And what a story—what an evil story. I shiver as I return to the living room, switch off the lamp. That poor woman. That poor child.

And *Jane*. Not Alistair, but *Jane*.

A tear runs down my cheek. I touch my finger to it and it gloms onto the skin; I look at it, curious. Then I wipe my hand on my robe.

My eyelids sag. I walk up to my bedroom, to worry, to wait.

I stand at the window, scanning the house across the park. No signs of life.

I chew a thumbnail until it leaks blood.

I pace the room, walk circuits around the carpet.

I glance at my phone. Half an hour has crept by.

I need a distraction. I need to calm my nerves. Something familiar. Something soothing.

*Shadow of a Doubt*. Screenplay by Thornton Wilder, and Hitch's personal favorite among his own films: a naive young woman learns that her hero isn't who he pretends to be. "We just sort of go along and nothing happens," she complains. "We're in a terrible rut. We eat and sleep and that's about all. We don't even have any real conversations." Until her Uncle Charlie pays a visit.

She remains oblivious a bit too long for my liking, frankly.

I watch it on my laptop, sucking at my wounded thumb. The cat wanders in after a few minutes, bounds into bed with me. I press his paw; he hisses.

As the story coils tighter, so too does something within me, some unease I can't name. I wonder what's happening across the park.

My phone buzzes, crawling across the pillow next to me. I seize it.

Going 2 police

11:33 p.m. I drifted off.

I step from bed and snap the curtains to one side. Rain batters my windows, sharp as artillery fire, turning them to puddles.

Across the park, through the smear of the storm, the house is dark.

"There's so much you don't know, so much."

Behind me, the film is still playing.

"You live in a dream," sneers Uncle Charlie. "You're a sleepwalker, blind. How do you know what the world is like? Do you know, if you rip off the fronts of houses, you'd find swine? Use your wits. Learn something."

I slope toward the bathroom, in the length of light falling through the window. Something to help me get back to sleep—melatonin, I think. I'll need it tonight.

I swallow a pill. On-screen, the body falls, and the train shrieks, and the credits roll.

"Guess who."

This time I can't dismiss him, because I'm asleep, though aware of it. A lucid dream.

Still, I try. "Leave me alone, Ed."

"Come on. Talk to me."

"No."

I don't see him, don't see anything. Wait—there's a trace of him, just a shadow.

"I think we need to talk."

"No. Go away."

Darkness. Silence. "Something's wrong."

"No." But he's right—something *is* wrong. That stirring in my gut.

"Man, that Alistair guy turned out to be a freak of the week, didn't he?"

"I don't want to talk about it."

"I almost forgot. Livvy has a question for you."

"I don't want to hear it."

"Just one." A flash of teeth; a curving grin. "A simple question."

"No."

"Go on, pumpkin. Ask Mommy."

"I said—"

But already her mouth is at my ear, piping her hot little words into my head, her voice that full-throated rasp she uses when she's sharing a secret.

"How's Punch's paw?" she asks.

I'm awake, with instant clarity, as though I've been doused with water. My eyes spring wide. A spine of light runs across the ceiling above.

I roll from bed and pad to the curtains, throw them back. The room fades to gray around me; through the windows, through the rain, I see the Russells' house shouldering an unholy sky. A jagged seam of lightning up above. A deep toll of thunder.

I return to bed. Punch whines quietly as I settle in.

*How's Punch's paw?*

That was it—the knot in my stomach.

When Ethan visited the day before yesterday, when he found the cat draped along the back of the sofa, Punch slid to the floor and wriggled underneath. I squint my eyes, replay the scene from every angle. No: Ethan didn't see—couldn't have seen—his lame leg.

Or could he? Feeling for Punch now, closing my fingers on his tail; he rustles against me. I check the time on the phone: 1:10 a.m.

The digital light spangles in my eyes. I squeeze them shut, then peer at the ceiling.

"How did he know about your paw?" I ask the cat in the dark.

"Because I visit you at night," says Ethan.

## MONDAY, NOVEMBER 15

# 95

My body bucks in shock. My head twists toward the door.

Lightning ignites the room, torches it white. He stands in the doorway, leaning against the frame, his head haloed with rainwater, scarf loose at his neck.

Words lurch off my tongue. "I thought—you went home."

"I did." His voice is low but clear. "Said good night. Waited for them to go to bed." His mouth curls in a soft little smile. "Then I came back here. I've been coming here a lot," he adds.

"What?" I don't understand what's happening. "I have to tell you," he says, "I've met a lot of psychologists, and you're the first who *hasn't* diagnosed me with a personality disorder." His eyebrows lift. "I guess you're not the world's best shrink."

My mouth clacks shut and creaks open, like a faulty door.

"You interest me, though," he says. "You do. That's why I kept coming back to you, even when I knew I shouldn't. Older women interest me." He frowns. "Sorry, is that insulting?"

I can't move.

"Hope not." A sigh. "My dad's boss had a wife who interested me. Jennifer. I liked her. She liked me, kind of. Only..." He shifts his lanky body, angles himself against the other side of the frame. "There was... a misunderstanding. Right before we moved. I visited their house. At night. And she didn't like that.

Or she said she didn't." Now he glares. "She knew what she was doing."

Then I see it in his fist. A bolt of silver, glinting.

It's a blade. It's a letter opener.

His eyes travel from my face to his hand and back again. My throat has closed up.

"This is what I used on Katie," he explains brightly. "Because she wouldn't leave me alone. I told her, and told her, *so* many *times*, and she just..." Shaking his head. "Wouldn't stop." He sniffs. "Kind of like you."

"But," I croak, "tonight—you..." My voice dries, dies.

"What?"

I lick my lips. "You told me—"

"I told you enough to—sorry, but to shut you up. I'm sorry to say it like that, because you're really nice. But I needed to shut you up. Until I could take care of things." He fidgets. "You wanted to call the *police*. I needed a little time to—you know. Get stuff ready."

Motion in the corner of my eye: the cat, stretching himself along the length of the bed. He looks at Ethan, cries.

"That darn cat," he says. "I loved that movie as a kid. *That Darn Cat!*" He smiles at Punch. "I think I broke its leg, by the way. I'm sorry." The letter opener winks as he wags it at the bed. "It kept following me around the house at night and I kind of lost my temper a little. Plus I'm allergic, like I told you. I didn't want to sneeze and wake you. I'm sorry you're awake *now*."

"You came here at night?"

He takes a step toward me, the blade liquid in the gray light. "I come here almost every night."

I hear my breath catch. "How?"

He smiles again. "I took your key. When you were writing down your phone number that day. I saw it on the hook the first time I visited, and then I realized you wouldn't even notice it was missing. It's not like you use it. I made a copy and put it back." Another smile. "Easy."

Now he giggles, presses his free hand over his mouth. "Sorry. It's just—I *so thought* you'd figured it out when you called me tonight. I was like—I didn't know what to do. I actually had this in my pocket." Waving the letter opener again. "Just in case. And I was stalling like crazy. But then you just lapped it all up. 'My daddy has a bad temper.' 'Oh, I'm so scared.' 'Oh, they don't let me have a phone.' You were practically drooling. Like I said, you're not the greatest shrink.

"Hey!" he exclaims. "I've got an idea: Analyze me. You want to know about my childhood, right? They all want to know about my childhood."

I nod dumbly.

"You'll love this. This is, like, a therapist's dream. *Katie*"—he practically pushes the word over with disdain—"was a druggie. A crack whore, except for heroin. Heroin whore. She never even told me who my dad was. And, man, she should not have been a mother."

He looks at the letter opener. "She started using when I was one. That's what my parents told me. I can't remember most of it, really. I mean, I was five when they took me away from her. But I remember being hungry a lot. I remember some stuff with needles. I remember her boyfriends kicking the shit out of me whenever they felt like it."

Silence.

"I bet my real father wouldn't have done that."

I say nothing.

"I remember seeing one of her friends overdose. I saw her die right in front of me. That's my first memory. I was four."

More silence. He sighs faintly.

"I started misbehaving. She tried to help me, or stop me, but she was too strung out. And then I went into the foster system, and then Mom and Dad got me." He shrugs. "They... Yeah.

They gave me a lot." Another sigh. "I cause trouble for them, I know. That's why they took me out of school. And my dad lost his job because I wanted to get to know Jennifer. He was mad about that, but, you know..." His brow darkens. "Tough luck."

The room goes lightning-bright again. Thunder rumbles.

"Anyway. Katie." He's looking out the window now, across the park. "Like I told you, she found us in Boston, but Mom wouldn't let her talk to me. And then she found us in New York, just showed up one day when I was alone. She showed me that locket with my picture in it. And I talked to her, because I was interested. And especially because I wanted to know who my father was."

Now he swings his eyes toward me. "Do you know what it's like, wondering if your father is as screwed up as your mother? *Hoping* he isn't? But she just said it didn't matter. He wasn't in her photos. She *did* have photos. All that was true, you know.

"Well..." He looks sheepish. "Not *all* of it. That day you heard her scream? I had my hands around her neck. Not even that hard, but I was sick of her by that point. I just wanted her to leave. She went crazy. She wouldn't shut up. My dad didn't even know she was there until then. He was like, 'Get out of the house before he does something bad.' And you called, and I had to pretend I was all scared, and then you called *again*, and my *dad* pretended it was all *cool*..." He shakes his head. "And the bitch *still* came back the next day.

"By that point I was bored with her. Seriously bored. I didn't care about the photos. Didn't care that she'd learned to sail or was taking sign-language classes or any of it. And like I said, she wouldn't say anything about my father. Probably she *couldn't*. Probably didn't even know him." He snorts.

"So, yeah. She came back. I was in my room and I heard her arguing with my dad. I couldn't stand it anymore. I wanted her gone, I didn't care about her sob story, I hated her for what she did to me, I hated her for not telling me about my father,

I wanted her out of my life. So I grabbed this from my desk"—he waves the letter opener—"and went downstairs, and ran in, and just..." He drives it downward. "It happened really fast. She didn't even scream."

I think of what he told me just a few hours ago: how Jane stabbed Katie. And I remember how his eyes darted left.

Now his eyes are bright. "It was kind of, like, exhilarating. Just pure luck you didn't see what happened. Or not all of it." He looks at me hard. "You saw enough, though."

He steps toward the bed slowly. And again.

"My mom has no idea. About any of it. She wasn't even there—she got back the next morning. My dad made me swear not to tell. He wants to protect her. I feel kind of bad for him. That's a pretty big secret to keep from the person you're married to." He steps a third time. "She just thinks you're insane."

One more step, and now he's standing beside me, the blade level with my throat.

"So?" he says.

I whine with terror.

Then he sits on the edge of the mattress, the base of his back against my knees. "Analyze me." He cocks his head. "Fix me."

I recoil. No. I can't do this.

*But you can, Mommy.*

No. No. It's over.

*Come on, Anna.*

He has a weapon.

*You've got your mind.*

All right. All right.

One, two, three, four.

"I know what I am," says Ethan, soft, almost soothing. "Does that help?"

Psychopath. The superficial charm, the labile personality, the flat affect. The letter opener in his hand.

"You—grew up hurting animals," I say, trying to steady my voice.

"Yeah, but that's easy. I gave your cat a rat I cut up. I found it in our basement. This city is disgusting." He looks at the blade. Looks back at me. "Anything else? Come on. You can do better than that."

I draw a breath and guess again. "You enjoy manipulating others."

"Well, *yeah*. I mean... *yeah*." He scratches the back of his neck. "It's fun. And easy. You're *really* easy." He winks at me.

A tap at my arm. I flick a glance to my side. My phone has slid down the pillow, lodged against my elbow.

"I came on too strong with Jennifer." He looks thoughtful. "She got—it was too much. I should've gone slower." He lays the blade flat on one thigh, strokes, as though whetting it. It zips against the denim. "So I didn't want you to think I was a threat. That's why I said I missed my friends. And I pretended I might be gay. And I cried all those fucking times. All so you'd feel sorry for me and think I was this..." Trailing off. "And because, like I said, I sort of can't get enough of you."

I close my eyes. I can see the phone in my head as though it's illuminated.

"Hey—did you notice when I undressed in front of the window? I did that a couple of times. I know you saw me once."

I swallow. Slowly I pull my elbow back into the pillow, the phone dragging along the flesh of my forearm.

"What else? Daddy issues, maybe?" He smirks again. "I know I've been talking about him some. My real father, not Alistair. Alistair's just a sad little man."

I feel the screen against my wrist, cool and slick. "You don't..."

"What?"

"You don't respect other people's space."

"Well, I'm here, aren't I?"

I nod again. Brush the screen with my thumb.

"I told you: you interested me. That old bitch down the block told me about you. Well, not *everything*, obviously. I've learned a lot since. But that's why I brought that candle over. My mom had no idea. She wouldn't have let me." He pauses, considers me. "I bet you used to be pretty."

He moves the letter opener toward my face. Slips the blade beside a lick of hair on my cheek, flicks it away. I flinch, whimper.

"That lady just said that you stayed in your house all the time. And that was interesting to me. This weird woman who never went outside. This freak."

I wrap my hand around the phone. I'll swipe to the passcode screen and let my fingers walk out those four numbers. I've tapped them so many times. I can do it in the dark. I can do it with Ethan sitting next to me.

"I knew I had to get to know you."

Now. I touch the button on the phone, press it. Cough to mask the click.

"My parents—" he begins, turning to the window. He stops.

My head turns with him. And I see what he sees: the glow of the phone, reflected in the glass.

He gasps. I gasp.

I snap my eyes to him. He stares at me.

Then he grins. "I'm kidding." He points at the phone with the letter opener. "I already changed the code. Right before you woke up. I'm not stupid. I'm not going to leave a working phone right next to you."

I can't breathe.

"And I took out the batteries from the one in the library. In case you were wondering."

My blood stops.

He gestures toward the door. "Anyway. I've been coming over at night for a couple of weeks, just walking around, watching you. I like it here. It's quiet and dark." He sounds thoughtful. "And it's kind of interesting, the way you live. I feel like I'm doing research on you. Like a documentary. I even"—he smiles—"took your picture with your phone." A grimace. "Was that too much? I feel like that was too much. Oh—but ask me how I unlocked your phone."

I say nothing.

"Ask me." Threatening.

"How did you unlock my phone?" I whisper.

He smiles broadly, like a child who knows he's about to say something clever. "You told me how."

I shake my head. "No."

His eyes roll. "Well, okay—you didn't tell *me*." He leans toward me. "You told that ancient bitch in Montana."

"Lizzie?"

He nods.

"You—were spying on us?"

He heaves a deep sigh. "God, you really are stupid. By the way, I don't teach disabled kids how to swim. I'd rather kill myself. No, Anna: I *am* Lizzie."

My mouth drops open.

"Or I was," he says. "She's been getting out of the house a lot lately. I think she's all better. Thanks to her sons—what are their names?"

"Beau and William," I answer, before I can stop myself.

He giggles again. "Holy shit. I can't believe you remember that." Laughing more now. "*Beau*. I swear I just made that up on the spot."

I stare at him.

"That first day I came over. You had that freak website on your laptop. I created an account as soon as I got home. Got to know all sorts of lonely losers. DiscoMickey, or whatever." He shakes his head. "It's pathetic. But he put me in touch with you. I didn't want to just write you out of the blue. Didn't want you—you know. Wondering.

"Anyway. You told *Lizzie* how to code all her passwords. Switch out letters for numbers. That's NASA shit right there." I try to swallow, can't.

"Or use a birthday—that's what you said. And you told *me* that your daughter was born on Valentine's Day. Oh-two-one-four. That's how I got into your phone and took that picture of you snoring. Then I changed the code, just to have fun with you." He wags a finger at me.

"And I went downstairs and got into your desktop." He leans toward me, speaks slowly. "Of *course* your password was Olivia's name. For your desktop and for your email. And of *course* you just swapped out the letters. Just like you told Lizzie." He shakes his head. "How fucking stupid are you?"

I say nothing.

He glares. "I asked you a question," he says. "How fucking stupid—"

"Very," I say. "Very what?"

"Very stupid."

"Who was?"

"I was."

"Very *fucking* stupid."

"Yes."

He nods. Rain slaps the windows.

"So I made the Gmail account. On your own computer. You told Lizzie that your family was always like, 'guess who' when you talked, and that was just too good to pass up. Guess who, Anna?" He giggles. "Then I sent the picture to your email. I wish I'd seen your face." He giggles again.

The room is airless. My breath is short.

"And I just *had* to put my mom's name on the account. I bet *that* got you excited." He smirks. "But you told Lizzie other stuff, too." He leans forward again, the letter opener pointed at my chest. "You had an affair, you slut. And you killed your family."

I can't speak. I've got nothing left.

"And then you just got so freaked out about Katie. It was insane. *You* were insane. I mean, I *kind of* get it. I did it right in front of my dad, and *he* freaked out, too. Although I think he was relieved to have her gone, to be honest. I was. Like I said, she pissed me off."

He shuffles up the bed, closer to me. "Move over." I fold my legs, brace them against his thigh. "I should have checked the windows, but it all happened too fast. And anyway, it was so totally easy to deny it. Easier than lying. Easier than the truth." He shakes his head. "I feel, like, *bad* for him. He just wanted to protect me."

"He tried to protect you from me," I say. "Even though he knew—"

"No," he tells me, voice flat. "He tried to protect *you* from *me*."

*I wouldn't want him spending time with a grown woman*, Alistair said. Not for Ethan's sake, but for mine.

"But, you know, what can you do, right? One of the shrinks told my parents I was *just bad*." He shrugs again. "Fine. Fucking fine."

The anger, the profanity—he's escalating. Blood surges to my temples. Focus. Remember. Think.

"You know, I kind of feel bad for the cops, too. That one guy was trying so hard to put up with you. What a saint." Another sniffle. "The other one seemed like a bitch."

I'm barely listening. "Tell me about your mother," I murmur.

He looks at me. "What?"

"Your mother," I say, nodding. "Tell me about her."

A pause. An ache of thunder outside.

"Like... what?" he asks, wary.

I clear my throat. "You said that her boyfriends mistreated you."

Now he glares. "I said they beat the shit out of me."

"Yes. I bet that happened a lot."

"Yeah." Still glaring. "Why?"

"You said you thought you were 'just bad.'"

"I said that's what the other shrink said."

"I don't believe that. I don't believe you're just bad."

He tilts his head. "You don't?"

"No." I try to steady my breath. "I don't believe people are made that way." I sit up straighter against the pillows, smooth the sheets across my thighs. "*You* weren't made that way."

"No?" He holds the blade loosely in his hand.

"Things happened to you when you were a child. There were... things you saw. Things beyond your control." My voice is gaining strength. "Things you survived."

He twitches.

"She wasn't a good mother to you. You're right." He swallows; I swallow. "And I think that by the time your parents adopted you, you were very badly damaged. I think..." Do I risk it? "I think they care about you very much. Even if they haven't been perfect," I add.

He looks me in the eye. A tiny ripple distorts his face.

"They're afraid of me," he says.

I nod. "You said it yourself," I remind him. "You said that Alistair was trying to protect me by keeping you—by keeping us apart."

He doesn't move.

"But I think he was afraid *for* you, too. I think he wanted to protect you, too." I extend my arm. "I think that when they took you home, they saved you."

He's watching me.

"They love you," I say. "You deserve love. And if we speak to them, I know—I'm sure—they'll do everything they can to keep protecting you. Both of them. I know they want to... connect with you."

My hand approaches his shoulder, hovers there.

"What happened to you when you were young wasn't your fault," I whisper. "And— "

"Enough of this bullshit." He jerks away before I can touch him. I reel my arm back in.

I've lost him. I feel the blood drain from my brain. My mouth goes dry.

He leans toward me, looks into my eyes, his own bright and earnest. "What do I smell like?"

I shake my head.

"Come on. Take a whiff. What do I smell like?"

I breathe in. I think of that first time, inhaling the scent of the candle. Lavender.

"Rain," I answer.

"And?"

I can't bear to say it. "Cologne."

"Romance. By Ralph Lauren," he adds. "I wanted this to be nice for you."

I shake my head again.

"Oh, yes. What I can't decide," he continues, thoughtful, "is whether it's a fall down the stairs or an overdose. You've been so sad lately, and all. And so many pills on the coffee table. But you're also a fucking wreck, so you could, you know, miss a step."

I don't believe this is happening. I look at the cat. He's on his side again, asleep.

"I'm going to miss you. No one else will. No one will notice for days, and no one will care afterward."

I coil my legs beneath the sheets.

"Maybe your shrink, but I bet he's had enough of you. You told Lizzie he puts up with your agoraphobia *and* your guilt. Jesus Christ. Another fucking saint."

I squeeze my eyes shut.

"Look at me when I'm talking to you, bitch."

With all my strength, I kick.

# 96

I connect with his stomach. He doubles over and I reload my legs, kick him again, in the face. My heel cracks against his nose. He spills to the floor.

I rip the sheets back and spring from the bed, run through the doorway into the black hall beyond.

Above me, rain drills into the skylight. I stumble on the runner, sink to my knees. Seize the banister with one flailing hand.

Suddenly the stairwell glows white as lightning flares overhead. And in that instant I glance through the spindles of the banister, see every step illuminated, spiraling down, down, down, all the way to the bottom.

Down, down, down.

I blink. The stairwell is plunged into darkness again.

Nothing to see, nothing to sense, except the percussion of the rain.

I haul myself to my feet, fly down the steps. Thunder rolls outside. And then:

"You *bitch*." I hear him stumble onto the landing, his voice wet. "You *bitch*." The banister creaks as he barges into it.

I need to get to the kitchen. To the box cutter, still unsheathed atop the kitchen table. To the slivers of glass glittering in the recycling bin. To the intercom.

To the doors.

*But can you go outside?* asks Ed, just a whisper.

I've got to. Leave me alone.

*He'll overtake you in the kitchen. You won't make it outside. And even if you did...*

I hit the next floor and whirl like a compass, orienting myself. Four doors surround me. The study. The library. The closet. The half bath.

*Choose one.*

Wait—

*Choose one.*

The bathroom. Heavenly Rapture. I grasp the knob, tear the door open, step inside. I lurk within the doorway, my breath short and shallow—

—and he's coming now, rushing down the stairs. I don't breathe.

He reaches the landing. Stops, four feet away from me. I feel the air stir.

For a moment I hear nothing except the drumbeat of rain. Sweat creeps down my back.

"Anna." Low, cold. I cringe.

Gripping the frame with one hand, hard enough to prize it loose, I peek into the dark of the landing.

He's faint, just a shade among shades, but I can make out the span of his shoulders, the floating white of his hands. His back is to me. I can't tell which hand holds the letter opener.

Slowly, he rotates; I see him in profile, facing the library door. He gazes straight ahead, motionless.

Then he turns again, but quicker this time, and before I can draw back into the bathroom he's looking at me.

I don't move. I can't.

"Anna," he says quietly.

My lips part. My heart hammers.

We stare at each other. I'm about to scream.

He pivots away.

He hasn't seen me. He isn't able to look deep in the dark. But I'm used to it, the low light, the no-light. I can see what he—

Now he moves to the top of the stairs. The blade flickers in one hand; the other dips into his pocket.

"Anna," he calls. He pulls his hand from his pocket, lifts it in front of him.

And light blasts from his palm. It's his phone. It's the flashlight.

From the doorway I see the stairs burst into view, the walls bleached white. Thunder rumbles nearby.

Once more he rotates, the ray of light sweeping the landing like a lighthouse beam. First the closet door. He strides over to it, throws it open. Points the phone inside.

Next, the study. He walks in, scans the room with his phone. I watch his back, brace myself for a flight downstairs. Down, down, down.

*But he'll catch you.*

I have no other way out.

*You do.*

Where?

*Up, up, up.*

I shake my head as he retreats from the study. The library is next, and after that, the bathroom. I've got to move before—

My hip brushes against the doorknob. It twists with a tiny whine.

He rounds sharply, the light glancing past the library door, and aims it directly into my eyes.

I'm blind. Time stops.

"There you are," he breathes.

Then I lunge.

Through the doorway, slamming into him, burying my shoulder in his gut. He wheezes as I push. I can't see, but I drive him to one side, toward the staircase—

—and suddenly he's gone. I hear him collapse down the stairs, an avalanche, the light crazed across the ceiling.

*Up, up, up,* Olivia whispers.

I turn, my vision still starry. I knock one foot against the base of the staircase, stumble, half crawl another step. Push myself upright. Run.

On the landing I spin, eyes adjusting to the dark. My bedroom looms ahead of me; across from it, the guest room.

*Up, up, up.*

But upstairs is just the spare room. And your room.

*Up.*

The roof?

*Up.*

But *how? How* could I?

*Slugger,* says Ed, *you don't have a choice.*

Two floors below, Ethan charges up the steps. I turn and scramble upstairs, the rattan burning my soles, the banister squeaking against my palm.

I burst onto the next landing, streak to the corner below the trapdoor. Flap my hand above my head, find the chain. Wrap my fingers around it and yank.

# 97

Water sprays my face as the door yawns open. The ladder barrels toward me with a scream of metal. At the bottom of the stairs, Ethan shouts, but the wind whips his words away.

I screw my eyes shut against the rain and climb. One, two, three, four, the rungs cold and slick, the ladder squealing beneath my weight. On the seventh step I feel my head breach the rooftop, and the sound...

The sound nearly knocks me back. The storm is roaring like an animal. Wind claws the air, shreds it. Rain, sharp as teeth, bites into my skin. Water licks my face, washes my hair back—

His hand clutches my ankle.

I shake it loose, frenzied, and haul myself up and out, rolling to one side, between the trapdoor and the skylight. I prop a hand against the curved glass of the dome and struggle to my feet, open my eyes.

The world tips around me. In the thick of the storm I hear myself moan.

Even in the dark I can see that the roof is a wilderness. Plants boil over in their pots and beds; the walls are veined with vines. Ivy swarms the ventilation unit. Ahead of me stands the hulk of the trellis, twelve long feet of it, canted to one side beneath the weight of its leaves.

And across it all rain isn't falling but billowing, in sails, vast sheets of water. It drops like a weight onto the rooftop, fizzes on the stonework. Already my robe clings to my skin.

I revolve slowly, weak at the knees. On three sides, a four-story drop; to the east, the wall of St. Dymphna's rears up like a mountain.

Sky above me. Space around me. My fingers curl. My legs buckle. My breathing is ragged. The noise rages.

I see the dark drop beyond—the trapdoor. And emerging from it, one arm bent against the rain, Ethan.

Now he rises onto the roof, black as a shadow, the letter opener a silver spike in one hand.

I falter, stumble backward. My foot brakes against the dome of the skylight; I feel it give slightly—*Flimsy*, David warned me. *Branch falls on that, it's gonna take out the whole window.*

The shadow nears me. I scream, but the wind rips it from my mouth, whirls it away like a dead leaf.

For an instant Ethan rocks back in surprise. Then he laughs.

"No one can *hear* you," he calls above the howl. "We're in a..." Even as he says it, the rain pounds harder.

I can't back up any farther without treading on the skylight. I step sideways, just an inch, and my foot grazes wet metal. I glance down. The watering can that David upset that day on the roof.

Ethan approaches, soaked with rain, bright eyes in a dark face, panting.

I stoop, seize the watering can, swing at him—but I'm woozy, off balance, and the can slips from my grasp, sails away.

He ducks.

And I run.

Into the dark, into the wild, afraid of the sky above but terrified of the boy behind. My memory maps the rooftop: the row of boxwoods to the left, the flower beds just beyond. Empty planters on the right, sacks of soil slouched among them like drunks. The tunnel of the trellis directly ahead.

Thunder riots. Lightning blanches the clouds, drenches the rooftop in white light. Veils of rain shift and shudder. I charge through them. At any moment the sky could cave in and crush me to rubble, yet still my heart is pumping, blood heating my veins, as I hurtle toward the trellis.

A curtain of water drapes the entrance. I burst through it into the tunnel, dark as a covered bridge, dank as a rain forest. It's quieter in here, beneath the canopy of twigs and tarp, as though sound has been walled off; I can hear myself gasping. To one side sits the shallow little bench. *Through adversity to the stars.*

They're at the far end of the tunnel, where I hoped they'd be. I bolt to them. Grasp them with both hands. Turn around.

A silhouette looms behind the waterfall. It's how I first met him, I remember, his shadow piling up against the frosted glass of my door.

And then he steps through it.

"This is perfect." He mops water from his face, moves toward me. His coat is sodden; his scarf sags around his neck. The letter opener juts from his hand. "I was going to break your neck, but this is better." He cocks an eyebrow. "You were so fucked up that you jumped from the roof."

I shake my head.

A smile now. "You don't think so? What have you got there?"

And then he sees what I've got here.

The gardening shears wobble in my hands—they're heavy, and I'm shaking—but I lift them to his chest as I advance.

He isn't smiling anymore. "Put that down," he says.

I shake my head again, step closer. He hesitates.

"Put it *down*," he repeats.

I take another step, snap the shears together.

His eyes flicker to the blade in his hand.

And he recedes into the wall of rain.

I wait a moment, my breath heaving in my chest. He's melted away.

Slowly, slowly, I creep toward the arch of the entrance.

There I stop, the spray misting on my face, and I poke the tip of the shears through the waterfall, like a divining rod.

Now.

I thrust the shears ahead of me and leap through the water. If he's waiting for me, he'll be—

I freeze, my hair streaming, my clothes soaked. He isn't there.

I scan the rooftop.

No sign of him by the boxwoods. Near the ventilation unit. In the flower beds.

Lightning overhead, and the roof blazes white. It's desolate, I see—just a wasteland of unruly plants and frigid rain.

But if he isn't there, then—

He crashes into me from behind, so fast and so hard that the scream is knocked out of me. I drop the shears and fall with him, my knees collapsing, my temple slamming against the wet roof; I hear the crack. Blood floods my mouth.

We roll across the asphalt, once, twice, until our bodies ram into the edge of the skylight. I feel it shudder.

"Bitch," he mutters, his breath hot in my ear, and now he's righted himself, his foot pressing on my neck. I gurgle.

"Don't *fuck* with me." He's rasping. "You're going to walk off this roof. And if you don't, I'll throw you off. So."

I watch raindrops seethe on the asphalt beside me.

"Which side would you choose? Park or street?"

I shut my eyes.

"Your mother..." I whisper.

"What?"

"Your mother."

The pressure on my neck eases, just slightly. "My mother?"

I nod.

"What about her?"

"She told me—"

Now he presses harder, nearly throttling me. "Told you what?"

My eyes pop. My mouth flaps open. I gag. Again he lets up on my neck. "Told you *what?*"

I breathe deep. "She told me," I say, "who your father is."

He doesn't move. Rain bathes my face. The tang of blood sharpens on my tongue.

"That's a lie."

I cough, rock my head against the ground. "No."

"You didn't even know who she was," he says. "You thought she was someone else. You didn't know I was adopted." He pushes his foot against my neck. "So how could—"

"She told me. I didn't—" I swallow, my throat swelling. "I didn't understand at the time, but she told me..."

Once more he's silent. Air hisses through my throat; rain hisses on the asphalt.

"Who?"

I stay silent.

"*Who?*" He kicks me in the stomach. I suck in air, curl up, but already he's seized me by the shirt, hauling me to my knees. I slump forward. He drives his hand into my throat, squeezes.

"What did she say?" he screams.

My fingers scrabble at my neck. He starts to lift me and I rise with him, my knees quaking, until we stand eye to eye.

He looks so young, his skin bathed smooth in the rain, his lips full, his hair slicked across his forehead. *A very nice boy.* Beyond him I see the spread of the park, the vast shadow of his house. And at my heels I feel the bulge of the skylight.

"Tell me!"

I try to speak, fail.

*"Tell me."*

I gag.

He relaxes his grip on my throat. I flick my eyes down; the letter opener is still clasped in his fist.

"He was an architect," I gasp.

He watches me. Rain falls around us, between us.

"He loved dark chocolate," I say. "He called her 'slugger.'" His hand has fallen from my neck.

"He liked movies. They both did. They liked—"

He frowns. "When did she tell you this?"

"The night she visited me. She said she loved him."

"What happened to him? Where is he?"

I shut my eyes. "He died."

"When?"

I shake my head. "A while ago. It doesn't matter. He died and she fell apart."

His hand grasps my throat again, and my eyes fly open. "*Yes*, it matters. When—"

"What matters is that he loved you," I croak. He freezes. He drops his hand from my neck. "He loved you," I repeat. "They both did."

With Ethan glaring at me, with the letter opener gripped in his hand, I breathe deeply.

And I hug him.

He goes stiff, but then his body slackens. We stand there in the rain, my arms around him, his hands at his sides.

I sway, swoon, and he holds me as I twist around him. When I'm back on my feet, we've traded positions, my hands on his chest, feeling his heartbeat.

"They both did," I murmur.

And then, with all my weight, I lean into him and push him onto the skylight.

# 98

He lands on his back. The skylight shudders.

He says nothing, just looks at me, confused, as though I've asked him a difficult question.

The letter opener has skidded to one side. He splays his hands against the glass, starts to push himself upright. My heart slows. Time slows.

And then the skylight disintegrates beneath him, soundless in the storm.

In an instant he drops out of sight. If he screams, I can't hear it.

I stumble to the edge of where the skylight used to be, peer over it into the well of the house. Shreds of rain swirl in the void like sparks; on the landing below glitters a galaxy of broken glass. I can't look any deeper—it's too dark.

I stand there in the storm. I feel dazed. Water laps at my feet.

Then I step away. Move carefully around the skylight. Walk toward the trapdoor, still flung wide.

Down I go. Down, down, down. My fingers slip on the rungs.

I reach the floor, the runner soaked with water. Tread to the top of the stairs, passing beneath the gouge in the roof; rain showers onto me.

I reach Olivia's bedroom. Stop. Look in.

My baby. My angel. I'm so sorry.

After a moment I turn, walk downstairs; the rattan is dry and rough now. At the landing I stop again, cross below the waterfall, and stand, dripping, in the doorway of my bedroom. I survey the bed, the curtains, the black specter of the Russell house beyond the park.

Once more through the shower, once more down the steps, and now I'm in the library—Ed's library; my library—watching the rain gust across the window. The clock on his mantel chimes the hour. Two A.M.

I avert my eyes and leave the room.

From the landing I can already see the wreckage of his body, disarranged on the floor, a fallen angel. I descend the staircase.

A dark crown of blood flames from his head. One hand is folded over his heart. His eyes look at me.

I look back.

And then I step past him.

And I enter the kitchen.

And I plug in the landline so that I can call Detective Little.

# SIX WEEKS LATER

## 99

The last flakes sifted down an hour ago, and now the midday sun floats in an aching-blue sky—a sky "not to warm the flesh, but solely to please the eye." Nabokov, *The Real Life of Sebastian Knight*. I've devised my own reading syllabus. No more long-distance book club for me.

It *does* please the eye. Likewise the street below, paved with white, high wattage in the sunshine. Fourteen inches dropped on the city this morning. I watched for hours from my bedroom window, saw the snow tumbling thick, frosting the sidewalks, carpeting doorsteps, piling high in flower boxes. Sometime after ten the four Grays streamed from their house in a happy herd; they shrieked amid the flurries, lurched through the drifts and down the block, out of sight. And across the road Rita Miller emerged on her front stoop to marvel at the weather, wrapped in a robe, a mug in one hand. Her husband appeared behind her, circled her in his arms, hooked his chin over her shoulder. She kissed him on the cheek.

I learned her real name, by the way—Little told me, once he'd interviewed the neighbors. It's Sue. Disappointing.

The park is a field of snow, so clean it sparkles. Beyond it, windows shuttered, hunching beneath that dazzled sky, is what the more frantic newspapers have dubbed KILLER TEEN'S

$4M HOUSE! It cost less, I know, but I guess $3.45M! doesn't sound as sexy.

It's empty now. Has been for weeks. Little visited me at home a second time that morning, after the police arrived, after the EMTs had removed the body. His body. Alistair Russell was arrested, the detective said, charged with accessory to murder; he'd confessed immediately, as soon as he heard about his son. It happened just as Ethan described it, he admitted. Apparently Alistair broke down; Jane was the tough one. I wonder what she knew. I wonder *if* she knew.

"I owe you an apology," Little muttered, shaking his head. "And Val—man, she *really* owes you one."

I didn't disagree.

He dropped by the next day, too. By that point reporters were knocking on my door, leaning on my buzzer. I ignored them. If nothing else, over the past year I've gotten good at ignoring the outside world.

"How you doing, Anna Fox?" asked Little. "And this must be the famous psychiatrist."

Dr Fielding had followed me from the library. Now he stood at my side, gawking at the detective, at the sheer scale of the man. "Glad she's got you, sir," said Little, pumping his hand.

"I am, too," Dr Fielding replied.

And so am I. The past six weeks have stabilized me, clarified me. The skylight's repaired, for one thing. A professional cleaner swung by, spit-polished the house. And I'm dosing properly, drinking less. Drinking not at all, in fact, thanks in part to a tattooed miracle worker named Pam. "I've dealt with all kinds of people, in all kinds of situations," she told me on her first visit.

"This might be a new one," I said.

I tried to apologize to David—called him at least a dozen times, but he never answered. I wonder where he is. I wonder if he's safe. I found his earbuds coiled beneath the bed in the basement. I took them upstairs, tucked them into a drawer. In case he calls back.

And a few weeks ago I rejoined the Agora. They're my tribe; they're a sort of family. *I will promote healing and well-being.*

I've been resisting Ed and Livvy. Not all the time, not fully; some nights, when I hear them, I murmur back. But the conversations are over.

# 100

"Come on."

Bina's hand is dry. My own is not.

"Come on, come on."

She's yanked the garden door open. A shivering wind blows in.

"You did this on a roof in the rain."

But that was different. I was fighting for my life.

"This is your garden. In the sunshine."

True.

"And you've got your snow boots on."

Also true. I found them in the utility closet. I hadn't worn them since that night in Vermont.

"So what are you waiting for?"

Nothing—not anymore. I've waited for my family to return; they won't. I've waited for my depression to lift; it wouldn't, not without my help.

I've waited to rejoin the world. Now is the time.

Now, when the sun is blasting my house. Now, when I'm clearheaded, clear-eyed. Now, as Bina leads me to the door, to the top of the stairs.

She's right: I did this on a roof in the rain. I was fighting for my life. So I must not want to die.

And if I don't want to die, I've got to start living.

*What are you waiting for?*

One, two, three, four.

She releases my hand and walks into the garden, tracking footprints in the snow. She turns, beckons me.

"Come *on*."

I close my eyes.

And I open them.

And I step into the light.

H. Rider Haggard
MR. MEESON'S WILL

Melville Davisson Post
MASTER OF MYSTERIES
THE COMPLETE UNCLE ABNER COLLECTION

Jack London
THE ASSASSINATION BUREAU LTD.

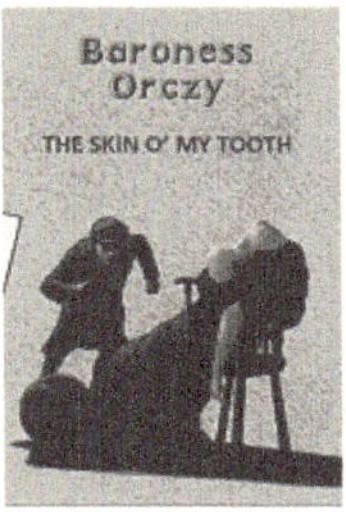
Baroness Orczy
THE SKIN O' MY TOOTH

Earl Derr Biggers
SEVEN KEYS TO BALDPATE

Horace Walpole
THE CASTLE OF OTRANTO

Sexton Blake
THE SEXTON BLAKE COLLECTION
VOLUME 1

Francis Beeding
THE HOUSE OF DR. EDWARDES

A. E. W. Mason
AT THE VILLA ROSE

Fergus Hume
THE MILLIONAIRE MYSTERY

Donald Henderson
A VOICE LIKE VELVET

Richard Hallas
YOU PLAY THE BLACK AND THE RED COMES UP